FLYING INTO DARKNESS

DON VALLEE

Published by Parker Publishers

Editing and Interior Design by Silvestra Z. Griffin & Dianne Williams

ISBN (Digital): 978-1-970751-75-8
ISBN (Paperback): 978-1-970751-76-5
ISBN (Hardback): 978-1-970751-77-2

First Edition

For permissions, inquiries, and additional information, contact: **donvallee.author@gmail.com**

Dedicated to my step-daughter

Mercedes Matzen

A beautiful and compassionate soul

Taken much too soon.

PROLOGUE

Nine-year-old Evan sat on the edge of his bed. A dim light from a full moon seeped in through threadbare curtains, casting long shadows across his cluttered room. In his small hand, he held the thirty-eight special he had taken from his father's tool chest earlier in the day. He trembled as he tried to hold back tears, but it wasn't easy with the sounds he could hear. His mother's screams blasted through the wall that separated their bedrooms, a regular occurrence since his father, Ray, had lost his job as an auto mechanic at a local car dealership.

Ray hadn't always been this way. Before losing his job a year earlier, he enjoyed life and was a man full of laughter and compassion. Then life had considerably changed, and not for the better. Ray felt like he had lost a large part of who he was and descended into a deep depression, turning to the bottle for solace. Drinking became his escape, and as his alcohol dependence grew, so did the abuse that transformed a once-happy home into a place filled with anger and pain. Ray was not just a drunk — he was the kind that turned mean.

Evan squeezed the butt of the revolver with both hands as he listened to his father beating his mother. The yelling, the slapping, the punching, and the kicking seemed to bounce against his bedroom wall. He made the fateful decision that he could no longer sit idly by while his mother screamed in pain.

Evan rose from his bed and slowly opened the door to his bedroom. He quietly tiptoed down the hall to his parents' bedroom. His heart beating loudly in his chest, his mother's screams amplifying in his ears. He reached for the doorknob to his parents' bedroom, carefully turned it, and inched the door open. When Ray glimpsed the bedroom door opening, he turned away from his wife and looked over at Evan.

Ray had fire in his eyes and drool running down his chin. He was breathing heavily, and the knuckles on his hands were raw and bloody. Evan slowly lifted the revolver as his arms shook, tears streaming down his cheeks. He pointed the gun at his drunken father, pressed his eyes shut, and squeezed the trigger. It was the first time Evan had ever fired a gun. The powerful recoil shocked him as the revolver jerked back against his face. The pistol split open Evan's bottom lip.

Blood trickled over his chin, dripping to the floor. The bullet entered Ray's chest, causing him to fall to the floor in agony. Evan's mother, still in a fetal position, got on her hands and knees and crawled to her husband. As Ray lay dying, she glanced up at Evan in shock and horror. When she saw him holding the gun in his small hand and Ray lying on the floor in a pool of blood, she shrieked, "Evan, what have you done!"

Evan calmed down as he looked at his father. Firing the gun felt good to him. He sensed a power he had never known existed. He dropped the gun and slowly walked to his mother, falling to the floor next to her. After holding each other for what seemed like an eternity, but was in reality only a few minutes, Evan's mother crawled to the bedroom phone, which sat on the nightstand and dialed 911. The house went quiet except for the sirens that approached minutes later.

A uniformed officer interrogated Evan and his mother as they sat in the living room, waiting for the coroner to remove Ray's body from the home. After several hours of questioning, Evan was handcuffed and placed in the backseat of a patrol car and transported to the county jail's juvenile section, where he awaited trial.

After a short hearing in juvenile court, Evan pleaded guilty to voluntary manslaughter after accepting a plea deal agreed upon by the judge and the district attorney's office. The district attorney offered incarceration until Evan reached his eighteenth birthday. The judge remanded him to a juvenile detention center located in Syracuse, New York. Evan's mother visited Evan only a few times, travelling the four hours from her home to see her son.

Evan tried to explain to his mother during her visits why he had killed his father, telling her that he could no longer watch the abuse inflicted upon her. He said he wanted to protect them from Ray and thought killing him was the only way to stop the violence they endured.

"Mom, you know how bad the beatings were. I couldn't let him continue to hurt and abuse us," Evan said.

"Evan, I know your father hit me occasionally, but that was just the alcohol. He truly struggled with being out of work," Betsy replied.

"But Mom, he hurt you all the time. Why did you let him do that to you?" Evan cried.

"He didn't mean it, Evan. It was only when he would drink."

"Yeah, excuses, and you always believed him."

They eventually stopped discussing Ray and the violence and the killing.

Evan was released from the detention center on his eighteenth birthday, having served eight and a half years. During his incarceration, he obtained his GED and took several computer classes. He loved computers and had a natural aptitude for newer technology. He even assisted the center's staff with computer problems and questions.

As part of the plea agreement, the courts sealed his juvenile records, and the incident was never brought up again. Evan was able to attend a college located in Albany, New York and earn a Bachelor of Science degree in Information Technology. In his early twenties, he accepted a job in Albany, where he met the love of his life and married.

CHAPTER 1

25 Years Later

October 19th

The Long Island Expressway, known as the L.I.E. to locals, is not anyone's favorite place on a Wednesday during rush hour traffic. However, it was precisely where Jenna and Evan found themselves for the third time in as many months. Traffic was stop-and-go, with speeds at their quickest reaching ten miles per hour. A cacophony of horns blew everywhere.

They were there because Evan had received a phone call stating that his mother had been rushed by ambulance to the hospital and admitted. Betsy, now 73 years old, had advanced brain cancer, and for the past six months, suffered with horrible headaches. She had undergone several chemotherapy treatments and two surgeries in the hopes of remission. Still, unfortunately, the doctors said the cancer had been discovered too late in the disease's progression for any real possibility of a positive outcome.

The drive to Long Island from Albany typically takes a little over three and a half hours. It involves heading south on the New York State Thruway, through New York City, and onto the L.I.E., when the trip is planned in advance.

They usually timed hospital visits for late evenings or weekends to dodge traffic. Not today. The call Evan received from the hospital at noon raised fears that his mother would not survive the evening, and they needed to be on Long Island as soon as possible. A planned trip to avoid traffic was not an option. Evan wanted and needed to be by her side as quickly as possible for the inevitable. As soon as Evan ended the call with the hospital, he contacted Jenna at work.

"Jenna Williams," she said when she answered her office phone.

"Hi Jenna, I just received a call from Long Island Medical Center. My mom was admitted this morning and is not doing well. The doctors don't think she'll make it through the night. I need to be there with her and would like you to come with me."

"Again? It's the fourth time she's been admitted to the hospital in the last three months. They told you the last time they called that your mother wasn't going to live through the night. Are you sure this will be the last time?" Jenna said with frustration and continued, "I also don't understand why you feel the need to be there. You and your mother didn't seem to have a very close relationship. My God, you don't even call her "mom".

You use her first name. That's just not normal!" Jenna finished.

"My mother is afraid to die alone. She needs my support. You know she is in hospice at home, living in a hospital bed in her living room. Strangers have been taking care of her. It is not the best of circumstances. I know you don't like these drives, but I wish you could understand how she must be feeling during something so distressing," Evan replied with scorn, then continued more softly, "I don't make these trips for myself. I go for my mother."

After the brief but heated exchange, they decided to meet at home at two in the afternoon to be on the road to Long Island no later than three. It required both Evan and Jenna to cancel meetings and delegate tasks to their co-workers for the remainder of the week.

Evan's office was closer than Jenna's, and he arrived home a half hour before her. He used the time to pack what he believed they needed for a few days away. When he had the suitcases filled, he changed out of his business clothes and into jeans and a sweatshirt.

Jenna arrived home just as Evan placed the suitcases in the trunk of his Audi S6. She pulled her bright red Porsche Boxster into the adjoining stall in the garage just before three.

When he noticed the look on her face, with her lips pressed tight, forming a straight line, Evan knew she was not pleased. Her eyes barely opened into an angry slit. Jenna never liked visiting Long Island. She could always tell something was not right between Evan and his mother, and she sensed an unbearable tension whenever they were together.

"I have everything packed and ready to go," Evan said as Jenna climbed from her car.

"Do I have time to change into something more comfortable for a long drive?" Jenna asked with noticeable frustration.

"Of course, but don't take too long. I want to get out of Albany before rush hour starts. It's going to be bad enough when we get closer to New York City," Evan replied.

"I'll be changed and in the car in fifteen minutes."

Albany's rush hour traffic had yet to begin when they began the trip to Long Island, and most of the drive down the New York State Thruway was smooth and uneventful. Jenna worked on her laptop while Evan drove. They had not uttered one word to each other. The only sounds heard inside the vehicle were the music playing through the car's speakers and the hum of tires rolling on pavement.

However, as they neared New York City, traffic reduced to a crawl. The highway was jam-packed with cars, trucks, motorcycles, and every other possible motorized machine. It was like all of Manhattan's entire workforce had escaped from their daily grind—cars, trucks, bikes, all at once, like the whole island trying to get home for dinner. Jenna closed her laptop and placed it on the back seat.

"We've entered hell," Evan said with exasperation and continued, "This traffic is horrible. Why don't these people take the train, bus, or work from home?"

Jenna ignored Evan's comment. They remained silent towards each other while Jenna thought about the tension between Evan and his mother. She attempted to raise the subject again.

"What is the issue between you and your mother, anyway?" Jenna asked, then continued, "You never told me, but I see the way you two look at each other. I've never seen you have a mother-and-son conversation, even at our wedding. Your traditional mother and son dance seemed strained, too."

"It's very personal and too upsetting to talk about. I don't think I can..." Evan stopped mid-sentence and drifted back to the day he killed his father.

"Evan. Evan!" Jenna shouted.

Jenna startled Evan, and he jumped in his seat.

"Where the hell did you go? You looked like you were in outer space. Didn't you see the cars start moving again? Didn't you hear the horns honking behind us?" Jenna asked curtly.

"Sorry, I was just thinking about something," Evan replied tensely.

"I'm sorry, Evan, if I sounded heartless earlier. These trips have been difficult for us both. I do understand how your mother must feel. It is just sitting here in this traffic again, and so soon after our last trip that makes it so damned frustrating," Jenna attempted to sound sympathetic without success.

"I know Jenna, but other than taking the Amtrak or getting a plane ticket, both of which would be nearly impossible to obtain and very expensive at the last minute, this is the only way to get there," Evan replied.

"Of course," said Jenna as she looked up in the sky, observing a small plane as it flew overhead, and added, as an afterthought, "If only you knew how to fly an airplane. How nice would it be to be able to zoom over this parking lot on a highway? We could be at your mother's home in an hour and not feel the stress from all of this driving up and down New York State."

Jenna stunned Evan when she mentioned flying, and he thought she couldn't be serious, although it did interest him that she would bring up such a strange suggestion.

"That is an interesting thought, me flying an airplane, but that must take years of training and cost more than we could comfortably afford."

"I am not sure that is completely true. I once dated a guy who flew a small airplane. He was only eighteen at the time and fresh out of high school. He told me he had always loved airplanes and signed up for flight school during the summer before starting college. How long could it have taken him to get his license, and how much could it have cost? Seriously, I don't think it's that unrealistic," Jenna replied.

"It's something I never considered doing. Not in a million years," Evan said, then added, "Well, I guess that's not entirely true. Maybe once I thought about it. It was a long time ago when I had a friend whose father was a pilot. He was in the Air Force. He took my friend and me up in a small airplane when I was around seven years old. It was called a Skyhawk, I think. We flew over my house, the Long Island Sound, and past the Statue of Liberty. It was a lot of fun and quite exhilarating! That night, while lying in bed, I thought it would be cool to learn how to fly an airplane. Unfortunately, I knew it was not something I could do. I was only a kid. I didn't think it would be possible. I never really thought about it again."

Jenna remained silent for a moment, then said, "Let me do a little research to get some accurate and detailed information. I know there is a flight school at the Albany International Airport, because I have seen a sign for one and noticed small airplanes lined up alongside a building. Would you like me to investigate it for you, Evan? If I did and it was something attainable, would you go for it?"

"Yeah, I guess you could look into it. I don't think it's all that realistic, though, but it can't hurt to find out."

Jenna and Evan continued their enthusiastic conversation about airplanes and flying during the rest of the ride. They fantasized aloud about all the possibilities available for extended weekends around the Northeast if they had access to an airplane. They mused how much smaller the world would become without being confined to *simple* roads. They chatted about finally getting to Nantucket and Martha's Vineyard without having to deal with the long ferry rides. They discussed how they could take off at the last minute and go anywhere they chose without adhering to airline schedules.

All this conversation between Evan and Jenna eased the tension and reduced the stress they felt at the trip's start. The final miles of the drive to Evan's family home were much less strained. As he drove, Evan looked over at Jenna and thought he caught a glimpse of her smiling for the remainder of the ride to his childhood home, the corner of her lips ever so slightly curved upward.

CHAPTER 2

It had been four months since Evan's mother died. The last trip to Long Island, when Jenna had brought up flying lessons, was indeed the last time that he saw her alive. Betsy had succumbed to cancer the evening they arrived. It was heartbreaking for Evan as he watched his mother take her last breath. Evan's mom genuinely needed the emotional support from him, and Evan was grateful to give it to her. Her last words spoken were, "I forgive you."

Evan spent the time since his mother's death on Long Island, cleaning out her house, making repairs, and getting it ready for sale. Evan spent considerable time removing his parents' possessions from the house, donating much of the belongings to local churches. He was fortunate that the company he worked for had a satellite office in Manhattan. Evan would commute to Manhattan on the Long Island Railroad, returning home in the afternoons to work on the house. He gutted the kitchen and two bathrooms, retiled the floors, installed new carpeting in the bedrooms and living room, and painted the entire interior of the home. He also repaired the exterior siding and window trim before adding a fresh coat of paint. He finished the remodel with new landscaping. Evan was extremely handy and able to complete most of the work himself, with occasional assistance from local handymen.

Evan would return to his home in Albany on the weekends, leaving Long Island after seven on Friday evenings to avoid the horrendous downstate traffic jams. He would return to Long Island the following Sunday evening. Evan always arrived back in Albany with just enough time to have a glass of wine with Jenna before heading off to bed, too exhausted to have meaningful conversations with her. His extended absences had weakened the relationship between him and Jenna, and their sexual relationship had become nonexistent. They had indeed drifted apart.

* * *

Jenna was not pleased with Evan leaving her alone every week for four months. Weekends were the only time they had to enjoy each other, but he always commented that he was too tired to engage in any fun activities with her. He had tried explaining the need to be on Long Island, readying his mother's house for sale. However, Jenna never fully accepted his reasons and began feeling isolated and estranged.

When Evan was home, he never gave Jenna the attention she desired and needed. She wanted more, so while Evan was away, she found ways to entertain herself. Jenna always told Evan that she was spending time with her girlfriends, tending to the gardens, reading books, or catching up on work. If he knew what she was really doing to stay busy while he was away, it would most definitely end the marriage.

As promised, Jenna investigated flight schools and flying lessons. To Jenna, though, she wondered if flying was just a fleeting desire for Evan. She thought he had given up on the idea because he had never brought it up again since their trip to Long Island the night his mother died. Whenever the two were outdoors, however, and a small airplane flew overhead, she found he stared at the sky and watched them fly over and disappear into the horizon. She knew deep down that Evan was fascinated with airplanes.

She did not immediately tell Evan she had investigated flight training, and he never asked. Jenna wanted to learn as much as possible before saying anything, as she didn't want to raise his hopes only for him to be disappointed. She feared the cost of training and the time it took would be prohibitive, and if that were true, she would drop the idea and move on. Evan would never have to know.

Jenna was surprised to discover that flight lessons were not only affordable but also within their financial reach. She learned that a person could receive a certificate as a VFR pilot in as few as forty flight hours. She discovered that VFR stood for *Visual Flight Rules*, which restrict pilots from flying in bad weather. The

Federal Aviation Administration's minimum requirement to obtain a VFR pilot's certificate was thirty hours of actual flying time with additional classroom training, known as ground school. She did not realize until her internet research that a pilot received a certificate, not a license. What the distinction or difference was, she did not understand.

Jenna was enthusiastic as she scoured the internet. With what she learned, she decided to do a Google search for local flight schools. She wanted to choose a school that received the best reviews for both the instructor and the school itself.

Jenna also looked at the various airplanes used for training. She discovered one type appeared most frequently, a Cessna 172, also known as a Skyhawk. She recalled Evan had mentioned a Skyhawk when he told her about his flight with a friend's father. She didn't know much about planes, but it did look safe.

With the best reviews based on over one hundred graduated and certificated students, the school and instructor Jenna chose was James Robinson at *TIME2FLY* Inc., located at Albany International Airport. Jenna decided this would be the perfect place for Evan to train. Not only was the instructor and school highly rated and the favorite of the area, but it was also conveniently located near their home. Jenna believed a facility nearby would be an added benefit and incentive for Evan to sign up for lessons.

Since Evan had stopped traveling to Long Island after he sold his mother's house, Jenna thought it was time to get serious about flying. She looked at her watch, seeing it was just after 9:00 in the morning.

There should be someone at the school to talk with, Jenna thought.

She picked up the phone and dialed *TIME2FLY*. The call was answered almost immediately by what sounded like an enthusiastic and young teenage girl.

"Good morning, thanks for calling *TIME2FLY*. My name is Liz. How may I help you?"

"Hi, my name is Jenna. I'm inquiring about flight lessons. I don't know much about the subject and found your name online."

"I'm so glad you picked us. Many of our first-time callers don't know much about flying or airplanes, and that's why we are here," Liz replied, continuing, "James Robinson is our school instructor, and everyone says he's excellent. He is my father and has been teaching me since I was thirteen. I'm seventeen now and just became eligible for an FAA examination. I hope to take it next week."

"Wow! Someone can become a pilot at seventeen years of age, and you've been flying since you were thirteen years old? That's incredible. I thought a person had to be older to fly an airplane," Jenna replied, surprised.

"Anyone can learn to fly. There is no age restriction for when someone can start training. It's a lot of fun, and my father is excellent, and I'm not just saying it so I don't get grounded, pun intended." Liz chuckled aloud at her little joke and added, "So, are you interested in learning to fly? It is a rewarding experience."

"No, I am calling for my husband. I'm doing a little exploration. He doesn't know I've been looking into it." Jenna went to explain her last conversation with Evan she had about flying, "So, I thought I would look around, see what I found, and make a call. Honestly, he might be too afraid to be in such a small airplane. How safe are they?"

"Ha-ha, you don't know how many people think small airplanes aren't safe, but I can assure you they are extremely safe." Liz laughed and continued, "I'll tell you what we can do that may help you and your husband's decision. We are offering a $50 introductory flight. If you'd like, my father would be happy to take your husband and you up for a short one-hour flight around the area and over Lake George. It might just hook your husband into signing up after realizing how beautiful it is. If, after the flight, you decide you don't want to sign up for training, the worst thing that happens is you get a nice scenic view of the Adirondacks. If you think your husband might want to learn how to fly, why don't you go ahead and purchase the intro flight? It's a way we help people determine if it is something they want to pursue."

Liz's sales technique was quite good.

"Let's do it! Is this something I can schedule over the phone for Saturday?"

"Yes, and we can set you and your husband up for this Saturday at noon. Let's get you on the schedule before someone else takes it."

Although only seventeen, Liz excelled at signing up new students. It is the very reason her father loved having her in the office.

After furnishing her credit card information and arranging the introductory flight for Saturday, Jenna hung up the phone. She had considered calling Evan to tell him the great news immediately. However, she decided to wait until dinner, enjoying a glass of wine together.

Evan, hopefully, she thought to herself, smiling, *will be delighted! Flying will allow me my free time.*

Her cell phone beeped with a text message notification as she hung up her office phone. She picked it up and read the sender's name displayed. The message was from *Mercedes*, but Jenna knew it was only a ruse. She secretly hid this type of message from Evan under a false contact on her cell phone.

CHAPTER 3

March 7th

When Jenna downloaded the *Boredwives* app onto her device three months ago, it was not with the thought of joining a dating site. She had stumbled upon the web version one day while surfing the Internet on her smartphone and, out of curiosity, checked it out. Unfortunately, the loneliness she endured with her husband away all those months drove her to explore more deeply than intended.

The curiosity Jenna first felt had quickly transformed into something much more. While on the website, she browsed various member profiles and looked at photos of handsome men who sought casual hookups. The men on the site searched for women they could connect with, meet up with, and have brief but exciting sexual encounters.

When Jenna learned that *Boredwives* offered a guarantee of anonymity, privacy, and promised safety, she downloaded the app to her cell phone. She created an account and began filling out a profile. After a few moments, Jenna caught herself, briefly stopping when she experienced overwhelming guilt. She considered removing the app but continued to press on the phone's keyboard instead as she fantasized about the possibilities. The loneliness she suffered was a much stronger pull than any guilt she felt.

Jenna carefully completed filling out the profile. She did not want to add any information that might readily identify her. She feared her friends and, more importantly, her husband, would find her profile on *Boredwives*.

How embarrassing and disastrous it would be if anyone discovered my association with such a salacious website, she whispered to herself.

Although Jenna was a little apprehensive as she created a profile with some of the limited personal information it sought, she found herself drawn in. The app seemed designed for people like her who wanted to meet a friend without any commitments, which she thought she desperately needed. She felt lonely, unwanted, and undesired by Evan.

At forty-two years old, she was still a beautiful woman who stood five feet eight inches tall, weighing one hundred and twenty-five pounds. She had long, shimmering chestnut brown hair. Her friends often complimented her stunning green eyes; obviously, they were her most attractive feature.

She never doubted her desirability. The constant, unsolicited remarks—many from complete strangers—

made that clear enough. She had no doubt that once her profile went live on *Boredwives*, the messages would start coming in, men eager to know if she really meant them.

Would I regret cheating on my husband? Would I even want to meet a man I did not know? She questioned herself but ignored her self-doubt and continued with her profile.

She found a photo on her cell phone that Evan had taken of her standing on Lake George's shore during one of their numerous drives to the tourist town. She was apprehensive about adding a photo, but it was needed to complete the registration. As she uploaded it, she let out a sigh.

The profile was complete, and she looked over the information on her screen. She felt she did not need to worry about a stranger showing up on her doorstep, violating her safety, because precise locations were not collected or revealed.

There was a fee to use *Boredwives*, which was renewed each month automatically using the credit card information stored in her profile. When she realized a credit card was necessary, she became concerned. However, she was relieved when the site said the charges would show up as "online services" on credit card statements with no other discernible information. She could easily explain "online services" to Evan as something associated with her job.

With her profile, picture, and credit card supplied, she had one last step to finish the registration. It was to create a unique username, and the username she conceived was "*LonelyandLooking.*" Jenna smiled as she entered it because she never actually looked for someone, even when she was lonely. She always made sure she was the courted one, never desperate, and always had someone interested in her for as long as she could remember.

After ending the call with *TIME2FLY*, feeling good about scheduling a flight for Evan on Saturday, she looked back at her cell phone and the message she received from her veiled sender. It was brief.

"Tonight at 6? Frear Park, Pagoda? JT."

When she saw the message and the initials JT, she knew it came from Jason Tanner. She had begun chatting with Jason via text messages and the app's chat feature shortly after she joined. Although they started texting each other daily, it took Jenna a few weeks before she felt comfortable enough to meet in person.

The first meeting took place at Frear Park, a nearby locale. They chatted and commiserated about their lives, and their connection was immediately organic and natural. Although the app was developed for lonely homemakers seeking friendly companionships, sexual encounters, and liaisons without commitment, Jenna fell for Jason the moment she laid eyes on him.

They had met several times since, although there was never any intimate contact other than light kissing, hand-holding, and warm embraces. Jenna was careful and slightly guilt-ridden, but her desire for Jason had become much more difficult to ignore as they continued to meet. She had felt herself draw closer to him while, at the same time, retreating from Evan.

Is this natural after twenty years of marriage? Do people really fall out of love? Is this what really happens? She wondered inwardly.

Jason was younger than Jenna by nine years, at only thirty-three years old. However, neither Jason nor Jenna was bothered by the age difference. Jenna found him to be incredibly attractive physically.

Jason stood tall at six feet, two inches, and weighed a muscularly toned one-hundred-eighty pounds with thick brown hair and beautiful, bright blue eyes. It was his eyes that drew Jenna to him from the moment she saw him. Just being around Jason made her feel invigorated and young again. She wondered to herself why he needed to chase wives on an app.

She simply replied to JT's message with a "yes."

A reply returned reading "great," and included a smile emoji.

Frear Park, where Jason and Jenna had been meeting, is a lovely place situated on a large hill in Troy, New York. It is a two-hundred-forty-seven-acre, eighteen-hole public golf course and hockey arena. It has many amenities, including a cozy little restaurant, nature trails, and a pagoda.

Jenna liked meeting Jason at Frear Park in Troy and across the Hudson River from Albany. She felt secure and confident she would not run into anyone who knew her, especially Evan, since he never frequented the park and rarely crossed the river.

Well, this changes tonight's plans. Instead of over dinner, I'll tell Evan about the new adventure I have planned for him tomorrow morning before I leave for the office. Jenna said to herself.

CHAPTER 4

March 7th

Jenna was startled back to reality when Debbie, her program lead, knocked on her office door jamb.

"Hey Jenna, a penny for your thoughts. You looked like you were in la-la land. Is everything okay?" Debbie asked as Jenna looked up from her cell phone.

"Oh, yes. I was just thinking about my plans for tonight. Is there something I can help you with?" Jenna asked.

"I just wanted to tell you the database testing went well. I think we will be able to implement the enhancements this weekend. We are looking to do it on Saturday afternoon now that we have received approval from change management. Will you be available Saturday if we need your help?" inquired Debbie.

Jenna was the Lead Database Administrator at Healthy Northeast Insurance, Inc., a large health insurance company located in Schenectady, New York. She had been promoted recently after ten years of database design and development.

She loved her position as the database administrator since it required less of her evenings and weekends.

Her new responsibilities included technical reviews of database changes and designs to ensure that everything the development staff created was accurate and efficient. She managed a staff of ten developers, two system analysts, and Debbie, her project lead. She was good with people and built a formidable team that worked efficiently together.

Although she was not required to be on-site after hours, she was always there during implementations involving significant design changes in the unlikely event that a catastrophic failure occurred. Fortunately for her, it was a rare event. The downside of this new position was that she wore the burden of leadership backlash if something went wrong. Although it didn't happen often, it was unpleasant when it did.

Jenna wanted to be with Evan on Saturday for his first flight, but she also knew she needed to be available for the implementation.

"Yes, Deb, I should be available Saturday. I may be out of pocket for an hour or so at noontime. Hopefully, that won't be a problem for the team."

"No, that shouldn't be an issue at all. We won't start the implementation until after one. We need to wait until operations shut down all systems and ensure everyone is logged out before we can begin. I am sending an email to all users today informing them of the shutdown."

"Excellent. It sounds like your team is well prepared. I am sure all will go as smoothly and efficiently as usual. You are a great team. I am fortunate to have you all."

Jenna always tried to reply positively to boost morale. It was why her team was considered one of the best at Healthy Northeast.

As Debbie smiled and turned to walk back to her desk, Jenna picked up her cell phone, located Evan's name, and pressed 'CALL'.

"Evan Williams."

"Hi, Evan. I just wanted to let you know I need to work late again tonight. We plan to implement our database changes on Saturday, and I need to be here to ensure everything is ready."

"You're working late again?" Evan asked.

"Yes, I'm sorry. Go ahead and make dinner for yourself, and I'll grab a bite to eat here at the office."

"Alright, but it seems you've been working a lot more lately. I was hoping your promotion would reduce the time you were needed at the office. What time will you be home?"

"I know I've been working a lot, and I'm sorry. I'm not sure what time I'll be home. Look, I have to run. See you at home. Bye."

"Bye," Evan said as he ended the call and groaned.

Evan didn't know it at the time, but working late was a deception Jenna had used frequently on Evan.

The remainder of Jenna's workday was busy and filled with meetings. The time passed quickly, and when she looked at her cell phone, she noticed it was already 5:30. She needed to log off her computer, pack up her briefcase, and set out for her encounter at 6:00 with Jason in Frear Park. It was a fifteen-minute drive across the Patroon Island Bridge into Troy, and she did not want him waiting for her.

Jenna departed her office and rode the elevator down to the parking garage. She felt anxious but also a little excited.

After all, she thought, *I didn't join Boredwives and download the app to my smartphone to fall for someone, yet I think I did.*

Jenna settled into her Boxster and gazed at herself in the rearview mirror. She wanted to ensure her makeup still looked fresh after a long day spent in the office. Jenna added a touch of blush and eyeliner to give herself a younger appearance for Jason.

Although he knew she was older than he was, Jenna never wanted to remind Jason of that fact. She ran her fingers through her long, thick hair, gave it a fluff, peered into the mirror one last time, and decided she looked good. She lowered the top of the Boxster and pushed the start button to begin the drive for her rendezvous with her new companion.

* * *

It was 6:10 p.m. when Evan arrived home, drained from a long and stressful day. As the Data Architect at Bank Trust and Financial, Evan provided detailed information and reports for all business aspects using data collected electronically. The business community used the information to form financial decisions, track customer preferences, identify fraud, and provide financial health to leadership. The data necessary demanded extreme accuracy and had to be delivered with immediacy. The chiefs of the corporation considered data to be their most valuable asset. Evan certainly felt pressure to deliver on time.

Evan knew he would arrive home to a dark and empty house. When Jenna called him earlier in the day, she said she had to stay with her programming staff late and did not know when she would be home. He was aware of the large project Jenna was responsible for because he often heard her on the phone with her developers when she received calls at home. At the moment, he did not think twice about her having to remain late at work again.

When Jenna wasn't working late, Evan made dinner for them, but decided that this was a night for pizza and beer. He called the local pizza parlor, ordering his favorite, a meat lover's with extra bacon and cheese.

With his order placed, he dragged himself upstairs to the primary bedroom, undressed, and jumped into a hot shower. Although he showered every morning before he left for work, Evan often showered again when he returned home and before dinner to clean off the office grime, as he frequently referred to it.

Evan stood under the hot water as it flowed over his head and down his chest, exhaling deeply to alleviate the day's stress. As the water streamed, he started to think back to all the recent late nights Jenna had spent in the office. Jenna led him to believe her new position as the administrator would reduce her hours, but this was not the case. She had spent more time in the office than at home over the last few months.

After a ten-minute shower, Evan threw on a T-shirt and a pair of comfortable sweats and lumbered downstairs to the kitchen. He walked to the refrigerator and pulled out a six-pack of beer. He entered the family room, falling into his favorite leather recliner.

Evan reached for the TV remote and tuned to his favorite reality crime channel. Jenna had believed the only reason men owned TVs was to watch sports and sports-related programs. She marveled at how Evan did not. Evan was never really a fan of the competitive sports world. He would always tell Jenna that he considered sports figures a group of overpaid men who only played the same games children played in their backyards and neighborhood parks.

Evan's favorite programs were true-life crime documentaries, particularly those involving murder. He loved to watch them religiously to follow advancements in forensic science. Evan primarily took an interest in how the authorities eventually captured their suspects. He would often try to solve the mystery as it unfolded before the program's host revealed the murderer's identity. He became adept at examining details and could point out to Jenna where a criminal made their mistake.

When the pizza arrived at 6:45, Evan took a slice, set the box beside his chair, and ate without taking his eyes off the screen. After three slices of pizza and four beers, he drifted off to sleep with the TV still playing a documentary about serial killers.

CHAPTER 5

March 7th

J enna arrived at Frear Park a few minutes earlier than Jason, as intended, because she liked to watch as he approached her. When Jason neared the pagoda, Jenna thought he looked exceptionally handsome. He donned a two-piece pinstripe business suit coordinated with a light salmon-colored shirt and a contrasting geometric tie. When he was close enough for her to see his blue eyes, she smiled.

Damn, what a beautiful man! She nearly blurted aloud.

Jason was a phenomenally successful defense attorney in New York's Tri-Cities—Albany, Troy, and Schenectady. He was a familiar face on local news, often interviewed after yet another client's acquittal. He very rarely lost and was paid quite well. Jenna loved to listen to his smooth, baritone voice. She found him to be comforting.

Jason arrived at the pagoda where Jenna was seated.

"Well, hello, beautiful!" Jason said.

He reached down to give her a warm kiss on the lips as he placed a hand on her thigh. Jenna cherished his touches and kisses. She tried, yet could not remember feeling this attracted to another man, not even Evan.

She often dreamt of running away with Jason to start a new life, but realized it was impossible. Raised in the Mormon Church, Jenna was aware that marriage is considered sacred — not a contract you could simply walk away from, and a dilemma Jenna could never resolve.

Jason sat down, and they discussed each other's day, making Jenna feel comfortable. She was always incredibly nervous whenever they met, knowing these rendezvous could destroy her marriage. However, Jenna calmed down quickly once they started talking.

Jason always put her at ease, and the connection she initially felt during their online chats and text messaging grew stronger after they met. Jenna's feelings confused her. She tried to comprehend how an attraction and desire for another human being could happen this quickly.

Was this how I felt when I met Evan? She tried to remember without success.

They sat and chatted about their day until Jason asked, "Jenna, we have sat in this pagoda for several weeks now. Don't get me wrong, I love our talks, but I thought maybe we could go get something to eat or drink tonight?"

Jason had fallen for Jenna, wanting to discover everything about her. He sought to bring their relationship to a new level, but Jenna was unsure if they should. She believed it would transform an innocent conversation into a real affair. Dinner and drinks were indeed a significant step.

What if there were people around who knew me? Knew Evan? she asked herself.

The thought of getting caught terrified her. She did not want to hurt her husband, which is not what she intended to do when she started this journey. Yes, she may be pulling away, losing her love for Evan, but she still cares deeply for him for all the good days they had had. Jenna always felt he was a gentle, kind, compassionate, and generous man, and she knew that if he found out she was having an affair, it would crush him. Evan always cared exceptionally for her, and she knew he did. Jenna never needed anything more except *maybe* this. She felt dinner with Jason was worth the risk as she recognized a desire to spend more time exploring a deeper relationship.

"Okay," was all Jenna said.

Jason and Jenna walked along the nature trail to a restaurant and bar located alongside the park's golf course. She felt safe as she believed no one who knew her would dine there. Golfers frequented the restaurant, but Jenna did not know anyone who golfed. Evan was undoubtedly not a golfer. When they arrived at the restaurant, they entered.

"Could we sit in a booth in the back of the restaurant?" Jenna asked Jason.

"Absolutely! Anything you like, Jenna," Jason replied.

Although Jenna was sure no one would recognize her, she still positioned herself so she could keep watch of the door for anyone who entered. She was attentive regardless of how safe she had felt.

They continued the small talk that had started at the pagoda. Jenna was nervous. She wasn't sure what to say, but when she saw Jason's watch, she grabbed his hand and lifted his wrist off the table to look closely.

"That's a beautiful watch. Is it a Rolex?" Jenna asked.

Jason smiled and felt a shiver as Jenna held his hand.

"Yes, it is. I purchased it right after winning my first big case. I wanted to reward myself. I wear it all the time. As odd as it sounds, I also wear it to bed. It feels like, at least to me, that I'm wearing a medal of accomplishment and don't ever want to remove it. Hell, I even wear it while jogging each morning," he laughed and continued, "The only time I remove it is when I shower or go swimming, but only to protect it."

"Well, it's a beautiful piece of jewelry, and you should be proud. I've seen you on TV—you really are as good as they say," Jenna replied.

A waiter arrived and asked if they wanted anything to drink. They both said yes. Jason ordered an Old Fashioned for himself and a Chardonnay for Jenna. Neither Jenna nor Jason had yet mentioned *Boredwives* or the reasons each had joined until now.

"Why are you on *Boredwives*? Are you really a bored wife?" Jason finally asked.

"I honestly don't know why. Initially, it was just a curiosity, but I started feeling lonely with Evan traveling to Long Island so often to care for his mother and then sell her house. To be honest, I never really expected to meet anyone," Jenna replied, asking in return, "Why did you join?"

"For fun. I am so busy with all the court cases. I don't really have any time for dating and serious relationships. A guy has to be with someone for fun from time to time if you know what I mean," Jason gave a playful wink.

"I do know what you mean. I think that is why I'm on here, too. I feel like the intimacy in my marriage is gone. Evan and I just don't have the same connection. We both seem too tired and can never initiate anything other than a peck on the cheek lately. When we are intimate, I don't feel the same sparks I did when we first met. It always feels more like a chore than anything else."

"That doesn't seem like an incredibly joyful home life, Jenna. You are a beautiful woman and deserve more. And to be honest and blunt, I don't think I'd be able to control myself around you. Not even after years together. You're extremely sexy, and I find you very desirable. It certainly would not feel like a chore to me!" Jason flushed a little.

"Thank you, Jason. I really needed to hear those words. It's been a long time. I know Evan loves me, but I'm not sure he's *in love* with me. Does that make any sense to you?"

"It does, Jenna. It happens to many couples, and I think it's unfortunate," Jason said sincerely.

"It makes me sad, also. On the other hand," Jenna said, smiling, her green eyes sparkling with energy, "I'm very attracted to you and find you extremely handsome."

Jenna's face reddened. She broke eye contact and gulped down her wine. She had difficulty believing she spoke those words to someone other than her husband.

"Well then, I guess we know what we need to do next, don't we?" Jason grinned widely.

"You don't even know how much I desire that, but not yet. Let's have a nice dinner and enjoy each other's company. I don't know if I'm ready to commit the ultimate marital betrayal quite yet. I hope you understand and will be patient. *Boredwives* was a lark for me, but now it is beginning to feel all too real. Just give me a little more time. Can you do that?"

"Absolutely, Jenna! Also, just so you know, since meeting you, I've stopped communicating with everyone else on the site. I only have eyes for you! I want to see if this could become something more meaningful," Jason said excitedly.

They smiled at each other as the waiter arrived to take their food orders. A brief time later, the dinners arrived: a hamburger for Jason and a chef's salad for Jenna. They dined while they talked about everything new couples talked of—their family, friends, life, religious beliefs, and especially desires.

Jason and Jenna finished their dinners and enjoyed a couple more drinks. It was dark and late. Jenna felt she needed to leave. She did not want Evan to wonder where she was or to become suspicious. She reluctantly told Jason it was time for her to go.

They exited the restaurant, walking through the park as they held hands like young teenagers in love. When they arrived at Jenna's car, they embraced and passionately kissed. Jenna's feelings deepened for him. Jason opened Jenna's car door for her, and she settled into the driver's seat.

"I hope we can do this again really soon. I miss you when I'm not with you. Drive safe, Jenna," Jason said.

She looked up at Jason and took in his dazzling blue eyes. She smiled, put the car in gear, and drove home.

CHAPTER 6

March 7th

Jenna arrived home close to midnight. Evan was asleep in the recliner, the TV flickering across his face, four beer cans at his feet and a half-eaten pizza cooling on the end table. She thought he looked tranquil and felt a wave of shame. Here was a man who was kind, yet she left him at home alone to eat takeout while she was out with another man.

How could I do this to my husband? she inwardly thought. *How unfair it is to be disloyal to such a nice man.*

She knew, though, that she was no longer physically attracted to Evan and no longer in love with him. She had desires that she needed to fulfill. Evan was no longer the man who could give her what she needed. She promised herself she would be careful and not hurt him, continuing to live in a marriage where she was no longer happy.

I have no choice, she thought. *It's what my faith demands—endure, no matter the cost.*

After Jenna watched Evan sleep in the recliner for a time, she entered the kitchen, reached into the refrigerator, and pulled out an already-opened bottle of Chardonnay. She poured herself a glass and sat at the island. She thought fondly about Jason and the wonderful dinner they had together.

Evan awoke when Jenna walked into the house. He heard her rustle in the kitchen and decided to join her. He walked to the refrigerator to grab a cold beer. He sat with Jenna at the island, where she sipped from a glass of wine.

"You're home late," Evan said.

"I know, Evan, and I'm sorry, there is a lot of preparation needed for this weekend's implementation," Jenna quickly replied.

"Are you close to being ready to implement?"

"Very close," Jenna replied, marveling at how easy it had gotten to deceive Evan.

"Will you be back to normal hours after this weekend?" Evan asked.

"I don't know, we have many projects in the works," Jenna said.

She knew she wanted to see Jason as often as possible and needed to keep her deception alive.

Jenna added, "I have some great news for you, I think you'll like."

"Oh yeah?"

"Remember when we were driving to Long Island the night your mother had died, and I mentioned something about wishing you could fly airplanes? I also said I would investigate it for you. Well, I kept my end of the bargain and did some research."

"Seriously? What kind of research and what did you learn?" Evan asked.

"A lot of research, and what I found out is three things. One, it's not that expensive; two, it doesn't take much time, and you can train on weeknights and weekends; and three, there is a flight school at Albany International Airport. It's convenient since we live nearby."

"Wow, you did a lot of research, but what does not expensive mean, and what is not much time?" Evan asked, cautiously excited.

"It means you can get your certificate in as little as thirty flying hours, and it will only cost between $10,000 and $15,000, depending on how fast you can learn. I know $10,000 sounds like a lot of money, but we never really splurge on trivial nonsense. We can afford it. You have the time, and I don't think this is trivial nonsense."

"I'm surprised it only takes thirty hours because that doesn't seem like a lot of time, but I'm not sure about spending $10,000. Do you think we should spend that kind of money on something like this?"

"I don't think it's as difficult as we think, Evan. I spoke to a seventeen-year-old girl on the phone who is taking her FAA flight test next week. It amazed me that she was so young. If a seventeen-year-old can do it, I'm positive you can. I do not doubt it. Is it something you still want to do? If you do, I say do it. Don't regret not taking the chance while you can and while we can easily afford it."

"Well, I guess I could try it. Did you learn how to sign up and what the steps are to enroll in training?"

"I've already taken care of it. I have booked an introductory flight for noon this Saturday. The flight school is called *TIME2FLY*, and the instructor's name is James Robinson. His daughter was the seventeen-year-old I told you about. She said her father would fly you up and over Lake George to give you a feel for the airplane, to see if you like it. She said I could join you, and I think I would like to go. It sounds like fun. After the flight, you don't have to sign up if you decide it's not something you want to pursue. What do you think? I can call tomorrow morning to cancel and get a refund if you think it's a crazy idea."

"Let's do it! I must be honest, though, I'm a little nervous thinking about it, but you're right; if I do it, now is the best time. I have the time, and we have the funds. I think this would be a lot of fun. And like you say, there is nothing to lose if I don't like it or think I can't do it."

"I'm glad you want to go on Saturday, but right now, I have to get some sleep. I'm exhausted! Are you coming?" Jenna asked.

"Right behind you!"

Jenna and Evan went upstairs, brushed their teeth, and climbed into bed. Evan was excited about flight training, feeling grateful that Jenna had done the research. Evan rolled to Jenna and gently rubbed her back as they lay in bed. He held her by the chin to pull her closer and kissed her passionately. He wanted to make love to her because he was excited about the thought of learning to fly, and he wanted to celebrate it with his wife.

Jenna retracted from Evan. She was not capable of intimacy with him, feeling a tremendous sensation that she would be cheating on Jason. It bothered her to feel the way she did, but she could not deny it. She was falling in love with Jason. She kissed Evan briskly, telling him she was too tired after such a long day, and apologized. She rolled over onto her side with her back to Evan and fell asleep.

Evan lay in bed staring at the ceiling, feeling rejected. He had become all too familiar with this feeling when it involved Jenna.

Does she no longer love me? If she is pulling away and does not love me or desire me, why would she encourage me to learn how to fly so we could go on small vacations together? were thoughts running through his mind.

He had trouble falling asleep as doubts about his marriage stirred through his head. Evan believed they had a decent relationship, but sensed something was wrong with the marriage. He was not quite sure what it was or why. He thought it was probably because he was away taking care of his mother's house all the time, but it was something he needed to do.

CHAPTER 7

March 11th

Evan climbed from the bed with excitement and anticipation. It was the day he would take his first flight on a small airplane, possibly signing up for lessons. He had barely slept with the thoughts that ran through his mind about this new adventure.

When he did sleep, he dreamt about flying off to fun locations with Jenna in an airplane they owned and taking friends for dinners to Nantucket and Martha's Vineyard. He also dreamt about other places they could explore, but never had the time to visit by car.

Evan jumped into the shower, setting the water to a temperature colder than his preferred hot setting. He wanted to wake up feeling invigorated after a poor night's sleep. He also wanted to be as alert as possible. He shaved, dressed, and swiped on extra deodorant—just in case nerves got the better of him. He really did not know what to expect.

Jenna woke up while Evan was in the bathroom, and when he saw she was up, he walked over to her and gave her a light kiss on the lips.

"Good morning, Jenna. How did you sleep?" Evan asked.

"I slept well. Are you excited about today?"

"I feel like a teenager going off to his Junior Prom! I'm excited and incredibly nervous."

"I'm sure you're nervous. This isn't something everyone does every day."

"We should go to the airport early to watch some airplanes take off and land. Check out some of the pilots who are flying. I want to see if they are regular people like me," Evan laughed as he said it.

"That sounds great. I can be ready by eleven. We can drive to the airport any time after then if you like."

"Great! I'm going downstairs to put on some coffee for us and maybe whip up some scrambled eggs and toast unless there is something else that you'd prefer."

"Scrambled eggs and toast are perfect. I just want to take a shower and get ready. I'll be down in about an hour," Jenna said.

Evan opened the closet door and stared at his clothes. He was unsure what to wear on a small airplane. He never imagined it would be something he needed to contemplate. Evan decided jeans with a sweatshirt would be appropriate and got dressed.

He left the bedroom and bounced down the stairs to the kitchen. Evan filled the coffee maker with fresh filtered water, added their favorite Colombian coffee, and hit the start button. He put a couple of slices of wheat bread into the toaster but did not start the browning process. He then cracked open a couple of eggs into a bowl, added seasonings, and whipped them into a frothy mixture.

Besides the coffee he sorely needed, Evan did not want to start cooking until Jenna was down from the bedroom. He wanted to enjoy the hearty and hot breakfast together.

* * *

Since meeting Jason, the first thing Jenna did each morning was pick up her cell phone to look for messages from *Mercedes*. She felt a wave of disappointment when she saw none received.

Jenna remained under the sheets, thinking about Jason for several minutes before she finally rose from the bed and entered the bathroom. As she was about to step into the shower, she heard her cell phone beep. Jenna put on her bathrobe, exited the bathroom, and walked to the nightstand. She smiled when she saw the sender was *Mercedes* and read the message.

"Would love to see you today, JT".

Jenna thought about it for a moment. She knew she had to go with Evan to the airport at noon. She was not sure how long they would be gone. Jenna also knew it was a possibility that she would be needed for the implementation later in the day. She wanted to see Jason, but she didn't think it would be possible.

She texted back, "Busy today. Not sure how long."

"Tonight then," came the reply.

"I'll text u when I can, 2 or later."

"Looking forward to it," Jason typed and added a winking emoji.

When she finished texting with Jason, Jenna deleted the conversation. She made it a habit to delete all messages she received from *Mercedes* immediately after receiving them. She did not want her husband to find the texts, not that he examined her phone, but safety first, she always believed.

Jenna stood in the shower, daydreaming about Jason and his beautiful blue eyes.

How can I manage to see him after the flight? she wondered. *I could always use the office pretext.*

It had been working since Evan didn't seem suspicious about the supposed time spent at the office.

Yes, she thought, *I'll tell him I need to go into the office,* and grinned.

Jenna finished getting ready and descended the stairs to the kitchen. She found Evan seated at the island with his coffee as he read the morning newspaper. She walked over to the coffee pot, poured herself a cup, and added a touch of cream before moving to the island and sitting opposite him. Evan looked up from the paper, smiled, and said he would start breakfast.

Evan browned the toast and cooked up the eggs. They sat in silence while they ate. Evan watched Jenna as she chewed and wondered why she seemed so distant. She appeared deep in thought. He had assumed they would be lively discussing flying, but that was not the case.

Jenna was indeed deep in thought of meeting up with her handsome new companion later in the day. She wanted to break the news that she had to go to work, but did not know how to approach Evan. Of course, she knew it would not be about having to go to the office. No, she understood it was something entirely different and much more exciting.

"What are you thinking about?" Evan was the first to break the silence.

"I don't know how to tell you, but the office contacted me just before I got into the shower. They need me to go in today. I told them it wouldn't be until later, after our flight. I'm sorry."

"More time at the office? Why have they needed you so much lately? I don't understand. I know you're working on a big implementation, but I thought you'd be spending less time on the details since your promotion," Evan said, annoyed.

"I know it's been a lot lately, but they need me," Jenna tried apologetically.

"They seem to need you a lot more than they used to. Will this all stop after your implementation?" Evan was now angry rather than annoyed.

"I don't know, Evan. You know, the beginning of the year always brings in many changes. Once open enrollment closes in February, several changes will take effect, including new health plans, new regulations from the Department of Health, and updates to payment plans, among others. So much occurs in the health insurance industry starting in January that must be completed by April 1st."

Jenna tried to justify her increasing absence from home.

"All right, Jenna, I don't mean to sound angry. I just feel left alone more often than I used to. I guess I will have to put up with it. If I decide to learn how to fly, now would be the perfect time, given your busy schedule at work. It'll give me something to do while you're spending time at the office."

Evan tried to ease the tension, but his anger was still apparent.

Evan and Jenna finished the rest of their breakfast in silence. When they finished eating, Evan picked up the dishes and placed them in the dishwasher. He scrubbed the frying pan he used to cook the eggs and rinsed the coffee cups before putting them in the dish strainer. It was already 10:50, and they were off to Albany International Airport.

CHAPTER 8

The drive to the airport was a brief 15 minutes, something that had worried them back when they were considering purchasing the house. They expected to hear a lot of noise from airplanes flying overhead, but the house was in foreclosure. With the realtor's recommendation, Jenna and Evan made an offer much lower than the asking price, and the bank accepted the terms. They were pleasantly surprised to discover that the home was not under any flight paths after they moved in, and they scarcely heard aircraft overhead. It was a peaceful neighborhood, considering the proximity to the airfield.

As they exited the highway and reached the airport entrance road, Jenna pointed Evan toward Albany Aviation. Liz informed Jenna that the Albany Aviation F.B.O. was located on the airport's outskirts, approximately one-half mile from the main passenger terminal.

"Turn here. We have to go to the F.B.O. called Albany Aviation," Jenna said.

"Okay. What is an F.B.O.?" Evan asked.

"Liz said it stands for Fixed Base Operator. They are found at most larger airports. She said it's like a service or gas station for private aircraft," Jenna explained.

They drove past the airport's main terminal and turned onto a small road leading to Albany Aviation. Evan was pleased that it was not part of the main terminal and had a dedicated parking lot.

"This is great! We don't go anywhere near the main terminal. I won't have to worry about paying for the expensive parking garage either! That would get pricey if I spent time here taking lessons," Evan said.

Evan and Jenna arrived at Albany Aviation and were impressed by the building. It was a large steel structure with enormous dark blue-tinted glass windows. After Evan pulled his car into a slot next to an expensive-looking Mercedes convertible, they climbed out and walked towards the entrance.

As Evan approached the building, he began to feel more anxious than when he first awoke. It seemed almost unimaginable that he would be flying in a small airplane later in the day. Although he felt tense, he was also enthusiastic.

As they moved closer, both front doors slid open. They entered and discovered a beautiful environment.

They found a large room immediately to the right of the front entrance. They looked in and observed several oversized leather recliners facing a flat-screen TV. Further in the room were several comfortable-looking sofas, a couple in use. Lined against one of the walls were several vending machines.

They spotted a door with a small sign reading 'Break Room' and walked to it. When they swung it open, they discovered a room full of cubicles with small beds. Along the back wall was a row of lockers like the type you would find in a train or bus station. They closed the door.

As they exited the main room and reentered the lobby, they saw a sign on the open door that read 'Pilot's Lounge'.

"Cool!" Evan remarked.

"Yeah, this *is* pretty cool. They have everything in there!"

"Yes," Evan answered as he tried to absorb it all.

Next to the pilot's lounge was a smaller room with computer terminals and monitors. Two older gentlemen in their early sixties were looking at one of the monitors. Weather radar was displayed on the monitor, remarkably, Evan thought, very much like what he saw each evening during weather forecasts on the local television news broadcast. Both gentlemen looked up at Jenna and Evan, smiled, and produced a welcoming wave. A sign on the door identified the room as the 'Weather Station'.

As they moved further into the building, they entered the main lobby. Again, the lobby had several wrap-style, comfortable-looking leather sofas and chairs. A large counter was in the center of the room with a coffee pot and an assortment of freshly baked cookies. There were small bags containing several types of snacks and chips. A small refrigerator stood beneath the counter. They assumed there would be refreshments for visitors and pilots.

Large glass walls began at the floor, and two full stories climbed to the ceiling surrounding the lobby. The blue-tinted windows formed a quarter circle around the lobby, providing incredible views of the airport's runways. From these large windows, they saw various types of airplanes parked on the tarmac. Several people could also be seen scattered around the tarmac and planes, animated in conversations.

"Wow, this is getting even more impressive! I never knew this was here at the airport. We always went directly to the main parking garage and into the main terminal," Jenna said.

"It is pretty impressive," Evan replied and continued, "They must all be pilots coming and going. Did you see the big fuel truck filling the small airplanes?"

Jenna noticed a large counter with a young girl behind it and nudged Evan.

"That must be where we need to go."

"Okay."

Evan's stomach began to twist, and he felt apprehensive. It had started to feel all too real.

As they moved toward the main counter, Evan glanced to his left and saw another small room, enclosed by a glass window. He saw a man seated behind a desk, toiling away at a computer. On the glass window was a sign reading "*TIME2FLY* Aviation."

"Jenna, I think we should go here. Didn't you say the school was named Time to Fly? That looks like it."

"Yes, that's the school. I guess we go in there then; let's go!"

They approached *TIME2FLY*, knocked on the door jamb, and caught the man's attention. He looked up from his computer.

"Hi there. What can I do for you?" the man called out.

"Hi, I'm Evan Williams. My wife phoned on Tuesday about taking an introductory flight. I believe she spoke with your daughter, Liz."

"Well, hello, Evan! Welcome to *TIME2FLY*. My name is James Robinson. You can call me Jim. I believe we have you booked for a flight at noon. You're a little early, but that's not a problem. We can get up into the sky anytime."

He stood, presenting a large hand as he spoke. Evan reached for Jim's hand and gave it a hearty shake. Jim Robinson appeared to be in his late sixties with thinning salt and pepper hair and a thick mustache. He stood close to six feet tall and was in reasonable shape for someone his age, weighing approximately 190 pounds.

"Sounds good, Jim. This is my wife, Jenna. She is the one who started my interest in flying."

"That's great! I think it's a wonderful pastime or profession, depending on your goals," Jim said and continued, "Not to sound offensive, but you might be a bit too old for a flying profession," he laughed and continued, "It takes years before you can make a living from flying. Most professional pilots start right out of high school, some even earlier. I will assume you're looking at flying as a pastime."

"Ha-ha, I'm not offended, and yes, it will be a pastime. I imagine it could open the world for me and Jenna. I'm hoping it will allow us to see places we wouldn't be able to by car, or at least easily by car," Evan explained.

"That's why many folks want to learn. We can do this in one of two ways; it is entirely your preference. We can go up in the airplane first, have a nice scenic tour of the area so you can get a feel for flying, then talk about the steps required to obtain a pilot's certificate when we land, or we can talk about those steps first and fly afterward. Your choice, what do you think?" Jim asked.

"I think I'd like to go up in the airplane first," Evan replied enthusiastically.

"All right then, let's go fly. Are you joining us, Jenna? You're more than welcome; there is room in the plane for you."

"I would love to go with you. I think that would be great. I guess I need to know if it will be something I like too if Evan becomes a pilot," Jenna replied.

"That's great, follow me!"

Jim grabbed three sets of headphones and led Jenna and Evan through the lobby, and out of another set of automated doors, onto the tarmac.

CHAPTER 9

Jenna and Evan were surprised to discover how breezy it was when they exited the building. Evan tried to remember if it was windy when they arrived, but he could not recall. As they moved along the tarmac, Jim told them to remain vigilant for running airplanes. He stated they would not want to walk into a spinning propeller. He also wanted Jenna and Evan to be alert for airplanes moving along the tarmac and asked them to stay at his side as he walked them to his plane.

The airplane Jim stopped at was white with gold stripes and displayed a number on the side. It looked old, and it made Jenna a little wary.

"This is a 1972 Cessna 172. It's also known as a Skyhawk. It's a popular airplane that flight schools and private pilots use because they are easy to fly, inexpensive to purchase, and not too costly to maintain. It's called a high wing because the wings are above the cockpit." Jim explained while they neared the plane.

"Wow, a 1972 airplane? Isn't that a bit old? I mean, I wouldn't want to drive a 1972 car! Is it safe?" Jenna asked incredulously.

"I understand your concern. Everyone says that when they first hear how old it is, but yes, it is safe. Airplanes are very well-maintained and robustly constructed. They are made from aluminum, so we don't worry too much about parts failing due to rust. They receive extensive yearly maintenance and inspections. These inspections are much more thorough than your typical car inspection. The engines are also rebuilt after a set number of flying hours as defined by the FAA. Trust me. We are safe," Jim explained.

"I guess that sounds okay then," Jenna was a little comforted, but still worried about the plane's age.

Jim reached the airplane, opened the pilot's door, and pressed switches. The rear of the wings hummed and slowly moved. Lights illuminated and blinked. When he turned away from the plane, he held a small book and a plastic tube in his hand.

Jim said he would start the flight with a check of the airplane, commonly called a pre-flight check. The purpose of this was to ensure the aircraft is in good flying condition, all lighting worked, and sufficient fuel was on board. He explained that the book he was holding was a checklist he would follow.

Jenna and Evan were a bit surprised to hear Jim say he used a book for the pre-flight check, as he called it.

Evan could not hold back his curiosity and questioned Jim.

"Jim, why are you using an instruction manual? Don't you already know what to do?"

"Yes, and I could easily perform the pre-check from memory, but it is always wise to use a checklist. The FAA requires all pilots to follow a checklist. Even commercial pilots, with hundreds of hours of experience, must follow a checklist for the jet they are piloting," Jim explained.

"Oh, okay, that makes sense, I guess," Evan said.

"Everyone asks me that very question the first time they fly. It's understandable. Follow me while I do the pre-flight, and I'll explain what I am doing as I go."

Jim walked to the front of the plane and pointed at the various solid and blinking lights.

"The first check is lighting. All lights must be in proper working order before taking off on a flight," Jim said as he described each light's purpose and specific color.

Jim walked around the aircraft, manipulating various sections as he moved.

"What I am doing now is checking each of the movable surfaces of the wings and tail, ensuring they are working smoothly. I also look at the yoke, making sure it moves as expected," Jim said.

"There's an awful lot to know," Evan said.

"You'll learn all this in ground school. It's also why we follow this checklist," Jim said as he pointed to it.

"Ground school? What is that?" Evan asked.

"I'll explain all that after our flight. Just relax and enjoy."

Evan pondered what Jim said about ground school. He had forgotten that Jenna mentioned a class. He always thought that learning to fly would be in an airplane only. As he thought more about it, he realized it did make sense. There had to be much more to flying than steering through an open sky.

Jim used the plastic tube he removed from the cockpit and drained fuel under each wing. He explained that he was looking for the possibility of water seeping into the tanks from fuel caps located on the top of each wing or from a tainted fueling pump.

"I am looking for water in the fuel. If there was water present, you would see it settle at the bottom of this little tube because water is heavier than gasoline."

After inspecting the fuel for water, he retrieved a step ladder, a small stick, and a paper towel from the rear of the airplane.

"A step ladder? Why do you need a step ladder? And what is that stick used for?" Jenna asked.

"We use the step ladder to reach the gas caps on these wings. The stick measures how much fuel is in each wing."

"Aren't there fuel gauges in planes?" Evan asked.

"Yes, there are, but you always want to check physically. If your car's fuel gauge stops working correctly and you run out of gas, you can pull over to the side of the road and call AAA. In an airplane, if you run out of fuel because of a bad gas gauge, you certainly can't pull over to the nearest cloud and park!" Jim chuckled as he said this.

After he ensured the fuel tanks were full, Jim opened the engine compartment and checked the oil using a dipstick. It reminded Evan of the times he checked the oil in his lawnmower and giggled to himself.

When Jim completed the pre-flight checks and returned the step ladder to the airplane's rear, he turned to Evan and Jenna.

"All right, guys, are you ready to see what your city looks like from above?" Jim heartily asked.

Jim opened the right-hand door for Jenna. He pulled the front seat forward and helped her climb into the back of the airplane. When Jenna settled and buckled in, he rolled the seat back into place. Evan tried to take the seat in front of Jenna, but Jim stopped him.

"Hey, that's my chair!" Jim laughed.

"What? I thought the pilot sat on the other side, like in a car. Aren't you going to sit over there?" Evan asked.

"Nope. That seat's reserved for you. I'm going to fly from over here. This is the side where instructors always sit, unless the student is working on their flight instructor certificate. If you hadn't noticed, the airplane has dual controls and is usually set up that way in most, if not all, airplanes. They can be flown from the left or right seat. As an instructor, I always sit in the right seat. As a matter of fact, I act as an instructor so often I find myself in the right seat even when I'm flying alone!" Jim said and continued, "And besides, I'm going to let you do a little of the flying once we are in the air! You'll have fun!"

Evan looked at Jim, astonished. It was supposed to be an introductory flight, and piloting an airplane was not what he expected. He felt a mix of enthusiasm and fear as he thought about it, walking to the other side of the aircraft and climbing in.

CHAPTER 10

March 11th

Jenna and Evan glanced at each other after they settled into their seats. She had an apprehensive look on her face while Evan beamed from ear to ear. They were going flying, and he was overjoyed. What was just a passing idea a few months ago had become a reality.

Evan looked over the console at the various dials and gauges. He saw buttons everywhere and what looked to be radios. Jim was correct; there were two sets of controls, and they moved in unison as though they were connected with invisible wires as Jim manipulated them.

Jim pulled on a choke, pushed a lever slightly towards the console, and turned the key. The airplane roared to life, becoming extremely loud in the cockpit. Traveling in relative silence inside commercial airplanes did not prepare Evan for how deafening it would be.

Jim looked at Evan and yelled, "This is why we wear headphones. It gets loud. Go ahead and put yours on."

Jenna watched Jim and Evan as they placed the headphones on their heads and over their ears and followed their lead. Jim reached towards Evan, grabbed a wire that hung from his headset, plugged it into the firewall, and did the same with his own. He reached back towards Jenna, grabbed the wire hanging from her headset, and plugged it into the ceiling.

"There, that's a little better. Can you hear me, okay?" Jim's voice radiated through the cups of the headphones.

"Yes, I can hear you," Evan replied.

"I can hear you, too," Jenna followed.

"Great. Now we can talk with each other more comfortably. We will also be able to hear the controllers talk to us. This little red button on top of the yoke is what I press to talk back to them. Please try keeping your hands and fingers off it, Evan."

Evan looked at the yoke and became apprehensive about accidentally hitting buttons, which could cause an issue.

"Okay, I'll be careful."

"For the next few minutes, I will contact ground control to introduce us and let them know where we are going. I'm going to ask you not to speak during this time. We call it a sterile cockpit. So, from now on, no talking until I tell you when it is okay to speak again."

"Okay," Jenna and Evan responded simultaneously.

Evan glanced over at Jenna again. She looked a little frightened, he thought.

"Albany Ground, Cessna Five One Six Sierra Mike," Jim's voice heard over the headsets.

"Cessna Six Sierra Mike, go ahead," a reply returned.

"Cessna Six Sierra Mike, we're a Skyhawk VFR to the northeast practice area at three thousand, request flight following," Jim responded.

"Cessna Six Sierra Mike, squawk three three one two, tower one twenty-two point two, let me know when you're ready to taxi."

"Six Sierra Mike squawking three three one two, tower on one twenty-two point two."

After the exchange with ground control, Jim entered 3312 into a device on the control panel.

"This is called a transponder. It provides air traffic controllers with the ability to track us. This number we were assigned will allow air traffic control to distinguish us from the other aircraft displayed on the radar screen," Jim explained.

Jim asked if his passengers were ready to go, and Evan enthusiastically gave him a thumbs-up. Jim eased the airplane from its location and rolled it towards the tarmac's center, away from other parked planes. He reminded them again about the need for silence as he spoke to the control tower.

"Albany ground Six Sierra Mike, Albany Aviation, ready to taxi."

"Six Sierra Mike, taxi to runway one via Charlie, then Bravo."

"Taxi runway one, Charlie and Bravo, Six Sierra Mike."

Jim steered the airplane off the Albany Aviation tarmac and onto a taxiway. Evan noticed Jim did not steer the aircraft with the yoke and assumed he used his feet. Evan looked down and saw the foot pedals move on his side of the plane while observing movement in Jim's legs as the airplane made its way to the runway. He tried looking behind the aircraft at the rudder to see if it moved, but could not find it from where he was seated.

Jim entered a small parking area at the end of the taxiway, spun the plane toward the direction they had just traveled, and stopped.

Jim spoke up, "This is called a run-up area, and we are going to do what is called the run-up. A run-up ensures the engine runs properly and the plane is ready for flight. I will also recheck the ailerons and vertical stabilizer for proper movement with the yoke."

Jim reached for the same book he used while performing the pre-flight check and opened it.

"You will notice I am using a checklist again. That is to ensure I don't miss a step," Jim said when he noticed Evan and Jenna looking at the manual in his hand again.

Jim moved the yoke while looking out the window at the ailerons and vertical stabilizer to ensure proper and smooth function. When he finished, he pulled on a lever marked carb heat. The engine's sound reduced as if it were about to shut off.

"This is carburetor heat. We always check that before a flight. Carburetor heat will melt any ice formation that may have built up in the carburetor during flight. That can occur on the warmest of days. I am looking for a slight reduction in power by looking at the RPMs," Jim explained.

When the airplane's engine roared, Evan watched Jim push a lever toward the control panel. Evan assumed it was the equivalent of an accelerator in a car.

"Now I am checking our magnetos, the spark required to run the engine. Every airplane has dual magnetos for redundancy, and we always want to ensure both function properly.

"I will turn the key one click to the left. That will cause the engine to run on the left magneto only. I should observe a slight RPM drop since the plane will run on only one side. I don't want to see too much of a drop, and I also don't want to feel the engine sputtering. Since the airplane has two magnetos, I'll do the same, turning the key to the right."

When Jim turned the key, Evan heard the RPMs drop slightly each time, but the engine sounded fine otherwise.

Jim pushed the carburetor heat lever in and hit a button marked flaps. It displayed several numbers that seemed to be percentages.

"I set the flaps to twenty percent," Jim explained and continued, "The proper setting for takeoff on this airplane, according to the checklist."

Jim pointed to a chart in the book.

"Although I know this airplane, I verify our rotation speed. That is the speed we need to reach before I can pull back the yoke to climb into the air. According to this airplane, that is seventy knots," Jim pointed to the book and a gauge on the firewall as he spoke.

"Are you guys ready for takeoff?" Jim asked.

"Sure," replied Jenna nervously.

"Yes," Evan also replied, but with excitement.

"Okay, let's go and, once again, sterile cockpit."

Evan watched as Jim changed the radio frequency to 122.2 as instructed earlier and spoke into his microphone.

"Albany Tower, Cessna Five One Six Sierra Mike, runway one ready for departure."

"Cessna Six Sierra Mike, hold short."

"Cessna Six Sierra mike holding short."

Jim pushed on the throttle, and the airplane moved from the run-up area to the runway, but stopped before it rolled onto it. They waited a few minutes before the control tower instruction came across their headsets.

"Cessna Six Sierra Mike cleared for takeoff," came a call from the tower.

"Cessna Six Sierra Mike, cleared for takeoff," Jim responded.

Jim rolled the airplane forward, tracing a white line painted on the runway with the airplane's nose wheel. When he was centered, he applied full power, and the plane raced forward.

After what seemed like only a few seconds to Evan, Jim pulled back on the yoke, and Evan could feel the airplane release its grip from the ground as it ascended into the sky.

CHAPTER 11

March 11th

J enna and Evan were airborne, and Evan's mind filled with marvel. It felt like a dream to him. When the radio crackled, Evan returned to reality.

"Cessna Six Sierra Mike climb to two thousand. Contact departure one two seven point five."

Evan tried to listen and understand the radio conversation but was too fascinated by the airplane's movement. He peered out his window, trying to locate the street and house they lived in, but he had trouble finding it among all the rooftops.

He was disoriented as he looked down at the ground from where they were. It was an unfamiliar view from the sky. Yes, he had arrived and departed from the airport commercially. However, the views from a small airplane window appeared larger and less restricted.

As he watched the ground falling away, Evan suddenly remembered he was deathly afraid of heights and began to feel dizzy. He had never told anyone about this fear, not even Jenna. It was then that he realized he could never learn to fly.

Unexpectedly, Jenna reached from the backseat and tapped Evan on the shoulder, causing him to jump at the sudden touch. He turned to face her. She smiled from ear to ear. She really enjoyed the flight, and she wanted Evan to know. It was her way of telling him she was ready to fly everywhere, and Evan had her approval for the training. The fear of an old, small, noisy airplane no longer worried her.

They continued to travel northeast as Jim pointed out several landmarks to Jenna and Evan.

"Look down there on your left. That is Round Lake. It was named correctly, as you can see. It really is round!" Jim continued after a drastic turn, "Over on your right, you can see the Green Mountains of Vermont. The river looks pretty small from this vantage point, don't you think?" Jim pointed at the Hudson River.

"Yeah," was all Evan could spit out.

"If you look straight ahead, you can see the Adirondack Mountains. That is where we will be heading. It will take us over the city of Glens Falls and the Glens Falls Airport."

"There's an airport in Glens Falls?" Jenna asked.

"Absolutely!" Jim replied and continued, "There are airports everywhere. To the left, you can see Schenectady County Airport. There's also a small airport in Rensselaer."

"Really, I never knew that! They must be for small airplanes."

Evan's first complete sentence since the climb out of the airport.

"They are small airports, although Schenectady County Airport has the Air National Guard, and Glens Falls can handle small private jets," Jim explained.

"There on your left is the Saratoga County Airport. If you were there during the Saratoga horse racing season, you would see several large private jets. They are the rich and famous who attend the track each year."

"Oh yes, I remember people talking about an airport for jets in Saratoga. Cool!" Evan said.

Evan became more comfortable in the airplane as it moved through the sky. His initial fear faded quickly; the height no longer bothered him. They continued to fly northbound and soon left Albany's controlled airspace.

Jim suddenly announced, "All right, Evan, I'm going to relinquish control over to you. All you need to do is take the yoke and hold it very lightly."

"I don't know. Should I? I'm a little nervous. What if I crash us?"

"Not to worry. You won't crash. I want you to get a feel for the airplane. All you have to do is hold the yoke, and I'll manage the rudder pedals. It will be quite easy," Jim assured him.

Evan was hesitant as he took hold of the yoke, and the airplane descended. It frightened him, and he immediately let go.

"Don't push on it. Just hold it lightly in your fingertips."

Jim demonstrated as he took the yoke back in his hands and leveled the airplane. He let go of the yoke, and Evan gently wrapped his fingers around it. To Evan's astonishment, he was controlling an aircraft. Initially apprehensive, he calmed down after a few minutes and fixated his eyes straight ahead. Evan feared that turning his head would cause him to lose control of the plane.

"You're doing great!" Jim assured Evan and continued, "Just do what you're doing. Remember, I have my controls over here, too. Nothing bad can happen. I want you to relax if you can and enjoy the ride."

"Okay, I'll try. Do I need to do anything differently?" Evan asked.

"No, you're doing fine. Let's just fly!" came Jim's cheerful reply.

They flew over Lake George and the Adirondack Mountains' southern tip. The skies were crystal clear, with nary a cloud seen, and the wind was calm. Jenna and Evan were surprised at the smoothness of the plane. They had always heard that small airplanes bounced and shook.

"Okay, folks, how about we turn back towards the airport? Evan, just turn the yoke very easily to the left, and I'll work the pedals," Jim said to him.

"Ok, I think I can do that," Evan replied timidly.

"You'll be fine. Just turn gently and slightly. I'll tell you when to stop."

As instructed, Evan turned the yoke gently to the left and was surprised by how easily it moved as the plane banked to the left.

"That's good. Keep the yoke right there," Jim said.

They continued to bank left and made a complete turn to the south.

"Far enough; let's go straight now. I'm going to contact the airport to let them know we are returning, so sterile cockpit," Jim said, then contacted Albany.

"Albany approach Cessna Six Sierra Mike returning to land," Jim spoke into his microphone.

"Cessna Six Sierra Mike, heading one eight zero, descend to two thousand," came the reply.

"One eight zero, two thousand, Six Sierra Mike," Jim responded.

"Okay, Evan, I'll take the controls back. You did a fabulous job! I think piloting is in your future. We can discuss that after we land and tie down the airplane."

Jim was confident he had a new student.

The airplane sailed towards the airport while Evan gazed out the window. After several minutes, the control tower radioed more instructions to Jim. Evan tried to understand everything that Jim and the controllers exchanged, but all he could grasp was that they were landing on runway one.

As they neared, Evan spotted an enormous number *one* painted on the blacktop and realized it must be how pilots knew how to identify the proper runway.

Jenna and Evan were both impressed with Jim's landing. They told him it was one of the smoothest landings they had ever experienced, softer than the commercial airliners they traveled on. Jim looked over and smiled as he taxied to Albany Aviation onto the tarmac and near the place it sat before they left. He twisted the plane using the throttle and rudder pedals, then turned the key to shut down the engine.

After they got off the airplane, Jim and Evan pushed it back into the parking spot and tied each wing with ropes affixed to the ground by metal loops. Jim reached into the aircraft, gathered up the headsets, and closed the door.

They walked back to the building in silence. Evan was overwhelmed by the flight and pleased with his experience. He looked over at Jenna and saw that she smiled brightly. Apparently, she was feeling the same way.

After the flight and discussing all the details with Jim, Evan signed up for flying lessons and ground school and purchased a headset. Jim also handed him his very own logbook to log his flight hours and endorsements.

As they walked out of the Albany Aviation building, Evan turned to take one last look inside. This was going to be his new favorite place. He gazed at individuals in the lobby and watched as two young men entered the pilot's lounge. He wondered to himself if they would become new pilot friends.

It has always been challenging for Evan to make friends since his release from juvenile detention so many years ago. His traumatic youth, the aftermath of killing his father, and spending time locked up made it harder for Evan to trust others. Other than being with Jenna, he had preferred to keep to himself.

Jenna and Evan settled into the Audi and sat quietly for a moment. He reached over to hold Jenna's hand. Evan gazed at her with a glowing smile, leaned over, and gave her a warm kiss.

"I cannot believe I just signed up to be a pilot!" he exclaimed.

"You did! You really did sign up. I'm delighted and excited for you. I know you'll do great!" Jenna responded.

"It sounds like it will take up a lot of my time. I may not be around much for dinners and away from home on the weekends. Will you feel abandoned and alone like you did when I was away those few months taking care of my mother's house after she died?"

"No, I won't feel abandoned. Don't be so silly. I think this is great. I'm so busy at work, and I'm sure I'll have plenty to keep myself occupied," Jenna replied.

Evan pulled out of the parking lot and headed for home. The car ride was silent. Both Jenna and Evan were deep in thought, but not of the same things. Evan's mind was filled with airplanes, flying lessons, ground school, and the medical exam he required to have before his first lesson. His mind was mostly filled with the flight they were just on.

Jenna's mind was full of many different thoughts from the ones Evan held. She did not think about the flight or Evan signing up for flight training. Jenna did not worry about the time he would spend at the airport. Her visions were those of Jason.

Don't worry, Evan, she gleefully said to herself, *I'll have plenty to keep myself occupied!*

CHAPTER 12

March 11th

Evan pulled his Audi into the garage and shut down the engine. As Jenna and Evan climbed from the car, Jenna reminded Evan of her need to go into the office. She told him she did not know when she would be home. It all depended on how the implementation went. It was a lie she had become more comfortable exploiting.

"Yeah, I remembered," Evan replied, annoyed.

Evan wanted to sit down with Jenna and discuss flying, flight school, and the experience they had just enjoyed. He was excited about the flight, but then he felt let down by Jenna.

"I was hoping we could spend the afternoon discussing flight training and schedules. After talking with Jim today, it sounds like I won't be around the house too often for the next several months."

"I realize it's going to take up a lot of your time, and I'm good with it," Jenna replied.

"Are you sure, Jen?"

"Yes, I'm sure, but I really need to go now. We'll talk later. Make dinner for yourself, and I'll eat when I get home," Jenna said as she climbed into her car parked alongside Evan's in the garage.

Jenna backed out of the garage, turned, and drove away. She desperately wanted to contact Jason, but she waited until she had left her neighborhood. Jenna traveled several blocks and made a couple of turns before she pulled alongside a curb. She grabbed the cell phone from her purse and typed.

"Are you there? JW," Jenna typed into her phone and pressed 'SEND'.

Jenna waited several minutes for a reply. She started to think her day with Jason would not happen when her cell phone finally beeped.

"Hey, beautiful!" The text message included a heart emoji.

"Hi. I am free. Are you?" Jenna typed with nervousness. She wanted him to be available for her.

"Yes. Frear Park?"

"25 mins!" Jenna typed back. She added a smiling emoji.

Jenna placed the phone back into her purse, but with the excitement she was feeling, she neglected to delete the messages she had exchanged with Jason. She pulled from the curb and began her drive to Frear Park. She had decided earlier in the day, while on the airplane, that she could no longer resist Jason. She decided that today was the day they would make love for the first time.

The airplane ride had invigorated her much differently than it had Evan. She had no idea why the desire came to her during the flight, but she anticipated that Jason felt the same way. She knew Evan had assumed that when she smiled during the airplane ride, it was because she was enjoying the flight, not because she was thinking about Jason. Of course, he was wrong.

When she arrived at Frear Park, Jenna approached their favorite pagoda bench to find Jason seated and waiting. She smiled radiantly when he looked up and waved to her. His eyes gripped her attention, sparkling ever more brightly than she remembered.

"Hi, Jason," Jenna said.

"Hey, gorgeous," Jason replied.

Jenna sat down next to Jason and reached for his hand. She leaned against him to feel his warmth and inhale his aroma. They kissed passionately, wrapping each other in a tight embrace.

"Let's go to your place," Jenna blurted while she had the nerve. She did not want to hide behind her anxiety any longer.

"Seriously? I would love that! Are you sure?" Jason asked in surprise.

"Yeah, I am sure. Nervous, but sure," Jenna replied.

"Then let's go before you change your mind!" Jason softly chuckled in response.

"I'll follow you back to your place. Don't lose me in traffic!"

"That would be great, and don't worry, I'll keep an eye on you," Jason said, smiling.

Jenna and Jason rose from the bench and walked to Jason's Jaguar parked alongside Jenna's convertible. Jenna felt her stomach churn with butterflies as she climbed into her Boxster. She would be with someone who was not her husband, and she tried to remember how she got there.

It doesn't matter, she thought.

Her desire for Jason was too strong to ignore. Jason navigated his Jaguar across the Hudson River to Washington Park, located in downtown Albany. Jenna followed closely behind.

Jason bought his place in Washington Park once his defense practice started to take off. The area—known for its restored, high-priced century-old townhomes—gave him exactly what he wanted: a way to show clients he was successful, and a chance to live that image himself.

Jason parked his car along the curb and watched in his rearview mirror as Jenna pulled in behind him.

They reached for each other's hands when they met on the sidewalk.

"Are you sure you're ready? I know I am."

"Absolutely sure!" Jenna exclaimed, though she felt slightly uncertain.

They walked down the street hand in hand past two beautiful townhomes before arriving at Jason's. Jenna was immediately impressed with the tall three-story stone and brick structure, painted a medium brown and trimmed in hunter green. Bright red double-entry doors dominated the view from the bottom of several concrete steps. There was a large porch overlooking the park with several high-end wicker chairs artfully arranged.

"This is beautiful!" Jenna exclaimed.

"Thank you. I purchased it a few years ago. Wait until you see inside," Jason replied.

Jason led Jenna up the stairs, inserted his key into the lock, and opened the door. He stood aside so she could enter first. Jenna's mouth fell agape when she noticed the two-story foyer and sizeable grand staircase gracefully curving to the floor above.

She looked to her left and viewed a large room with a fireplace soaring from the floor to the ceiling. In the corner was a white grand piano. She looked to her right and found another stunning room exhibiting overstuffed leather furniture and a huge flat-screen TV mounted to the far wall.

"So, what do you think?" Jason asked Jenna with pride.

"It's amazing! I've never been in a townhome like this. I'm impressed for sure!" Jenna replied.

"I'm glad you like it," Jason said and continued, "What do you want to do?"

"I want a tour of the whole magnificent place!"

Jason gave Jenna a complete tour of his three-bedroom, three-bathroom townhouse. He pointed out several wall paintings, statues, and artifacts he collected over the years. He explained that many were inherited from his grandparents, including the piano that he didn't know how to play. They toured the entire place before they ended at a doorway to the primary bedroom. Jason made sure it was the last stop on the tour.

"This is the primary bedroom," Jason said as he entered.

"Very nice," Jenna replied.

Jenna looked around the room. She saw a large, ornate, wood-framed king-size bed with two matching, huge dressers on opposing walls. The bedroom was wrapped in large floor-to-ceiling windows located on the corner walls. To her left, she saw a door to what she presumed was the bathroom.

Although she was equally impressed with this room as the rest of the house, only one thing filled her head. Jenna felt as if the butterflies she had in her stomach when she left for the park had grown into full-sized birds. She was in another man's bedroom.

Jason moved closer to Jenna, pulled her to him, and gently kissed her on her lips. Jenna pulled him in tighter, kissed him harder, and reached for his belt. As she unclasped the hook, Jason reached into her blouse to explore her erect nipples and gently caressed them between his fingers.

They swiftly undressed each other, fell onto the bed, and started to make love. They did not spend unnecessary and wasteful time removing the covers. They made love all afternoon, only taking breaks to sip champagne and nibble on strawberries that Jason had retrieved from the kitchen. Jenna was in heaven.

Sometime later, Jenna woke to find herself curled against Jason, which felt natural. The butterflies fluttering in her stomach were gone and replaced with a calm she had not felt in a long time. She listened to Jason breathe quietly, and it soothed her.

Jason rolled over to face her. When he smiled at her, she thought he looked even more handsome. His blue eyes sparkled as the setting sun's rays streamed through the impressive bedroom windows. He kissed her, wrapped an arm around her, and gently stroked her back.

While she knew she was married and had just committed the ultimate sin, she felt incredibly relaxed.

The peacefulness was shattered suddenly when Jenna's cell phone startled her back to reality. She was lost in another world, a place she yearned to stay. She had overlooked the need to be available for the implementation at work. She presumed it was Debbie on the other end of the call and reached for her phone. She did not look at the caller ID when she answered.

"Hello."

"Jenna! Where are you? I tried to reach you at the office, but they said you hadn't been in all afternoon. I thought you had a big implementation to worry about?" Evan was infuriated.

"Oh, yeah. After leaving the house, I called them to let them know I was on my way. They said they didn't need me, and I thought I would do some shopping since I was already in the car. I'm sorry, I should have called you to let you know," Jenna impressed herself with her ability to lie so easily.

"Oh, okay. You've been gone for a few hours. When will you be home?" Evan calmed slightly.

"I should be home soon. Did you make dinner?" Jenna asked.

"I was just about to start, which is why I called. I'm going to make chicken cordon bleu with a side of broccoli. It should be ready by 8:30. Will you be home in time to have dinner with me?" Evan asked.

"Yes, I should be. I'm almost done here at the mall. I never did find anything I liked."

Jenna ended the call. She started to feel anxious again and wondered if her husband would be able to sense she was with another man. She questioned if she could look at him the same way without guilt drawn over her face. The butterflies returned, but this time for a different reason.

"I need to go," Jenna said with sorrow.

"Do you really have to? I wish you could stay forever," Jason meant it.

"Yes, I do. That was Evan. He asked where I was. I lied, but I do need to get home before he becomes too suspicious," Jenna said, then asked, "Is it okay if I use your shower before I go?"

"Of course. Fresh towels are in the closet inside the bathroom, and a hairdryer is hanging on the wall next to the sink. Do you want me to join you?" Jason smiled.

"Do I want you to join me? Yes! Should you? No."

Jenna excused herself to the main bathroom and walked to a large mirror hanging over a massive marble sink. She stared at herself and tried to determine if she looked any different. "Would Evan sense a difference?" she wondered to herself. She was unsure if he would, but she knew she had to shower to remove Jason's heavenly scent from her body. She wished she could keep it on her forever.

CHAPTER 13

March 11th

Jenna pulled into the garage and shut down the Boxter's engine, but remained seated. She wanted to collect her emotions and feelings before she entered the house. Those emotions wavered between excitement for Jason and guilt for Evan. She had to calm herself down to appear as normal as possible. She thought about how she would look and, even more so, how she would act. She had crossed a line, a line that would destroy her marriage, and it worried her.

She finally gathered her emotions, got out of her car, and moved across the garage to the inner door leading to the kitchen. As she walked in, she found Evan enthusiastically preparing dinner.

She placed her purse and cell phone on the island counter where she stood to avoid getting too close to him. Even though she had showered before leaving Jason's townhome, she was convinced Jason's scent and the scent of lovemaking still emitted from her, and she did not want Evan to smell it.

"Great, you're home!" Evan called out.

"Yes, I am. I see you have dinner started. Do I have time to go up and take a shower?" Jenna asked.

"Sure. Dinner will be served in an hour. Take your time."

"I'll be back down soon."

***

Jenna walked out of the kitchen and moved swiftly up the stairs. She felt the need to shower again quickly to prevent the aroma she imagined she smelled from lingering around the house.

She undressed in the bedroom and immediately placed her bra and panties in the hamper. She believed Jason's smell still adhered to them and would fill the bedroom if she left them on the floor. She entered the bathroom, turned on the shower, and climbed in.

***

Evan was laser-focused as he prepared the meal, whistling as he moved around the kitchen. He had learned to cook from his mother as a young boy before being sent off to juvenile detention. They would make the meals and bake cakes and cookies. Evan absorbed a lot from his mother and gradually improved his cooking skills over the years.

Whenever Evan was in the kitchen with his mother before the events that changed his life, Ray had never missed a chance to spew nasty comments about a man in a kitchen instead of working in an engine bay, but Evan ignored him. It was just one of numerous unpleasant remarks Evan learned to disregard.

As Evan placed the chicken into the oven to bake, he heard Jenna's cell phone beep. He was surprised she left it in the kitchen, especially recently, because it never left her side. He thought Debbie was texting Jenna about the implementation and picked up the phone.

He felt a sudden, gut-wrenching punch when he saw who sent the message and read its contents.

"Had a great time today," read the message with a kissing emoji.

He saw the message was from a *Mercedes,* but it did not make sense. His curiosity turned to a sudden feeling of sickness. He looked up *Mercedes* in Jenna's contact list and saw it assigned to a local Albany area phone number. He returned to the messaging app to read all the messages Jenna had received from *Mercedes.* The messages he found were dated only for the day and appeared to be a conversation between *Mercedes* and Jenna. He read them.

"Are you there? JW," Sent by Jenna moments after she had left the house.

The rest of the conversation didn't make sense to Evan. He had it all in front of his eyes and still was confused.

Who is she meeting at Frear Park? Evan wondered.

"Whoever it was, Jenna met this person 25 minutes after we returned home from the airplane ride," Evan mumbled to himself.

Evan felt incredibly nauseous, rushed to the downstairs bathroom, and dry heaved into the toilet. He felt overpowered by disbelief. Jenna was having an affair, and Evan never suspected a thing.

How could she do this to me? Why would she have an affair? Why didn't I see it? How long has this been going on? Evan sat on the cold bathroom floor and seethed with all these questions rushing through his mind.

After a time, Evan gathered himself, rose from the floor, walked into the living room, and fell onto the couch. He still held Jenna's phone. While he sat and waited for Jenna to finish her shower, he contemplated what he would say about her apparent infidelity. Evan was angry and felt betrayed.

Jenna started walking downstairs but stopped halfway when she noticed Evan on the couch. She felt uneasy as she watched him stare blankly into her cell phone. She could see that his face was distorted and red with anger. Jenna immediately knew something was wrong and did not wonder what it was. She knew she had been caught.

*** * ***

"How could you do this to me?" Evan yelled when he saw her on the stairs.

"I'm so sorry, Evan. I never meant to hurt you," Jenna quietly replied.

"Who is this? How long has this been going on?"

"It's someone I met a few months ago while you were in Long Island. I felt alone. I wasn't looking for an affair, honestly. I certainly wasn't looking to ruin our marriage. It just happened. I don't know how. It just did," Jenna tried to explain as she continued down the stairs and towards the living room.

"How? Where? Is it someone from your job?" Evan asked.

"No, Evan, it's not."

"How? Where? Tell me!" Evan yelled.

"Not now, Evan. It doesn't really matter how or where."

Jenna didn't want him to know she had signed up for a dating site.

"Are you a lesbian now? Who is this *Mercedes*?"

"No, Evan, I am not a lesbian. It's a man. I just hid his name under *Mercedes*."

"I never imagined you would do this to me in a million years, Jenna. Make me out to be a fool. To believe we were happy. I was happy. I *am* happy. I love you. You are everything to me. I took care of you. How dare you embarrass me like this?!"

Jenna stood in silence. She knew there was nothing to say, no way to justify, no explanation that would ease Evan's pain.

"I need to think. Make your own fucking dinner. I'm going out!" Evan yelled out in anger.

Evan snatched his car keys from the coffee table where he had placed them earlier, grabbed his coat hanging by the door, stormed into the garage, and dropped into his Audi. He hit the remote to raise the garage door, started the car, backed out, and squealed his tires as he sped away.

CHAPTER 14

March 11th

After Evan stormed out of the house, Jenna sat on the sofa and cried. She knew the marriage was over. Not because her husband would want it to end, but because Jenna could not stay. Her feelings for Jason were much too strong to ignore. She knew she could not remain married to a man she could easily betray. She had not been in love with her husband for quite some time and wanted to end the illusion of a happy union. It was against her religious upbringing, but she no longer cared.

***

Evan drove his car aimlessly, the radio blaring, as he thought about Jenna being with another man. He had no destination in mind and didn't know where he would go. He just needed to get away from Jenna to think.

He eventually found himself on the road leading to the airport. He decided it was a great place to be alone.

Why not? he thought to himself, *I'm still going to learn how to fly*. After his flight earlier, he was determined to become a pilot, and a failed marriage would not end the dream.

When Evan arrived at the airport, he parked in an observation area and watched airplanes move along the taxiways. He watched several of them take off and land, pondering his marriage, or what he thought was his marriage. He knew it was most likely over. He was unsure if he could forgive Jenna or get past what she had done. Evan now realized, he wasn't just angry, but was utterly, devastatingly heartbroken.

* * *

Evan returned home just after midnight, pulled the Audi into the garage, and slowly exited. He entered the kitchen through the inner garage door, surprised to find the dim family room lights glowing with Jenna on the couch, holding a glass of wine. He could see rings of red lining her eyes and knew she had cried most of the evening.

Evan entered the room, stepped over an empty wine bottle lying on the floor, and settled into his recliner to face her. He wanted to say something, anything, but remained silent.

Jenna sensed the tension and eventually spoke.

"Evan, I am really sorry for this and never wanted to hurt you, but I did. You're a great husband, and I was lucky to be married to you. I don't know how or when I chose to do what I have done, but here I am," Jenna began and continued, "I know how much you care for me, and I really do love you, but I have realized I am no longer *in love* with you. It isn't fair to either of us to remain in a marriage based on deception, and I think we should go our separate ways while we can," Jenna finished.

"I don't know what you're trying to tell me. You want to get a divorce?" Evan was consumed by rage at the thought that Jenna would end the marriage.

"What I am saying is, I think we should separate before anger takes over and we begin to hate each other. While you were gone, I moved most of my belongings into the guest bedroom. I am going to stay there until I find a place for myself. I didn't think we should share a bedroom or home any longer than necessary.

I really thought a lot about this while you were out tonight. I don't want to take the house from you or fight for half of your retirement account. I have my own savings. I destroyed the marriage with my choices, and I don't want you to suffer. I really do care for you. The only thing I ask is for you to allow me to take the family heirlooms I brought into the home and for you to leave my retirement funds to me. I think that would be more than fair for you."

"Geez, Jenna. It sounds like you have all this figured out. I appreciate you not making me suffer for your cheating on me!" Evan sarcastically snapped.

"Tell me how you met this other man. I want to know!" Evan yelled.

"Fine, Evan, it was on a dating app. There, now you know," Jenna replied and began to cry.

Evan stormed out of the family room and upstairs to the bedroom. He fell onto the bed, still dressed. He lay there for several hours before he fell asleep.

The following morning, Evan found Jenna seated in the kitchen with a cup of coffee.

"I will contact a divorce mediator later today. I've heard about them from others who have had positive outcomes. We can work out a divorce agreement using a mediator instead of a lawyer. I believe it would be better than having a nasty battle in the courts if we can come up with a mutual agreement," Jenna stated as soon as Evan entered the kitchen.

"Fine! Do what you want! You always do anyway!" Evan yelled as he stormed out of the kitchen and returned upstairs to the primary bedroom.

He lay on the bed and wondered how his life had changed so drastically in just one day. Evan did not leave the room until Jenna departed for work. When he heard the Boxster's distinct exhaust note fade into the distance, he returned downstairs to the kitchen and brewed a fresh pot of coffee. He was boiling with anger.

CHAPTER 15

May 16th

It had been two months since Jenna moved out of the home and into a two-bedroom apartment in the neighboring town of Halfmoon. It did not take her long to find a new place, and she moved just a few days after Evan discovered the affair. Jenna continued to see Jason regularly, and he was constantly begging her to move in with him. Still, she decided to live independently before committing to another serious relationship.

Jenna did indeed find a mediator and worked out the details of the divorce. They included everything she promised, and Evan agreed to the terms. They were not officially divorced because New York required a one-year legal separation before one received a finalized divorce decree.

* * *

Evan made good on his vow to attend flight school. He completed his ground school training and found most of the material intuitive. He took the FAA written exam, passing it effortlessly. He also passed the necessary FAA medical exam. Jim Robinson was correct when he said it was a simple physical exam performed by an FAA-certified doctor. It took less than 30 minutes.

Evan may have jumped headfirst into flight training, but the constant feeling of anger and betrayal did not fade away. He had thought learning to fly would ease the emotions of his failed marriage and Jenna's betrayal, but it did not. He was angry at Jenna, but mostly, he was furious at the scumbag who stole her from him. If not for this man interfering in their marriage, Jenna would still be his, and he would still be, what he thought, happily married. He suddenly felt a burning need to find out who this other man was.

While he sat at home, drinking a beer and reading his flight training material, the solution to seek revenge became clear. He felt rage, not from losing Jenna, but from betrayal. He knew what he needed to do and wanted to act immediately. It would require help from a friend, and that friend was John. He was Evan's coworker and a whiz with technology.

Evan glanced at the time in the corner of his computer and saw it was 9:30 p.m., but he knew John would still be in his office, toiling away at his desktop computer. John always said he had no one to go home to, and being in the office was where he enjoyed his time. Evan finished his beer and snatched his car keys from the dining room table. He got into his Audi to reach Bank, Trust, and Financial with a plan.

Evan arrived at the office building and walked through the entrance. He waved his badge at a guard on duty, then rode an elevator to the fifth floor. When he exited, he could see John's small office illuminated. He strode over, stepped inside, and tapped John on the shoulder. John always wore headphones, listening to heavy metal rock while he worked, and was never aware when someone entered. John jumped when Evan touched him, and he turned.

"Jesus, you scared the crap out of me!" he cried out.

"Sorry, John, I didn't mean to scare you. Got a minute?" Evan asked.

"Sure, what's up? You look like shit, by the way. Everything okay?"

"Yeah, just not sleeping well. I wanted to know if a cell phone can be cloned and, if so, how? Is that something that can be done easily, or is it just a fantasy I see in the movies?"

"No, not just in the movies. It can be done," John replied.

"Do you know how to clone one?" Evan asked.

"I do. It's not that difficult. Whose cell phone, and why do you want to clone it?" John was curious.

"I want to clone Jenna's. Can it be done without her knowing it was done?"

"Sure, as long as you share the same cellular provider and contract. You wouldn't even have to have the phone in hand. It can all be done over the internet. I just need to find an app that will do it. There are plenty to choose from. Most of them were initially created so parents could keep an eye on their kids, but these apps have been misused, so to speak," John stated.

"Good, then I want to do that now. Could you do it for me?"

"Sure, I can, but why Jenna's phone? Didn't she move out a while ago?" John inquired suspiciously.

"I just want to, that's all. Will you do it?" Evan asked again.

"Yeah, I can do it right here, right now. Do you know your login credentials for the cellular provider's website? If so, that's all I need," John instructed.

Evan provided John with the needed information, and he began clicking away. He was fast on the keyboard, his fingers a blur. After several minutes, John told Evan he was done.

"Already? Are you sure? How will I know?" Evan asked.

"Yes, it's done. I downloaded and remotely installed an app on her phone to duplicate calls and messages to your phone. She won't see the new app or even know it's there."

"How does it work?" Evan asked.

"When Jenna receives a phone call or text, you will also receive it. Your phone will ring or beep. Don't answer the phone calls. You'll know it's Jenna receiving a call because I assigned a distinctive ring to let you know the call is for her. The number calling will be displayed on your phone."

John played the ringtone so Evan could hear it and continued, "If Jenna doesn't answer, it will go to her voicemail. You'll have access and can play the messages without her knowing you did. You can also open and read a text message without her knowing. They will still appear as unread on her device," John explained.

"Will Jenna know her phone was cloned and that I'm also receiving the messages and calls? Will she see anything on her phone indicating it is cloned?" Evan nervously asked.

"No, she will not be able to tell. It's not actually a clone. It's just an app that duplicates the calls and texts to your phone number. Although if you're in the same room and your phones go off simultaneously, she might become suspicious," John laughed.

Evan thought to himself while John laughed, *Not a problem, we'll never be in the same room again.*

Evan looked down at his cell phone and grinned.

"Thanks, John. And let's keep this to ourselves."

"Not a problem, Evan. I hope everything is okay."

"Don't work too long. Have a good night, John."

"You too, Evan."

John resumed working as Evan left the building and strolled to his car. He felt great. He got in and stared at his phone again. When Jenna and Evan separated, Evan had intended to remove Jenna from the joint cell phone contract, but now he was happy he had not. He was pleased about the cloning, but his anger against this other man grew within him.

CHAPTER 16

May 16th

Evan returned home and settled into his favorite recliner with a beer. He looked over at his cell phone as it sat on the coffee table. He thought about the next steps he needed to complete. Evan was aware that the affair Jenna had during the marriage continued. He felt confident the identity of the man who destroyed his marriage would be revealed with the new spy app he had.

Evan awoke early the following morning to find himself in the living room, apparently having fallen asleep in the recliner. His back was sore from being twisted in a chair all night. Evan pulled himself up and strode to the bathroom because his bladder was full. Once he relieved himself, he started towards the kitchen when he suddenly remembered cloning Jenna's cell phone. He rushed back into the living room, picked up his phone, and looked for phone calls or text messages to or from Jenna's number. He was disappointed when he found none.

He returned to the kitchen and brewed a fresh pot of coffee. It was a Saturday morning, and he had a training flight planned with Jim at *TIME2FLY*. He needed the coffee to revive himself from the restless night's sleep. While the coffee brewed, he headed upstairs for a hot shower.

Evan felt refreshed after his shower. He dressed and returned to the kitchen to pour a mug of freshly brewed coffee. Sitting at the kitchen island, sipping from his coffee mug, he heard a ping from his cell phone. Evan had left it on the coffee table in the living room. He walked over to it, reached down, and grinned. "Finally," he thought, "a text from the loser." He read the text message.

"See you today?" It was from Jenna.

"Sure," came the reply a few seconds later.

"Meet at your place?" Jenna texted back immediately.

"2 pm," he replied.

"Great, see you then," with a kissing emoji.

Jenna's kissing emoji upset Evan, even though they were no longer together. He still had trouble visualizing Jenna with someone other than himself.

Perfect! Evan thought to himself. The app John placed on Jenna's phone the prior evening worked.

Evan had a flight lesson at 11:00 a.m. and knew he would be back on the ground no later than 12:30. Jim always kept the flying time to one hour because he said a student stopped learning if it was any longer. After the lesson, they would spend an additional thirty minutes talking about the flight and discussing concerns uncovered during the training. Evan knew he could be on his way to Jenna's by 1:00 p.m., just in time to follow her to her boyfriend.

The morning's flight lesson went quite well. Evan had been learning landing techniques, and it came naturally to him. He did bounce one landing and aborted a different approach to the runway, but Jim said he was pleased with Evan's progress in the short time he trained. They stayed the entire hour in the traffic pattern of the airport. It felt like they had performed a hundred landings to Evan, but the number was much lower.

After the typical after-flight review, Evan thanked Jim for an enjoyable day. He walked out of the Albany Aviation building to his parked Audi. He climbed in, pushed the start button, and noted the time on the digital display. It was 1:07 p.m., which gave him plenty of time to drive to Jenna's apartment complex, park his car where she could not see it, and wait for her to leave for her date.

Evan arrived at the complex at 1:39, backed the Audi into a parking spot, and shut down the engine. He had a clear view of Jenna's building and was sure she would not see his car. While he waited, he started to wonder why he was there.

What would I do when I saw this guy? Would I confront him? Scream at him for ruining my life? Would following him really solve anything? were all the questions running through his mind as he watched for Jenna.

It was just about 1:45 p.m. when Jenna emerged from her apartment. She bounded down the exterior staircase and over to her Boxster. It bothered Evan to see her looking so happy, knowing she was on her way to see her new boyfriend. It was how he remembered her back when they were young and dating.

How could she feel this way again and, worst of all, with someone that wasn't me? He wondered aloud.

Jenna pulled out from her parking spot and drove towards the exit onto Route 7. Evan pulled out a few seconds later. He followed Jenna, maintaining a safe distance. He knew she had a bad habit of not checking her rearview mirror, which annoyed Evan while they were married, but now he was grateful for her lapse of judgment.

They continued to travel east on Route 7 until she turned onto Route 787 and headed south towards Albany. Evan continued to trail behind, leaving at least one or two cars between them, a trick he picked up from watching all the true crime shows he enjoyed.

Jenna continued to drive south and exited the highway into downtown Albany. She followed State Street into Washington Park and slowed down. Evan stayed behind her, but when she began to slow, he pulled to the curb as soon as he found a clearing. No cars separated them, and Evan worried she would spot the Audi behind her.

Evan watched Jenna parallel park between two cars and realized one of the townhomes must be her destination. Evan decided he could park where the car idled and pushed the button to shut down the engine. He exited the vehicle and crept along the street, ducking behind raised staircases leading to various townhouses. He kept Jenna in his sights.

Evan felt an ache of envy when he saw Jenna climb a staircase to an impressive-looking townhome. Not only did this guy steal his wife, but it looked like he was someone who had it all. Evan watched as Jenna knocked and waited. When the front doors opened, he caught a glimpse of the man who ruined his life.

Evan returned to his car, feeling as nauseous as the night he learned of the affair. Although separated for the last few months, he was still in love, and seeing her in another's embrace disturbed him. He knew he was the better man and believed Jenna should have also known.

He pushed the start button to fire up his car and sped away from the curb. He needed to execute a plan. A plan that will fulfill his vengeance.

He had urges throughout his childhood, even his young adult life, to kill. He realized it when he killed his father, and he still felt those urges now. He would fulfill his craving by killing the man who destroyed his perfect life.

CHAPTER 17

June 2nd

Two weeks after following Jenna to the Washington Park townhome, the devil's den, as labeled by Evan, Evan decided it was time to exact his revenge. He could no longer accept that another man was with the woman he loved. The day he followed Jenna, he had taken note of the address and used his data and computer skills to retrieve all the information about the man he could find online.

Evan had learned the man's name was Jason Tanner, a local defense attorney. Evan knew little about Tanner, but he recalled seeing him occasionally on various local news broadcasts, *bragging*, Evan thought, to anyone who would listen about how good a defense lawyer he was. Evan recalled Tanner's narcissism during those interviews, which infuriated him. Evan wanted to end this man's life. He could not live with the thoughts of Jenna and Tanner together. Evan wanted Tanner gone, not just away from Jenna, but gone for good.

"It is time to put my plan of revenge into action." Evan decided. He carefully developed a strategy. The plan was simple, and Evan felt proud of what he had arranged to rid the world of Tanner. He would follow the 'devil', as he referred to him, to study his daily habits. As soon as he established Tanner's routines, he felt he could exact his vengeance once and for all. He even fantasized about reuniting with Jenna.

As a fan of true crime documentaries, he enjoyed watching them every night, from "A Body in the Basement" to "Very Scary People." Through these shows, he learned about forensics and the types of errors each killer made, which ultimately led to their arrests and convictions. Evan felt confident he could eliminate Tanner without being discovered, arrested, or convicted.

Evan, wanting to learn Jason Tanner's daily routine, set his alarm at 3:00 each morning to be downtown by 4:00. He parked in a darkened lot located near Tanner's townhouse that always seemed to be deserted, then walked to Washington Park, where he had a clear view of the townhome. He did not leave his post until Tanner departed in his Jaguar. He never brought his cell phone with him, leaving it powered up and on his bedside table to avoid leaving a trail for law enforcement to follow. He was well aware of law enforcement's ability to track cell phones and knew many criminals got caught and arrested because they kept their phones in their pockets or cars. Evan was not foolish and would not give law enforcement an edge.

He was delighted that Tanner was consistent with his morning routine. Evan discovered he left his apartment promptly at 5:00 each morning wearing the same jogging outfit and, for some odd reason, a Rolex watch. He always walked across the street and entered Washington Park on the east side to jog west along the stone-covered paths. To Evan, it seemed awfully early to be out jogging, but it worked perfectly into his plan. The park at that time of the morning was as dark as black ink and virtually empty.

He followed Tanner every morning as he traversed the paths to a small pond located at the park's far west end, where he turned east and jogged on an alternate route, returning to his townhome. Evan observed large trees and overgrown bushes circling the pond and realized they would provide excellent cover, concealing any illegal activity, especially his intended action. It was the furthest from any building surrounding the park's perimeter, and neighbors would not hear the sound of gunshots. "A perfect location to exact my revenge," he muttered to himself.

Fortunately for Evan, Tanner always left for his office consistently at 8:00, giving Evan enough time to return home, shower, dress, and be at work by 9:00. It would be a tight and exhausting schedule to follow, but Evan was determined.

CHAPTER 18

August 17th

Evan was ready to execute his plan after he had staked out Tanner's routine. He felt he had everything worked out to the smallest of details. He would confront Tanner at the pond during his morning jog and explain that it was time to pay for ruining marriages. Evan would tell him Jenna was too good for him and then pull the trigger. He wanted to say Jenna's name to let Tanner know who was about to kill him.

He retrieved the Glock from the gun safe he stored under his bed. It was a powerful forty-caliber pistol with a sensitive six-pound trigger, weighing only thirty-eight ounces when fully loaded. He found the gun in Ray's things when he cleaned out the house after his mother's death. Evan was not surprised to find a second gun owned by Ray, which he never intended to keep, but he brought it back to Albany on his last trip to Long Island. Jenna was angry when he returned home with it in his suitcase and ordered him to get it out of the house.

Evan had planned to sell it to a pawn shop or a used sporting goods retailer. Still, he decided to keep it after discovering that his father had purchased it illegally and never registered it, just like the revolver. Evan visited gun ranges without Jenna's knowledge to practice shooting with it and became exceedingly accurate. When he held the gun in his hand, it made him feel alive. He had acquired a taste for blood at the age of nine, and it never completely left him.

While Evan worked on his revenge plan, he decided to purchase a silencer for the Glock. He found a website selling silencers without requiring a permit, something that was definitely illegal, but Evan didn't care. The silencer was delivered in a plain, unmarked package shortly after he began his planned attack on Tanner. The credit card statement simply displayed a purchase for sports equipment, eliminating any electronic trail to the acquisition.

CHAPTER 19

August 18th

E van was in bed early, but he couldn't sleep as his mind raced. All he could think of was what he would do to Tanner, punishing him for stealing his wife. Evan boiled with anger but knew it would ease soon. After he tossed and turned and realized sleep had evaded him, he climbed out of bed, walked to the bathroom, and splashed water onto his face. It was only 3:00 a.m., and Evan was weary, but he needed to be ready for Tanner at the pond. He was worried he would fall asleep if he lay his head back on the pillow.

He entered the walk-in closet to select appropriate clothing for the attack. He looked at everything he owned, picking the darkest materials he could find. He retrieved a black sweatshirt, black jeans, black sneakers, and a black knit cap. *Perfect,* he thought. He reached into his dresser and pulled out a pair of black leather winter gloves.

After he dressed, he studied his reflection in the mirror and was satisfied with what he saw. He left his cell phone, still powered on, atop his dresser.

As he approached the door leading into the garage, he reached for the gun safe he had set on a small table after he carried it from the bedroom, entered his combination on the digital keypad, and pulled the lid open. He extracted the loaded Glock, carefully placed it inside the waistband of his jeans, and obscured it with his sweatshirt.

Evan pulled out of his garage with the headlights turned off until he exited his neighborhood. When he felt he was clear, he turned on the Audi's lights and drove to downtown Albany.

Evan parked his car in the same dark lot he used when he staked out Tanner. Exiting his car, he watched for street movement and saw no activity. He continued to the park on foot, taking advantage of darkened areas to remain undetected.

When he arrived at the entrance to the park, he stealthily moved to the small pond and crouched in the thick bush to begin his wait. He felt the heat rise in his neck and face as he trembled uncontrollably with rage. It took all his effort to quiet his ragged breath while he waited to unleash the monster growing louder within him.

Evan kept a vigilant watch for his intended target. He began to calm and stop trembling as he thought about Tanner's unavoidable fate. At 4:55, with his breathing under control and his mind focused, he caught the first sight of Tanner as he jogged along the stone path. "Tanner was so dependable," he mused. He remained very still as his prey neared. Evan wanted to be sure Tanner did not escape his destiny.

As Tanner reached the pond and moved closer to Evan's location, Evan vaulted from the bushes. It startled Tanner, which caused him to stumble but not fall. When Tanner turned to see what caused the noise, he saw Evan with a gun pointed at his face. Tanner was frightened.

"I-I-I I don't have any money on me," Tanner stuttered.

"I don't want your money. I want you to die," Evan calmly said.

"D-D-D Die? Why? Who are you?"

"I'm the man whose life you ruined."

"I don't know you. How did I ruin your life?" Tanner was confused.

"You took Jenna from me, and now I take you from her!" Evan shouted as he pulled the trigger.

Evan jumped when the gun went off. The sound startled him. He assumed that because he had used a silencer, there would only be a slight pfft sound, like he had observed in movies. It became apparent to him that silencers only suppressed the sound but not eliminated it.

Evan looked around the park nervously to check for anyone who might have heard the gunshot, but he saw no movement. The park was still dark and empty. He placed the Glock back into his waistband.

Evan gazed down at Tanner as he lay on the ground. He was motionless with eyes open, staring blankly into the sky. Blood trickled from a small hole where the bullet entered the center of his forehead. Tanner was dead.

Bent over the body, Evan removed Tanner's Rolex and cell phone. He wanted it to look like a simple robbery. He also picked up the cartridge that was ejected from the gun when he pulled the trigger. He was determined not to leave any useful evidence behind.

After examining the park one last time for any activity, he walked swiftly back to his car as he remained in the shadows of the buildings. He was relieved to find the streets still dark and quiet and was confident he remained unseen. As he walked, he removed the battery from the stolen phone and discarded both pieces into a nearby sewer grate. He placed the Rolex into the pocket of his jeans. It was his trophy.

He returned to his car, dropped into the driver's seat, fired up the engine, and sped away. His revenge was complete. He knew his anger would be relieved. As he continued his drive home, he shook. It suddenly occurred to him that he had just committed his second murder. Until that moment, it was just a plan, a dream, an idea, but now it was real. He stopped trembling, felt a rush of adrenaline, and grinned, feeling the same sense of calm that he had felt after he killed his father.

When Evan returned to his neighborhood, he extinguished the Audi's lights to move invisibly over the streets. He pulled into his garage and lowered the door with the remote. He looked at the digital clock. It was only 5:51. He sat briefly before shutting down the engine.

After several minutes, he climbed out of the car. As he entered the house through the kitchen door, he pulled the Glock from his waistband and placed it back in the safe. Weakened as the adrenaline left his body, Evan strolled upstairs to the primary bedroom and returned the safe under his bed.

He removed his gloves and examined them for blood. He could not find any stains but held them under the sink's faucet for several minutes to rinse any unseen blood from them. He laid them over the rim of the tub to dry. He walked to the bed and dropped onto it. He was exhausted. Before long, he fell into a deep sleep in the clothes he wore for murder.

CHAPTER 20

Homicide Detective Kirk Fisher entered Washington Park at 6:25 a.m. to a crowd of uniformed officers and gawkers. When he received the morning wake-up call about the homicide, he did not find it unusual. Drug dealers and prostitutes actively used the park, and Fisher assumed it was just another drug-related homicide. Detective Fisher folded his large frame under the crime scene tape protecting the area and proceeded to where he found the Albany County coroner standing over a body. His name was Dr. Richard Propp, but everyone called him Doc.

"Hey Doc!" Detective Fisher greeted.

"Good morning, Detective. Another lovely day, wouldn't you say?" Doc mused.

"What do we have here? He looks like a jogger based on the clothing and sneakers."

"Yeah, one famous jogger! This is the well-known defense Attorney Jason Tanner. I recognized him from the news, and I was called to testify in a couple of trials where Tanner was the defense counsel. He lives over there in that townhouse. It looks like he was out for a jog and got popped in the forehead," Doc said.

"Robbery?" Detective Fisher asked.

"Looks like it. His watch and cell phone are missing," Doc replied.

"Any witnesses?

"None. The attorney jogs in the park before sunrise, according to the neighbors. He was always wearing his Rolex as if it were a badge of honor. It's probably what got him killed," the Doc lamented.

"So, you're telling me he was wearing a Rolex while he was out jogging? That seems odd. How can you be sure?"

"Based on a neighbor's statement. That elderly woman standing over there said he never leaves his place without it," the medical examiner pointed to where the woman was standing and continued, "Also, see these abrasions on the wrist and thumb?" They are fresh and appear to be caused by something yanked across his wrist."

"Who found the body?" Fisher asked.

"That woman over there," Doc replied as he pointed to a young female and continued, "She looks like a hooker if you ask me. She said she was walking through the park on her way to the shelter. You won't get much information from her; she is higher than the Empire State Building!"

"Get the body to the morgue, and we'll canvass the neighborhood. We're probably not going to learn much. More than likely, the perp was just some addict out looking for cash. It's been happening too often," Detective Fisher finished as he started walking towards the young woman who found the body.

Detective Fisher discovered Doc was right about the streetwalker. She was strung out on methamphetamine and not much help. He thought his questioning of the neighbors would be more helpful, but to his disappointment, it was not. No one had valuable information to offer. According to everyone the detective spoke to, Tanner kept to himself and did not socialize with the neighbors. The only helpful information came from one neighbor who said she thought he had started dating a new woman. She said she did not know her name, but the detective imagined it would be easy to find out.

***

Evan awoke after an hour of deep sleep. Looking down at his legs, he realized he still had on the same clothes he wore when he shot Tanner in the park. Evan jumped out of bed and rushed to the bathroom. He stared at his reflection in the large mirror mounted above the sinks. Evan wanted to make sure he had no blood on him. He also looked at his hands for any traces of blood.

Although he could not see blood, he swiftly undressed, tossed the clothing on the floor, and jumped in the shower. He scrubbed his face, hands, and arms raw to remove any potential specks of blood. He shampooed his hair twice to ensure he got everything clean. When he was confident there was no blood on him, he exited the shower and tossed on a robe hanging off the bathroom door.

He reached down to the floor and picked up the clothing he had removed before he showered, examining it for bloodstains. He did not see any, but was not convinced. They were black and could easily hide blood from the naked eye, but not from DNA testing. It was another fact he learned from his favorite shows. He decided it would be safer to destroy them. He carried the clothing to the basement and tossed it on the concrete floor. He would burn it all later.

He returned to the primary bedroom, removed the bathrobe, and dressed in sweatpants and a T-shirt. He rushed back downstairs to the family room. He flicked on the TV to watch the local morning news programs. Evan wanted to know if the murder had been discovered.

***

Jenna rose from bed and entered her tiny kitchenette to turn on the coffee maker. She had a fantastic night's sleep, and work had been a breeze after the large implementation a couple of months earlier. Jenna felt great. Her life moved in the direction she wanted. While she waited for the coffee to brew, she sat on her sofa in the small living room and flicked on the TV to the morning news. She liked to catch the weather forecast to prepare her outfit for the day.

A reporter was in the middle of her story about a homicide. However, Jenna missed the beginning and paid little attention. Murders never affected someone like her. As the news story continued, Jenna heard the coffee maker beep. The coffee was brewed. She rose from the sofa, walked into the kitchen, and filled her mug.

As she returned to the living room, she heard the reporter wrapping up the homicide story,

"Again, it looks like a robbery. Attorney Tanner will be missed," she heard the reporter say.

Jenna's coffee mug fell from her hand, shattering across the floor. She quickly ran into the living room walking over the shattered ceramic and stared at the TV, not even feeling her right foot bleeding. Unfortunately, it was too late, as the anchor had moved on to other breaking news of the day. Jenna picked up the remote, feverishly scanning all the local channels to look for the story elsewhere.

She was frantic. She thought she must have heard it wrong. Jason could not be dead. She picked up her cell phone and dialed his number. The call went immediately to voicemail, which was unusual, elevating her panic. Jason always answered his phone when he knew Jenna was calling. The story reappeared on her TV screen just as she put her phone down.

"Jason Tanner, a prominent Tri-City area defense attorney, was found shot to death while jogging in Washington Park. Authorities are saying it appears to be a crime of opportunity. The victim's Rolex watch and cell phone were missing. We will offer more information as we receive it. Back to you, Tom."

When Jenna saw Jason's picture on the television screen as the news hit her, she fell to the floor sobbing. The man she fell in love with was gone, dead.

"How could Jason be dead? Why was the world so cruel?" she mumbled as she cried.

Jenna was distraught and needed to talk to someone, anyone. She could only think of one person. She picked up her phone and dialed his number.

* * *

"Hi Jenna, I'm surprised to hear from you," Evan said when he answered the phone.

"Evan..." a shaky voice whispered. There was a pause, like she was gathering herself to speak.

"I... I don't know who else to call," she admitted, her voice breaking. "Something terrible happened... something I can't handle alone."

"What's going on?" Evan asked, tension creeping into his tone.

"It's Jason... he's—he's dead," Jenna sobbed, the words barely audible through her tears.

"Who is Jason?" Evan asked.

Jenna swallowed the lump in her throat, knowing she had kept this from him. Jenna never told Evan whom she met when they were married, and Evan never asked. He acted ignorant when Jenna told him his name because he did not want Jenna to know he knew about Tanner. It could get back to the police, and Evan would become the primary suspect.

"He's the man I've been seeing. I never told you who it was, but it was Jason Tanner." Jenna continued to cry.

"That scumbag lawyer? That's too bad," Evan replied calmly.

Jenna sobbed louder.

"Do the police know who did it?" Evan asked coolly.

"I don't know. The news is saying it was a robbery. Why are you being so flippant?" Jenna cried out.

"I'm sorry to hear this, Jenna, but you can't expect me to feel sorry for a guy who stole my wife, do you?" Evan snickered.

"That's cruel, Evan! He's a human being, and he's dead."

"I know Jenna, but you're telling me this is the man who tore my life apart, killed my marriage. I can't feel any empathy for him. Listen, it's getting late, and I need to get dressed for work."

"I don't know why I called you. It was a mistake. I'm sorry I bothered you. Goodbye!" She hung up before he could respond.

CHAPTER 21

August 19th

Detective Fisher was at his desk when Doc called from the morgue with a cause of death for the victim found in Washington Park the morning prior. It was from a forty-caliber, single-shot to the forehead, the doctor told the detective.

When Fisher ended his call with Doc, he searched a database for homicides with similar M.O.s but found none. The shooting appeared to be a random robbery, and he was surprised the killer used a 40-caliber weapon. It was not the average gun of choice among drug dealers, addicts, or typical street thugs.

While he looked, his partner, Detective John Byrd, approached with a handful of paper.

"I just got the cell phone records for our vic."

"Has his phone been used since yesterday morning?" Fisher asked.

"Nope. Dead silent. Probably tossed," Byrd replied.

"Okay, let's look at the phone records, see if we can determine who he's been in contact with leading up to his death," Fisher said.

Byrd handed over the documents and plopped into a chair alongside Fisher's desk.

"We should also canvas local pawn shops, see if anyone tries or has already tried to sell a Rolex," Byrd said when he sat.

"Yes, good idea. Send some uniforms out. Let me know if they find anything."

Detective Fisher scanned the cell phone records. He noted a number repeated frequently, with numerous calls and daily text messages exchanged. The night before the homicide was when the number sent the last text message.

"Look at this. I wonder if it's his girl?" Fisher pointed at the number.

"Could be. I'll find out who the number belongs to and get back to you," Byrd replied, copying the number to his notepad.

* * *

Jenna did not go into the office the day of Jason's murder and called in sick to work for a second day.

Jenna was dressed in pajamas and sobbed most of the morning. She could not force herself to get dressed for the drive to the office. Jenna remained glued to her television, flicking from station to station. She wanted to learn more about Jason's murder, hoping there would be information coming from local news broadcasts.

Jenna could not understand or even comprehend how Jason got snatched from her instantly. Just the night before his murder, they enjoyed a beautiful dinner at her favorite Italian restaurant and made love. She was upset with herself because she had insisted that she leave Jason's townhouse before midnight. She wanted to be in her place in the morning so that preparing herself for work the next day would be easier.

If only I had stayed, she thought, *he wouldn't have been out jogging so early in the morning.*

* * *

Evan also stayed glued to the morning news while he prepared for work. He was interested in any information the police may have reported.

"Did I leave any clues behind? No, I don't think I did. Did any witnesses see me? I doubt anyone saw me, but could I be sure?" Evan asked himself aloud.

Although he questioned the execution, he was incredibly calm and at ease. When he first returned home after shooting Tanner, he was running on adrenaline, but now he was relaxed and surprised to discover he was not bothered by the killing.

What kind of man am I? He wondered, *Am I the psychopath I thought I was when I killed Ray? Yes, I think I am!"*

CHAPTER 22

August 19th

Detective Fisher was reviewing the notes he received from the morgue when Detective Byrd called out to him.

"I have the owner of that number."

"Who does it belong to?" Fisher asked.

"It's registered to an Evan and Jenna Williams in Latham," Byrd replied.

"Do we have anything on them?"

"Nope, they appear to be a normal couple. Could be a client of Tanner's, but I didn't find any arrest reports with them listed," Byrd said.

"Well, I guess we need to make a trip to the Williams' residence. Have an address?" Fisher asked.

"4604 Van Patten Drive," Byrd said and stood.

"Well, it's after six. Everyone should be home from work. Let's roll," Fisher replied, grabbing his coat from the back of his chair.

Detectives Byrd and Fisher climbed into their unmarked patrol car and drove to the Williams' residence. They didn't believe they would retrieve any helpful information regarding the homicide. The Williamses appeared to be an upper-middle-class family living in an upscale suburban neighborhood with no prior arrests, not even a speeding ticket. They expected the visit would lead to a dead-end, but their combined experience told them never to take anything at face value.

The detectives arrived at a large custom colonial address with pristine gardens and a meticulously manicured lawn. The home was perfectly maintained and matched the other homes on the block. It did not look like the usual place to search for a park murderer or common thief.

Detective Byrd reached for the doorbell, pressed it, and heard a musical sound emanating from inside the home.

"Fancy!" he snickered.

* * *

Evan was surprised to hear the doorbell peal and leaped from the sofa to peer out the large living room window. He saw two gentlemen on the front landing and a prominent unmarked police car in the driveway. He walked over to the television and flicked it off.

Evan didn't expect to see the police at his door so soon after the murder.

Well, that was quick, the little, incompetent fuckers. Time to turn on my actor's charm! He thought to himself with a grin as he approached the front door and swung it open.

"Can I help you?" he asked, smiling.

"Mr. Williams?" Byrd asked.

"Yes, I'm Evan Williams. How may I assist you?"

"I'm Detective Fisher, and this is my partner, Detective Byrd. Mind if we come in?"

"No, not at all," he replied as he stepped back to allow the detectives entry.

"We're here about Jason Tanner. Do you know him?" Byrd asked.

"No, I don't. Is that the guy who got murdered downtown yesterday? I saw something on the news just tonight about it."

"Yes, he is. We are here because the victim was in constant contact with a cell phone number registered to your name. Are you sure you don't know him?" Fisher asked with suspicion in his tone.

"I'm positive. Are you sure it's my phone number?"

Evan knew it was probably Jenna's cell phone number they were referring to, but he pretended not to know.

"Here is the number right here. That's not yours?" Fisher pointed to his notepad.

"Oh, that's my wife's cell phone. She doesn't live here any longer. We separated a few months ago," Evan explained.

"You're separated? Was she dating Tanner?" Byrd spoke up.

"I don't know. She was seeing someone on the side while we were married. It's why we split, but I never asked who, and I didn't want to know. I just didn't care."

"You didn't want to know who your wife was sneaking around with while you were married? That's unusual," Fisher stated.

"I didn't care. It didn't matter to me. The marriage was over, and I just wanted to move on. It wouldn't change anything for me to know who the dude was. It was just over," Evan calmly said to sound nonchalant about the affair as if he no longer cared.

"All right then. Could you give us your wife's address so we can speak to her, or did you not ask her for that either?" Byrd asked sarcastically.

"I have it written down somewhere."

Evan knew her address but wanted to make it appear that he was not interested in her new life. Evan walked into the kitchen, opened a drawer, and pulled out a small sheet of paper. He returned to the living room, where the detectives milled about.

"Here it is. 3344 Anderson Lane, the Lakeview Apartments, apartment 212. It's up in Halfmoon, I think."

Detective Byrd copied the address to his notepad.

"Thank you for your time. If you think of anything, please give us a call. Here is my card," Detective Fisher said while handing out a business card to Evan.

Evan inhaled deeply as he closed the door. He was confident with his acting skills and knew he would not become a suspect.

* * *

The detectives returned to their vehicle.

"What do you think?" Byrd asked.

"I'm not sure. He seemed like an arrogant ass to me. A bit of a narcissist. He said he didn't know Tanner, which is a little hard to believe. He also doesn't look like a killer, but they usually don't. Let's drive up to see the missus and get her feelings on the murder," Fisher said as he backed out of the driveway to begin the drive to Jenna Williams' apartment.

CHAPTER 23

August 19th

Jenna was asleep on the sofa when she was startled awake by the sound of a knock on her apartment door. She had exhausted herself, crying most of the day as she thought about Jason's murder. She had fallen sound asleep with the television still turned on.

Jenna rose from the sofa, tightened her bathrobe, and walked to the door. When she opened it, she was surprised to see two gentlemen standing on the landing who appeared to be police detectives, dressed in cheap suits, wrinkled shirts, and stained ties.

"Hi," was all Jenna could verbalize.

"Hi, are you Jenna Williams?" Detective Fisher spoke.

"Yes, I'm Jenna," she said, not in the mood to talk.

"I'm Detective Fisher. This is Detective Byrd. Can we come in to talk?"

"Is this about Jason?" Jenna asked as her eyes filled with tears.

"We'd prefer to talk inside if that is okay," Detective Byrd said.

Jenna backed away from the door to allow Byrd and Fisher room to pass by and into the apartment. She moved to the sofa and sat with her legs curled under her. She did not offer the men seats.

"We are investigating the homicide of Jason Tanner," Detective Fisher said.

Jenna sobbed when Detective Fisher mentioned the homicide and Jason in the same sentence.

"Did you know Jason Tanner well, Mrs. Williams?" Detective Byrd asked.

"Yes, I know… I mean, I knew him," Jenna said through tears.

"He was killed in Washington Park early yesterday morning. According to cell phone records, you were the last one to have contact with him. How did you know him?" Byrd questioned.

"We have been dating for the last few months. I was there the night before he died. We were out for dinner and returned to his townhome afterward," Jenna explained, her crying subdued.

"Did you stay the night?" Detective Fisher asked.

"No, I didn't. I left a little before midnight. I wanted to be home so I could get ready for work in the morning," Jenna said, and wept again. "I should have stayed. Maybe he would be alive today!" Her sobbing intensified.

"You shouldn't blame yourself. There was nothing you could have done," Detective Byrd said.

"Was your husband aware of who you were dating?" Fisher asked.

"No, he wasn't. He never asked me. I never told anyone," Jenna replied.

"Could your husband have found out without you knowing?" Fisher continued.

"No, I don't think so. Besides, Evan is a gentle soul, a passive man. He wouldn't be able to kill anyone, even if he did know who I was dating. Are you trying to imply Evan is a suspect?" Jenna asked.

She did not like what the Detective suggested.

"Do you know anyone else who might have wanted to see him dead? Anything he mentioned to you about people he was defending?"

"No, he never really talked about his work. I thought he got killed while being robbed. Why all these questions?" Jenna was confused.

"Yes, it does look like a robbery. We just need to cover all our bases. Here is my card. Call us if you think of anything."

Detective Byrd placed his business card on the coffee table in front of Jenna.

Jenna got up from the sofa and walked the detectives out. She returned to the couch and sobbed again. The detective's visit refreshed the memory of Jason's death. The heartache she had felt the day before furiously returned.

* * *

Detectives Fisher and Byrd returned to the precinct after interviewing Jason and Jenna Williams. They had not learned anything new after their morning's investigation of the Williams'. Evan Williams seemed unaware of Jenna's new partner, and Jenna Williams was visibly emotional over Tanner's death. It still looked like a robbery gone horrifically wrong. Tanner, they speculated, refused to turn over his precious Rolex and died for it. Fisher and Byrd never understood why people put so much value on material objects.

They pushed Evan Williams to the back burner and turned their focus to local gangs and addicts, but something still ate at Detective Fisher. It was the forty-caliber bullet found inside Tanner's brain.

CHAPTER 24

November 4th

Evan continued his flight training and prepared for his first cross-country solo flight the previous evening. He created a flight plan according to the FAA requirements for a pilot's first solo cross-country trip. Pilot trainees for both single and multi-engine aircraft were required to complete at least five hours of solo cross-country flights. The first solo cross-country had to cover at least one hundred fifty nautical miles with landings at three different airports. The originating airport, Albany International, for Evan, was considered the third landing when he returned from the flight. He selected an airport in Massachusetts for his first landing and an airport in Vermont for the second.

While planning his cross-country trip, Evan studied the aviation map he purchased the day he signed up for his lessons and attempted to commit much of the topography to memory. Although he would have the map attached to a kneeboard that he wore in flight, he wanted to memorize landmarks, rivers, mountains, or anything else he saw outside of the plane's windscreen. Evan worried he would find himself lost, his first time alone on the airplane. He also studied each airport's printed diagram for radio frequencies, taxiway configurations, and runway orientation to familiarize himself with their layouts.

Evan arrived at the airport early, dressed for the wintry weather, and went directly to the 'Weather Station' room. It was a Saturday morning, and the room was a flurry of activity with weekend pilots. His first task, taught by Jim, was to check the weather radar and NOTAMS issued. NOTAMS are 'notices to airmen' reporting closed airports, airspace, or other critical information that pilots must be aware of before taking flight.

Evan became exceptionally competent in his understanding of the required weather maps. He also learned about weather patterns and how they might change throughout the day. He was pleased to discover the conditions looked great around the Northeast. The skies were crystal clear and perfect for a VFR flight.

When he had gathered all the information he could from the computer, Evan strode out of the F.B.O. and over to the Skyhawk he would pilot on the trip. He felt good knowing he was nearing the completion of the training.

When he arrived at the airplane, he retrieved the checklist from the door's pocket and completed a full pre-flight inspection of the airplane.

Evan was pleased with the plane's condition and felt anxious about beginning his flight. He returned to the *TIME2FLY* office with his flight bag to meet Jim. Evan needed him to review his flight plan and sign his logbook to authorize the solo flight, but Jim had not yet arrived.

While Evan waited for Jim, he sat in the lobby and watched numerous airplanes take off and land. After what seemed like hours to Evan, but in reality, only twenty minutes, Jim strolled into the F.B.O. shortly after 10 a.m.

"Hey, Evan—sorry I'm late," he said, brushing off his coat. "Busy morning."

"No worries," Evan replied, standing up. "I'm ready whenever you are."

"Good. Let's take a look at your plan," Jim said, motioning toward the pilot's lounge.

They sat down at the small table as Evan spread out his flight paperwork.

"So," Jim asked, scanning the route, "any concerns before you go?"

"None," Evan said. "I think I'm set."

Jim nodded with a small smile. "You're well prepared. You've got this."

He reached out, shook Evan's hand firmly, and said, "Good luck out there."

Evan exited the F.B.O., walked to the airplane, settled into the pilot's seat, and took a deep breath. He felt anxious even though it was not his first time flying the aircraft alone. He had completed his first solo two weeks earlier, but it was just a short flight that required Evan to remain in the airport's traffic pattern. This solo would be the first time he would fly a considerable distance independently.

Evan was nervous but also excited. He fired up the engine, contacted ground control with his flight plan, and requested flight following. Although flight following was not mandatory, Evan wanted the air traffic controllers to keep him in their sight and follow along on radar. Ground control approved the request, assigned a transponder code, and instructed Evan to taxi to runway two-eight.

Runway two-eight pointed west, so Evan knew he would have to turn the plane around after takeoff to head east toward Pittsfield. The control tower would guide him onto the proper route once he was airborne.

Evan taxied to the run-up area for runway two-eight. After he completed the run-up procedure, he contacted the control tower and received a clearance for an immediate takeoff. As he rolled onto runway two-eight, he breathed deeply and held it. He aligned the plane on the runway's centerline and pushed the throttle to the instrument panel. As he rolled down the runway, he exhaled.

"Here I go," he said aloud to no one.

Evan felt his takeoff was perfect. Smooth and controlled, the way Jim had trained him. He switched to the departure's frequency and received a clearance to climb to three thousand and five hundred feet on a heading of one-two-five. Evan could not have felt more thrilled as he flew on his own to a location of his own. He gripped the yoke of the airplane with confidence.

He relaxed as he flew towards Pittsfield. In the serene environment of the sky, his mind wandered to Jenna. He thought about the conversations they had had the year before. They dreamt of taking flights to vacation hideaways in an airplane Evan piloted. Evan imagined the life they would have been living if it were not for her infidelity.

A sudden image of him killing Jason Tanner appeared in his mind. He had not thought about Tanner since he shot him dead in the park. He had erased it from his memory and moved on with his life. During the solo flight, his memory of that fateful day came back to him for the first time.

Alone in the airplane, Evan realized that his anger had never truly left him. It had been eight months since Jenna moved out of the home and three months since the murder, but nothing really changed for him. He felt angrier than when he first learned of the betrayal and could not understand why those emotions still swirled within him. He fought to eliminate the thoughts from his mind so he could concentrate on the flight.

As Evan neared the Pittsfield Airport, an uncontrolled airport with two runways and the first airport planned for his cross-country flight, he pushed Jenna and Tanner out of his mind. He needed to concentrate on flying and returned his focus to the airplane.

Evan looked at the flight plan clipped on his kneeboard for the airport's radio frequency. He entered it into his radio and obtained the current weather conditions. He needed to know the prevailing wind direction and speed. The wind determined which runway to use. Airplanes must always take off and land directly into the wind to gain the necessary airspeed and lift.

The airport's automated weather observation system, or AWOS, indicated the wind was two fifty-five at five knots. Evan referred to the airport diagram attached to the kneeboard, choosing runway two-six for his landing. As he entered, he announced his position over the radio and moved through the airport's traffic pattern.

Evan landed smoothly, and he felt proud. He shut down the airplane engine and climbed out. He located the entrance of the F.B.O. situated on the field and walked toward it. He needed to have his logbook signed by the attendant to prove he arrived and landed as planned.

When he entered the building, he saw no one behind the counter. He found a small table placed against a back wall and sat to wait for someone to appear. While he waited for an attendant to return to the front desk, he thought more about the phone call he had received from Jenna the week before.

***

Jenna never recovered from the death of Jason. Although they had not been in a long-term relationship, she enjoyed his companionship and had fallen in love. After Jason's murder, Jenna loathed what her life had become and felt she needed a change. At the time, she considered her separation from Evan and her new relationship with Jason a fresh start. However, it was no longer enough with Jason gone. She needed new surroundings, new friends, and a new life.

Jenna joined a national employment networking website and interviewed for several positions nationwide almost immediately. Her final phone interview was with a similar-sized health insurance company as Healthy Northeast Insurance, Inc., located near Philadelphia, Pennsylvania. All her interviews went very well, and she received an offer for a Vice President, Information Technology position. She considered the job for a few days before deciding to accept it. She felt this was the rejuvenation she so desired. She contacted the HR department with her decision to take the position and made arrangements to onboard within a few weeks. They offered a generous relocation package to cover her moving expenses.

When Jenna called Evan to tell him of her decision to leave and move out of state, she did not do so out of consideration. She felt she needed to tell him because the divorce was not yet final. Evan would need to know her location so a final divorce decree could be delivered and signed.

* * *

As Evan sat in Pittsfield, waiting and thinking about the phone call from Jenna, he recalled feeling both surprised and indifferent by her decision to leave the area. He grew to hate her for the betrayal and destruction of his perfect life. While on the phone call with Jenna, he felt hate towards her and suddenly realized why he had not sensed relief from his feelings of anger after he murdered Jason Tanner.

As Evan waited for someone to sign his logbook, it hit him like a freight train hitting a concrete wall. He had looked for relief in the wrong place. He knew he was angry at Tanner because he destroyed Evan's and Jenna's marriage, but Tanner would not have been able to destroy the marriage or Evan's life if it were not for Jenna.

When he thought back to the phone call with Jenna, Evan realized he should have focused his rage on her. She had created the events that led to their estrangement.

She was a wife who had started an affair. A wife who had looked for someone else. A wife who had joined a dating site. Evan snapped back, looking around the F.B.O. lounge, and it occurred to him that he was a stranger in a strange town, unknown to everyone.

Evan waited close to ten minutes before a young girl returned to the front of the F.B.O. and positioned herself behind the main counter. Evan asked if she was the attendant, and when she told him she was, he had her sign his logbook with the date and time.

With his logbook signed, Evan returned to the airplane. Although he never lost sight of the aircraft as he waited in the F.B.O., Jim said no matter how long you were on the ground, you always needed to do a pre-flight inspection, so he did one. With the check completed, he climbed in, started the engine, taxied to the active runway, and departed.

The rest of the cross-country flight went well. Evan chose the Edward F. Knapp State Airport in Barre, Vermont, as his second destination. Commonly referred to by pilots as Montpelier Airport, it was uncontrolled as well. He followed the same procedures as he did in Pittsfield, and then he returned to Albany International Airport.

He arrived in Albany without issue, taxied the Skyhawk to its parking slot, and tied it down. When he entered Albany Aviation, he found Jim seated in the lobby with other pilots. Jim watched as Evan approached, stood, and smiled. He asked Evan about the flight, and Evan told him it went well, proudly showing Jim his signed logbook. Jim looked at his watch to check the time and noted that Evan returned to Albany within fifteen minutes of the planned flight time. He congratulated Evan for his solo cross-country flight and the meticulous planning that he put into it.

Evan was delighted with his cross-country trip and Jim's compliments. He left the F.B.O. to return home feeling satisfied, pondering his revelation while waiting for the attendant in Pittsfield.

CHAPTER 25

November 6th

Monday morning rolled around, and Evan arrived at work just before 9:00 with a new goal. He hurried past his own office and went directly to see John. He needed John's technical expertise once again. Evan wanted to reach him before the day's typical data emergencies arose, which would take away everyone's available time.

Evan knocked on John's door jamb, and again, he jumped in his seat. It still amazed Evan that he flinched whenever someone knocked on his door.

"Hey, John!" Evan greeted.

"Hi, Evan. I wish you'd stop scaring me," John replied and laughed.

"Stop wearing those headphones, and maybe I will."

"Ugh, Whatever. What's up?"

"I need another non-work-related favor from you. I want to know if there is a way to find apps installed on a cell phone."

"Sure, that's easy. All you need to do is look at the phone under apps," John sarcastically replied.

"I know that, John, but what if I don't have the phone to look at?"

"Is this about Jenna again?" John squinted.

"Yeah. I want to know what apps she has on her phone."

"If she is still on your account, just look online. All paid apps will be listed. Of course, if it's a free app, it will probably not be displayed."

"That sounds easy. I should have done that first before bothering you."

"Yeah, you probably should have. See ya later!"

John dismissively waved at Evan as he turned to leave.

It never occurred to Evan to look at Jenna's cell phone information online before he went to John. It had become apparent as soon as he said it, and Evan could have avoided him altogether. He did not want John to become suspicious about anything related to Jenna, especially after he had asked him to clone her phone several months earlier.

Evan entered his office with a plan to log onto the cell phone provider's website. However, his administrative assistant, Rachel, immediately intercepted him before he could get started.

"Mr. Allen called down. He wants to meet with you about yesterday's reports. He thinks the financials look a little low," Rachel said.

"Ok, I'll call him," Evan replied.

Evan spent the day pulled into multiple departmental issues, postponing his investigation of Jenna's phone. Although senior leaders flagged concerning financial data, none of the problems required Evan's intervention, leaving him mostly answering questions and guiding his team. It was 7:00 p.m. before Evan finally arrived home after another hectic day, and again, he felt drained. However, it was something he had learned to accept in his chosen career. He took a quick hot shower and changed into his favorite sweats. He ordered Chinese takeout for dinner.

After Jenna moved out, he no longer enjoyed preparing meals and had most of his dinners delivered. Cooking for one depressed him. Whenever Evan tried to cook a meal for himself, the leftovers would linger in the refrigerator until they went bad and then be discarded in the trash. He never enjoyed the leftovers. Evan preferred freshly cooked dinners, and when he discarded what he considered delicious food, it bothered him.

Evan uncorked a bottle of white wine and moved to the family room as he waited for his food to be delivered. He picked up his laptop from the coffee table, sat in his favorite chair, and logged into his cell phone provider's website to start researching Jenna's cell phone.

The doorbell sounded as soon as he logged onto the cellular provider's website. Evan was surprised to have someone at his door. The food he ordered would not be delivered for another thirty minutes. He began to worry it was the detectives back for another interview, even though he had never heard anything further about Tanner's murder. Evan rose from the recliner and looked out the front window. He saw Jenna's Boxster parked in the driveway.

He strolled to the front door and swung it open. When Evan saw Jenna, he felt a rush of fury.

"What do you want?" he asked curtly.

"I'm sorry, Evan. I wanted to pick up some of the things I left in the basement. You know, those boxes I didn't have room for in the apartment," Jenna replied.

"Why do you need them now? You should have called instead of just showing up unannounced," Evan retorted.

"I know I should have, but I'm moving to Philadelphia next week, and I wanted to have everything ready for the moving company. They are coming this weekend to begin loading the truck."

"Okay, come in. I just ordered Chinese, and it will be here soon. I'll walk you down to the basement."

"I can go down by myself. Why are you ordering take-out? You love cooking, and you used to make us delicious meals."

"I prefer take-out instead of cooking. I'll go down with you. It might be a mess because I've moved things around since you left."

Evan followed Jenna to the basement door, opened it, and allowed her to go down first. He was still a gentleman. Some habits were hard to break.

While descending the steps, Evan stopped dead in his tracks, frozen by what he saw on the floor at the bottom of the staircase. It was the clothes he wore the night he killed Tanner. His flight training had kept him busy, and he completely forgot they were still there. He needed to destroy them before the police returned, found the clothing, and took it to the lab for testing. The police could find evidence left on them. He didn't believe the police considered him a suspect in Tanner's murder or would show up with a warrant to search his house. However, he learned from reality crime shows that people often get caught when they leave evidence lying around.

"Not a good place to leave your clothes, Evan," Jenna pointed at them.

"I know. I got them dirty while cleaning the car and tossed them down the steps." Evan attempted to sound nonchalant.

"Do you want me to bring them upstairs to the laundry room for you?"

"No, I got it," Evan said, rushing to the bottom of the stairs.

He did not want Jenna to pick them up and possibly find blood.

Evan pushed past Jenna as she stepped off the last step into the basement and picked up the pile of clothes. He bunched them into a ball to hide descriptive details.

"Your boxes are there by the furnace. Take whatever you need. I'm going back upstairs to wait for my dinner," Evan said as he pointed to an area where Jenna's boxes were stacked.

When Evan was at the top of the staircase, his mind swirled with options for the clothing he held. He looked around the room, then decided to place it in the trunk of his Audi to burn later.

"I *must* remember to get that done soon," he muttered when he closed the car trunk.

Evan returned to the basement after his food was delivered and found Jenna had moved her boxes to the center of the room. She had burrowed through a particular box of photographs and documents. When she heard Evan on the staircase, she turned to him.

"These are all the wedding photos. I want to keep some," Jenna softly said.

"Keep them all, Jen. I don't want them. Burn them for all I care!"

"Don't be like that, Evan. We were married and in love once."

"Yeah, well, that was before, and this is now. I don't want any of them!"

"You can't make believe our marriage didn't happen. I'll leave you some. You'll change your mind and be sorry if you didn't have the photos."

"I SAID I DON'T WANT THEM!" Evan shouted.

Jenna turned back to the box of photographs, placed the pictures she held inside it, closed the lid, and stacked it with other boxes she had packed. She only had three.

"Could you help me bring these to my car?" Jenna asked.

"Yeah, I guess I could."

Jenna had spent an hour in the basement. The Chinese food Evan ordered for dinner remained untouched on the kitchen island, getting cold. He had no desire to eat while Jenna was in the basement. Evan wanted her gone from his house. He bent over, lifting two of the three boxes she had packed. They were heavy, but he managed.

"You don't have to do this in one trip, Evan," Jenna said.

"Yeah, I do, Jenna," Evan replied, wobbling up the stairs under the weight of the load.

Jenna picked up the remaining box and followed Evan up the stairs, out the front door to her car. Evan had to place the two boxes he carried onto the front seat of her Boxster since her frunk, the trunk in the front of the vehicle, was much too small to hold all three. Jenna popped the frunk and placed the box she had carried inside. Evan turned to walk back into the house, but Jenna had grabbed him by the arm to stop him.

"Evan, this is the last time we will see each other. I'll be moving to Philadelphia in a couple of weeks. Shouldn't we sit down and talk?"

"No, Jenna, there's nothing to say. I wish you luck and hope you find what you need."

Evan really did not have anything to say to her.

"My food is getting cold. I have to go."

Evan pulled away from Jenna's grasp and walked to the house. He entered, closing the door without looking back.

It was a long time after Jenna had pulled out of the driveway before Evan composed himself and calmed down. The hatred he felt for her grew stronger. He never imagined he could feel that way about Jenna. He got over his denial, disbelief and grief, and at this point, it was just hatred.

A Grubhub driver had delivered Evan's Chinese dinner at 7:45 p.m. while Jenna was in the basement collecting her belongings. The food cooled while it sat on the kitchen counter because Evan had lost his appetite while she was there. When Jenna left, the appetite returned, and Evan considered reheating the food in the microwave but chose to eat it cold.

He polished off the bottle of wine he had opened just before Jenna arrived. He didn't intend to drink the entire bottle, but needed something to ease his nerves after Jenna's unplanned visit. Evan tossed the cardboard containers that held the dinner and the empty wine bottle into the trash bin and returned to his laptop. He resumed what he had started before Jenna sounded the doorbell.

John was correct about the information he could find on the cellular provider's website. The cell phone information he sought was there, although what John told him about unpaid apps was incorrect.

Evan noticed that Jenna had several commonly used apps, including Uber, Lyft, various department stores, streaming music services, and email, installed on her phone. Those, Evan knew, were free. He did not see anything out of the ordinary.

He located a tab reading 'Paid Apps,' clicked on it, and found what he was looking for. The app that ruined his life. It was called *Boredwives*. Evan had never heard of it and wanted to learn more about it. He opened a new tab in his browser, went to Google, and searched. He was stunned by what he found.

The narrative for *Boredwives* disturbed Evan. It promoted infidelity among married couples with promised confidentiality. A married woman could join this site, create a profile, and meet men for sex. Evan could not comprehend why an app like this would even exist. It went against everything he believed in. He once thought Jenna felt the same way.

Evan browsed several photos of women scattered around the country, but he couldn't see any details about them because he wasn't a paid member. Many looked to be beautiful, professional women.

What was wrong in their lives to warrant such a pursuit? Evan questioned internally. Then he thought about Jenna.

Nothing. Jenna had nothing wrong with her life. I made sure she had everything!

Evan considered the site to be a disgrace to morality and an attack on family values. The women who became members of the site were undeserving of the men they were married to. These unsuspecting husbands believed they were in happy, loving marriages, but they were not.

These men are being deceived and betrayed, much like Jenna betrayed me!

Evan, severely bothered by what he saw, didn't know what to do next. It angered him to know Jenna placed an app like this on her phone, created a profile, and became a member. She was not the person he thought he had married. He never envisioned her considering something so vile. Evan searched for Jenna's picture on the app, but was unsuccessful because there were too many photos and he didn't know her profile name.

Evan slammed shut his laptop in disgust and rose from his seat. He paced the family room for several minutes before he walked to the liquor cabinet, poured three fingers of bourbon, and plopped back down on his favorite recliner. He flicked on the television to watch his favorite crime documentaries while his anger brewed.

It was close to midnight, and Evan needed sleep. He felt drained after his strenuous day at work, the unexpected visit from Jenna, and the outrage he felt when he learned about the dating site. He lay in bed for several hours, unable to fall asleep as he thought about *Boredwives*. He had seen several photos of women on the site who reminded him of Jenna, smiling back at him. More wives he knew were destroying their husbands' lives, making them all look like fools. The visual sensation of all those *Jennas* staring back at him kept him awake.

It was as if the pictures were playing like a slide show, behind his closed eyelids, when the solution to ease his anger was formed. He would punish the women who thought cheating on their unsuspecting, loving husbands was okay.

He now realized that his targeted anger at Jason Tanner was misguided. Evan knew Tanner deserved to die for ruining the marriage, but Jenna was the catalyst.

"Jenna did this. She started this. She betrayed me and cheated on me using that damned, vile app. All those wives are doing the same thing to their husbands. Making them out to be fools!" Evan muttered to himself.

Evan decided he would create a profile on *Boredwives* of his own. He would find those women who, like Jenna, were destroying their marriages and lure them to their deaths.

He knew he could kill. He actually enjoyed it. The act awakened something inside him—a dark hunger, a taste for blood that both terrified and exhilarated him. He finally understood the cruel satisfaction of it, the intoxicating pull of the kill, and knew there would be more, if he could just get away, like the last time.

CHAPTER 26

November 7th

Evan awoke the following morning at 5:00 after very little sleep. The first thought that entered his mind when he opened his eyes was the *Boredwives* app and the awareness that he had developed while lying in bed the night before. He wanted to destroy that site and the women who used it. He knew the best way to do it was to create a profile for himself as a man looking for commitment-free sex. He could post a photo, lure these horrible cheating wives to him, and destroy them.

As Evan internally developed his plan, he wondered how to kill without being identified or discovered. The biggest problem for Evan was the photo he had to post on *Boredwives*. If women started turning up dead, and it was found that they were online dating, he knew the police would eventually make a connection to *Boredwives*.

Evan climbed out of bed, put on his bathrobe, and descended the stairs. He moved through the kitchen, opened the basement door, and walked down. He wanted to see if the items he once owned were still there. He searched all the shelves and pulled boxes from crevices built into the walls. After hunting for some time, he found what he sought, buried behind old storm windows stacked in a basement corner. It was the box labeled 'Drama Club, SUNYA.'

While attending the State University of New York in Albany, referred to locally as SUNYA, he had a girlfriend in the Drama Club who convinced him to join. He was unsure whether it would be something that would interest him, but it did not take long before he became immersed in the acting scene. He had a natural ability to act, and directors had frequently chosen him as the lead in several plays. During his sophomore year, he decided to purchase an entire professional-grade theatrical makeup kit for himself. He wanted to be the best actor he could be and immersed himself in the characters he imitated.

He carried the box upstairs to the family room. He pulled off the lid and reviewed the contents. Everything was there. Blonde, black, and brunette wigs. Some with long hair, some with short. One was curly-haired and red. There were various shades and lengths of sideburns, mustaches, and beards. Various prosthetics that changed the shape of the nose and chin were present. There were jars of liquid makeup and powders. The make-up kit contained everything he needed to bring justice to those who had compromised their marriages.

This is perfect. I'm glad I held on to this stuff. I can be anyone I want to be. I'll be on stage once again! Evan gleefully thought.

Once he uncovered everything he needed to begin the mission, he mapped out several profiles on paper based on what he had in his kit. He wanted to ensure they were distinct enough to conceal his natural appearance. He pulled two blonde and brunette wigs from the box and placed them on the floor. He selected several styled mustaches and beards to match the wigs he chose.

He combined the wigs, mustaches, and beards in various combinations, creating several different men. But still something felt off. He needed something better. Suddenly, Evan opened his phone and found an ad on an app about colored contacts. It never made sense to him how apps knew what he needed and advertised exactly that when he only just thought or talked about it. He rummaged through the website and found a few pairs of colored contacts in blue, green, grey and brown. He placed an urgent-delivery order with a local vendor. They were delivered within the hour and had accepted cash on delivery, *how fortunate.*

Evan happily included colored contacts to construct the disguises with more detail. He would make his choice after he had something to eat.

Pleased because he found the make-up kit, he returned to the kitchen and brewed a fresh pot of coffee.

He also cooked himself a delicious breakfast of chocolate chip pancakes with a side of bacon.

Evan, immersed in character creations and visions of revenge, didn't remember it was a working day. He glanced at the time on his phone and groaned, knowing he needed to be ready for work. He gathered up the wigs and other pieces of disguises, returned them to the box, and placed it behind the sofa.

He climbed the stairs to the bathroom and jumped in the shower. While he showered, Evan continued formulating a vision of the different profile identities he would create. His anger at Jenna increased as hot water streamed down his back. He wanted to apply his newly discovered form of justice to immoral women he felt deserved punishment.

He exited the shower, dried off, and stared into the mirror at a changed man. He would no longer pretend to be the gentle and passive human being everyone thought he was. He was just an actor playing a role he thought the world needed. The anger and betrayal Jenna brought to him had exposed the real man hiding behind the actor's mask.

"God, it's so tiring hiding my true self. Time to stop making believe I'm someone I'm not," Evan said into the mirror.

Evan walked to the closet to choose a suit and tie for work. As he reached in, he stopped himself. He decided he didn't feel like going into the office. He wanted to stay home to create a profile and photo for *Boredwives*.

"I have much more important things to tend to!" Evan muttered aloud.

His self-appointed mission to seek justice for all married men had begun at that very moment. He picked up his cell phone, dialed his administrative assistant, Rachel, and informed her he had a slight fever and would not be in the office. It was an excuse everyone used, and it always worked. If Evan needed another day or two, he would develop the fever into a full-blown flu.

When Evan ended his call with Rachel, he snatched the sweats and t-shirt he had worn the previous night from the floor and put them on. He returned downstairs to the kitchen to brew another fresh pot of coffee. He needed more caffeine to maintain his vigilance, especially after having such a restless night's sleep.

CHAPTER 27

November 7th

While the coffee brewed, Evan retrieved the make-up kit from behind the sofa and selected two blonde wigs with a couple of color-matching mustaches. He also selected a prosthetic that would alter the shape of his nose. He wanted to create a suitable disguise for his *Boredwives* profile photo.

He tried the two wigs and mustaches in various combinations and studied himself with a handheld mirror he pulled from the kit until he chose a blend he thought was the best. It was a medium-length blonde wig with a full mustache draped slightly over his upper lip.

He attached the prosthetic that enlarged the width of his nose and used the liquid makeup to blend and hide the exposed edges. He pulled on the wig and glued the mustache to his upper lip. He thought he looked younger and, more importantly, unrecognizable.

He pulled out the pair of blue contacts and placed them over his hazel-colored irises to complement the blonde wig. He looked into the mirror again.

"I look like a completely different person! I haven't lost my touch in the make-up department!" Evan laughed when he saw a completely different man staring back at him.

The makeover was complete. Evan picked up his cell phone, held it out, and took several selfies. He reviewed the pictures he snapped, choosing a slightly blurry photo. Evan thought it would help conceal his real identity and make it difficult for law enforcement to identify him. He was sure they would use facial recognition software to try to identify the killer if his image was captured on CCTV or security cameras.

He stared at the photo for several minutes, wondering if this was a new character he was about to portray in a play he wrote, directed, and produced. A play not performed in a college auditorium but on a much larger stage.

Evan was satisfied with the photo. His next step was to download *Boredwives* onto his cell phone. As the app loaded for installation, a sudden thought occurred to Evan that led him to hit 'CANCEL' right then.

"What are you? Some kind of an idiot. You're much smarter than this!" Evan said aloud.

The police can track cell phones and apps, so he canceled the installation and deleted the selfies he had just taken. If the police connected *Boredwives* to the married women they found murdered, they could eventually connect the murders to him.

He decided to use a burner phone instead. He knew criminals purchased these phones at various drug or department stores, always paying with cash, making it nearly impossible for law enforcement to trace them back to the owner.

Evan swallowed the remainder of his coffee, placed the mug into the dishwasher, hand-washed the coffee carafe, and tidied up the kitchen. He was indeed a man of habit. When satisfied that the kitchen was spotless, he returned to the primary bedroom. He put on a pair of jeans and a sweatshirt with no logos displayed for his ride to the store.

Evan decided to continue wearing the disguise after learning from crime television programs that investigators use security videos from store and parking lot cameras to identify suspects, including those who use burner phones during crimes. He knew he would be visible on one of those cameras. Once Evan got dressed, he opened his bedside table drawer, where he kept emergency cash available, and pulled out $500.

Evan got into his Audi, backed out of the garage, and drove towards town. It was only eleven in the morning. He was not concerned about bumping into co-workers who might be out and about for lunch so early in the day. He was supposed to be home, sick with a fever, and did not want to be seen by anyone he worked with. He had hoped to run into someone he knew who didn't work with him. He had donned a wig, mustache, prosthetic, and blue contacts for his selfie picture and thought it would be a great assessment of his disguise.

Hopefully, someone I know is out and about. Let's see if they can recognize me. If they do, I can say I decided to try community theater and that I am on my way to a dress rehearsal. If they don't, I know I did a perfect job! Evan thought to himself.

Evan drove into town to a local strip mall and spotted a smaller drug store at the far end of the mall's long building. He entered the parking lot at the most distant entrance, gazing up at the poles that supported large parking lot lighting fixtures. He searched for mounted security cameras but could not locate any. He parked his car in the first open slot he found.

Before he exited the car, he placed a plain blue baseball cap on top of his head to conceal his identity even further from store security cameras covering the mall. His obsession with reality TV crime shows continued to pay off with the knowledge he gleaned from them.

Evan walked to the drug store and stopped to look through a large pane window for phones, but could not see them. He spotted a security camera above the pharmacist's stand as he entered through the automatic doors. It was too far away and did not concern him.

Evan browsed the aisles until he found the burner phones in a display case near the store's front wall. He walked up to the display and peered into the glass. Several types of phones were available.

Evan examined each phone until he selected a bargain-priced, lower-end smartphone. The phone's price was $109, and he believed it was worth every penny.

Once he selected the cell phone, he moved to a carousel where gift cards of all types hung. He spun the rack, looking for an AT&T minutes card he could use with the burner phone.

After selecting an AT&T card providing one hundred minutes of use, he also retrieved a $100 Visa gift card. *Boredwives* required membership fees to be paid online with a credit card, and he did not want to use one issued in his name.

The total cost of everything with tax came to $319.33. The money Evan carried with him was enough to cover the purchases, but he needed to remember to replenish the emergency cash he kept at home. When the minutes on the phone card depleted, he would have to return to purchase additional AT&T minutes for the burner.

As he approached the cash register, Evan observed a security camera mounted above the ceiling. He kept his head lowered as he paid for his items, though he was not overly concerned.

On his way home from the store with his purchases, Evan stopped at a local deli to grab a Reuben sandwich to go. Even though he had eaten a substantial breakfast, he was famished. He had hoped again that someone he knew would be in the deli, but that wasn't the case.

Everyone I know must be working. Evan thought.

Evan returned home, heading directly to the family room with his Reuben, burner phone, and Visa and AT&T cards. He dropped onto the sofa. He was tired from his lack of sleep the night before and drained from the energy it took to plan a murder career.

"Murdering Career," he laughed. "Is that what they call it?" He muttered to himself.

Do serial killers consider it a career? Or is it a hobby? He thought about it momentarily, deciding it would be his hobby since he already enjoyed a full-time career in data management.

He placed the items he brought home from the store onto the coffee table and walked to the kitchen. He grabbed a cold beer from the refrigerator to help wash down his Reuben. While he ate, he tried to think of a profile for *Boredwives* that would encourage responses from the disgusting married female members. He assumed it should be a profile promising discretion without strings.

Evan pulled the burner phone from the drugstore packaging and powered it up. The initial screen indicated no service was available. He reviewed the accompanying manual. It instructed him to enter a code from a phone card. He reached into the store bag, extracted the phone card, and found a validation code under a wax-based coating he scratched off with a coin. After he entered the code, the phone continued with its initialization. When it finished, he turned off the location services option in the settings menu.

After the device completed its power-up routine, an assigned telephone number displayed on the screen, Evan made sure to write it in his notepad.

Evan looked for the Play Store on the burner phone, opened it, and searched for the *Boredwives* app. When he found it, it took less than a minute to download after he clicked on 'INSTALL.'

Evan opened the app and clicked on 'new member.' He was surprised that it only required a limited amount of information to join. It did not ask for much personal data.

No wonder Jenna could keep it a secret from me, he thought.

He began creating his membership profile, identifying himself as a forty-three-year-old single male, five feet, eleven inches tall, one hundred eighty pounds, with blonde hair and blue eyes. It asked for the member's current county of residence. Evan wanted to target women in his local area without disclosing his actual location and chose Montgomery County because it was only thirty minutes west of Albany. Since Montgomery County was nearby, he knew he would still receive replies from local women.

Evan described himself as a professional businessman with no time for serious relationships. He finished with *"looking for companionship without strings"* as his tagline. It asked him to create a username. He thought about it briefly before concocting the perfect name, *'FlyWithMe.'*

Yes, he thought, *that is perfect!*

All that remained was to pay the fee to become a member. He reached into the drugstore bag, pulled out the Visa gift card he purchased, activated it, and entered the payment data. *Boredwives* was an auto-renewal membership site that required him to monitor the current balance on his Visa card. When the amount was depleted, he would need to purchase a new Visa card.

He had to take new selfie photos using the burner phone for his profile. He took several, again choosing one slightly blurred, and uploaded it to the site.

With everything complete, he sat back to reflect on his mission so far. He was on his way to fulfilling his pursuit of vengeance and the beginning of the end from the anger he felt because of Jenna's betrayal. He carefully removed his disguise, placed all the pieces in the emptied drugstore bag, and set the bag in the box holding his makeup kit. He wanted to ensure he had the exact items used when he created the mask in his profile photo.

He observed many women on the site who looked like Jenna, with the same color hair, similar stature, and close in age. It triggered something deep inside his soul.

He needed to go after *specifically* those women. He believed that killing all the Jennas he found would end his feelings of betrayal and rage. He searched for women who looked like Jenna within his hunting ground. He tried to locate women with the same shimmering green eyes, but they were so unique to his real Jenna. That wasn't as important to Evan as long as the women resembled her.

Evan spent much of the afternoon sending messages to local women on *Boredwives* through the online messaging app. He waited anxiously for replies but was disappointed when he did not receive any. He figured at least one of the women on the app would fall for it.

"Come on, ladies. Here I am. Come and get me!" He muttered.

He felt discouraged and placed the burner phone on the coffee table. He lay down on the sofa to take a nap. He was exhausted.

CHAPTER 28

November 7th

Evan awoke from his nap a little after 5:00 p.m. and picked up his burner phone. He opened the app, looking for replies to the messages he had sent earlier. There were none.

This is going to be more challenging than I thought, he realized.

"I will not give up! It's only the first day, and not even an entire day at that," Evan said to himself.

He had an evening flight lesson scheduled for 7:00 p.m. with Jim. Evan left the burner phone at home and drove to the airport.

Flights after sundown were an FAA requirement to complete the training for a pilot's certificate. All pilots needed to learn to navigate the dark skies while identifying airport beacons among the numerous lights glowing and winking from the ground.

In his ground training, Evan learned that all public airport towers had rotating beacons emitting one green light and one white light in succession to identify themselves. Military airports cast two green, followed by one white. These rotating beacons were extremely bright, but with traffic lights, streetlights, building lights, and all other lighting mixed in, finding airports at night was challenging.

Another reason for night training was to give pilots experience with landings on runways illuminated by various colored lights. Pilots needed to establish each of the different strings of colors and what they indicated. Blue lighting lined the taxiways, while white lights bordered the runways. Informational signs identifying taxiway and runway assignments were in yellow. With all the lights glowing from an airfield, runways appeared as black holes when viewed from the sky. Nighttime landings were much more challenging to execute smoothly.

Evan's night lesson went well, with Jim telling him he was remarkably close to scheduling the FAA flight examination. Evan had completed fifty-four hours of training and felt confident he would pass the FAA flight exam. His initial fear of heights was no longer an issue, and he was surprised when Jim told him many pilots had acrophobia but were fine when in an enclosed object. Evan felt the same.

The only requirement Evan had left before scheduling with the FAA was to perform one more cross-country flight. This cross-country flight would differ from his last one. It had to be at least three hundred fifty nautical miles with three separate landings, not including the originating airport.

Evan returned home, tired from the nighttime training. Although he did not go into the office, his day was more intense than usual. It took effort to purchase what he needed, build the disguise, and create the online profile. It felt like work to him, but he also assumed he felt drained from the intense emotions he suffered.

He changed into sweats and a bathrobe, discarding his worn clothes. He went to the kitchen to grab a beer from the fridge. Evan wanted to relax in the recliner, drink his beer, and wait for messages from unsuspecting women.

Again, he was disappointed after he checked the burner phone throughout the evening without receiving any messages.

"Hmm, maybe Jenna was the only slut on that app," he muttered.

It was nearly midnight, and he decided he could no longer stay awake. He climbed the stairs and went to bed. It did not take him long to fall asleep.

CHAPTER 29

November 20th

E van completed his second cross-country flight the week prior. It went as well as his first trip. He and Jim also went on several more night flights. Evan thought he was ready for the FAA flight review, and Jim agreed.

They contacted the local FAA field office to schedule the flight for 2:00 p.m. on Monday, December 4th, as long as the weather cooperated. If it snowed or the skies filled with low-lying clouds, they would need to reschedule the test. Evan trained for a VFR pilot's certificate, which limited his flying to conditions with no clouds in his flight path and a minimum visibility of ten miles.

Evan would need to take the day off from work for his flight test, but he knew it was not an issue since his superiors and co-workers all knew about his training and had been supportive throughout it all.

Evan eventually received responses on *Boredwives*. However, most of the messages he read were from women who only wanted conversations with men, never intending to meet them physically. He was uninterested in chatting with these women and deleted those messages without a reply.

Why would a woman pay just to chat? That makes no sense, he thought. However, he was comforted knowing they weren't physically cheating on their husbands.

He did chat with one woman daily who wanted more than just conversation. Her profile name was '*INeedMore.*' She contacted Evan on *Boredwives* for the first time two weeks earlier. He reviewed her profile before he initially replied to her original message. He saw she was an attractive, fortyish woman who looked very much like Jenna. Her profile said she had been married for nineteen years and was the mother of two teenage children. She had the familiar wording all the women used, '*Bored wife looking for more.*' Evan hated that expression, which infuriated him every time he read it. It was a similar phrase Jenna had used on her profile.

After messaging on the website for a few days, Evan offered to send '*INeedMore*' his telephone number, and she accepted. He gave her the number of his burner phone and not his cell phone, which Evan thought was ironic because she considered herself cautious, wanting to get to know him through messages and phone calls before meeting him in person.

During those phone conversations, she told Evan her name was Laura. He had given Laura the name Stephen because he did not want her to know his real name, in case she mentioned him to a friend about meeting someone from *Boredwives*.

They spoke several times as he tried to understand why she betrayed her husband. When he asked her directly, her reply made him boil inside. She said it was to have some fun. She stated she still loved her husband, saying he provided well for her, but he couldn't satisfy her as much as he did when they first met. Laura finished by saying she required much more sexual stimulation than he could give.

Evan had become furious to think she was so cavalier about the purity of her marriage. Relationships meant more than just sex, he believed.

During their calls, Evan asked her several questions about the website. He asked her if she knew anyone else using the site or if her husband had suspicions. She told him no one knew, not even her best friend. It was all Evan needed to know to remain on his quest to admonish her.

CHAPTER 30

November 30th

Evan lay in bed, listening to the sound of rain as it pounded on the roof, and thought about Jenna. He continued to hate her for what she had done to their marriage, yet he still thought he loved her. He was a jumble of uncontrolled emotions.

Jenna had surprised Evan with a phone call while he was eating dinner the previous night. He never expected to hear from her again, or at least not until their divorce papers were available to sign. She had phoned to remind him that she was leaving for Philadelphia on Saturday and asked if he would meet her for lunch. He initially declined because all he wanted was for her to go away and to forget about her betrayal. However, he relented and agreed to meet her at 1:00 p.m. for sushi.

As he lay in bed, he became enraged and recalled his arrangement with Jenna to meet for lunch. He really did not want to see her and regretted accepting the invitation. She wanted to say goodbye to Evan, but he did not care.

"After she ruined my life, she believes we are old friends," he snickered.

She wrecked his life, and he would never consider her his friend. He felt an immediate urge to release his fury. He reached over to the nightstand and picked up the burner phone. He looked for messages from *Boredwives* but found nothing. He didn't care because he intended to text Laura.

"Want to meet tonite?" He typed.

While waiting for Laura to answer, Evan grabbed the laptop on the nightstand alongside his bed. He powered it up, and when it came alive, he googled area parks in the city of Schenectady, where he thought they could connect.

He chose Schenectady because it was where Laura said she lived, and Evan thought she would be more likely to meet if it were convenient for her. He found Central Park in his Google search. The large park included an area referred to as The Rose Garden.

He discovered a map of the park online and looked for the Rose Garden. He found it at the far west end of the park, bordered by homes. He navigated back to Google to search for photos of the Rose Garden. He found several photos in posts left by previous visitors to the park and observed that most of the homes were shrouded from direct view with several large trees and thick bushes.

The perfect place to kill, he thought.

He deemed it the perfect location since he would be wearing black. He would also have his Glock fitted with its silencer, and although it did not silence the gun, it would suppress the blast of a gunshot enough to prevent the sound from reaching the homes. He also liked the fact that there was a gazebo in the Rose Garden where he could meet Laura.

Evan used the weather to his advantage. It was the end of November in upstate New York, and temperatures hovered in the lower thirties. The late fall weather kept most people indoors at night, and Evan didn't think anyone would wander through the park in the frigid air. He felt confident the location would make a perfect meeting place.

He pulled a street map up on his screen for the area and found where he would park the car. He wanted to know as much about the route as he had when he killed Tanner. He determined he would enter Central Park on foot.

He waited several minutes with intense anticipation until his burner phone finally beeped with a reply.

"Love to," Laura responded and added a kissing emoji.

"Central Park Schenectady?" Evan asked.

"A park?" Laura questioned.

"Go from there if we like each other," Evan typed.

"Ok," Laura replied.

"The Rose Garden," Evan typed.

"In the Gazebo," Laura instructed.

"See you at 9."

Evan was excited about meeting Laura to put his vengeance against immoral, cheating women in motion. He wondered how it would feel.

"Will my anger ease with each dishonest wife I eliminate?" he asked himself.

After he exchanged texts with Laura, he climbed out of bed and danced downstairs to the kitchen to start a pot of coffee. He had awoken in a foul mood, thinking about meeting Jenna for lunch against his better judgment, but now he felt positive energy when considering what he had planned for later that evening. It was turning out to be a fabulous day!

While brewing coffee, he returned to the main bathroom to shower, shave, and brush his teeth. He had big plans for the night, but he still had a full-time job to think about. After he dressed, he looked at the burner phone for more messages, but there were none. He slid it into the pocket of his slacks along with his cell phone and bounded downstairs to plan better by the kitchen island.

He would include a stop at Hertz Rental Agency on his way home from the office to rent a nondescript car using the Visa gift card. His self-described mission started over three weeks ago, and it was the third gift card he purchased. He would choose a Toyota Camry, a common car seen on the streets. He knew he would be required to show his driver's license and insurance card at the rental agency, but thought using the Visa gift card would reduce some of the electronic trail. He wanted to rent a car because he did not want to drive his distinctive Audi into Schenectady, where it could be later described to the police by potential witnesses.

He reaffirmed his plan internally as he poured himself another cup of coffee. When he returns from the office, he would pull the rented Camry into his garage. He would instantly change out of his business clothes and put on the disguise he used for the *Boredwives* profile photo. He would also prepare a lovely steak dinner as a pre-celebration for the night he has planned.

When Evan began his drive to work, the rain had subsided into a slight drizzle. Clouds were forecast for the remainder of the day, with temperatures dropping to the mid-twenties after sunset.

"Weather conditions could not be more perfect," Evan mused.

He arrived at work excited about the activities he had planned for later in the evening, and it showed. Rachel, his administrative assistant, greeted him as soon as he entered his office.

"Good morning, Mr. Williams. You're in an excellent mood today!"

"I am. I had a perfect night's sleep," Evan replied.

"That's nice," Rachel said and continued, "There are no issues to report today. Hopefully, it stays that way."

"I hope so!" Evan exclaimed.

After Rachel left Evan's office, he logged into his desktop computer to read the morning's data reports. Evan spent the morning reviewing overnight reports and responding to routine emails from his team. He then went through the new design proposals on his desk, approving, rejecting, or suggesting changes as needed. John knocked on Evan's office door before he finished.

"Good morning, Evan."

"Hey, John! How's your day so far?" Evan asked.

"Going well. Pretty quiet for a change!" John replied.

"Yes, let's hope it stays quiet. We could use a break."

"So Evan, how are things with Jenna? Did she leave town yet?" John asked.

"Funny you ask. I am meeting her at 1:00 today for sushi. She is leaving for Philadelphia on Saturday and wanted to meet one last time."

"Really? And you're going to meet her? I'm surprised you said yes."

"I wasn't going to, but I gave in. It's only lunch, and it will be the last time."

"Well, hope it goes okay," John replied, then asked, "Oh, by the way, did she ever find out you were spying on her phone?"

The question caught Evan off guard. He had hoped John would not remember they had cloned her cell phone. Evan really wanted him to forget it. It alarmed him when he asked.

"No, she never found out, but I also never learned anything. She wasn't doing anything behind my back like I thought she was. She just didn't want to be married any longer," Evan lied.

Evan did not want John to know he had found out about her cheating, especially with Jason Tanner. Tanner was a well-known attorney in the area, and his killing stayed in the news. Fortunately for Evan, it did not seem like the police made much progress in identifying his killer. John never knew the reason for the marriage ending. Evan never told anyone.

"Oh, that's good. I'm glad to hear," John replied and nervously chuckled, "Well, not that part about not wanting to be married."

"No problem. I guess she outgrew herself," Evan retorted sarcastically.

"Alrighty then, enjoy your lunch," John said with a smile and a wave as he left Evan's office.

Evan remained bothered by John's question about Jenna's cell phone. He had hoped John would not mention it again. More importantly, Evan hoped the police would not find out and approach John with questions.

Evan arrived for his lunch with Jenna just before 1:00 at the Hana Japanese Steakhouse in Guilderland, a small town outside Albany close to his office building. Jenna had texted as he walked through the restaurant's door, saying she was running late. Evan proceeded to the bar to wait and ordered himself a Japanese beer.

While he sat, he continued to think about the plans he had made for the evening. He needed to remember to leave his cell phone behind, like he did the night he killed Tanner. Evan knew that many suspects were captured and convicted because they were foolish enough to leave their cell phones on their persons or in their cars while committing a crime.

Evan also decided to contact the rental agency when he returned to the office after lunch to reserve a Toyota

Camry in advance. He would be disappointed to show up after work without a reservation and be turned away because they had no cars available.

Jenna arrived fifteen minutes later, saw Evan at the bar, and weaved around tables to join him. She sat on a barstool and ordered a white wine. A Chablis. As she waited for her wine, she remained quiet, and it felt awkward to Evan. It was like they were strangers. She was no longer the woman he married. When Evan looked over at her and saw that she just stared straight ahead, he sensed love and rage simultaneously. He hated those mixed feelings and felt that he needed to speak before the tension grew thicker.

"How was your drive over?" Evan asked, nonchalantly.

"It was good. Traffic is light today," Jenna replied.

The bartender returned with her glass of wine and placed it on the bar in front of her. She picked it up and took a sip.

"Let's get a table," Evan said as he stood and walked to the front of the restaurant.

Jenna followed behind him. They stood silently at the hostess stand while waiting for her to return from seating another group of people.

The hostess returned to her station, greeted Evan and Jenna, and then grabbed two menus from her stand before asking them to follow her. Evan called out to the hostess and requested a booth. He wanted a booth to avoid sitting in the middle of the restaurant at a table exposed to others. The booths lined the outer walls, providing a modicum of privacy.

"So, Jenna, why did you want to have lunch?" Evan asked as soon as they settled into their seats.

"I just wanted to say goodbye in person," Jenna replied and continued, "I want us to part as friends, and I didn't think leaving town without seeing you in person one last time would be appropriate. We were married, after all. And I did love you, Evan."

"Well, you hurt me badly, Jenna, and I don't know if I'll ever forgive you. I am glad you're leaving town. It will make it easier for me to avoid running into you out in public."

"I hope you will forgive me someday. I don't want you to hate me. It's not what I ever wanted," Jenna said.

"I don't think I'll forgive you. And I do hate you. I never thought I could hate you, but I do, and that's that."

"I'm sorry you feel that way, Evan."

Jenna's eyes filled with tears.

The waiter appeared at the table as Jenna finished speaking. They both ordered the Sushi Lunch Special: five sushi pieces with a California roll. Evan had another beer while Jenna slowly sipped her first glass of wine. She tried to hold back her tears.

They finished their lunch in silence. There was not much more to say to each other. Jenna was leaving town, and Evan was happy she was departing. Jenna had barely touched her food, her plate remaining full, but Evan, excited about his evening, was famished and finished everything on his plate. This chapter in his life with Jenna ended, marking the beginning of a new one. He looked forward to his mission to make married women pay for their sins.

When Jenna said she wanted to leave, Evan reluctantly walked her to her car. She gave him a peck on the cheek before she settled into the driver's seat of her Boxster, said goodbye, and drove away. Evan hoped it would be the last time he would ever see her again. He walked to his car, climbed in, and returned to the office.

CHAPTER 31

November 30th

Evan looked at the wall clock in his office, saw it was 5:00 p.m., and decided it was time to wrap up the day. He had dealt with no emergencies or dreadful meetings with leadership and felt refreshed. He left the building with a bounce in his step, yet he also felt anxious. Although he had killed in the past, killing a woman would be a new experience for him.

On his way home, Evan stopped at the rental agency but did not drive into the lot. He felt leaving his car there and driving off with a rental would appear suspicious to the agent at the counter. He parked a few blocks down, around a corner from Hertz, and walked the rest of the way.

Evan lied in response to the many questions that the overly chatty rental agent asked. The agent wanted to know why Evan needed a rental car since he was local to the area. Evan told him that his car was in the shop. He asked Evan how long he needed the rental, and Evan said he only needed it for the night. The rental agent questioned the Visa gift card, and Evan told him he had received it from a friend sometime back. He wanted to use it before it expired. Evan regarded his responses as reasonable enough to avoid suspicion.

The agent gave Evan a choice of a black, red, or silver Camry, and he chose black. Evan reasoned that a black car would fade into the darkness of the night, blending in with other vehicles parked along a curb. If the police were to ask witnesses, the answers would most likely be '*a black sedan*' or '*a black car,*' and there were thousands of them everywhere. Evan's Audi was also black. He was sure his neighbors would not easily spot the changed vehicle.

On his way home from the rental agency, Evan pulled into an apartment complex near his home. Since New York required a front and rear license plate, he needed to replace both on the Camry. He searched the complex's lot for security cameras but found none. When he arrived at the back of the lot, he saw several cars parked with their noses pointed against a concrete barrier.

How fortunate. No one will see me removing license plates, he thought.

He chose two separate cars and removed the front plate from each with a screwdriver he had placed in his briefcase before leaving for work. He thought taking just a front plate would go unnoticed by the owners for quite a while before they reported it stolen or replaced.

He looked around one last time to ensure he was alone, stood, and concealed both plates inside his raincoat. He was confident the mismatched plates would go unnoticed by police cruisers passing by him. If someone saw the Camry parked in Schenectady during the murder and remembered the license plate number, it would not tie back to the rental car's registration.

Evan arrived home with the rental car, pulled it into the garage, and lowered the door. He picked up the two license plates from the passenger floor of the vehicle, along with the screwdriver. He removed the front and rear plates from the Camry, replacing them with the ones he stole. He set the original plates on a worktable in the garage.

Evan changed out of his suit into black jeans and a sweatshirt. They were the very same clothes he wore when he killed Tanner. He had made the decision a few weeks back to keep them. No witnesses had reported seeing anyone suspicious in Washington Park, and the police never returned for more interrogation. Eventually, Evan put the clothes through the washer twice, thoroughly examining every inch for bloodstains. He did not see anything. He looked in the mirror after he dressed.

"My new uniform!" he muttered and laughed.

Dressed in black, he walked to the basement to retrieve the makeup kit. He had stored it behind boxes of holiday decorations to keep it hidden from view. He retrieved the drug store bag containing the disguise he used for the profile photo from the case. He took it to the kitchen, laying it on the island.

Evan fired up the gas grill and threw on a thick ribeye steak with a russet potato. He wanted a special dinner before he headed out to meet Laura. While the steak and potatoes were grilling, he entered the first-floor bathroom to put on his disguise.

With the disguise in place, he stared into the mirror at a different man. He loved how he appeared, and his lips curled into a cunning smile.

Perfect! He thought.

By the time he finished with his makeup, his steak and potatoes had finished cooking. Evan took the food off the grill and grabbed a beer from the fridge. He sat at the dining room table, eating his dinner.

While enjoying his meal, Evan thought he should text Laura to confirm that she still planned to meet him. He wished he had texted her to confirm the date before he spent the effort to get into his disguise. Evan, however, was much too excited to think about it earlier.

Evan picked up the burner phone and typed.

"Are we still on tonight?"

It was a few minutes before he received a reply, continuing to eat while he waited.

"Yes, looking forward to it!" his phone beeped.

He finished his dinner calmly. He was surprised to find himself so relaxed, knowing what he had planned to do in just a couple of hours. He placed his dirty plate and silverware in the dishwasher and discarded the emptied beer bottle. Evan sat back in his recliner and closed his eyes. He waited for his quest to begin. He did not have to wait long.

When Evan rose from the recliner, he felt a calm overtake him. He picked up his cell phone to ensure it was powered up and placed it back on the coffee table. He tucked his Glock inside his waistband and pulled on his black leather gloves. Evan grabbed the rental car keys from the kitchen's island, where he had set them down earlier. He climbed into the Camry, lowering the garage door using the remote control he had removed from his Audi earlier after he backed out. He turned off the daytime running lights feature of the car, driving with the headlights extinguished until he left his neighborhood.

CHAPTER 32

November 30th

Evan departed an hour before the scheduled rendezvous. He wanted to have plenty of time to find a parking spot on the street he had chosen. He would walk the remaining distance to wait for his prey. He had memorized the name of the street where he would park, which was conveniently close to the Rose Garden. It was close enough to walk on foot without being seen. Due to the darkness, if someone happened to see him, they would not be able to describe him to the police easily. If the street were full of cars without a place to park, he would find an alternative.

As he drove, his calmness shifted to apprehension, especially the closer he got to his destination. He knew he was undertaking what needed to be done and knew he could do it, but he was nervous, nonetheless. He considered how he felt. He determined it was not because he was killing again, but because he never wanted to be locked up in prison. He needed to be cautious.

The drive to Schenectady took less than thirty minutes. He arrived at Central Park with plenty of time to spare and parked the Camry on the nearly deserted street he had chosen from Google Maps. It was mostly empty, as he had expected due to the frigid winter temperatures. It was only a five-minute walk to the park, where three distinct stone-covered paths led to the Rose Garden. He chose one that would keep him the furthest from many of the homes that lined the street.

Evan entered the park undetected and found the gazebo. He arrived twenty minutes before Laura, sitting on a wooden bench inside the gazebo to wait. It was chilly, and he shivered. He was unsure if the shivering was from the cold or something else. He was delighted that the rain had stopped.

Laura arrived a little after 9:00 p.m. and approached the gazebo. Evan watched her walk from the street onto the grounds and was surprised that he hadn't seen her exit a car. He surmised that she was worried about being seen and parked further away, just like he did. He stood up to greet her.

"Hi, are you Laura?" he asked as he rose from the bench.

"Yes. Are you Stephen?" she asked.

"Yeah, I'm Steve. Great to meet you in person," Evan answered, then asked, "Do you want to sit here and talk?"

"Only for a few minutes. It's pretty cold out here. I hoped we could go somewhere warm to be alone and have fun. There's a hotel close to here," Laura replied.

Her response raised Evan's blood pressure. This woman had just met him, yet she already wanted to be alone for sex. Evan remembered how he felt when he found out Jenna was cheating on him, and he also thought about Laura's husband and how he would feel. He continued to string her along, just for a few more minutes.

"Yeah, we can, but let's talk a little first to understand our expectations better," Evan said.

They both sat down on the bench, and she kissed him on the cheek. It caught Evan by surprise, and his anger grew, but before he acted, he needed to ensure she did not tell anyone where she was or with whom.

"Where's your car? I saw you walking," Evan asked.

"Oh, I live just a few houses down that street."

Evan looked at the homes in the direction she pointed.

"That's why I said yes to meeting you here in this park. What a coincidence, right?" She laughed.

"You walked? Wouldn't your husband or kids see you coming to the park?"

"No. My husband is out of town on business until tomorrow, and my kids are off to their friends. No one knows I'm here."

It gave Evan the ease and confidence he needed.

"So, do you want to get out of the cold and get a room somewhere? I can ride with you," Laura asked again as she grabbed Evan's hand.

He pulled it away.

"I am not here for sex. I am here because I cannot stand women like you ruining marriages and betraying the men who take care of you!" he yelled.

"I don't understand. Why are you yelling at me? Why did you contact me if you're not interested in hooking up?" Laura asked, confused.

They both stood facing each other.

"It's simple. I'm here to punish you," Evan said when he pulled the gun from his pocket and pointed it at her. Evan wanted to ask her why she would deceive her husband, but he worried he would be spotted if he spent too much time with her. He just wanted to complete the mission quickly.

He could see fear wash over her, and she turned to run.

"Stay right there, or I'll shoot you in the back," Evan growled.

Laura stopped moving forward and turned back to him. She noticeably trembled with panic, and Evan saw tears stream down her face. He looked around the park, seeing no movement. He was confident they were alone. He gazed at the string of homes lining the street, realizing they were too far away for anyone to see or hear.

He pointed the Glock at Laura's face. As he was about to pull the trigger, he caught a glimpse of Jenna. Laura looked just like her. He fired the gun directly into Laura's face, destroying it. He smiled.

When Laura fell to the ground, he pictured Jenna and had the urge to do more. He considered this a punishment for how she had betrayed her husband. As he gazed at Laura's motionless body, he spotted the rings on her left hand.

Evan knelt over the body and rolled it flat on its back, straightening the legs. He grasped each hand and folded the arms over the chest while eying the rings again. It incensed him to know she was willing to have sex with another man while she wore the symbol of unity blessed by the church. He concluded she no longer deserved to wear that symbol and slid the wedding and engagement rings from her finger.

"You won't be needing these any longer," he muttered with a grin.

He placed her left hand on top of her right hand, laying them back on her chest. Evan put the rings in his pocket along with the gun and felt satisfied. He also picked up the forty-caliber cartridge that had ejected from the pistol.

Evan then reached into Laura's purse and extracted her cell phone. He saw it used biometric security, requiring a fingerprint to unlock it. He held the phone under the index finger of Laura's right hand, and the phone came alive.

He tried to type on the phone, but his glove prevented the touch screen from working, forcing him to remove his right-hand glove. Evan searched for the *Boredwives* app, located it, pressed the uninstall option, and watched as the icon disappeared. He opened her messaging app and looked for the messages they sent to each other. When he found them, he deleted them.

When Evan had finished erasing all evidence of conversations between Stephen and Laura from her cell phone, he wiped his fingerprints from the device on his pant leg and slipped it back into her purse. He put the glove back on.

Evan stood up and studied how he had positioned Laura's body. He smiled when he pictured her in a coffin at a funeral. It is how Laura will appear when her husband mourns the disgraced marriage. Of course, Evan realized her husband wouldn't know that his wife was betraying him. When the thought occurred to Evan, he concluded he wasn't killing women. Evan was erasing infidelity. It was how he justified his mission.

Evan bolted from the park. He used a path leading away from the Rose Garden behind a pond. It terminated on a different street than where he had entered. It was also a separate entrance from the one Laura had used.

He slowed to a comfortable stride when he reached the sidewalk outside the park. He did not want it to appear like he was rushing away from something, drawing attention to himself.

He looked up and down the street and didn't see anyone, grateful the streets remained empty. People really did hide when it was cold outdoors. He walked along the sidewalk before turning left, back onto the road where he had parked.

Evan shook when he fell into his car. He breathed much heavier than he expected. He trembled, not due to remorse, he concluded, but from the adrenaline rush he felt when he killed Laura.

"Oh my God, that was exhilarating! That bitch didn't know what was happening to her. She deserved to die because she betrayed her marriage. She will never deceive her husband or anyone else who loved her ever again," he said aloud to his reflection in the rearview mirror.

It took Evan a few minutes to regain control of his breathing and stop trembling. He fired the engine and sped away. Evan felt fantastic the entire drive home. He pulled the Camry into the garage, climbed out, and pressed the wall control to close the door.

Evan entered the house and walked directly to the refrigerator, grabbing a beer before he flopped into the recliner. His energy spent. He experienced many emotions caused by the lunch with Jenna and the murder. It was only 10:45 p.m., but Evan felt as if he had been awake for days. He quickly fell asleep where he sat.

When Evan awoke two hours later, he found himself still settled in the recliner. He was tranquil, and it astounded him. He had murdered a woman, yet it did not repulse him. He was only comforted instead. He questioned if Jenna's betrayal inadvertently released the killer he knew was hiding within him. He thought only a trained psychologist could tell him, and he certainly would not visit one to find out.

Evan rose from the chair and walked to the bathroom to remove the wig, mustache, nose prosthetic, and contacts. He returned the items to the make-up kit, placing it back behind the boxes full of holiday decorations in the basement. He took the rings he yanked from Laura's finger and put them in a small jewelry box that held Tanner's Rolex watch. He admired the items, thinking he was building a collection. After watching his favorite crime documentaries, he learned it was something serial killers do to remember their killings. They all saved mementos, and now he collected his own trophies.

Evan returned to the first floor, removed his clothes, and placed them into the washer for cleaning. He added detergent and color-safe bleach before he pressed the button to start the wash cycle. He ascended the stairs to

the primary bedroom, fell into bed, and slept quietly and
peacefully.

CHAPTER 33

Detective Christina Hart awoke to the blast of her cell phone at 3:15 a.m., just after falling into a deep sleep. Hart was a homicide detective for the Schenectady Police Department and was on-call for the entire month of December. Her superiors had recently initiated the monthly schedule for the homicide division, which evenly rotated late-night calls among the staff. She was annoyed to receive a call out on her first day in the rotation, exhaled sharply, and picked up her phone.

"Hart."

"Detective Hart, this is Schenectady Dispatch," came the voice over the phone.

"Yeah, I know who it is. Where am I going?"

Detective Hart did not have to ask the reason for the call. She already knew from the numerous times she received similar sleep disruptions during her last rotation.

"Central Park detective, near the Rose Garden. We have a deceased woman. Her teenage daughter found her," dispatch advised her.

"Okay, I'll be there in twenty minutes. Have you contacted my partner, Detective Sullivan? If not, please do, and tell him I'll meet him there," Detective Hart said.

"Yes, ma'am, will...," Detective Hart ended the call mid-sentence.

Hart dragged herself out of her warm, cozy bed and reached for the pants and blouse she had worn the previous day. There was no time to shower or search her closet for something fresh to put on.

She quickly dressed, brushed her hair, and swished a shot of mouthwash around her teeth to clean off the fuzz. Hart reached into her night table, pulled out her service revolver with its holster, and clipped it to her slacks' waistband. She looked in the mirror, sighed, and headed out the door.

Detective Hart lived in a two-bedroom condominium near the location of the homicide and knew the twenty minutes she told dispatch would be closer to fifteen. She expected her partner, Detective Bill Sullivan, who lived even closer to the park, to be on the scene shortly before she arrived.

The Detective climbed into her department-issued Ford Explorer SUV, pushed the start button, and began her drive to the location given to her by dispatch. It was dark and cold, with temperatures hovering near twenty-five degrees, and the Detective cursed herself for not grabbing her wool scarf as she shivered in the cold truck.

Only after seventeen short minutes, she arrived at the park. She could see several patrol cars and uniformed police officers milling around a taped-off section near the Rose Garden gazebo. Blue and red lights danced brightly off the homes surrounding the area. It gave an eerie sense of the holidays. Several uniformed police officers, with flashlights illuminating the grounds and bushes, searched the area for evidence.

Detective Hart approached the dead woman and saw her partner as he spoke to the medical examiner, who was also called out in the cold. The M.E. walked away as Detective Hart neared. She pulled on latex gloves. When she got to the body, she looked down and immediately saw an apparent bullet wound to the face. She could see the woman's purse lying nearby.

"Hey, Sully," Hart called out to her partner.

Sully was how Detective Sullivan was known on the police force and among friends.

"Good morning, Tina," Sully responded.

"Looks like she was dressed for a night out," Hart said when she saw the victim's clothing.

"I thought the same thing. She doesn't look like someone you would expect to find killed in this park at one in the morning," Sully replied.

"Where'd the M.E. go off to?" Hart asked.

"He went back to his van to get a gurney."

"Was he able to give you an approximate time of death?" Hart asked.

"He thought between nine and twelve last night, but can't be sure. The cold temperatures make it harder for him to determine. He said he needs to examine her at the morgue," Sully explained.

"Okay. Let's see what we have here."

Hart knelt to get a closer look at the victim.

"Looks like a single shot to the face, nine mill, maybe. Fully dressed, so it doesn't look like a sexual assault. Is that her purse lying there?" Hart pointed.

"Yeah, looks like hers. I haven't looked inside of it yet. I just got here, too. And the uniforms didn't want to touch it," Sully replied.

Detective Hart reached for the purse and peered inside at the contents. She noticed a wallet along with a ring holding a few keys. The bag also had a cell phone, makeup, and other items typically found in a woman's handbag. She removed the wallet to examine it further.

"Nothing looks stolen. The wallet has $211 in cash, along with some credit cards. Her cell phone and car keys are still here, too."

"So, not a robbery. Not a rape. Definitely not a suicide since no weapon was found nearby," Sully replied.

"Not sure what we have here. The name on the license is Laura Emerson, aged forty-five. Victim matches the photo."

Detective Hart held up the license so Sully could see it.

"The body looks strange to me, too. Lying flat out on her back with her arms crossed over her chest. You see this, too?" Hart asked Sully.

"Well, that didn't occur to me until you said it, but yeah, looks like her killer posed her, maybe."

Sully looked back at the woman on the ground.

"Okay, after the crime scene guys are finished snapping pictures, have her brought to the morgue. Let's get an autopsy started immediately. Make sure they bag her purse and its contents, too," Hart said and continued, "Where's the daughter? I heard she discovered the body."

"In the back of that patrol car," Sully pointed.

Detective Hart stood and walked to the patrol car, where a teenage girl was seated in the back, rubbing her palms against each other, attempting to stay warm. The Detective hated this part of her job: talking to the victim's relatives. She was always uncomfortable asking tough questions, especially when they were feeling emotional. All Hart ever wanted to do was comfort them while they sobbed.

Detective Hart arrived at the patrol car and opened the door to find an approximately sixteen-year-old girl. She had long, dark blonde hair and brown eyes. She held a wad of tissue in her clutched hands, softly crying.

"Hi. I'm Detective Hart. I'm very sorry for your loss. What's your name?" Hart asked.

"I'm Bethany," She responded quietly.

"Hi, Bethany. Is it okay if I ask you a couple of questions? I'll be quick so that you can go home. I'll have the officer drive you when we are done," Hart tried to be as compassionate as she could.

"Ok," Bethany said through tears.

"How did you find your mother?" the Detective asked.

"I got home from my friends' house, and my mom wasn't there. Her car was in the driveway, and I knew she liked coming to the park, so I walked over. And then I saw her over there on the ground!" Bethany started to bawl uncontrollably.

Detective Hart needed to step back from the car to allow the young girl to sob. She waited several minutes until Bethany could compose herself before she continued her questioning.

"You said you walked over. Where do you live?"

"In that blue house over there," Bethany pointed at a house nearby.

"Okay. Do you know why your mom was in the park?"

"No. She just likes coming here sometimes."

"Do you know if your mother was supposed to meet someone?"

"I don't know. I don't think so. She never said anything," Bethany said, sobbing softly.

"Ok. Is there anyone else at home? Your father? Brothers or sisters?" Hart asked.

"My older brother should be home. He's eighteen. My dad is in Chicago and won't be back until tomorrow morning. Today, I mean."

Bethany started to bawl again, and Detective Hart stepped back from the car to give her room. When Bethany's crying slowed, Detective Hart returned to her.

"Is it okay if I have someone drive you home?" Hart asked.

"Yeah, I guess so."

"Ok. I'm going to have this officer take you home now. I will talk to you in a few hours, so try to get some sleep. I know it's hard. Here is my card if you can't sleep and want to talk. You can call me anytime, day or night," Hart said.

Bethany started to cry once more.

Detective Hart closed the car door and approached a uniformed officer who leaned against the hood with a cigarette between his lips.

"Officer," she paused to read the name on his tag and continued, "Fusco, please drive the young girl home. It's only four houses down the street. Ensure you walk her to the door, and her older brother is home. If he isn't, bring her to the station," Hart instructed the officer.

"Will do, Detective."

"She's distraught. Please be as gentle with her as humanly possible, understood?"

"Yes, ma'am!"

The officer threw his half-smoked cigarette onto the pavement, smothering it with the toe of his shoe. He moved to the driver's door, got in, and drove away.

Detective Hart rejoined her partner, who was chatting with the coroner. Laura Emerson's body lay on a gurney in the back of a dark, windowless van.

"Sully, let's get to the station. See if we can get a head start on this thing," Hart said.

Detectives Hart and Sullivan walked to their respective vehicles to begin another demanding day.

CHAPTER 34

December 1ˢᵗ

Evan awoke to the alarm sounding at 6:00 a.m., the morning after he killed Laura, feeling refreshed after his best night's sleep since Jenna left. What took place in the Rose Garden in Central Park the previous evening awakened a beast he knew existed but held in check until now, and he liked it.

He climbed out of bed and moved to the mirror to look at the new man he had become. Evan examined his face for signs of the creature that finally emerged, but all he saw was the same Evan. It amazed him as he caught sight of the man looking back, who appeared compassionate.

I've been able to fool everyone, he thought.

Evan loved that his performance as a caring, compassionate man had remained intact.

"No one will ever know what I am capable of!" Evan murmured into the mirror.

It was a Friday morning, and he needed to prepare for work. He liked going in on Fridays, especially after management instituted casual dress Fridays. They did not go as far as jeans and t-shirts, but he could wear a pair of casual slacks with a collared short-sleeve shirt. What he liked most was not having to wear the tie. He pulled his selections from the closet and placed them on the bed before he entered the bathroom to shower.

While the hot water streamed over him, he thought about the murder the night before. He recalled with delight the look of fear he saw on Laura just before he pulled the trigger. He cherished the memory he had created in his mind's eye. He also thought about the *Boredwives* app. He would have to cancel the membership for 'Stephen'. He will create a new profile, disguise, and photo. He would also destroy and discard the burner phone. Evan will need to pick up a new one.

Evan finished in the bathroom and dressed, then went downstairs for breakfast. He was extra hungry and filled with a vitality he had not felt in a long time. He started a pot of coffee and then walked to the pantry to get the pancake mix he knew would be there.

While he prepared the pancakes, it dawned on him. He did not urgently need to turn on the television to search the news for a found body in Schenectady. He recalled the morning after murdering Tanner, his anxiety, and the need to watch the news for information, but he was relaxed after killing Laura. He did not have an immediate desire to watch for the discovery of his murder.

When his pancakes were ready, he plated them, poured a second mug of coffee, and strolled to the family room. He flicked on the television out of curiosity, not concern. The news broadcast was in the middle of the weather forecast, and Evan was more interested in the weather because of his planned FAA exam on Monday. The weather looked promising. He clicked off the television, finishing his breakfast in silence.

Evan had to return the rental car on his way into the office. However, before he pulled out of the garage, he put on his leather gloves and removed the stolen license plates. He reattached the original plates on the rented car; then folded the stolen plates into thirds with the numbers turned inward and, using a hammer, pounded the creases flat to make them more difficult to unfold. He placed the folded plates into a brown paper bag and laid them on the car's passenger seat.

On his way to the rental agency, Evan spotted a dumpster behind a closed liquor store and pulled into the empty lot. He placed the paper bag holding the plates under the discarded trash inside the dumpster. He was pleased to see it packed full, indicating that trash collection was due soon. With the license plates taken to the landfill, they will be gone forever.

After he returned the rental car to Hertz, he walked to his Audi, still parked down the street, got in, and completed his ride to work. Although he had additional morning tasks, he still made it to the office before 9:00.

Evan greeted Rachel as he passed her and strolled to his desk to start his day.

CHAPTER 35

Detectives Hart and Sullivan were frantic when they returned to the precinct. They spent time collecting as much information about the victim as they could. The first forty-eight hours of any homicide were critical, with the chance of solving the crime diminishing exponentially after those hours passed. They did not want to waste a single minute of those hours.

The detectives did not take long to learn that Laura Emerson was a receptionist for a local auto dealership in the city. She had been married for twenty-two years with two teenage children. Her husband's name was Matthew, a forty-seven-year-old pharmaceutical rep for a drug manufacturer in Latham, New York.

Like most homicides, Detective Hart began her investigation with Laura's spouse. Hart searched her database for previous domestic violence calls to the home but found none. She looked for arrest records and violations Laura or the husband might have, but neither of them had even received a parking ticket. By all appearances, she was an unlikely homicide victim; her husband, an unlikely killer.

Detective Sullivan had the unpleasant job of calling Matthew Emerson to inform him of his wife's homicide and contacted him long before the Chicago sun rose. The detective believed the husband to be genuinely shocked and distraught. When asked, Mr. Emerson told the detective that he would take the earliest flight out of Chicago and inform him when his flight landed in Albany. He expected to be home by noon.

The coroner had contacted Detective Hart with the preliminary cause of death: a single gunshot to the face, piercing the brain. The projectile extracted from Mrs. Emerson's brain was identified as a .40 caliber bullet. They also identified recent indentations on the victim's left hand ring finger, indicating she had recently worn rings. There was no sign of a sexual assault or any abrasions or bruises found on the body.

When Detective Hart received the coroner's report, the details bewildered her. The victim did not appear robbed, there was no sexual assault, and there was no sign of a physical attack. No discernible DNA was found on her body or clothing to help identify a suspect. Detective Hart was discouraged by the report. It looked like some type of execution, but she could not find any information in Mrs. Emerson's background supporting her conclusion.

With so little learned, the detectives discussed an approach to solve the homicide.

"There is nothing here to start with," Hart said to Sully.

"I know, nothing to explain why the victim was killed other than being in a darkened park late at night. If she were raped or robbed, we would have found something," Sully agreed.

"I have a subpoena in the works for Emerson's cell phone records, but we won't receive them for another couple of days," Hart said.

"So, with nothing obvious, where do you want to start?" Hart questioned.

"We need to start with family members. See what they can tell us," Sully replied.

"Yeah. What about the spouse? Did you get a read from him? I find it convenient that he was out of town while his wife was being killed. Do you think he could have hired someone to do her in and used being out of town as an alibi?" Hart asked.

"I agree it's convenient, but he did sound pretty shook up on the phone. He is flying back this morning and should be in town by noon."

"Okay. I'd love to talk to the kids. However, without a parent or guardian present, I don't want to risk losing a conviction if it does turn out to be a family member. I did question a minor with no legal guardian present, but only as a witness."

"Agreed, but isn't the son eighteen? We could talk with him."

"True, but the daughter will be there, so it could look like we were taking advantage of the situation. Let's wait until Matthew Emerson returns to town," Hart concluded.

"Agreed," Sully said.

While they waited for the victim's husband to return to town, the detectives continued to review the crime scene photos for clues and the coroner's report. Detective Sullivan looked for other similar homicides in the city, including any involving a .40 caliber pistol.

After the crime scene investigation unit completed the ballistics, a report would be entered into New York State's Combined Ballistics Identification System (CoBIS) database. Detective Sullivan said he would search for other crimes committed with the weapon when the report became available.

CHAPTER 36

December 1st

Detectives Hart and Sullivan returned to the precinct after interviewing Matthew Emerson and his two children. As promised, Mr. Emerson returned to Albany at 11:45 in the morning and contacted the detectives immediately. He told them he would be available at his residence by 12:30. The detectives arrived shortly thereafter.

According to Matthew, they were a happily married couple. They never fought, other than when his wife complained about the time he spent out of town. He said they were financially stable. The Emerson children confirmed this, both saying they never witnessed fighting other than the normal disagreements all spouses typically had from time to time. Based on their conversation with the family, the marriage looked unusually pleasant.

Detective Hart asked uniformed officers to canvass the neighborhood and question the neighbors. Everyone they spoke with described the Emersons as friendly and outgoing. They always offered to help others in the community. The neighbors said they never heard loud arguments emanating from the home or observed physical altercations between Mr. and Mrs. Emerson.

When told his wife's wedding ring was missing from her ring finger, Matthew Emerson was surprised to hear she was not wearing them. He offered to search for the missing rings in her jewelry box. He had stated she never removed them from her hand, not even to bathe.

He searched the jewelry box, the primary bedroom, and both bathrooms but could not locate them. He told the detectives the killer must have taken the rings.

Detective Hart asked Mr. Emerson if he would allow them access to their cell phone records. Mr. Emerson did not have an issue with the request, supplying the detectives with access to the documents. Detective Hart was thrilled since she would no longer need the subpoena to retrieve them. He was highly cooperative and appeared genuinely anxious to have the murder solved. Although he would be thoroughly investigated, the detectives almost immediately eliminated him as a suspect after meeting him.

Unfortunately for the detectives, the interviews with the husband and children yielded no helpful information to jump-start their investigation.

"We have nothing here to go on," Hart said.

"It doesn't look good, I agree," Sully replied.

"It's weird that the perp would take her rings but nothing else. She had over $200 in her purse, along with her phone and keys. She was also wearing an expensive watch."

"None of it makes sense," Sully agreed, then continued, "I have entered the ballistics report into CoBIS. Hopefully, that turns up something."

"Let's look at the cell and home phone records next, see if they turn up anything. I'll take the phone, and you take the records," Hart said.

Detective Sullivan snatched the phone records from the top of Hart's desk and plopped down at his own to begin his research. At the same time, Detective Hart started to look at Laura's cell phone.

After he scanned the phone records for a few minutes, Sully called out.

"Hey, I may have something here, Tina."

Detective Hart looked up from her desk. Sully waved her over, and she walked to him—almost running.

"Look at this. She texted this number a few times last night. I don't have the actual texts, but she contacted somebody," Sully said.

"I wonder if they were meeting up?" Hart asked, saying, "Let's look at her contacts on the phone and see if we can find the number."

Detective Hart picked up Laura Emerson's cell phone and started scrolling through the contact list, checking each number against the number Sullivan discovered.

"Nope, not in her contact list," Hart said and continued, "The text messages were deleted too."

"I think we should try calling the number and see who answers. Should we use the precinct phone or Emerson's cell phone?" Sully asked.

"I think from the cell phone. If this is our perp and he sees the precinct name on his caller ID, it might spook him," Hart said.

At that, Detective Hart entered the phone number and pressed 'CALL.' She turned on the phone speaker so she and Sully could listen together. The phone was answered immediately. What they heard exasperated them.

"We're sorry, the cellular number you dialed is no longer in service. Please check the number and try again."

"Well, that sucks!" Sully said, clearly frustrated.

"It does, but it doesn't. We have a number Laura Emerson texted the night she was killed. It's something, not much, but something," Hart said.

"Okay, let me track this number down and see where it goes," Sully said as he returned to his desk.

***

Evan arrived home from work at 6:30, still feeling the high from his previous night's activity. He prepared a dinner of spaghetti and meatballs with items he picked up at an Italian food market on his way home from work.

There was a time when he cooked dinner every night for Jenna and himself, but he stopped when she moved out. He tried to prepare dinners after Jenna left, but was always depressed when he cooked for one.

Things had changed, with his new purpose in life to punish adultery. He had begun to enjoy cooking again, taking the leftovers to work the following day and eating them for lunch.

After dinner, he relaxed on the sofa with a glass of red wine and watched reality crime television shows. He began to view them as training materials, similar to those he used for his flight training.

He paid closer attention to the programs' details and listened more intently to the various techniques law enforcement uses to capture perpetrators. He committed everything he learned to memory.

"These documentaries are great training tools! I wonder if the creators or producers know they help us by teaching us how to get away with murder?" Evan muttered and laughed.

Although he was anxious with a yearning to kill again, he knew he needed a cooling-off period to reduce the chances of being captured.

CHAPTER 37

December 4th

Evan was excited when he awoke in the morning. He had his FAA flight review scheduled for later and was confident he would pass. Evan needed to take the day off from work, but he knew it was not an issue, as his superiors and co-workers all knew about his training and had been supportive throughout it all.

He had devoted the entire previous weekend to studying the type of questions he expected from the examiner during the oral component of the exam. He also spent the weekend at the airport, practicing numerous takeoffs and landings, known as 'touch-and-gos'. He wanted perfect, smooth landings to impress the examiner with his aircraft handling skills.

Evan ensured he ate a large lunch and drank a highly caffeinated soft drink to be alert and ready. Before he drove to the airport, he examined his flight bag to confirm he had everything he needed. Those items included his logbook, charts, and headset. He had arrived at 1:20 p.m., well prepared.

When Evan arrived at the airport, he found Jim sitting in the F.B.O. lobby, chatting with several people. He approached the group to let Jim know he had arrived. Jim greeted Evan with a smile and led him back to his office, where they talked without interruption.

Jim reviewed Evan's logbook and then asked him several aviation questions, all of which Evan quickly answered confidently. Jim agreed Evan was ready, telling him he knew he would be a certificated pilot by the day's end. His faith in Evan helped to put him at ease.

When Evan completed his review with Jim, he returned to the lobby, sat by the large plate-glass windows, and watched several aircraft departing and arriving. He rated every landing and decided he could do much better than many of the pilots he saw. Yes, he was that confident with his aviation skills at this point.

While seated, a young woman approached and asked Evan if she could join him on the lobby's sofa. Evan preferred to be alone but conceded and said it would be fine.

Just as she settled, she wondered and asked Evan out of curiosity, "Are you a pilot?"

"Not yet, but hopefully, by the end of today, I will be!" Evan answered enthusiastically.

"Taking your FAA flight today? That's great. Good luck!" She replied, then added, "I'm Tanya."

"I'm Evan. Nice to meet you. Are you a pilot?"

"Yes, I am. About three years now. I'm heading out for a charity flight."

"Charity flight? For what?" Evan asked, interested.

"It's called *Angel Wings*. It's a volunteer organization that arranges flights for people who need medical care but can't afford to fly commercially, and treatment is too far away to travel by car. The flights are usually within four hours of flight time. I'm going to Poughkeepsie to pick up a young boy and his mother and fly them to Boston for medical tests. The poor thing has leukemia, and the Children's Hospital in Boston has been treating him," Tanya explained.

"That must be expensive. Do you get reimbursed?"

"No, I can't be reimbursed. Pilots can't accept payments or reimbursements unless they have a minimum of a commercial pilot's license. So, no, we do it on our dime, but I like it. It gives me places to fly and a reason to be in the air. I also get to land at airports like Boston's Logan that normally turn away small aircraft like ours."

"Wow, that is cool. It must feel nice to be able to help people in need. Can anyone join *Angel Wings*? I might want to do something like that," Evan was curious.

"Yes, anyone can sign up. Here is the information," Tanya said when she handed Evan an *Angel Wings* card.

"Looks like my plane has refueled. I have to run. Maybe I'll see ya around!" Tanya rose and smiled.

Evan watched as Tanya walked across the tarmac to a Piper Cherokee. It looked like a nice low-wing airplane. Seeing the aircraft prompted Evan to consider his options after getting his pilot's certificate. He had never considered buying a plane and had no idea how much they cost, but it was something he'd need to think about soon.

After Tanya departed, he watched aircrafts coming and going and observed fuel jockeys as they refilled aircraft wings. He dreamt about buying an airplane when he suddenly heard his name called out, breaking him from his dream state. He turned to see Jim walking toward him with another gentleman who looked to be in his seventies. Evan stood to greet them.

"Hi, Jim!" Evan called out.

"Hey Evan, ready for today?" Jim asked.

"I think I am. I'm feeling terrific."

"This is Art Dickens, your FAA examiner. He's an outstanding pilot. I think you'll enjoy flying with him today. I wouldn't be surprised if he taught you a couple of things, too!" Jim said.

"Hi Evan, nice to meet you," Art said as he reached to shake Evan's hand.

"You too," Evan said.

Butterflies immediately invaded Evan's stomach, and his palms began to sweat. Although convinced he was ready, Evan was intimidated when he met Art, aware that he was from the FAA.

"So, Evan, we will start with the oral part of the exam. Let's go over to the pilot's lounge and grab a table in the back," Art said when he pointed towards the pilot's lounge.

Evan picked up his flight bag from the floor, threw it over his shoulder, and walked with Art to the lounge. They walked in silence, mainly because Evan was too terrified to speak.

Art questioned him on several aspects of flying. He also questioned Evan about aircraft mechanical systems. Evan could not answer every question, but Art said he did very well. Some of the questions Art asked were not required by the FAA or a part of the oral exam, but Art liked to help educate new pilots. He was a very personable and knowledgeable man. After Art was satisfied with Evan's knowledge, they walked out on the tarmac to the Skyhawk.

Art observed Evan's use of checklists and performance while inspecting the airplane. After completing a full pre-flight check and a run-up, Evan and Art ascended into the sky. They flew for forty-five minutes, with Evan executing several types of maneuvers, before Art provided Evan with directions to fly to Saratoga County Airport, an uncontrolled airfield. Art said it was to ensure Evan could handle communication at a non-controlled airport and to observe him enter the traffic pattern while he announced each leg of the approach over the radio. Art had Evan perform a touch-and-go, then directed him to the Schenectady County Airport. Art said he wanted to observe how Evan handled entering an unfamiliar, controlled airspace.

Evan was confident, and the nervousness he felt when he first met Art evaporated. He handled the airplane flawlessly, and all his landings were smooth and graceful. Evan knew he had passed when Art said he wanted to take the controls and land back at Albany. He told Evan he didn't fly as often as he wanted, so he used the opportunity to practice.

After they landed at Albany, Art and Evan pushed the plane back into its parking space. After tying down the wings, walking across the tarmac, they discussed flying, the weather, Art's wife, and Evan's goals once he had his 'ticket,' as Art referred to it.

As they entered through the F.B.O. doors, Jim stood and approached them. He must have received a discreet gesture from Art because he had begun to smile. Jim must have known Evan passed the flight exam. Jim joined Evan and Art as they walked to the *TIME2FLY* office.

"Great job, Evan," Art spoke first.

"Thanks! Does that mean I passed?"

"Absolutely. As soon as I fill out this form, sign the bottom, and hand it to you, you will officially be a private pilot. Congratulations!"

Evan looked at Jim, who had a strong smile with a thumbs up. It must be an excellent feeling for instructors when their students do well. Art handed Evan his certificate, shook his hand, and exited the office.

"Congrats, Evan!" Jim said as he shook his hand.

"Thanks, Jim. You're a great instructor!"

"What are your plans now? Are you going to buy an airplane? They aren't too expensive to buy. Just expensive to maintain," Jim said.

"I don't know. What other options would I have?"

"There is a flying club here called *Above and Beyond*. It's limited to twenty members, but I know one member who is relocating for his job and wants to sell his membership share. You could buy his membership for half the initiation costs. If you wanted, I could call him now."

"What will joining the club do for me? Would I have planes to use when I wanted? How much does it cost?"

"The club has five airplanes, three high-wing and two low-wing. It costs $100 a month for membership dues, covering airplane maintenance expenses. You can rent one of the planes for $120 or $150 an hour wet, depending on the plane you select. It's a great deal."

"What does an hour wet mean?"

"Wet means it includes the fuel. The F.B.O. bills the club if you have a plane refueled here on the tarmac. If you purchase fuel somewhere else, keep the receipt and submit it to the club for reimbursement," Jim explained.

Evan thought about it, and it seemed like a great idea. He could easily afford the monthly fees, which would provide him with airplanes to fly. Evan did not think an airplane purchase at this time was an option, but vowed to investigate it in the future.

"Yes, call the guy. I'll buy his membership," Evan said.

"Excellent. The only additional cost will be for a flight instructor to check you out on each airplane. I would be willing to do that with you."

"Sounds like a deal!"

Jim made the call while Evan waited. When he hung up, he told Evan that his friend had accepted the offer and that Evan was in the club. Evan wrote Jim a check for the initiation fee and the first month's membership dues. Evan then asked Jim if he could meet him over the weekend to get an introduction to the club's president.

He told Evan he would and that he would have time to check him out on a couple of the club's airplanes.

Evan returned home from the flight exam feeling great. He was officially a licensed private pilot, able to fly anywhere he desired. He didn't have an airplane to fly, but he knew that would change after the weekend when Jim checked him out on the club's planes.

Evan was starving and decided to grill a burger. He found ground beef in the refrigerator that he had purchased a few days before. He rolled a piece of cheddar cheese into the center of the patty he formed, a trick he had learned from his mother. He fired up the grill and, once it reached temperature, slapped the hamburger onto the grill to cook.

He found tater tots at the bottom of the freezer and threw a few in the toaster oven to brown while the hamburger grilled. He loved tater tots, especially with a burger. Evan considered it a fun meal after a fun day.

CHAPTER 38

December 9th

Evan arrived at Albany Aviation on Saturday morning to meet with Jim and the *Above and Beyond* club's president, Randy Vogt. After Jim introduced Evan to Randy, they walked into the large hangar. Randy pointed out various available club airplanes, stating that a member must receive a minimum of a one-hour assessment on each aircraft with a certified flight instructor before they are authorized to rent the specific plane. It was a requirement enforced by the club's insurance underwriter. The underwriter also required an annual reassessment in each plane.

It was a clear morning and a perfect day to fly.

Jim turned to Evan, "I have a couple of free hours this morning. Do you want to get checked out on a couple of planes today?"

"Sure," Evan replied.

Evan chose a Skyhawk and a Piper Cherokee. He would return another time for an assessment on the others, but he believed having at least these two available was sufficient for the time being.

Evan was confident in his capabilities with the club's Skyhawk, as it was the model he had trained on. The Piper Cherokee, however, was different, with its wings placed below the cockpit. Evan wasn't sure if he could pilot a low-wing airplane, but Jim promised he would do fine. Jim also said he would provide Evan with additional flying time in the Cherokee if he thought it was necessary.

While Evan waited for Jim and the club president to finish a conversation, he looked up *Angel Wings* on the pilot's lounge computer that reminded him of his conversation with Tanya.

According to the narrative he read, *Angel Wings* offered free travel for ambulatory patients who could not otherwise afford commercial transportation for various medical reasons. A pilot who joined could select from a comprehensive list of flight requests for the region where they were based.

Evan pulled up a list of open requests and saw most were for flights to Boston, New York City, Buffalo, and Philadelphia, with a few smaller towns and cities included. Patients requesting transportation were scattered throughout the Northeast, living in remote areas without extensive medical facilities. Evan learned that many large airports would also waive expensive landing and tarmac fees for all *Angel Wings* operations.

After reading the *Angel Wings* narrative, Evan opened the new member registration page and filled out an application to join. When he started on his journey to learn how to fly, he was still married to Jenna, and they had planned to fly to various destinations for pleasure. Now that she was gone, *Angel Wings* gave Evan a different purpose to pilot throughout the Northeast. He would transport patients from areas he would never see on his own and land at large airports he would otherwise never experience due to the prohibitive landing and tarmac fees those airports imposed.

Jim finished his conversation with Randy and walked to the pilot's lounge. When Evan saw him approach, he logged off the computer.

"I asked to have the Skyhawk and Cherokee pulled out of the hangar. Let's head out on the tarmac," Jim said.

The flight in the Skyhawk went very smoothly, and Jim cut it short since Evan could easily handle the club's plane. It was equally equipped like the airplane he had trained on, and he looked and felt comfortable behind the controls. After thirty minutes and three landings, Jim asked Evan to return to the airport so they could spend more time in the Piper.

The Piper Cherokee took Evan much longer to adjust to piloting. The wings below the cockpit altered its handling, particularly during landings. It suddenly clicked after the sixth or seventh landing, and Evan became comfortable and confident. They returned from the Saratoga County Airport to Albany, where Evan executed a perfect landing. Jim agreed he was capable in the Cherokee and signed Evan's logbook. Evan had authorization to rent both aircraft from the club.

It was a fabulous day, and Evan felt great until he returned home and settled on the sofa with a beer. He thought about what he had accomplished over the past several months. Evan reached his goal of becoming a pilot with access to airplanes. He could fly anywhere he wanted or needed and whenever he desired.

As he rested on the sofa with his thoughts, he was saddened when he remembered it was Jenna's idea for him to become a pilot in the first place. However, he was without Jenna to enjoy his new skill, and his mind wandered to her betrayal. The happiness he felt when he first arrived home had quickly turned into rage. It was what he endlessly felt, with brief moments of pleasure occasionally tossed in.

To feel calm and distracted, Evan rose from the sofa and went to the basement to retrieve his makeup kit. He needed to create a new disguise and online profile and find the next woman he would punish.

He returned to the family room with his kit, dumping the contents on the coffee table. He picked an assortment of wigs and mustaches, laying them on the floor. He wanted to create a new identity different from the one he used when he killed Laura Emerson.

Evan chose a brunette wig with shoulder-length hair parted in the middle, a coordinating brown mustache, and a closely cropped beard. He also selected brown contacts. To complete the disguise, he added a rounded prosthetic nose.

Evan put on the disguise pieces and moved to the bathroom to examine his altered appearance in the mirror. He was satisfied with the transformation. He had created the new persona that would be the man who would execute the next sinner.

After retrieving $500 in cash from his bedroom, Evan walked to the garage and settled into his Audi to return to the drug store in disguise. He needed a new burner phone and an AT&T phone card. He also needed a new Visa gift card because the one he had had nearly depleted.

When he returned home from the drug store with his items, he powered up the burner phone and applied the AT&T minutes. With the new burner phone prepared, he installed the *Boredwives* app and created a new profile with the username '*FlyAway*.'

He enjoyed correlating his two new hobbies, killing and flying. When he arrived at the registration section asking for his location, he stopped.

He had suddenly realized that if he continued killing in his local area using the same weapon, the chances of being discovered were much greater. Then it occurred to him, he could use flying as another tool in his arsenal. It would complete the fusion of his unconventional hobbies.

Evan needed to think about ways to lure women from different cities to their deaths since it would not be an easy achievement. He would need to establish a time to meet, a location for the execution, and transportation from the destination airport to the site and back to the airport.

Evan put the phone down to take a nap while considering his options. He was tired from all the flying he had done earlier in the day, and maybe after a rest, he thought, he would have everything all figured out.

CHAPTER 39

December 11th

Detective Kirk Fisher was sitting in the Albany precinct reviewing evidence gathered over the last several months since Jason Tanner's homicide in Washington Park. He was no closer to solving the case than he was the night he had begun his investigation.

He could not identify viable suspects or find witnesses who might have seen the killer. Extensive forensic testing of the body and crime scene yielded no clues. Detective Fisher was frustrated, believing the case would go cold, becoming another unsolved homicide in the city.

Fisher pushed the Tanner murder book to the side. He was in the midst of focusing on other cases he was also investigating when Detective John Byrd walked in and enthusiastically slapped a sheet of paper on his desk. It startled Fisher.

"What the hell?" Fisher cried out.

"I thought you'd like to see this."

"What is it?" Fisher asked.

"I received a hit from CoBIS on the bullet pulled out of Tanner," Byrd answered.

"Really? The same gun was used in the city in another crime?"

Fisher was excited, not because of another crime, but due to a hit in CoBIS.

"Not in Albany. This one was in Schenectady last month. A woman shot in the face who died instantly."

"Do they have any suspects or leads?" Fisher asked.

"I don't know. There aren't many details given. I have a call over to their homicide division. I'm waiting to hear back," Byrd answered.

"I hope they contact us soon. I'm out of ideas. The Tanner case is going ice cold."

Detective Fisher felt a rush of excitement. He hoped the information he received from the Schenectady police would help push the Tanner case forward.

* * *

When Detective Hart observed the blinking light on her desk phone indicating voicemail, she rolled her eyes. She returned her focus to the Emerson murder case file, looking for any information to help her solve the case. She had interviewed Matthew Emerson several times over the past few weeks, but learned nothing new and believed he had nothing to do with her homicide.

Hart spent several minutes reviewing the case file, but only hit a dead end. She pushed the file to the side of her desk, closed her eyes, and sighed. She could not find anything to lead her to a probable suspect. When she opened her eyes and saw her phone's light still flashing red at her, she decided to pick up the receiver to listen to her messages.

"Hi Tina, I have a request for you to call Detective Kirk Fisher in Albany's homicide division regarding a homicide they had back in August. They believe it was the same murder weapon used in a recent Schenectady homicide."

The message was from Jill, who worked in the precinct's communication department. Hart was intrigued and pressed a button on the phone to disconnect from voicemail. She looked up the number for the Albany Homicide Division and dialed. She asked for Detective Fisher when a receptionist answered. She hoped it was the break in the Emerson case she needed.

When Detective Fisher answered the phone, Detective Hart introduced herself and briefly summarized her case. Detective Fisher then filled her in on his open homicide investigation. He told Hart that CoBIS had matched the bullet found in his homicide victim to the bullet used in the Schenectady homicide.

They compared notes about each victim, recognizing the need to work together to solve the crimes. If they could solve either homicide, the corresponding one would fall into place.

The detectives spent an hour on the phone discussing each other's case information. They agreed they needed each other's assistance to close the books and catch the killer. Fisher and Hart decided to meet at the Albany precinct in person.

Before the detectives met, they agreed to dig deeper into each victim's background to see if they could find a common denominator linking the homicides. After the call ended, Detectives Fisher and Hart were invigorated to have each other's assistance, feeling confident they would find their suspect.

* * *

Angel Wings accepted Evan as a member of the organization. He received login credentials to their website, logged in, and created a required pilot's profile. He reviewed a listing of requests for flights. He could choose any available missions he felt he could easily fulfill.

While logged into the site, Evan found flight requests organized geographically. He selected the Northeast region, which encompassed several states. The submissions ranged from short one-hundred-mile flights to much longer missions spanning the country as pilots handed off the patient to the next volunteer. It reminded Evan of a relay race at a track and field event where the patient represented the baton.

As Evan scanned the *Angel Wings* list, it struck him. The solution he needed to continue his mission to kill. After looking through the *Angel Wings* website, it occurred to him that the *Angel Wings* missions would make a great cover to continue his quest to punish women. Most of the requests were for future dates. If he could select a date at least two or three weeks in advance, it might be possible for him to have enough time to attract a woman who lived in the destination city. He could kill her, get back on his airplane, and fly home, far away from the crime scene.

"This just might work. It would provide me with an opportunity to kill away from home. Flying an airplane just got a lot more useful," Evan said, smiling.

He recalled his first cross-country flight when he sat in the F.B.O. in Pittsfield, Massachusetts. He remembered he was an unknown in an unknown city. He would just be another ordinary pilot passing through. Also, if he could schedule the *Angel Wings* mission, he certainly could schedule a rental car. Many of the destination airports had rental car agencies on-site. He could kill just like he did with Laura Emerson. Rent a car, steal a license plate, lure the woman to a remote location, end her infidelity, and return home in less than a day.

The task that challenged Evan the most was finding remote locations to carry out a killing. He would not be familiar with the areas he flew into. It would be a significant disadvantage for him. He would have to rely heavily on Google Maps to find a suitable place for a murder.

After much thought, he concluded he could safely continue the mission he started months ago. The quest Jenna initiated was a result of her disloyalty. Although he always felt angry when he thought about Jenna, he now felt jubilant from his strategy to continue killing. He had become accustomed to his continually mixed emotions.

Evan was happy and hungry and decided it would be another celebratory night. After logging off the *Angel Wings* website, he fired up the grill and cooked dinner. He enjoyed a thick, juicy steak and a baked potato. He washed it down with a glass of red wine.

CHAPTER 40

Detectives Hart and Sullivan climbed into Hart's department-issued Explorer for their trip to Albany's police precinct to meet with the detectives working on the Tanner homicide. The investigations into Tanner's and Emerson's cases led to dead ends for both teams. The only component they could connect to both murders was the .40 caliber firearm.

The detectives felt exasperated. They decided to meet in a conference room to lay out all the information they had from both investigations, hoping to identify anything that would help them move toward a suspect.

Hart and Sullivan entered the Albany precinct carrying a very thin folder. It amplified the limited amount of information gathered during their probe. As they approached a tall counter where a uniformed officer hovered behind, Detective Fisher called out from across the room. He had expected the detectives and waited in the lobby to greet them.

"You must be Detective Hart?" Fisher called out.

"Yes, I am. This is Detective Sullivan."

"Call me Sully," Sullivan said and offered his hand in greeting.

"I'm Detective Kirk Fisher. Detective Byrd is in the conference room waiting for us."

"Sounds great. Where can we grab some coffee?" Sully asked.

"We have a pot already brewed and waiting."

Detectives Hart and Sullivan followed Fisher. He led them down a hallway and onto an elevator to the third floor. When the doors slid open, Detective Hart snickered to herself as she looked around the room. All precincts were identically decorated and furnished, she concluded. Shabby, with peeling paint and packed with antiquated desks placed indiscriminately around an open space.

Upon entering the conference room, Detective Hart observed someone writing on a whiteboard with a black marker and assumed it was Detective Byrd. He turned to greet her.

"Hi, I'm Detective John Byrd. You must be Detectives Hart and Sullivan."

"Yes, I'm Hart, and this is Sully."

"Great. Grab a cup of joe, and let's get started."

Detective Byrd returned to the board and drew a vertical line using a red marker to divide the surface into two equal sides. He handed a second black marker to Detective Hart.

"I'm writing everything we know about Tanner on my side. You write what you know about Emerson on your side, and maybe it will indicate something in common between the two homicides," Byrd said.

Detective Hart grabbed the marker from Byrd, opened her folder, and began to write. After several minutes, Byrd and Hart stepped back to see what was displayed. Detectives Sullivan and Fisher, seated at the conference table, also examined the board.

"I don't see anything," Sully said.

"Neither do I," Fisher agreed.

"Let's scan the cell phone records for both. Maybe they were connected somehow," Byrd said.

The detectives pulled out the phone records for each victim. Detective Fisher scanned Tanner's for Emerson's number while Detective Hart checked Emerson's for Tanner's. They both came up empty and were discouraged. Their hope about a connection between the two victims or a sign that they were acquainted quickly evaporated. It did not look like the victims knew each other or ever made contact.

They returned to the whiteboard, looking for anything connecting the two victims or homicides. However, all they had in common was a forty-caliber weapon. The only other common theme was the crime scene, since each homicide occurred in a city park. The detectives spent several hours reviewing each other's cases, tossing up possible motives and theories, but they continually arrived at a dead end.

* * *

When he returned to the office after eating lunch at a nearby deli, Evan fired up his desktop computer and logged on to the *Angel Wings* website. He craved another killing and needed to find a place to do it. *Angel Wings* would help him decide.

He entered the site and searched for requests scheduled for the next month. He found one he thought was ideal for him. The flight indicated it was for a young girl who needed to travel from Boston to her home in Penn Yan, a small village in the Finger Lakes Region of upstate New York. Evan searched Penn Yan on Google and learned it included several isolated areas surrounding a lake.

He uncovered a Chamber of Commerce article stating that many residents were seasonal, living in summer homes that they would shutter during the winter months. During the summer, the Finger Lakes were overwhelmed by a bustle of events while tourists visited the numerous wineries and lakes. However, since it was winter, it would be deserted.

Evan returned to the *Angel Wings* website and looked up information about the young patient needing the flight. The ten-year-old girl had survived a fire at her family's home and suffered third-degree burns on over half of her body. She has traveled to Boston for frequent skin grafts and treatments over the last several months.

With so many required treatments, the cost and time to travel by car had become prohibitive for the family, so they turned to *Angel Wings* for assistance. Evan learned that the girl's mother always accompanied her on the flights, acting as her escort. The request Evan found had a scheduled pickup at Boston's Logan Airport at 5:00 P.M. on January 4th. It would be a Thursday evening.

Evan opened the bottom drawer of his office desk and pulled out a flight map he kept readily available. He reviewed the Penn Yan area for a local airport, finding a small airfield on the city's outskirts. He then plotted the course he would need to follow from Boston to Penn Yan and noted the number of air miles he would travel on the flight.

He did not know which aircraft would be available for his use and realized he needed to sign in to the *Above and Beyond* club's site to ensure he would have an airplane available that day.

He found both planes he was authorized to fly were unreserved for the evening of the *Angel Wings* mission and selected the Skyhawk. He felt the passengers would prefer a high-wing airplane as it allowed better views from the windows to the terrain below. They would have an enjoyable flight with the ability to see familiar landmarks as they crossed the Northeast.

After determining the number of miles and the airplane he would use, he returned to the computer and pulled up a pilot's website that included options for flight planning. Evan entered the required information, including the arrival and destination airports, aircraft type, and average airspeed. The software returned an estimated flight duration of a little over three hours.

Evan then plotted Penn Yan's distance to Albany and determined that the return flight home would take less than two hours. It would work well to meet a woman in the dark, kill her, and return undetected in Albany. He would be at home and in bed by midnight.

Still logged into the flight planning website, Evan looked up the Penn Yan Airport's information. He found it was within a few miles of the city limits, but with no rental car agency available. He decided he would call a taxi to pick him up at the airport, which could drop him off at a restaurant in town, as if he were having dinner. The restaurant could be the place where he met his next target.

After examining the *Angel Wings* request, the flight routes, airport information, and the Penn Yan area, and knowing he had an aircraft available, he volunteered for the flight. Evan returned to the club member's page and reserved the Skyhawk for January 4th from three p.m. until midnight. He had a plan he believed would allow him to continue his mission to eliminate infidelity from society.

Evan logged into *Boredwives* when he returned home after work to complete the profile he had begun the previous week. He chose Yates County, where Penn Yan was located, as his location. Evan searched and found a few *Boredwives* members in the area, but only two that reminded him of Jenna. He messaged them.

Evan was euphoric when he had everything in place. Then he thought about the juxtaposition of his mission. He joined *Angel Wings* to help people in need, but he also used it as a tool to kill. Evan knew if he were ever captured alive and incarcerated, psychologists would line up to study him, and if he were dead, they would surely crack open his skull to examine his brain.

"The doctors would have a field day with me," Evan laughed.

But I'm not killing for fun. I'm getting rid of sinners for God. Evan justified his mission.

CHAPTER 41

January 4th

Evan slept well, knowing he was helping a young girl and her family. However, he also dreamed of the plan he had in place to execute another cheating wife.

There weren't many women on *Boredwives* in the Penn Yan area because the city was small. It had a total population of less than five thousand and was off-season.

Evan was surprised when the both women he had contacted replied on the day he sent his first messages. Evan thought they must have felt they led a lonely existence in the sleepy town of Penn Yan to reply so quickly.

Anne Roberts was one of the two women who readily accepted an invitation to meet. Her profile described her as thirty-seven years old with a seven-year-old daughter. She had only been married eleven years, yet already out cheating on her husband. She bore a striking resemblance to Jenna.

"No one has sparkling green eyes like Jenna, but she'll do," Evan muttered to himself.

Anne had used the same excuse as all the others on the site. She said her husband was always out of town on business, and he could not satisfy her. She also believed he was stepping out on her and felt it was only fair she did the same. She told Evan she had been on *Boredwives* for seven months and had already connected with five men. Anne said she only wanted casual sexual encounters, telling Evan he would not have to worry about unwanted phone calls.

"You won't be around to make even *wanted* phone calls, Anne!" Evan laughed to himself.

Evan could not believe how cavalier she was about her marriage. Willing to meet strange men for sex outside of her marriage incensed him. It was her time to pay. Evan and Anne talked several times by phone before planning to meet on January 4th.

On the morning of Evan's planned *Angel Wings* mission, Anne texted Evan early in the morning, asking where they would meet. Evan told her she could pick him up at 8:30 in an automotive tire shop's parking lot across the street from the Penn Yan Diner. Evan lied, telling her he had an appointment to replace the tires the following day and wanted to drop his car off the night before. Anne said she would, and Evan was astonished. They had only briefly spoken over the phone, yet she

was unconcerned about allowing a stranger in her
vehicle.

Evan wrapped up his workday early. He left his cell
phone powered up and in his desk drawer. Rachel and
John wished him a safe flight on the way out of the
office. They praised Evan for his willingness to spend
personal time and money on something as commendable
as *Angel Wings*.

Evan arrived at Albany Aviation and prepared for his
first *Angel Wings* mission with plenty of time. He
wanted to have the airplane ready for departure by 3:00
to be at Boston's Logan Airport before 5:00. He didn't
want his passengers to wait.

Evan checked his flight bag one last time before he
climbed onto the airplane. He also checked the bag with
his disguise. He wanted to ensure he had everything he
needed for both of his planned missions.

Evan departed for Boston at 3:05 under primarily
clear skies. Some scattered cumulus clouds looked like
cotton balls floating in space. The airplane bounced
more than he expected, caused by warm air currents
rising from the earth and colliding with the colder air
aloft. Though he felt some turbulence, he was not
concerned about his passengers having an
uncomfortable flight.

An air traffic controller instructed Evan to change to
Boston's tower frequency when he entered the airspace
surrounding the Logan Airport. When he heard rapid-
fire instructions called out by the control tower to

aircraft arriving at the airfield, his anxiety levels rose, and he was intimidated. His palms had become wet, and a bead of sweat rolled down his forehead. He sat up straight in the pilot's seat, erasing all thoughts from his mind other than what he needed to do to land the airplane.

With all the different aircrafts arriving in Boston, Evan had to listen intently for his plane's tail number when called by the control tower. He wanted to ensure he didn't miss any of the instructions given to him. He certainly did not want to be responsible for delays with any of the commercial airliners arriving at the airport. He was indeed a tiny fish in a large pond.

Evan received instructions to enter right-hand traffic for a landing on runway two-two right. He studied the airport diagram clipped to his kneeboard and peered out the plane's window as he gathered his bearings and located the runway. He was amazed by the vastness of the airfield and the numerous runways he saw. It made Albany International seem like an insignificant landing strip.

He continued to receive directions from the control tower and found himself on a final approach to the runway. He followed the vertical approach slope indicator known as the VASI, maintaining two red lights over two white lights to keep the plane on a steady and proper descent. Evan repeated the common GUMP acronym several times aloud during his final approach to the runway: Gas set to a full tank, Undercarriage down, Mixture lean, Prop set. He did not pilot a retractable gear airplane with an adjustable prop, but he wanted to ensure the plane had been properly configured for landing.

When he was lined up on the runway's centerline and ready to touch down, the tower called. They wanted him to exit the runway as quickly as possible after landing to make way for an approaching Southwest airliner. If he did not exit the runway in time, the airliner would need to do a go-around, costing thousands of dollars in jet fuel.

As soon as the plane's wheels touched the ground, Evan applied the brakes. Evan slowed the plane quickly and left the taxiway at the first available exit. When he was clear of the runway, the controller praised him for a job well done and asked him to switch to the ground control frequency.

Evan taxied to Signature Flight, the F.B.O. servicing Logan, following the ground crew's batons as they directed him to park. After he received the ground crew's signal, he shut down the aircraft engine, removed his headset, and wiped the sweat from his forehead. He relaxed as he thought about his first landing at a large commercial airport hub. He also thought of Jenna, who should have been with him for the monumental achievement.

Evan sat and contemplated the flight for a few minutes before he climbed from the cockpit and strode to the F.B.O. to wait for his passengers. He walked through the doors, surprised to find the mother and daughter already seated on a sofa. The mother had a cup of coffee in her hand while the young girl held a Diet Coke.

He walked to them and introduced himself. He was surprised they had already arrived. Evan saw that the young girl had severe scarring caused by a horrific fire, her face disfigured, and her nose missing. The fire had also scorched both her ears from her head. Evan felt incredibly sorry for her, but her enthusiasm and bright smile quickly erased his pity.

A child's innocence is utterly amazing. An innocence I will never understand because of my father, Evan thought.

The girl's name was Marissa, and her mother's name was Michele. They were excited to fly back home and told Evan they enjoyed traveling in small airplanes. Evan discovered Michele was married with two other children from a previous marriage. They sat and talked while waiting for Signature Flight to refuel his plane.

When the F.B.O. attendant told Evan his plane was ready, he paid for the fuel, placing the receipt in his logbook to be submitted to the club when he returned to Albany. After completing his pre-check of the airplane, he returned to the F.B.O. to gather his passengers. Marissa chatted with delight about all her airplane rides as they walked across the tarmac to the plane. Her injuries and painful treatments did not seem to affect her joy for life. Michele rode in the back so her daughter could ride in the front seat with Evan.

Evan fired up the engine and contacted Logan Ground with his flight plan and requested a taxi from Signature Flight to the active runway. He received his instructions, taxied to the departing runway, and soared into the sky. He was delighted with the knowledge that his new skills benefited those in need.

CHAPTER 42

January 4th

The flight from Boston to Penn Yan was uneventful. The Penn Yan Airport was an uncontrolled field with small hangars lining the single runway. A building constructed of concrete block housing restrooms stood nearby. A self-service refueling station was available at the far end of the airfield. The airport stood deserted and dark.

Marissa told Evan she enjoyed the ride, proclaiming he was her favorite pilot. Evan supposed she said the same thing to all the pilots who flew her to and from Boston, but it felt good to him to hear it, nevertheless. They thanked him for the flight and walked to a waiting car to complete their trip home.

When he saw them disappear into the night, Evan walked to the lone building housing the restrooms and entered a foul-smelling men's room. It was empty and dark. He searched for a switch on the wall, found it, and flipped on the lights. It did not appear to be a well-maintained facility. He walked to a dingy mirror mounted over a rusted sink to assemble his disguise. When he finished, he pulled on a knit cap to complete his transformation. He was pleased with his appearance when he examined himself in the mirror.

"I'm just a stranger in a strange town!" Evan muttered and grinned.

He pulled the burner phone from the flight bag and dialed a number for the local taxi company he had previously stored in the phone's contacts, requesting a ride from the airport to the Penn Yan diner. He waited at the airport's front gate for the taxi to arrive.

Evan was at the Penn Yan diner at 8:25, after a brief fifteen-minute ride by cab from the airport. He was thrilled with the airfield's proximity to the restaurant. After climbing out of the cab, he waited until it was out of sight. He then used his burner phone to text Anne Roberts and walked across the street to the tire store to wait.

Anne Roberts pulled into the parking lot shortly after Evan sent the text, driving a new Range Rover. Evan was sure she got her fancy SUV thanks to her husband, convinced she took everything he provided to her for granted and cheated on him without remorse. Evan was outraged yet felt comforted with the knowledge that he was about to deliver justice for her husband.

When Evan approached the SUV and heard the distinct click of doors unlocking, he pulled the passenger door open. He peered inside to find Anne clad in a not-so-modest dress under an expensive-looking fur coat.

"Hi, are you Michael?" Anne asked.

Michael was the name Evan had given Anne when they messaged on *Boredwives* and talked on the phone.

"Yes, I'm Michael. You must be Anne."

"I am. Climb on in!"

Evan climbed into the Range Rover's passenger seat and closed the door. He wore gloves to avoid leaving fingerprints. The wintry weather helped shroud the real reason he had them on. Evan scanned Anne closely, wondering why a woman would risk ruining her husband's life for meaningless sex. Evan was incensed but managed to conceal it from her.

Anne looked at Evan with a big smile while she suggestively slid her tongue across her teeth and lips. Evan thought this woman was much sleazier than Laura Emerson. He would enjoy killing her.

"My husband and I have a camp house on Keuka Lake. It's closed for the season, but we can go there if you like," Anne said.

Evan thought about it and considered it the perfect place. He knew the surrounding camps were closed for the winter.

"Sounds good," Evan quietly replied.

Anne put the SUV in gear for the drive to her family camp. Evan became furious when he discovered that she had turned a place where her family had enjoyed quality time into a house of decadence. Evan had been angry when Jenna cheated on him, but at least she did not use their home.

The family's camp should be a sanctuary and not stained by infidelity! Evan raged to himself.

Anne's decision to use the family retreat proved that killing her was justified and much needed. They traveled to the camp in relative silence but occasionally glanced at each other. Anne's look was a look of desire. Evan was sure his look was not.

Anne pulled onto a gravel road when they exited the main street, less than a mile from the diner. Just off the main street, Evan spotted a sign for the Indian Pines Park. He knew it was the place he would kill her and pulled his Glock from his jacket pocket. Evan raised it and pointed it at Anne's face.

"Pull in here," Evan instructed.

She looked horrified when she saw the gun, nearly driving into a ditch.

"What are you doing?" Anne cried out.

"Pull into the park," Evan growled.

"Why, what are you going to do?" Anne asked with tears.

"JUST DO IT!" Evan yelled.

Anne turned onto the entrance road to the park as instructed. She stopped under large pine trees covering a picnic area. Evan ordered Anne out of the SUV with the gun still pointing in her direction. Evan climbed out when she moved around to the front of the truck.

The park was an excellent location for a murder, especially in January. With the winter's cold, it was abandoned and dark. Evan walked Anne deep into the woods while he kept the gun pointed at her back until they reached an area wholly hidden from view of the road. He asked her to stop moving and to turn around. When Anne faced Evan, she looked terrified, tears streaming down her cheeks.

"This is for your husband!" Evan exclaimed when he pulled the trigger, shooting her in the face.

He positioned the body like he had with Laura Emerson and removed her wedding and engagement rings. He returned to the SUV to get her cell phone. Evan was relieved to find she had no security on the phone. He erased phone calls, text messages, and the *Boredwives* app, wiped it clean of fingerprints, and placed it back in the purse. Evan stared down at Anne lying on the ground, feeling relieved from his anger. He looked around the park, ensuring he was still alone. It was empty.

"Another successful mission," he muttered to himself.

Before Evan left the park, he returned to the SUV and scoured it for any evidence he might have left behind, but found nothing. Evan knew he left no fingerprints because of the gloves. He believed no DNA was present because he wore a coat and a winter cap.

Satisfied, Evan traveled down a dirt trail, following it as it wound toward the main road. When Evan arrived at the trail's end, he caught sight of neon lights and realized the diner was nearby. He arrived back at the restaurant before 9:30, amazed that the execution took less than an hour. He used his burner phone to call the cab company for a return ride to the airport.

After the cab dropped Evan at the front gate of the airport and he was sure the taxi was out of sight, he returned to the men's room to remove his disguise. When he finished, he stared into the dingy mirror to ensure no makeup remained from the prosthetic nose. He placed the pieces of his disguise in the pockets of his coat.

Evan taxied the Skyhawk to the fuel farm located on the airfield. He filled both wings of the plane and placed the receipt spit out by the pump into his logbook. He prepared the airplane for flight, including the proper pre-flight check and run-up. Evan did not want to rush because Jim emphasized the importance of always performing complete pre-flight checks and run-ups before every flight. Evan departed Penn Yan Airport en route to Albany at 10:13.

The flight plan estimated a ninety-minute flight time back to Albany. However, when the westerly winds picked up, they provided Evan with a tailwind. He expected the flight to be shorter.

Evan felt peaceful on the plane during the trip back home. He thought about the little girl, Marissa, and the battle she faced as she grew into an adult. It saddened Evan, but he also felt noble for having helped her with her continuing struggles.

Evan's mind shifted to the murder, and he felt calm. His evening started with a rage boiling inside him when he got into Anne Robert's SUV. However, Evan replaced that emotion with tranquility. He also counted the murders he had committed, realizing he would now be considered a serial killer. It made him smile, and he wondered what moniker the media would place on him.

While en route to Albany and over the Mohawk River, he opened the cockpit window, tossing the burner phone from the plane after he broke it into several pieces. He would purchase a new one when he needed it the next time.

As Evan neared Albany International Airport airspace, he dialed in the Albany approach radio frequency, announcing his arrival and planned landing at the airfield. The radio remained silent, with only very few aircrafts arriving or departing the area. The controller advised Evan to navigate for a direct approach to runway one.

Evan arrived back in Albany at 11:25 p.m. after a tranquil flight. He discovered how peaceful flying at night was during this trip. Evan had one of his best landings and taxied to Albany Aviation. He powered down the airplane, grabbed his flight bag, and notified the ground crew he was back. They would refuel the aircraft before rolling it back into the hangar. He placed his fuel receipt into a wooden receptacle attached to the interior hangar door.

On his way home, Evan returned to his office to retrieve his cell phone. As soon as he entered his house, he changed into sweats, grabbed a beer, and relaxed in his favorite recliner. He played the day through his mind, finding it glorious. He was exhausted and fell asleep, fully dressed.

CHAPTER 43

January 5th

The Yates County Sheriff's Department was called out to Indian Pines Park at dawn to find Anne Roberts lying dead. An early morning hiker had found the body. Because the sheriff's department was small and the Sheriff knew they did not have the resources to investigate a homicide, he immediately contacted the New York State Police for assistance. Sergeant Stephen Miller, a ten-year veteran, and his partner, Detective Kevin Fowler, from the Bureau of Criminal Investigation, responded.

Sergeant Miller and Detective Fowler arrived at the scene of the homicide shortly after 8 a.m. They noted the victim's position as she lay on the ground with her arms folded across her chest, legs positioned straight, and a bullet hole to the face. The State Police crime scene unit arrived a few minutes later. Sergeant Miller instructed the C.S.U. to search and bag any evidence found on and around the body.

As Detective Fowler looked around the area, he spotted the victim's SUV parked under a row of pine trees. He walked over and looked in. He observed a purse still lying on the back seat. He opened the rear door to retrieve it. Fowler combed the contents, locating a cell phone and a wallet containing $80 in cash. He asked a forensic technician to dust the exterior of the Range Rover for fingerprints before it was towed from the park.

Unable to find anything of value at the crime scene, Sergeant Miller and Detective Fowler returned to the police barracks to await autopsy results from the county coroner. While they waited, they searched on their computer for similar crimes in the county, but found none. When the coroner sent over the bullet retrieved from Anne Roberts, they had the lab enter ballistic information into CoBIS. It quickly returned a match.

* * *

Schenectady Police Detective Christina Hart was sitting at her desk reviewing open cases when her desk phone rang. She yanked the receiver from its cradle. Her curiosity was triggered when the caller identified himself as Sergeant Miller with the New York State Police. It was not often she received a phone call from the state authorities.

"Detective Hart."

"Hi, this is Sergeant Miller with the State Police, BCI division, Troop E."

"Troop E? Where are you located?"

"Central New York. I'm calling about a homicide we are investigating that occurred in Penn Yan, and I hope you can help," Miller replied.

"I'm not sure how I can, but shoot," Hart said.

"Our murder victim was shot with a forty-caliber handgun. We ran the ballistics through CoBIS and received a hit from a homicide you're investigating. We also found a third homicide in Albany connected to the same weapon," Miller stated.

"Who was the victim?

"A thirty-something married female."

"Really? Interesting. Was her wedding band removed?" Hart asked.

"I don't know. Why are you asking?"

"Our victim had her wedding and engagement rings removed. They were the only valuable items taken during the crime. It was odd," Hart explained.

"Interesting. I'll follow up with the husband. It's not in my report."

Detective Hart and Sergeant Miller talked for another thirty minutes, discussing the similarities between the homicides. Sergeant Miller then told Detective Hart that the State Police BCI division would take over the investigation of all three homicides. It was no longer a local police matter because the murders occurred in various cities across the state, connected to the same weapon.

He asked her to send all the information she had about Emerson's homicide to him. Before ending the call, Hart informed Miller that the Schenectady and Albany police departments were working together on the Capital District's two murders.

"That's just peachy. I hate it when the staties scoop down like they're saving the day," Detective Hart mumbled as she hung up the phone.

After Miller ended the call with Detective Hart, he contacted Detective Fisher to discuss the Jason Tanner homicide. Before he ended that call, he also informed Fisher that the BCI would handle the investigation.

Sergeant Miller and Detective Fowler received the case files for Laura Emerson and Jason Tanner from the respective city police departments later in the afternoon. Together, they reviewed the details gathered.

They could not find anything connecting Tanner to the two female victims. However, when they reviewed the crime scene notes, Sergeant Miller did find similarities with the homicides of both women. The bodies had been found in identical positions, looking as if they were posed, with their wedding rings removed. Anne Roberts' husband confirmed her wedding band was missing.

Miller knew those homicides were related because the modus operandi was the same, but Tanner's murder baffled him. Sergeant Miller had started to consider that a serial killer roamed the state, but the killer's motivation eluded him.

While Sergeant Miller reviewed crime scene notes, Detective Fowler examined the three victims' phones as well as financial, personal, and travel records, but found no commonalities.

Detective Fowler interviewed Laura Emerson's husband but found nothing unusual. After they spoke with Anne Roberts' husband, the only red flag raised was the money she spent. They interviewed friends of the Roberts's, confirming she fought with her husband about her spending habits. It provided Anne's husband with a potential motive. However, Mr. Roberts had a solid alibi. He had been playing poker with colleagues.

The State Police investigators took a deeper dive into Jason Tanner's homicide. They reasoned that if they could discover the motive for Tanner's murder, they might find a connection to the two women.

When they read Tanner's murder book, they learned about Tanner's girlfriend. Sergeant Miller reached out to Jenna Williams, who informed Miller that she had only briefly dated Tanner. She had let Miller know that she was married when she had met Jason, which led to the end of their marriage. That detail aroused the Sergeant's attention.

"How did your ex-husband react when he found out about the affair?" Miller asked.

"He was understandably upset, as you would expect."

"Did he know you were dating Jason Tanner?"

"No, he didn't know. I never told him, and he never asked."

"Is there a possibility he did know, and you weren't aware?"

"No, he did not know about Jason. I'm sure," Jenna replied with conviction.

Sergeant Miller asked her if she knew of anyone else who would want to kill Jason. She told him she did not.

There was a question he asked, but no other detective posed.

"How did you meet Jason Tanner, Mrs. Williams?"

"This is embarrassing, but I met him on a dating app called *Boredwives*."

"Nothing to be embarrassed about. Many people use dating apps in this day and age. Thank you, Mrs. Williams, for your time. If I need anything else, I'll reach out to you."

Sergeant Miller ended his call with Jenna Williams. After learning about the dating app she used, Sergeant Miller wanted to examine the cell phones of the other two deceased women to determine if they had also used *Boredwives*. The app, designed to be used by married women, was the only connection they could see with the two female victims. The women were indeed married.

Jason Tanner's tie to the other homicides, Miller thought, was because he used the app to meet a married woman at the time of his murder.

Sergeant Miller called Detective Fowler over to his desk, passing on the information he had gathered from Jenna Williams. He then asked Fowler to help him power up the cell phones to look for the *Boredwives* app.

The first phone Detective Fowler pulled from the evidence box was Jason Tanner's. He needed to plug the cell phone into an electrical source because the battery had drained. When he powered it up and searched through the apps Tanner had installed, Fowler found the app he was looking for.

While Detective Fowler searched Tanner's phone, Sergeant Miller grabbed Laura Emerson's cell phone, which also needed to be plugged into a power source. After it initialized, he began browsing the installed apps but did not find *Boredwives*.

Sergeant Miller removed the last cell phone from the box, the phone belonging to Anne Roberts, plugged it in, and powered it up. Again, the *Boredwives* app was not there.

"Well, that was disappointing. I was hoping that was the lead we needed," Miller said.

"Yeah. We're back to square one," Fowler moaned.

"Could it be possible that our suspect deleted the app from the cell phones after he killed the women? The phones are wiped clean of any fingerprints. Not even the victims' prints were present," Miller said.

Sergeant Miller decided to contact both husbands of the deceased women to request internet access to their cell phone records. The husbands agreed and provided the usernames and passwords. Detective Fowler checked the Emerson account while Sergeant Miller logged into Roberts's account.

They were excited to discover that both phones had *Boredwives* installed in the past. Unfortunately, the logs did not indicate when they had been removed. Each phone also contained saved usernames and passwords in a password manager app.

Sergeant Miller and Detective Fowler logged into the app using the username and password for each woman's account. When they logged in, they looked for messages sent between the victims and any men who contacted them through the app. They searched for overlapping names and numbers.

The only problem they had was tying the victims together with Jason Tanner. Were these women killed because they had joined a dating site called *Boredwives?* If so, they couldn't understand how Tanner got mixed up in it. He had used the app to meet Jenna Williams, but she certainly did not appear to be a serial killer.

Sergeant Miller was able to find messages sent to Emerson and Roberts from men they met on the app. The messages included requests to continue contact on cell phones. The detectives compared the numbers given to call lists for each phone found on the cell phone provider's website.

They discovered text messages on each of the phone logs that were sent to and from each of these men's cell phones on the evening of the homicides. However, the phone numbers and names were different. One man was named Michael, while the other was Stephen.

Miller asked Fowler to look up the phone numbers, but both numbers led to prepaid disposable burner phones. Miller then sent the three cell phones to the New York State Police's electronic forensics division for further examination.

Sergeant Miller also sent the information they collected about *Boredwives* to the State Police IT department, requesting a thorough investigation into the website. He knew he was grasping at straws, but he wanted to find out who Stephen and Michael were. While he waited for IT to call him back with anything they could discover, he dug into Jason Tanner. He wanted to find out what tied him to the female victims.

Although the cell phones did not provide them with a solid lead, the two female homicide victims had met men through *Boredwives,* and those men supplied numbers to burner phones. The victims contacted these burner phones on the nights of their homicides. The men's names were different, but it did not suggest that the men were.

Sergeant Miller took a closer look at Jenna's ex-husband, Evan Williams. He could have killed Tanner due to a jealous rage. Jenna Williams said her husband did not know she was dating Jason Tanner, but that did not mean he didn't. Miller knew he had to look closer and pulled everything they could find on Evan Williams.

Sergeant Miller acknowledged a connection existed with *Boredwives*, the two female victims, Jenna Williams, and Jason Tanner. Both Sergeant Miller and Detective Fowler found it difficult to ignore since they had no other clue.

CHAPTER 44

January 20th

Evan had been relaxing in front of the television, sipping on a beer and enjoying a submarine sandwich he had picked up from the deli. He was thinking about where his life had taken him when he heard what he thought was a car pulling up to the house. He walked to the front window and looked out. He observed a car had parked in his driveway, immediately recognizing it as an unmarked police vehicle. The last time he had the police come to his house was after he killed Tanner, but he thought they had moved on from him as a suspect in the murder.

Evan's suspicions that they were police detectives were confirmed as soon as he swung open the door. The telltale cheap suits and black shoes gave them away.

"Hi, can I help you?" Evan asked.

"Are you Evan Williams?" Sergeant Miller inquired.

"Yes, I'm Evan. Who are you?"

"I'm Sergeant Miller with the New York State Police. This is Detective Fowler. Mind if we come in?"

"What is this about?"

"I would prefer to talk inside if that is okay."

"Sure, come on in. Can I offer you anything?" Evan replied, courteously.

The detectives looked around the room as they entered the house. Evan wondered why they were there. He thought the Albany Police were investigating the Tanner murder. The only reason he could think of for the State Police being in his home was that he had killed Anne Roberts in Penn Yan two weeks earlier, but he did not believe they could make a connection to him. Evan was confident that he had left no evidence or clues behind.

"Mr. Williams, we are investigating the homicide of Jason Tanner. My understanding is that your ex-wife was dating him at the time of his murder. Did you know him?" Miller asked.

"I thought the Albany Police were investigating it and said it was a robbery gone bad," Evan answered.

Evan was confused. He could not understand why the State Police were investigating a local homicide.

"We don't believe it was a robbery. Two more homicides have happened since, and we have reason to believe they are connected," Miller explained.

"Well, I knew my wife cheated on me, but I didn't know it was Jason Tanner until a detective from the Albany police department told me the day that he came to question me," Evan said, then added, "I certainly don't know about any other murders."

"Do you know how your wife and Tanner met?" Miller asked.

Jenna did tell him she used a dating app, but had not revealed which one. If Evan told the detectives he did not know they met on an app, and Jenna told them he did, it would look suspicious. If Evan told them he knew they met using a dating app, and they connected the murders to *Boredwives*, he would look suspicious. It was a problem. Evan decided a partial truth was best.

"I think Jenna said she used a dating app, but I never knew which one. I really didn't care. She cheated, and it didn't matter to me how she met the dude."

"Okay, so you were aware it was a dating app. Where were you the night Jason Tanner was murdered?" Fowler asked.

"It was a long time ago, but I believe I was at home alone and sleeping," Evan said.

"Have you ever been to Penn Yan, New York?" Miller asked.

This question posed another problem for him, and again, Evan was unsure how to answer it. Evan thought about it momentarily, then decided the detective would never learn about his flight.

"No, I've never been to Penn Yan. Why do you want to know?"

"Do you own a gun, Mr. Williams?" Miller asked.

Evan could see the detective's mind toil behind blinking eyes. Miller appeared intelligent and was likely good at his job, but Evan knew he was much more intelligent. Evan had never registered the Glock when he took it from his mother's home. If they asked Jenna about a gun, Evan was sure she would say he never owned one. She would have forgotten about his father's gun because, as far as she knew, Evan no longer had it.

"No, I don't. I don't like guns, and they are dangerous to keep around the house. My ex-wife never wanted one in the home," *that is primarily true,* Evan thought.

"Okay, Mr. Williams. Here is my card. If you think of anything, please call," Miller said as he handed his business card to Evan.

Evan walked the detectives to the door, said goodbye, then closed it behind them. He felt confident he had deceived the detectives. He knew they could never match his intelligence. Evan moved to the front window, pulling back the curtain to watch them drive away.

After the detectives' visit, Evan finished half his submarine sandwich while thinking about the murders. He worried a little about their questioning, especially Sergeant Miller's, but he was sure he had not left any clues at the murder scenes. He could tell the Sergeant tried to connect Evan to the slayings, but Evan knew he was too smart for them.

Evan needed to find his new target, but after the detectives' visit, he decided the next one would be somewhere outside New York State, far away from Sergeant Miller's prying mind.

CHAPTER 45

January 23rd

Although the detectives could not definitively tie him to any of the murder scenes, they considered Evan Williams a solid suspect as their investigation continued. He did not have an apparent motive to kill the two women, but he had a motive to kill Jason Tanner. Sergeant Miller could not ignore his hunch and intensified his scrutiny of Evan. After their previous conversation with him, the detectives felt he was hiding something from them.

The detectives asked for and received a search warrant for Williams' cell phone records. They compared the locations his phone pinged with each homicide. During the time of Jason Tanner's and Laura Emerson's homicide, Williams appeared to be at home. Sergeant Miller knew he could easily have left his cell phone in his house while he was out, but it would be hard to prove. The night of Anne Roberts' homicide, his cell phone pinged until midnight in his office, hundreds of miles from Penn Yan.

It could be just a coincidence that Evan Williams' wife had met Jason Tanner on *Boredwives*. The two female victims were on *Boredwives* as well as Jenna Williams, but that could also be coincidental. However, Sergeant Miller did not believe in coincidences. Sergeant Miller and Detective Fowler knew there had to be a connection, but they had no evidence.

Sergeant Miller attempted to obtain a search warrant for the Williams' home. Still, the District Attorney he approached said a judge would never sign a warrant because there was insufficient probable cause. He told them to gather more substantial proof. The detectives were frustrated because they thought they needed to investigate Evan further, although it was only based on their gut feeling.

* * *

Evan thought back to when the State Police knocked on his door, but he did not worry. Just because the detectives seemed convinced that he was their killer, or at the very least, their number one suspect, he was confident they couldn't tie him to the murders.

As he sat in his office at work, Evan felt a strong urge to continue with his *Holy Mission*, but knew it would be risky if he killed another woman in New York State. When he killed again, it would have to be elsewhere. Evan decided to log onto the *Angel Wings* website to select another mission.

Evan pulled up the list of requests on the *Angel Wings'* site. He found a few originating in New York and terminating in neighboring states, with many flights ending in the early evening hours. The timing would give Evan plenty of time to complete a flight, drive into a local town, pick up a victim, and complete his kill. The states where many of these flights terminated were Massachusetts, Vermont, and New Hampshire.

After considering the various requests, Evan chose one originating in Buffalo, New York. The request was for a twenty-three-year-old woman who needed to return to her home in Nashua, New Hampshire, after having surgery at a Buffalo clinic to correct her vision. The flight had a scheduled date of February 3rd, a Saturday. It would be a long day as Evan would have to leave Albany for a three-hour flight to Buffalo, then turn around for a five-hour return flight to Nashua. The return trip from Nashua to Albany added two more hours.

Evan would be in the air for almost eight hours before meeting with his prey. He worried he would be too exhausted from all the flying to have the stamina to kill someone, but the urge inside him was too great to ignore. He chose to sign up for the *Angel Wings* mission.

Evan returned home from work and felt excited. It astonished him how the thought of planning a fresh kill invigorated him. Evan immediately went to the basement to pull out his make-up kit, returning it to the family room. He was very eager to produce a new identity and did not think about eating. All Evan wanted to do was choose his disguise so he could create a new *Boredwives* profile to lure the next cheating wife into his trap.

Evan chose a short wig, a matching blonde mustache, and blue contacts. He selected the same prosthetic nose he used when he killed Laura Emerson in Schenectady. He applied the pieces and looked in the bathroom mirror. He was satisfied with his choices.

He left the house wearing the disguise and drove to the same pharmacy he had previously used, where he needed to purchase a new burner phone, an AT&T minutes card, and a Visa gift card. He considered using a different location for the purchases, but wore a disguise each time he entered the store and was confident none of the clerks could identify him to the police. He again used cash to avoid a financial trail.

On the way home from the pharmacy, Evan stopped at a local Italian restaurant and grabbed a Chicken Parmigiana to go. Although he did not think about food when he first got home from work, he was now starving.

While Evan ate dinner, he created his new profile. He took a photo with the burner phone and uploaded it to *Boredwives*. He used the name Jeffrey and sent several messages to women who resided in Nashua, New Hampshire, that reminded him of Jenna. He felt energized with anticipation.

It was not long before Evan received his first message from a married woman. It convinced him that all wives were unfaithful to their husbands based on how quickly he received requests to chat. The woman Evan selected from the replies was Amber Glenning because of her vulgar way of writing. Her first replies all contained sexual overtones, nauseating Evan.

Amber Glenning wanted to meet almost immediately, but Evan told her he was unavailable until February 3rd. He lied and said he would be out of town until that Saturday. She fell for it, saying she looked forward to a meet-up. Evan felt ill with her egregious attitude towards marriage. His anticipation of killing Amber grew after each of her replies. If it were at all possible, he would have taken her out that day. Unfortunately, it had to wait until the *Angel Wings* mission.

* * *

Sergeant Miller was frustrated with his investigation of the three homicides. He could not find any more clues leading him to Evan Williams or any other suspects. All he had was the *Boredwives* app connection and the weak link tying Williams to Jason Tanner.

Sergeant Miller and Detective Fowler received approval to remain in the Albany area after convincing their superiors that the best approach to solving all the homicides began with gathering as much information as they could about the Jason Tanner homicide.

Sergeant Miller, who still believed Evan Williams was their number one suspect, wanted to follow his movements, hoping Williams would make a mistake.

However, he did not have authorization from his superiors.

Miller ignored his orders and used his off-hours to follow Williams as he left for work and arrived home each day. He also followed him on weekends to the Albany International Airport, discovering Evan Williams was a private pilot.

He would watch as Williams boarded a small airplane, but he always returned after short flights. Sergeant Miller did not believe he had any time to commit other homicides in the short amount of time he was gone.

Sergeant Miller followed Evan Williams for a third time as he drove from work to the airport. When Williams entered the F.B.O. building, Miller considered following him inside but decided against it to avoid tipping off Williams that he was under surveillance and stayed in the car. When he saw Williams exit the building and approach an airplane on the tarmac, he knew it was safe to go in.

Sergeant Miller looked around the building and spotted a counter with a young gentleman chatting with a couple of men. Once the two men walked away, Miller approached the counter and introduced himself. He flashed his badge.

"Hi, I'm Sergeant Miller, State Police."

"Hello, how can I help you?" the young man replied cheerfully.

"Could you tell me where that pilot is flying off to?"

Sergeant Miller pointed towards Williams.

"He told me he was going up to Glens Falls to do some touch-and-gos."

"What is a touch and go?" Miller asked.

"That's where they land and take off immediately without stopping on the runway. It's to practice landings and takeoffs," the man replied.

"Okay. Thanks," Miller said.

"Oh, and please don't tell him I was asking about him," Miller added as he walked to the window and watched Williams pre-flight the aircraft.

When Evan Williams climbed onto the plane and fired up the engine, Sergeant Miller shook his head and returned to his patrol car. Miller felt deep in his gut that he had his man, but was unsure how to prove it.

Sergeant Miller waited in the F.B.O. parking lot until Evan Williams returned to the airport approximately ninety minutes later. Miller watched as he collected his things and exited the airplane. When Williams eventually left the F.B.O. and got into his car, Miller started his engine.

Sergeant Miller followed Williams back home and watched him pull into his garage. Miller sighed heavily because it was another failed attempt to gather evidence against Williams. Miller pulled away from the curb, returning to the hotel where he and Fowler occupied a residence.

CHAPTER 46

February 2nd

Evan spent several hours planning the flights he had scheduled for the next day. His first flight would take him from Albany to Buffalo to pick up the young woman who posted the *Angel Wings'* request. Evan learned her name was Lisa Lockett after he contacted her earlier in the day to confirm the flight and time.

Evan told her he would pick her up at 3:00 P.M. in Tac Air's lobby, the F.B.O. located at the Buffalo Niagara International Airport. She said she was flying alone and that her mother would pick her up at the Nashua Airport to drive her home. Evan needed to depart from Albany no later than noon to be in Buffalo by 3:00.

Evan researched the Nashua Airport for an F.B.O. and found Infinity Aviation Services. He called them and asked about courtesy cars. After discovering that such cars existed, he would always ask at his destination if any were available whenever he planned a flight.

Infinity said they had courtesy cars but could not guarantee one would be available the day he arrived. After Evan explained to the woman who answered the phone that he was performing an *Angel Wings* mission and hoped he had a car to drive into town for dinner, she said they could hold one for him until 9:00 that evening. Every airport seemed to reward pilots who flew *Angel Wings'* missions.

After Evan had the flights planned, he looked for parks in and around Nashua. He wanted to find a location near the airport but remote enough for a murder. He located the Mine Falls Park. It looked perfect to meet his requirements. It was only four or five miles from the Nashua Airport and contained several remote areas within its grounds.

The Nashua River flowed around the park's perimeter, and a lake was within its boundaries. The lake site had a private cove near a parking area surrounded by trees and brush. There were no homes located nearby. This location was where Evan would execute the duplicitous spouse.

Evan continued to message Amber Glenning throughout the week, even though it made him sick to reply to her sexual inferences. When he found the kill location, he informed Amber he could meet her Saturday evening around 9:00 at The Cove in Mine Falls Park and asked if she was available. She replied with a kissing emoji that irritated Evan, but it would be just one more day before he would apply his punishment to her.

He would eliminate another unfaithful wife from this world.

Evan decided he would enjoy a hearty breakfast in the morning because he knew he would be on an airplane for over eight hours. His day would include a flight originating in Albany and terminating in Buffalo. He then had to turn around to fly back over New York to Nashua with no time for a bite to eat.

Evan also made four peanut butter and jelly sandwiches to pack for the trip. He would be on a quest to kill Amber Glenning, with no time to patronize local restaurants after the long day he had planned to fly across the Northeast.

CHAPTER 47

February 3rd

Evan packed his flight bag with everything he needed for the day, including his burner phone, Glock, and the disguise. He backed the Audi out of the garage and headed for the Albany International Airport. As he started his drive, he felt like he was being watched and peered into the rearview mirror. He thought he recognized a car behind him.

He kept an eye on the mirror as he made direction changes. He observed that the car following was making the same maneuvers. Evan speculated it was a detective. *Could be Sergeant Miller?* When he realized that he was under surveillance, he grinned and muttered to himself, "Good luck, Sergeant!"

When Evan arrived at Albany Aviation and got out of his Audi, he spotted the unmarked police car parked alongside the road, several hundred feet away. Evan acted casually as he reached into the back seat for his flight bag. As he entered Albany Aviation, he glanced over his shoulder towards the car that had followed him, but could not easily identify the men seated inside.

***

Sergeant Miller and Detective Fowler realized Evan Williams spotted them as they followed him. He had made directional changes and traveled roads that created an indirect route to the airport, which was unusual and added time to the trip.

When they parked on the shoulder of the access road to Albany Aviation, they could see Evan Williams as he looked back at them. Their clandestine surveillance of Evan Williams was over. They only hoped it did not spook Williams enough to harm their chances to nail him for murder.

***

Evan thought about Sergeant Miller and Detective Fowler as he performed the pre-flight procedures for the Skyhawk. He wasn't overly concerned, as he thought they would have already arrested him if they had anything on him. He knew they had followed him to try to catch him in the act, but it would never materialize. Evan would never do that in his hometown or even his home state again. All his killings would take place out of the New York State police jurisdiction, away from their intrusive scrutiny.

Evan received his clearance for takeoff and departed Albany for Buffalo. He enjoyed the Western New York views. When he flew over the Finger Lakes region, he looked down at Penn Yan Airport, smiling as he remembered Ann Roberts taking her last breath. She deserved to die for her adulterous ways.

* * *

Sergeant Miller and Detective Fowler entered the F.B.O. when they observed Evan Williams' airplane lift off the ground, flying westward, and walked to the counter. They wanted to know where Williams was going. The woman behind the counter told them he had left for Buffalo on an *Angel Wings* mission, but did not know when he would return.

"I think we need to contact agents in Buffalo. Have them call us if there is a homicide that resembles our M.O. discovered later today or tomorrow in their area. He could be flying there to kill someone," Detective Fowler said when they returned to the car.

"I agree with you," Sergeant Miller replied.

Sergeant Miller started the engine, put the car in gear, and returned to their hotel.

CHAPTER 48

February 3rd

Evan found Lisa Lockett sitting on a sofa in the F.B.O.'s lounge, reading a magazine while she sipped coffee. She was pretty, with shoulder-length brown hair and doe-like brown eyes. She wore a heavy, pink colored parka and blue jeans. As Evan approached her, Lisa stood and smiled. As he neared, she reached out to give him a friendly hug and thanked him for helping her. She seemed incredibly grateful for the aid she received.

Evan told her he needed to use the restroom while his plane received fuel and headed to the lavatory. When he entered, he leaned onto the counter and looked into the mirror. Evan tried to reconcile with the man he was at the moment, willing to help others, with the man who would later commit murder. He tried to determine if he was a psychopath, a sociopath, or something in between. He could not make sense of it. All he knew was that he yearned to slaughter to end his anger and rage. He also knew he enjoyed the hunt and the kill.

When he returned from the restroom, he sat with Lisa Lockett. They drank coffee while chatting about her medical issues. After a few minutes, an F.B.O. employee approached Evan to let him know the plane had been fueled. Evan and Lisa walked through the F.B.O.'s sliding doors and out onto the tarmac. Evan explained to her that he needed to perform a pre-flight check of the aircraft and to verify the fuel tanks were full.

After completing the fuel check, Evan helped Lisa into the airplane's front right seat and showed her how to buckle the belt. He closed her door, ensuring it latched securely. He moved around the plane and climbed into the left seat. After securing his seat belt, he handed her a set of headphones, which he had previously plugged into the firewall.

Evan contacted ground control, activated his flight plan to Nashua, and received his taxi instructions. He taxied to the run-up area at the end of the taxiway to perform a run-up. He explained each step to Lisa as he performed them. She seemed interested and asked questions. Evan felt like a flight instructor and thought someday he could become one.

They departed Buffalo at 3:10 for Nashua, traversing crystal blue skies with little to no turbulence. Lisa was glued to her window as they sailed over buildings, cars, and lakes en route to New Hampshire. He sensed she appreciated the experience and was thankful for *Angel Wings*.

Evan arrived at the Nashua Airport at 8:20 after a wonderfully enjoyable flight. Lisa Lockett was inquisitive during the flight and asked questions throughout the trip. She asked about the various gauges and switches. When air traffic control gave Evan instructions, she wanted to know what they meant. He enjoyed the flight with her.

They departed the airplane and walked to the F.B.O. to find Lisa's mother standing at the large windows watching the tarmac's activity. Lisa hugged Evan, kissed him on the cheek, and thanked him for volunteering his time for her. After she introduced Evan to her mother, they left.

Evan walked up to a woman tapping away at a computer behind the counter of the F.B.O., giving her his name and the tail number to his plane. He asked for fuel for the airplane and the use of a courtesy car. He explained that one should have been reserved for him and that he only needed the vehicle for a few hours to drive into town for dinner.

She typed away on a computer and said she found a car held for him. She handed him the keys and a list of restaurants. She pointed to a couple she highly recommended. She did not ask for a credit card or a driver's license. Evan assumed it was because he arrived as an *Angel Wings* pilot.

Evan exited the F.B.O. and walked over to a Subaru Forester. He presumed they preferred the all-wheel drive vehicles due to the harsh New Hampshire winters.

Evan climbed in, placed the flight bag on the passenger seat, and pulled out a portable GPS. He entered the address of Mine Falls Park. The GPS indicated it was five miles from the airport. Evan backed out of the parking spot to begin his drive.

On his way to Mine Falls Park, he spotted a small gas station and pulled in, parking alongside exterior restrooms. He wanted to have his disguise in place when he entered the park. Before climbing from the car, he searched for security cameras but found none. It was already dark out, and the bathroom location provided privacy.

Evan left the bathroom wearing the wig, mustache, and contacts he had chosen to transform into Jeffrey. He returned to the Subaru to continue the drive to Mine Falls Park. He found the entrance he needed, which brought him directly to the private cove. Once parked, Evan pulled out the burner phone and texted Amber Glenning to let her know he had arrived.

Amber replied immediately and said she would be at the park within ten minutes. She also included a kissing emoji that disgusted Evan.

Evan watched as Amber Glenning pulled her vehicle alongside the Subaru. She was another rich married woman arriving in a large S-class Mercedes sedan. When she turned off the motor, she flicked on the interior light and waved at Evan to move closer. He climbed out of the Subaru. When he walked over to the driver's side window of her car, she lowered it.

"Hi, are you Jeffrey?"

"Yes, I am, and you must be Amber."

"It's finally nice to meet you in person," Amber replied.

She had on thick makeup with fake eyelashes, purple eye shadow, and bright red lipstick.

"Where do you want to go?" she asked.

"Well, I was thinking of a nice hotel where we could get some room service."

"Sounds great! I know the perfect place. You can follow me," Amber said.

"Okay, but I would love to go by the lake. I've never been to this park, and I would enjoy seeing the water. Let's take a walk down to the bank," Evan said.

"It's awfully cold out. Maybe another time?" Amber asked.

"Aw, come on. Just for a minute."

Evan wanted her down by the lake to relieve her of her sin. When she got out of her car, she hugged and kissed Evan. It sickened him, but he tried not to let her see how he felt.

As they walked towards the lake, Evan covertly pulled the Glock from his jacket pocket, secreting it at his side. He wanted to get Amber to the lake before he killed her.

When she stepped onto a dock leading from the lake's shore, Evan asked her to turn around, gave his speech, and shot her in the face. She had the same look of fear as the other two wives he killed. It made Evan smile. He checked his surroundings, feeling confident they were alone.

Evan considered rolling her off the dock into the lake's murky water, but decided against it. He had learned from his favorite true crime documentaries that serial killers usually had a standard way to kill or leave a victim. Experts called it a signature, and Evan wanted one for a reason unknown to him. He bent over her, placed her arms on her chest, straightened her legs, and removed her rings. She looked just like Laura Emerson and Anne Roberts had when he executed them.

Evan returned to the large Mercedes sedan, found Amber's cell phone in a cup holder, and removed all references to *Boredwives* and Jeffrey.

Satisfied, he walked calmly back to the Subaru and got in, driving away with his feeling of anger, once again, relieved.

It was only 9:15, and Evan realized he had plenty of time to stop for dinner in town because he had become more efficient with his kills, and the long day of flying and only eating breakfast had left him starved. He also developed a healthy appetite after he killed Amber Glenning.

Evan scanned the restaurant list he received at the F.B.O., selecting a tavern highly recommended by the older woman who handed it to him. He entered the address into the portable GPS and drove. He would save the peanut butter and jelly sandwiches he brought along, possibly having them for a snack as he flew home to Albany.

He stopped at the same gas station he had found on his way to kill Amber Glenning to remove his disguise before arriving at the tavern. He wanted to be recognized as himself to create an alibi for the murder. Evan enjoyed a delicious chicken salad sandwich with a side of curly fries.

Evan arrived back at Infinity Aviation Services at 10:15. He was able to kill a cheating wife and have dinner in less than two hours. The tavern's receipt displayed a timestamp of 9:53, which provided him with an alibi if approached by law enforcement about the murder. It was only ninety minutes after landing at Nashua, and he could easily explain the time. He would say he got lost driving to a restaurant in an unfamiliar town and ate slowly.

Evan turned in the keys to the courtesy car and paid for the fuel. He was in the air and on his way back to Albany by 10:35. He tossed the burner phone from the airplane as he crossed over the Connecticut River.

CHAPTER 49

Evan awoke much later than usual, feeling both tired and empowered. The previous day's flying exhausted him, but killing Amber Glenning made it all worthwhile. He dragged himself out of bed, took a long, hot shower, put on a pair of sweats, and then headed downstairs to the kitchen for breakfast.

As he entered the kitchen and saw the flight bag sitting on the kitchen floor, he had a desire to gaze at the new mementos he had taken from Amber's finger the evening before. He reached in to pull out the rings. The engagement ring had a two-carat diamond flanked by several smaller stones and appeared to be a costly item of jewelry. A circle of diamonds adorned her wedding band that glimmered beneath the kitchen lights.

Evan shook his head when he recalled the top-of-the-line Mercedes she drove to the park. He thought about the poor husband who purchased his wife nothing but the best, only to have her soil their marriage. Evan felt a mix of sadness and anger. Amber Glenning deserved what happened to her.

Evan also pulled the pieces of disguise from the flight bag. He took the jewelry and disguise to the basement. He opened the souvenir box and added the rings to his collection. He placed the pieces of his disguise into the makeup kit. As he returned the two boxes to their hiding place, he thought about the state police detectives. They had followed him to the airport, and it caused him some concern. He decided he could no longer hide the jewelry in the house and carried the souvenir box upstairs to the kitchen. He needed to think while he cooked bacon and eggs for breakfast.

He sat at the kitchen island, eating while he stared at the box containing his keepsakes. Evan pondered various locations where he could hide his mementos from the police. He considered the trunk of his car, but Evan knew a search warrant for his house would more than likely include the vehicle. He also considered a self-storage unit. However, based on the reality crime shows he watched on television, he knew the police always discovered them.

Evan was at a loss until he remembered the pilot's lounge at the airport. The lounge included a separate break room with lockers available to pilots who wanted to store flight equipment at the airport instead of dragging it around with them. The lockers were spacious enough to hold a pilot's flight bag, headsets, and other equipment, and were similar to those found at bus stations. They were inexpensive at only one dollar per day and modernized to accept credit cards for payment. Evan could use a Visa gift card, eliminating any electronic footprints. With these lockers inside the F.B.O.'s pilot's lounge, Evan was confident no one would attempt to break into them. He thought it would also be a great place to store the Glock.

He finished his breakfast and cleaned up the dishes. He wanted to get to the airport as soon as possible to secure the burner phone, gun, ammunition, and souvenirs. As he was about to leave, he thought about his laptop and the searches he had done. He had searched *Boredwives*, parks, and rental cars.

He returned to the family room, picked it up, and placed it in his flight bag with the other items. He grabbed his coat and keys and got into his Audi. As he drove away, he kept a vigilant watch for Sergeant Miller's unmarked car in the rearview mirror. He did not see it and assumed the Sergeant had given up following, since Evan never led him anywhere worthwhile.

Evan arrived at Albany Aviation and walked to the pilot's lounge. He was happy to see it empty. He pulled open the break room door, closing it behind him. He examined the numerous lockers before selecting one in the bottom row. He placed the laptop, burner phone, box of jewelry, and gun with extra ammunition inside. Evan removed the key and prepaid for the month using his Visa gift card. He slid the key into his coat pocket.

Since he was already at the airport, he decided to stay to observe airplanes arriving and departing. He went to

the main lobby, poured coffee, and sat on a sofa
overlooking the runway. Although there was very little
activity, he realized with humor that he still rated each
landing.

CHAPTER 50

February 5th

Detective Fowler approached Sergeant Miller as he was looking at the documents related to the homicides they were investigating. Miller could still not find any evidence tying Evan Williams to the three homicides. When Sergeant Miller saw Fowler approach, he dropped the documents on his desk and leaned back in his chair.

"I just got off the phone with the Buffalo office," Fowler said.

"And?" Miller asked.

"Nothing. No homicides. I even called the local police and the Sheriff's department. Nothing."

"Damn it. I really thought Williams would do something out there," Miller said, dejected.

"I left instructions for all of the agencies I spoke to and asked that they contact us if they stumble upon a murder. Are we really after the right dude? What now?" Fowler asked.

"I don't know. I still think Williams is our guy. We have to stay on him."

"I'll run another CoBIS check in a few days. Just in case he stopped somewhere else on his way to or from Buffalo," Fowler said.

"That's a great idea. In the meantime, I guess we keep digging."

Sergeant Miller groaned as Detective Fowler returned to his desk. They had not made any ground with their homicide investigations.

* * *

Evan arrived at work on Monday morning to find Rachel in the reception area. He greeted her with a broad smile. She said he looked exceptionally refreshed and cheerful. Evan told her it was because he had had a wonderful weekend.

Rachel assumed he meant the *Angel Wings* mission. She asked how it went, and Evan told her all about it. He said Lisa Lockett was a sweet young woman who appreciated the *Angel Wings* organization. Evan told her about the airports he landed at and described the scenic views he observed from the airplane.

Of course, Evan could not tell her he felt fantastic because of Amber Glenning. He wished he could, but it would be disastrous.

Evan attended several uneventful meetings throughout the morning with no problems reported from the weekend's data collection. Things ran smoothly, and Evan's job became dull and rote, with no new data to process or reports to generate. He was pleased to have discovered his latest hobby, which captivated him.

Evan awakened his desktop computer to search the internet for Amber Glenning's death in Nashua. He was careful not to use her name in the search criteria. He wanted to know if there were any reports of witnesses to the killing. He uncovered three major network news organizations that reported the murder and read each of their articles about the crime. According to all three networks, there were no witnesses, and authorities had not yet identified a motive. The police were baffled, saying it appeared to have been a random attack. It seemed Evan was able to execute the murder flawlessly.

CHAPTER 51

February 14th

It was Valentine's Day, and Evan arrived at work feeling depressed and lonely but primarily agitated. He was not a fan of the holiday that he believed was conceived by women, florists, and greeting card companies. While he was with Jenna, he had spoiled her with roses and chocolates every year. He always made dinner reservations at their favorite Italian restaurant several weeks in advance to ensure they would have a romantic evening. The day always ended with passionate lovemaking before falling asleep in each other's arms. After the unfortunate betrayal from Jenna, he realized it was simply a sham.

Evan's depression when he arrived at work became fury after he attended meetings throughout the building, walking past desks filled with flowers, chocolates, and stuffed animals. It reminded him of what Jenna did to him. It had only been ten days since Evan killed Amber Glenning, and he knew he should not consider killing again so soon. However, he needed to alleviate the anger burning within him.

Evan logged onto the *Angel Wings* site to look for his next mission. Again, he needed a flight that sent him outside the New York State boundaries and away from Sergeant Miller's scrutiny. He searched through the requests and discovered a flight beginning in Plattsburgh, New York, and ending in Boston, Massachusetts. It was for a five-year-old boy who needed heart surgery at the Children's Hospital in the city. It also stated his parents would travel with him. The mission had a scheduled date for March 10th, a Saturday.

The flight requirements were perfect for Evan. Since the boy's surgery was not until Monday morning, he could set the flight time to accommodate his needs. He would pick up the family in Plattsburgh late in the afternoon and be in Boston during the dark to perform his murder. He volunteered for the flight despite not conducting his usual research into local parks. He needed a mission to help alleviate some of the rage he felt.

* * *

Sergeant Miller and Detective Fowler made no progress in solving the three homicides they investigated. They stopped following Evan Williams two weeks earlier because he did not appear to lead them to any evidence. He went to work during the week, always consistent with the time he left in the mornings, returning directly home in the evening.

Williams flew on weekends, but his flights were never longer than two or three hours. They did not believe he had sufficient time to murder in such a short period. The detectives continued to monitor CoBIS for additional matches to the ballistics recovered from the three homicide victims, but did not receive new hits.

Sergeant Miller scoured western New York looking for homicides on February 3rd, the day Williams flew to Buffalo. He found several homicides reported, but none of them had the same M.O. as the three they investigated.

They could not find any new evidence and had no solid suspects besides Evan Williams. Their superiors requested that they return to Central New York's headquarters. Disappointed, the detectives packed up what little evidence they had and reluctantly returned to Syracuse, New York.

CHAPTER 52

February 21st

Sergeant Miller sat at his desk in the New York State Police's Central New York Headquarters, examining the evidence he brought back from Albany. He could not pull himself away from the challenging investigation. He still considered Evan Williams his primary suspect since there were no other leads, not even a teeny-tiny one. Miller believed there had to be something in the evidence collected that would tie him to the homicides.

As he analyzed the notes he took when he followed Williams, Miller focused on February 3rd, the day he flew to Buffalo. Williams had been gone the entire day. It occurred to Miller that an airplane provided plenty of opportunities for Williams to travel to bordering states. He could have easily flown elsewhere to commit murder. Miller decided to expand his investigation to encompass much of the northeast.

Sergeant Miller powered up his computer to search for homicides in New York, Massachusetts, Vermont,

New Hampshire, Connecticut, New Jersey, and Pennsylvania. It was a large geographical area. Miller knew he would have many homicides to sift through, but had no other leads to follow. When Sergeant Miller saw the list on his computer screen, he was stunned by the number returned. He had over one hundred homicides to review. He needed assistance to get through them all and called over to Detective Fowler, who sat across the room.

"Hey, Kevin!"

"What's up, Sarge?" Fowler asked.

"I was thinking about these killings and Evan Williams. He has access to an airplane. What if he killed outside of New York?"

"I guess that's possible, but if he crossed state lines, it's out of our jurisdiction. We would have to call in the Feds."

"Yeah, I know, but we would have to look first. I still think that bastard is our killer. I want to nail him. If we need to get the Feds involved, we will."

"Okay. So, what do you want to do?" Fowler asked.

"Well, I was thinking if he did kill again, it would have been on the third of February, when he was supposedly flying to Buffalo. I increased the search for homicides that day to include all of the northeast," Miller answered.

"That's crazy! There must be at least fifty or even a hundred of them!"

"One hundred twenty-five, to be exact. I sent the list to the printer. I need your help going through it. You game?"

"Sure," Fowler answered warily.

The antiquated printer took nearly ten minutes to print the list. When it stopped spitting out paper, Miller snatched up the thick stack and returned it to his desk. Each incident was printed on a separate page, accompanied by a brief description of the homicide reported. The list also included the victims' details and a contact number for the local investigating agency.

Sergeant Miller handed approximately half the stack of paper to Detective Fowler. When Fowler saw how many pages there were, he groaned, knowing it would take a lot of effort and time to examine the details of each murder. He looked up at Miller, observing the same expression of concern drawn across his face.

"How do you want to handle this?" Fowler asked.

"I think we should separate our lists into two piles. A pile for male victims and a pile for female victims," Miller answered.

"Okay. That makes sense. Then review the female list first?" Fowler asked.

"Yeah, and eliminate female homicides that include rape. If a family member or boyfriend killed them, push that aside as well. I guess we'll end up with three bundles, not two," Miller said and continued, "By eliminating homicides that don't fit our profile, we may be able to zero in on a similar homicide."

Detective Fowler returned to his desk to scour through the list of homicides while Miller worked on his.

The detectives worked all day, sifting through their lists. The only break they took was a short fifteen minutes to choke down vending machine sandwiches. Sergeant Miller sought to reduce the number of homicides reported by conducting a detailed review of each to identify those that he could eliminate.

As instructed, Detective Fowler completed separating the list of homicides he received into three separate designations—one designation he assigned to male victims and two to females. One of the female piles contained victims killed during a rape or domestic violence incident. The last stack included the remaining females. Fowler returned to Sergeant Miller's office with the information.

Miller completed his review just as Detective Fowler pulled up a chair and sat alongside him. Miller had also divided his original list of homicides into three distinct stacks, similar to Fowler's. When he looked up at Fowler, he spoke.

"How many females do you have?"

"I'm down to seventeen," Fowler answered.

"I have twenty-one," Miller replied.

"Now, what do we do?"

"Well, I think we need to break these down to women who were not killed during a robbery or in a drug-related incident," Miller answered, then continued, "The two homicides we are looking at were not robberies or involved drugs. The only items taken were wedding rings."

"Sounds like a plan," Fowler replied.

The detectives were able to quickly analyze each of the remaining lists they had. They tossed aside anything that looked like a robbery or a drug-related offense. It took them less than an hour before they decreased the number of remaining homicides to three. Detective Fowler had one homicide in Pennsylvania and another in Connecticut. Sergeant Miller had a homicide in New Hampshire.

"Okay, we have three to look at," Miller said.

"A little bit easier than one hundred twenty-five," Fowler agreed.

"What do we do now? How do we determine if Williams was in any of these locations that day?" Fowler asked.

"I don't know. We know Williams flew to Buffalo, or at least that's what the guy at Albany Aviation told us," Miller answered.

"I think, for now, we take a break. Go home, get some rest, and take a look at this in the morning. It's been a long day. Maybe something will come to us after a good night's sleep," Fowler said.

Sergeant Miller placed the remaining three sheets of paper detailing the homicides in his desk drawer. Both detectives called it a night.

Sergeant Miller had difficulty sleeping with the homicides roiling in his mind. He climbed out of his bed before dawn to take a hot shower. He knew sleep eluded him, and it was useless to lie in bed. After a quick breakfast of cold cereal and a mug of instant coffee, Miller climbed into his patrol car to return to the headquarters. He wanted to examine the remaining three homicides he and Detective Fowler identified to determine if their elusive serial killer perpetrated any of them.

Sergeant Miller arrived at the headquarters at 5:45, finding Detective Fowler at his desk working. It appeared he could not sleep either. Miller approached Fowler.

"You're in early. How long have you been here?" Miller asked.

"I got in about fifteen minutes ago. I couldn't sleep thinking about these three killings we discovered yesterday," Fowler replied.

"Same here. Find anything?"

"Not yet. There isn't much detail included in the reports. I hope you didn't mind me rifling your desk drawers without you here."

"Not a problem. Just don't touch my Playboys!" Miller laughed and continued more seriously, "I think we should contact the investigators working on these cases to see what they have."

"You think any of them are out of bed yet?" Fowler asked.

"We'll know soon!" Miller replied.

Fowler handed Miller the report for the homicide in Connecticut. As Miller approached his desk to make a call, Fowler lifted the handset from the phone's cradle to contact the Pennsylvania authorities.

When Detective Fowler completed his call, he walked over to Miller as the Sergeant placed the phone receiver into its cradle.

"Our Connecticut killing doesn't fit. The girl was dismembered and placed in trash bags. They have no suspects, but our guy isn't cutting up his women, at least until now," Miller said.

"The Pennsylvania homicide doesn't match our suspect's M.O. either. The girl was stabbed to death and tossed in a dumpster. Our guy uses a gun and poses his victims," Fowler said.

"Let me give a call to the New Hampshire guys."

Miller picked up his phone and called the New Hampshire investigating agency. Detective Fowler, wanting to listen in, pulled up a chair alongside Miller's desk. He hoped to receive the information they sought.

Miller was on the call for over thirty minutes with the Nashua police discussing the homicide. Based on the side of the conversation he heard, Detective Fowler knew the homicides were similar.

"Bingo!" Sergeant Miller yelled enthusiastically as he slammed down the phone's handset.

"Do we have a match?" Fowler asked.

"Yes, we do. There was a killing of a woman in a park in Nashua. The body had been posed, with her lying on her back and arms folded across her chest. She also had her wedding band and engagement ring taken. Her expensive Mercedes was in the parking lot with the keys still in the ignition. On the front seat of her car, they found a purse with her wallet still inside. The victim's cell phone was also left sitting on the dashboard. It sounds like our guy," Miller said.

"That sure does sound like our guy," Fowler agreed.

"It does. The hard part now is how to connect it to Williams. We know he has access to airplanes, but how do we know where he flew the day we followed him to the airport?" Miller asked.

"I don't know. We could contact the FAA, I suppose. We will have to know what airplane he had that day," Fowler said.

"I guess our day just got a whole lot busier! Let's talk to the Lieutenant, see if she will let us return to Albany," Miller said.

"She'll probably want us to contact the Feds, especially since it looks like it's turning into a multi-state investigation."

"She most likely will, but hopefully, she will also allow us to complete what we started here. I will take a walk to her office when she gets in. She's usually at her desk by nine." Miller said.

CHAPTER 53

February 22nd

When Sergeant Miller received permission from Lieutenant Hodges to return to Albany, the detectives were in their cruiser and on the New York State Thruway within the hour. The Lieutenant informed Miller that they could not make an arrest, obtain search warrants, or interrogate their suspect until they had the F.B.I. involved. He had to contact them as soon as possible.

Sergeant Miller was not pleased with the restrictions placed on him, yet he was committed to the investigation. He felt his instincts regarding Evan Williams were correct. Sergeant Miller also wanted to uncover as much as he could before he handed the case to the Feds. The detectives arrived in Albany at 1:00 and went directly to Albany Aviation.

When they entered the F.B.O., they approached a woman working behind the counter. They flashed their badges at her and introduced themselves. They asked her if she knew Evan Williams or what airplane he owned. She told them that she knew who he was, but that he did not own a plane.

The woman told the detectives that she had heard he belonged to the flying club located at the airport. When Miller asked how he could contact the club, she pulled a promotional pamphlet from an acrylic stand on the counter's far end and handed it to the Sergeant.

Jim Robinson approached as the detectives walked through the F.B.O.'s lobby to leave.

"Hi. Did I hear you were detectives asking about an Evan Williams?" Jim asked.

"Yes, we were. Do you know Williams?" Miller asked.

"He's a former student of mine. He's a really nice guy. An excellent pilot, too," Jim said.

"Do you know anything about this flying club? He's supposedly a member," Miller inquired as he held out the flyer he obtained.

"Yes, I do. I'm also a member. What's this all about? I can't imagine Evan being in any trouble. He's an outstanding guy."

"We just want to know what airplanes he flies. Would you know?" Detective Fowler asked.

"I do. I can even show you each of the birds Evan uses. All the club planes are in the hangar right here. Follow me."

The detectives followed Jim as he approached a door to the side of the F.B.O.'s lobby. It had a keypad lock restricting access. Jim punched in a code, and when he heard the sound of the lock releasing, he swung open the door. As the detectives entered the hangar behind Jim, they observed several small airplanes surrounding an impressive-looking private jet. Jim stopped at one of the small planes.

"This is one of the birds he flies," Jim said as he pointed at the Piper Cherokee.

"Is this the only one he has access to?" Sergeant Miller asked.

"No, he also has access to that one over there," Jim pointed to the SkyHawk parked nearby.

"Does he fly any others?" Fowler asked.

"No, these are the only two airplanes he's authorized to fly," Jim said.

"Are there any records the club keeps that indicate when an airplane is used and by whom?" Fowler asked.

"Yes, we have records. We keep a logbook inside the airplane that every pilot must fill out after each flight. All the pilots use an online application to reserve a plane under their name with the date and approximate hours they will need the airplane."

"Do you mind if we look at the logbooks for these two planes?" Miller asked.

"Not at all."

Jim Robinson opened the cockpit door and reached into a compartment in the firewall. He pulled out a small hardcover book resembling an accountant's ledger. He handed it to Sergeant Miller, who opened it and looked through February's activity. Miller did not find Evan Williams listed as a pilot. It appeared that the plane did not fly anywhere on the date of Amber Glenning's homicide.

Sergeant Miller handed the book back to Jim Robinson. He asked for the other airplane's logbook. The three men moved to the Skyhawk, and Jim retrieved it from the cockpit. He handed it to Miller. It looked identical to the one he had just examined.

When Sergeant Miller opened it and searched for February flights, he was excited to see Evan Williams' entry on February 3rd. He asked Jim if he could take the logbook with him, but Jim said it needed to stay with the airplane. Without a warrant and unable to force Jim to turn it over, Sergeant Miller took out his cell phone to snap a picture of the entry. He also found an entry for a flight on the day Anne Roberts was killed. He took a picture of that entry as well.

Sergeant Miller asked Jim if there was a way to determine where Williams flew on the dates in question. Jim said they do not normally log destination airports, but receipts are turned in for fuel purchased at an airport for reimbursement to the pilot. Sergeant Miller asked if there was such a receipt.

Jim walked over to a steel cabinet with the name of the flying club painted across the doors. It was standing at the back wall of the hangar, secured with a combination padlock. Jim removed the padlock, pulled open the cabinet doors, and retrieved a small metal box. Jim lifted the lid to the box. When Sergeant Miller looked inside, he noticed several tabs organized the paperwork by airplane.

Jim searched through the section for the plane Williams rented before pulling out a receipt. It was for fuel purchased at Nashua Airport, dated February 3rd, with Evan Williams' signature on the back. Another receipt was also found for a fuel purchase at Penn Yan, signed by Williams, and dated January 4th.

Sergeant Miller and Detective Fowler looked at each other and smiled. They knew they had their killer in their grasp. They were aware that it was all just circumstantial evidence, but more than enough to secure a search warrant for his residence. Miller asked Jim if he could take the receipts, and Jim again said he could not. Unable to take the receipts with him, Miller snapped photos.

The detectives thanked Jim for his cooperation, and as they passed through the building, they noticed a pilot's lounge and looked in. It was unoccupied. Sergeant Miller nodded to Detective Fowler, and they entered.

The detectives sat on a sofa furthest from the room's entrance so no one who entered could overhear their conversation. Sergeant Miller reached into his jacket to retrieve his cell phone. He looked over at Detective Fowler and grimaced.

"It might be time to call in the Feds."

"I agree with you. There is a pattern emerging with Evan Williams," Fowler said.

"I really don't want to make this call. I want to nail Williams myself. It's typical; we do the legwork, and the Feds get the collar," Miller said.

"I know it sucks, but if we try to bring Williams in for an interrogation and the Lieutenant finds out we didn't get the F.B.I. involved, we will get our heads handed to us."

"Well, let me call Lieutenant Hodges first. Let her know what we have. I'll ask her if we can stay and work with the Federal agents. I don't want to give this up," Miller said.

Sergeant Miller pulled up the number from his contact list and pressed 'CALL.' When Lieutenant Hodges answered, he described the circumstantial evidence he and Detective Fowler discovered regarding Evan Williams, including the plane flights and fuel receipts. Miller explained to her the connection to the first victim, Jason Tanner, through Williams' estranged wife. Miller also described the two killings discovered in Penn Yan and Nashua. He told her about the documentation they had just received that placed Evan Williams in both locations on the same night of the homicides. He requested authorization to remain in Albany before he ended the call to Lieutenant Hodges.

"Well, what did she say?" Fowler anxiously asked.

"She agrees with our assessment of Evan Williams."

"Do we get to stay in Albany and finish this out?"

"She wants us to contact the F.B.I. immediately, have a meeting, and fill them in on our investigation. If the Feds have no issues with our help, we can stay in Albany to assist them," Miller said.

Sergeant Miller googled the local F.B.I. field office and jotted down the address.

"Let's go for a ride. I don't want to make a phone call. I want to meet in person," Miller said as he stood.

The detectives left the F.B.O. and climbed into their cruiser, headed to the regional F.B.I. headquarters in downtown Albany.

CHAPTER 54

February 22nd

The detectives found the F.B.I. field office located on a four-lane boulevard directly off a highway. As they drove towards the building, Miller spotted a driveway leading to a parking lot in front of a grey five-story, concrete structure. All four sides of the building had darkly tinted vertical windows rising from the ground to the roof. Sergeant Miller pulled into an empty spot designated for visitors. He turned off the engine and looked at Fowler, sighing as he climbed from the car.

"You ready to give up our case?" Miller asked.

"No, not really," replied Fowler.

The detectives trudged to the building's front entrance, where they discovered massive double-entry glass doors. On each door was a vinyl decal with the FBI's insignia circled with the motto, *Fidelity*, *Bravery*, *Integrity*. Miller swung open one of the doors, and they entered the lobby.

The interior of the building was ancient, with cracked marble floors, dark wood, and worn carpets. They observed a young man wearing a dark blue suit with a name tag pinned to the breast pocket. He was seated behind a circular reception desk in the lobby's center, banging away at a computer. The darkly stained wooden desk matched the dark stain of the interior wood-paneled walls. As they approached the desk, they saw Todd Harlan's name printed on a silver colored name tag. He looked up from his computer when the detectives arrived at the desk.

"Hello, how can I help you?" Todd Harlen greeted.

Sergeant Miller and Detective Fowler presented their badges as they introduced themselves.

"We'd like to speak to an agent in charge," Sergeant Miller said.

When Todd Harlan asked why they needed to see an agent, Detective Fowler informed him they were working on homicides in multiple states and needed the FBI's assistance. Harlan's eyes widened to large circles as he picked up the receptionist's desk phone and pressed buttons.

Todd Harlan was on the phone for a few minutes before he hung up the receiver.

"Agent Santiago will be down in a few minutes. Why don't you have a seat while you wait?" Todd said.

Sergeant Miller and Detective Fowler sat on wooden chairs that also matched the dark stain of the desk and walls in the lobby. While they waited, Miller opened the folder he brought along to review its contents. As he flipped through documents, someone approached wearing a dark blue suit, a white shirt, and a blue striped tie.

Agent Hector Santiago was a heavyset Latino who stood five feet eight inches tall. His hair was graying, and he sported a thick mustache and goatee. He appeared friendly, displaying a smile. As he neared, Sergeant Miller and Detective Fowler stood.

"Good afternoon, detectives, I'm Agent Santiago."

"Good afternoon, Agent Santiago," Miller replied, shaking Santiago's hand.

"How can I help you?" the Agent asked.

"I'm Sergeant Miller, and this here is Detective Fowler. We're with the BCI unit of the New York State Police. We are investigating multiple homicides that we believe are connected. Three homicides occurred in New York, two here in the Capital District, but the fourth was in Nashua, New Hampshire. Because this fourth killing was outside of New York and our jurisdiction, we need the F.B.I. to step in and assist us," Miller explained.

"Interesting. Let's head up to my office," Santiago said.

The two detectives followed Agent Santiago past the reception desk and down a long corridor to a bank of elevators. Santiago reached out and pressed the 'UP' button. They stood in silence while waiting for the elevator to halt and the doors to slide open. Agent Santiago remained silent as they rode to the fifth floor, prompting Detective Fowler to give Miller a twisted glance. Miller smiled in return.

The three men exited the elevator and continued to a spacious office with views from large windows overlooking the same highway the Detectives had traveled a few minutes prior. Agent Santiago walked behind his desk while directing the two detectives to chairs positioned in the office.

Agent Santiago offered the detectives a beverage. However, both declined. After briefly exchanging general pleasantries, the detectives showed Santiago their paperwork on the four homicides with up-to-date investigation details. They told Santiago they believed Evan Williams was their primary suspect, listing several reasons for their conclusion.

Agent Santiago listened carefully to the details as the detectives spoke and was intrigued. Miller explained the link between Jason Tanner, Evan Williams, and Williams' estranged wife. Detective Miller described to Agent Santiago the murder in Penn Yan and Evan Williams' flight to the city on the same evening. After he told Agent Santiago about Amber Glenning's murder in Nashua, New Hampshire, Miller presented a picture of the receipt for aviation fuel, placing Williams in Nashua on the same day.

Detective Fowler explained to Agent Santiago the roadblocks they faced as they attempted to connect Evan Williams to each of the homicides. They felt he had a motive for killing Jason Tanner, but they could not determine a motive for the other homicides. While they could place him in the same cities, they could not put him at the exact locations.

They also could not place Williams at the location of the Capital Region murders because his cell phone did not ping near the crime scenes. However, they knew Williams could have left it at home, but had no way to prove it. Sergeant Miller told Santiago they did not have enough conclusive evidence to arrest Williams, but hoped to gather more as their investigation continued.

By the time Sergeant Miller and Detective Fowler finished presenting the details of each murder in their ongoing investigations to Agent Santiago, night had fallen. The agent agreed with the detectives' opinion of Evan Williams.

"This is certainly something for the F.B.I. to handle," Santiago agreed when Miller finished.

"We agree. It was our Lieutenant who wanted us to reach out to you guys. But I have a request. Detective Fowler and I have been working on these homicides for quite some time now. We would love to be able to assist you and remain involved with the investigation."

"That shouldn't be a problem. We only have a few agents assigned here in Albany. We are short-staffed. I am sure I can convince my superiors to allow you to continue with us." Santiago said.

"That would be great. We won't step on your toes. We'll follow your lead and instructions. We understand it is no longer our case, but we have a lot invested in this and would love to see it through to the end." Miller said.

"Sounds like we have a deal. I'll call my superiors and get back to you by ten tomorrow morning. Are you staying in town?" Santiago asked.

"Yes, we are staying at the Marriott on Wolf Road. Here is my card. We'll wait for your answer," Miller said.

"Thank you. My wife and I had dinner plans scheduled for tonight, so I'd better give her a call to tell her I'm going to be late. I'm probably in the doghouse already," Santiago laughed.

Sergeant Miller and Detective Fowler shook Agent Santiago's hand before they left his office.

When the detectives returned to their cruiser, they smiled at each other. They were encouraged after meeting Agent Santiago, knowing they would receive assistance from the Feds. Sergeant Miller was confident they would be allowed to remain on the case even though Agent Santiago could not commit before he reached out to his superiors. With assistance from the Feds, the arrest of Evan Williams was inevitable.

CHAPTER 55

February 23rd

Sergeant Miller had just finished eating breakfast in the hotel's buffet room when Agent Santiago called him to confirm the F.B.I.'s takeover of the homicide investigation. He also told Miller that he and Detective Fowler were welcome to stay and work with him. He asked that they return to his office as soon as possible. He wanted to examine the investigations underway for each homicide in more detail. The agent also wanted to discuss a strategy for proceeding.

As soon as Sergeant Miller ended his phone call with Special Agent Santiago, he reached out to Lieutenant Hodges. He informed her of their progress and their meeting with the F.B.I. agent. He also requested authorization to remain in Albany to continue working on the case alongside Agent Santiago. Lieutenant Hodges gave her consent.

When Detective Fowler strolled into the buffet room, Sergeant Miller told him about his phone calls. Fowler was elated and poured himself a cup of coffee to go.

They hurriedly left the hotel to return to Agent Santiago's office to continue the investigation of the homicides, along with the additional agents Santiago will be assigning to the case.

The detectives arrived at the F.B.I. field office, and after thoroughly reviewing the investigations with the detectives, Agent Santiago felt he had heard enough. He visited the United States District Attorney's office to present the facts about the homicides that the New York State Police were investigating. He was in the attorney's office to obtain a search warrant for Evan Williams' home and vehicle. Santiago felt there was sufficient evidence for the District Attorney to grant the request. He spent two hours presenting his case before the attorney approved the search warrant. He would find a judge to sign it immediately.

Sergeant Miller and Detective Fowler waited at F.B.I. headquarters while Agent Santiago was at the District Attorney's office. When Agent Santiago returned with the signed warrant, everyone gathered in a conference room to discuss their approach to search Williams' residence and car. On his way back from the District Attorney's office, Santiago had stopped to pick up a couple of pizzas at a local joint. They ate while they worked.

"Now that we have our search warrants, how do you want to attack this? These warrants are only valid for 24 hours," Miller inquired.

"I think we should stake out Williams' home and present the warrants to him when he gets back from work," Santiago said.

"Why do you want to wait until he gets home?" Fowler asked.

"Because I think it will catch him off guard and put him on the defensive. Once the search is underway, we can bring him in for questioning. Seeing the police rummaging through his house might put stress on him, and that stress might cause him to crack," Santiago explained.

"That could work," Miller agreed.

"Do you think he is reckless enough to leave any evidence in his house?" Fowler asked.

"I don't know where else he would keep it, especially the rings. When I followed him, he never went anywhere but to work and the airport. The airplanes are all rentals and flown by any number of pilots, so I don't think he would leave anything in them. I think if he kept the rings he took, they would be somewhere in his house or car. The only other place he might keep them is in his office, but we don't have a warrant to search it," Miller said and added, "Should we go back to the District Attorney and have the warrant amended to include his office? I didn't think about having to search it when you met with them earlier today," Miller asked.

"I didn't think to ask either," Fowler added.

"We should have it amended. Can you meet with the District Attorney again this afternoon before we start searching Williams' home and car?" Miller asked Agent Santiago.

"Sure, I can meet back with the District Attorney. It shouldn't take too long. I could probably have it in less than an hour," Santiago said.

"Great! Fowler and I will head to Williams' house and wait in the car. When you have the new search warrant, meet us there. We'll execute the warrant on the house and office simultaneously after Williams shows up at home," Miller said.

* * *

As Evan pulled onto his street, he saw two unmarked patrol cars idling in front of his house. It was apparent they were there for him. He slowed the Audi to consider his options. He could continue home and find out what they wanted or turn around and run. After a few seconds, he decided to continue home. He did not believe they were there to arrest him today.

On all the crime shows he watched, he saw suspects arrested while driving in their cars or at their places of employment, but rarely at home. The police even waited for the BTK killer to leave his house before they pulled him over and wrapped him in handcuffs. Evan did not believe they would arrest him at all. He was too smart to be caught.

As Evan drove past the parked patrol cars, he kept his head pointed straight to avoid eye contact with the men seated inside. He pressed the garage door opener button and slid his car in when the door rose. Evan peered into the rearview mirror at the parked cars before he pressed the button again to lower the door. He wanted to see if they got out of their vehicles, but the men remained seated. He did not get out of the Audi until the door settled entirely to the floor.

Evan walked into the living room, hastily removed his coat, and tossed it over the back of the recliner. He moved to the front window, slowly pulling back the curtain to see what the police were doing. The patrol cars remained parked, with the men still seated inside. He was confused by their presence.

Evan walked to the kitchen to grab a cold beer from the refrigerator. He popped the cap and took a generous mouthful. It tasted good. He continued to drink the beer while he thought about his options. He still did not know why the patrol cars were out front or why the police did not approach him as soon as he returned home.

Are they just watching me, or are they here to arrest me? Evan pondered.

He tried to recall his killings and was sure he did not leave anything at the scenes connecting him to the murders. The only evidence linking him could be his presence in the cities on the day of each murder, but he was confident it would not be enough to arrest him. He finished off the beer quickly and grabbed a second.

"If they are here to arrest me, then I'm going to enjoy a nice buzz on the way to the slammer," Evan chuckled.

* * *

Sergeant Miller and Detective Fowler were in their patrol car, parked in front of the Williams' residence. They brought additional New York State Police troopers seated in a second car behind them. The troopers were there to assist the F.B.I. in the search of the house and Williams' car.

Sergeant Miller looked in his rearview mirror and saw Evan Williams' Audi turn onto the street and stop. Miller assumed he must have seen the patrol cars parked in front of his house. The Sergeant wondered if Williams would turn around to drive away or continue down the street to his home. Sergeant Miller was ready to make a U-turn until he observed that Williams started moving down the road. They watched as he drove slowly past them, entered the garage, and lowered the door. They also caught it when he peeked at them through a crack in the living room curtain.

Agent Santiago arrived a few minutes after Evan Williams with three additional agents. Santiago and one agent exited the car that brought him to the location. Miller watched the other two agents drive away. They were headed to Williams' office to execute the search at that location. Santiago and the agent climbed into the back seat of Sergeant Miller's cruiser.

"Hey, detectives," Santiago said as he sat and continued, "This is Agent Poole. He will assist the troopers with the search. Since it's an F.B.I. matter now, I thought having a federal agent present would be best."

"Nice to meet you, Agent Poole. Our suspect arrived home a few minutes ago. How did you make out at the D.A.'s?" Miller asked.

"I have two search warrants. One for the house and car, and the other for his office. The agents that just pulled away are heading to the office now to search it," Santiago said.

"Excellent!" Miller exclaimed, asking, "How do you want to handle this?"

"We should bring Williams down to the State Police Troop G headquarters for interrogation tonight. We could take him to our offices, but you have a nicer building. Detective Fowler can stay here and assist in the search. He knows what we need to find. Jewelry and a forty-caliber handgun would be great, but anything that ties him to all the homicide locations would be good too," Santiago said.

"Sounds like a plan. Let's do it!" Miller said.

Agent Santiago, Agent Poole, and the detectives climbed from the state police cruiser. As they walked to the front door of Williams' home, Santiago waved his hand at Agent Poole to take a position at the garage door. He did not want to allow Williams an opportunity to drive away with evidence. He had two additional

State Troopers move to the back of the home to cover the rear exit.

Santiago, Miller, and Fowler walked up the front steps to the door, and Miller pressed the doorbell as they arrived on the landing. They saw Williams pull back the curtain and look out at them.

* * *

Evan smiled when he heard the doorbell ring and walked to the front windows to see if it was the men he had seen sitting in the cars. He recognized Sergeant Miller and Detective Fowler at the front door. He did not know the Latino who stood next to them. The Latino, dressed in a much nicer suit, did not appear to be your everyday average detective. Evan assumed he was a federal agent because he wore a dark blue suit and tie, typically required by the F.B.I., which made Evan smile even more. The doorbell chimed again.

"Let the games begin," Evan muttered as he opened the door.

"Good evening, Evan," Miller spoke first.

"Hi, Detective. What can I help you with?"

"Can we come in?" Miller asked.

"Sure," Evan said as he turned and moved to the family room.

"You remember Detective Fowler, I'm sure, and this is Special Agent Santiago with the F.B.I.," Miller said.

Evan was pleased to have an F.B.I. agent in his house. He believed they were more intelligent than the State Police, which would make it more challenging to play the game. He wondered how the F.B.I. got pulled in, then thought about the murders. He had killed in a different state when he killed Amber Glenning. It made sense that it became a federal matter.

"Hi, Agent Santiago. Can I get you guys something to drink?" Evan asked.

"No. We're fine. Let me get right to the reason for our visit. We are here to execute a search of your house and vehicle. Federal agents are also searching your office as we speak," Miller said.

"A search warrant? What for?"

"Why don't you come with us, and we will explain the whole thing," Santiago said.

"I don't understand. What are you looking for? I don't know if I want to go with you while you're tearing my home apart." Evan was angry, but he also acted scared. He loved the theater.

"We have reasons to believe you are connected to some homicides and want to ask you a few questions. You don't have to come with us, but it will be easier for you if you do. You are not under arrest right now, but

I'll get a warrant if I have to, and you will be coming in handcuffs. Your decision," Santiago said.

"Connected to homicides? Me? There must be some mistake!" Evan said, trying to sound shocked.

When Agent Santiago threatened to obtain a warrant to arrest him, Evan decided it would be wise to go with them voluntarily. He just needed to remain in control and not say anything to incriminate himself as they questioned him. Evan had seen numerous interrogations on his reality crime shows. He felt he knew their tactics very well and promised himself he would not fall for any of their tricks.

Evan expected to be interrogated for hours and hoped he did not get too exhausted. He knew the accused began to make mistakes, saying the wrong things when they became weary. Evan did not have a criminal lawyer he could call, but he did not think he would need one.

"Hell, I did not even have a divorce lawyer," he muttered to himself.

Evan decided it was probably best if he did not contact one immediately. He believed he would look innocent if he went voluntarily without requesting attorney representation. Evan would ask for a lawyer to end the interview if he felt too much pressure. It also made Evan realize he should look for a good defense lawyer as soon as he could.

Evan was not worried about the search warrants because he knew they would never locate anything in the house, car, or office to connect him to the murders. It was a timely decision to conceal the rings, laptop, and gun at the airport when he did.

"Okay. I'll answer any questions you want to ask me. I have nothing to hide, and I am certainly not some killer you're assuming I am. Let me grab my car keys, and I'll follow you there."

"I'm sorry, Mr. Williams. You'll have to ride with us. The search warrant includes your vehicle," Santiago said.

Evan knew the warrant included the Audi, but wanted to see if he could fool them. He should have known it would have been much too easy.

Evan grabbed his coat from where he had tossed it earlier. As he followed the Agent and detectives out the front door, he turned back to see several strangers rummaging through drawers, moving furniture, and touching his personal property, leaving a mess. He saw them pull pictures from the walls. They even removed a plaque he had purchased to memorialize the day he received his pilot's certificate. He was furious and wondered what they would do to his Audi.

Evan tried not to let it affect him too much because he needed to keep his head straight to get through an interrogation, though he was not too concerned. As he climbed into the back seat, he looked around at his neighbor's homes and hoped no one had watched. He did not see a soul.

Evan remained silent while sitting in the back of the unmarked police car. He did not want to say anything to the Agent or the detectives that might be used against him while they were in the interrogation room. He just listened to the rumble of tires against the pavement with his eyes shut as they traveled.

After a twenty-minute ride, they arrived at their destination. Evan lifted his head to peer out the window when Sergeant Miller shut off the car's engine. He was stunned to see they were at the New York State Police's Troop G building located in the town of Latham rather than at F.B.I. headquarters. Since the F.B.I. was at his house, he assumed it would be the F.B.I. who would lead the interrogation.

Evan recalled hearing on the news about the new State Police building. The Troop G headquarters was a 90,000-square-foot structure on 40,000 acres constructed when the former location became obsolete. According to the news reporting, this new building offered more capacity for the growing investigative teams and added state-of-the-art technology. Evan assumed that was why they were there.

Evan instinctively grabbed the door handle to get out of the back seat, but the door did not open. When he could not get out of the car, he recalled from the crime documentaries he had watched that police cars had mechanisms to prevent rear doors from opening from the inside, thereby preventing suspects from escaping. Seeing Evan's attempt to exit the cruiser, Sergeant

Miller smirked as he pulled on the exterior handle and opened the door to allow him through.

Evan followed Sergeant Miller while Agent Santiago and Detective Fowler walked behind him through the front entrance. The interior of the building was bright and airy, with ample open space and a three-story lobby. When Evan looked up, he observed modern LED lighting circling its borders. It didn't feel like a typical police station. It was reminiscent of a posh Fortune 500 building. They did not talk as they moved past the lobby through a long corridor until they arrived at a small room. Agent Santiago stepped aside to allow Evan to enter. Evan tried to sit in the first chair he saw. However, Santiago stopped him and asked him to sit in the seat located in the room's corner.

When Evan sat, he scanned the room and spotted a camera mounted to the ceiling pointing directly at him. The Agent directed Evan to that chair because they needed him to face the camera. Santiago asked if he wanted anything to drink. Evan requested a cold Mountain Dew because he knew he would be in the room for hours, enduring intense questioning, and the jolt of caffeine would help him get through it.

CHAPTER 56

February 26th

The questioning lasted for over eight hours. Evan lost count of how many times Sergeant Miller asked him if he had killed Jason Tanner or any of the women they had found murdered. It was just like on TV or in the movies, the good cop, bad cop routine on full display. Evan always thought it was just a myth or something created by Hollywood for entertainment. He enjoyed the game they played.

Sergeant Miller seemed to take on the role of the bad cop, constantly raising his voice and screaming while getting uncomfortably close to Evan. He repeatedly accused him of the murders as he threatened Evan with the death penalty if he did not confess, telling him the District Attorney would seek it. He said that because the homicides crossed multiple states, it was a capital case. Evan wasn't concerned.

On the other hand, Agent Santiago was the apparent good cop who controlled Sergeant Miller when he became too loud or aggressive. He talked to Evan like they were fishing buddies. Agent Santiago even offered Evan food and additional Mountain Dews several times throughout the interrogation. Detective Fowler had kept quiet in the corner of the room, observing Evan's behavior and only occasionally exclaiming his opinion of Evan's involvement in the killings.

Evan became fatigued and hungry, but he refused any food offer. He did not want the detectives to feel like he was their friend by letting his guard down. It became apparent how innocent people confessed to crimes they did not commit when exposed to such brutal questioning. However, because Evan was indeed their serial killer, he thought it made it easy for himself to lie, adhering to his assertion of innocence.

Evan was able to maintain his convictions even as he became exhausted. He felt confident that they would not find anything after searching his home, car, and office. Evan only used the burner phone and personal laptop for everything related to his killings. His office computer would be clean if they took it for an electronic forensic inspection. They would only find his applications for *Angel Wings* missions.

"Come on, Evan, just tell us the truth. It will be so much easier for you," Agent Santiago said.

"I have been telling you the truth, Agent. I don't know what else to say," Evan replied.

"We can put you in every city where there was a homicide. We know you did it!" Miller yelled.

"I have told you over and over. Didn't you say the killer used a gun? I don't even own a gun," Evan calmly replied and added, "I also don't know any of these victims. Why would I have a reason to murder them?"

"You knew Jason Tanner. He was banging your wife. That's a pretty good reason to put a bullet in his head, don't you think?" Miller said as he moved close to Evan's face.

"I didn't know about him until after the Albany police showed up at my home and told me his name. I don't know how many times I need to tell you!" Evan shouted.

"Why did you lie to me when I asked if you were ever in Penn Yann? We can place you there on the night of Anne Roberts' homicide," Miller asked.

"I'm sorry. I forgot all about the flight I made there, I wasn't a tourist. I have been flying a lot to and from many airports. I can't remember every city I've been to. Especially if the airports are small and unimpressive."

"You forgot you were in Penn Yann? That isn't very believable, Mr. Williams. You knew you were there, and you lied about it," Miller growled, and continued, "What about the make-up kit we found in your basement?" Why do you have that? Are you trying to hide your true appearance for some reason?" Miller asked.

"And again, I told you. It's from college. I was in the drama club. I used it in plays. I haven't touched it in a long time. I even forgot about it until you brought it up tonight.”

“Why did you keep it? Seems like something I would have thrown out,” Miller added.

“It was expensive when I got it. Also, it’s something from my college days. I always thought I might try community theater someday, but I never got around to it. Besides, I bet you kept your letterman sweater, Sergeant Miller. Something from your *high school* days,” Evan replied sarcastically.

“Where is your home computer, Evan? We didn’t find it when we searched your home,” Agent Santiago asked.

“I don’t have a home computer.”

“No home computer? That’s hard to believe. Everyone has a home computer or laptop, Evan. Where is it?” Miller asked firmly.

“I had one, but it died several months ago, so I trashed it after drilling holes into the hard drive. I spend all day looking at a computer screen. I don’t want to go home to stare at another one. Besides, with cell phone technology and smartphones, I can do everything I need to do on the phone. Having a home computer these days is so blasé,” Evan again replied sarcastically.

Sergeant Miller groaned as he aggressively pushed his chair away from the table where they were seated. The metal screeched loudly across the linoleum-tiled floor as he did. He looked over at Agent Santiago and sighed loudly. When Evan looked at Agent Santiago, he saw him glare without blinking. Agent Santiago knew they had no solid evidence that linked him to the murders. He turned away from Evan to look back at the two detectives. They all shook their heads, dejected. Evan knew they could not pin the murders on him, and he was eager to leave.

"I'm drained. You have kept me here for hours. You have nothing on me because I'm innocent of these crimes you're trying to pin on me. Either you arrest me now, or I am getting up and leaving. I have answered every one of your questions without even contacting a lawyer. I'm tired and I want to go now," Evan vehemently said.

Evan stood and glared at the men. Simultaneously, the three stood while they stared Evan down, but he just smiled at them. They all crookedly smiled back. Evan knew they were fake smiles.

"You are free to go, Mr. Williams. I appreciate your cooperation. I'm sure we will be in touch again," Agent Santiago said.

"Will one of you fine gentlemen give me a ride home? Or do I have to call an Uber? If you remember, you didn't allow me to drive my car here."

"Yes. Detective Fowler would be happy to give you a lift home," Santiago said.

Evan followed Detective Fowler out of the building to the parking lot without speaking. Evan reached for the front passenger door when they arrived at the patrol car. However, Detective Fowler instructed him to sit in the back. He said it was against department policy to allow a civilian in the front seat. Evan knew it was bullshit, but he climbed into the back as instructed. The detective's feeble attempt to display authority was wasted on Evan.

They returned to Evan's house in silence. Detective Fowler was quiet during the interrogation and still did not speak in the car. Evan began to believe this was his natural state since he never uttered a word. Evan didn't mind, however, as he thought it was much better than listening to Sergeant Miller spewing nonsense. They arrived back at Evan's house at 2:45 in the early morning. Evan waited for Detective Fowler to open the door to the patrol car and exited as soon as he swung it open. Evan did not say anything to him, not even goodnight, as he climbed the stairs to his front door.

* * *

When Evan Williams and Detective Fowler were far enough down the corridor and unable to overhear, Agent Santiago and Sergeant Miller discussed the interrogation results. They both felt they had their killer, but they could not trip up Williams into confessing or releasing details only the killer would know. The search of his property provided no evidence. They had hoped to find the stolen rings or the murder weapon, but were unsuccessful. The only item discovered of any significance was the makeup kit. However, Williams had a logical explanation for possessing it.

"Well, that was unproductive," Agent Santiago sighed.

"He's our guy. I know it! He's a smug son of a bitch. I wanted to smack that stupid grin from his face. It was all I could do not to haul off on him!"

"I agree with you. Williams was in every city where the homicides took place. I don't know what his motive could be, though. Other than killing Tanner because he was the wife's boyfriend, there is nothing to tie him to the other victims," Santiago said.

"He was careful not to leave any forensics behind. We could not even find a speck of DNA," Miller said, adding, "We have to stay on him. I could keep following him, see if he trips up."

"Yes, do that. The District Attorney will not issue an arrest warrant until we get some physical evidence. He is worried that without DNA or a weapon, he would not be able to win a guilty verdict. Too many jurors expect it. I'll assign a couple of agents to assist you. We need to keep him under surveillance twenty-four-seven. Because you will need to find some time to sleep, I'll have a couple of agents contact you so you can arrange a schedule."

"Okay. You want to grab a coffee while we wait for Kevin to return with the patrol car?"

"Coffee sounds good," Santiago answered.

***

When Evan opened the front door and saw the mess in the living room, he became more enraged than when he had left with the detectives. It looked like someone had broken in to ransack the place. The police were undoubtedly not careful while searching through his things. Couch and chair cushions littered the floor, with pictures hanging skewed on the walls. Paperwork and documents that Evan had brought home from work earlier in the day were scattered across several tables in chaotic piles. When he looked in other rooms, he found the same frenzied mess.

Evan walked into the garage to check the condition of his Audi. When he opened the car door, he found the entire contents of the glove box lying on the passenger floor. They had tossed everything from the center console onto the passenger seat and the driver's side floor. When he looked in the trunk, he found the cover to the spare tire compartment removed. The donut-sized spare tire was off its mount and lying sideways. They threw the bolts that had secured the tire in place on the floor. Evan concluded they did not care and purposefully wanted to rattle him.

Evan was exhausted and furious, but he was not ready to go to bed. He felt irritated after seeing the mess the searchers left behind. He went to the refrigerator for a beer, looked at the bottle, then placed it back on the rack. He wanted something much more potent. He pulled out a bottle of eighteen-year-old Scotch from under the kitchen island. He had saved it for a special occasion. His mother had purchased it for him as a gift for his wedding. The Scotch cost over $500 for the bottle, and Evan admonished his mother for spending so much money on liquor, but she said it was something she wanted to do.

Evan returned to the family room after he fetched a cocktail glass from a cabinet Jenna had purchased to store fancy glassware. He wanted to sit, but he had forgotten that the cushions were on the floor. He placed the Scotch bottle and glass on the coffee table so he could return the cushions to their proper place. He looked at the rest of the mess the police had made and considered cleaning it up, but realized he was too exhausted. It would have to wait until later in the day, he decided.

When Evan had the cushions positioned correctly, he sat down, poured the Scotch, and replayed the interrogation in his mind. He attempted to recall what he had said as Sergeant Miller questioned him. He did not believe he gave anything away. Evan assumed that if he had done so, he would have been arrested immediately and not permitted to leave the police station. He nodded off to sleep as he sipped his third glass of the soothing brown liquid.

CHAPTER 57

February 26th

Evan awoke after a sleepless night, having slept for only two hours before waking up on the sofa, exhausted. He still felt a buzz from the Scotch he had downed earlier in the morning after he had returned from the interrogation.

Evan took a hot shower and brewed a pot of strong coffee, but it didn't help. He had considered calling in sick, but did not want to bring attention to himself. He also did not want the detectives to believe they spooked him.

Evan arrived at work fifteen minutes late. When he saw Rachel in the lobby, he hurried past her, flashing a brief smile before continuing to his office. He did not want to give her the chance to start a conversation. Evan knew she would ask numerous questions about the F.B.I. searching his office. He did not want to explain why they were there. He shut the door to his office, sat at his desk, and closed his eyes to rest before his workday was underway.

Evan attended several meetings throughout the day, but did not participate very much. As he sat in the various conference rooms, he observed numerous curious and twisted stares directed towards him. Fortunately for Evan, no one mentioned the F.B.I. search at the meetings, and he offered no comments. Nosy coworkers had approached him throughout the day, attempting to elicit information by telling him he looked dreadful. Evan was clipped in his replies when he told them he did not sleep well but felt fine. Some inquired about the Federal agents' presence and their search of his office. However, he kept all discussions related to business. Evan was relieved that John had taken the week off for his annual trip to Las Vegas with his buddies and was not in the building.

* * *

Sergeant Miller and Detective Fowler awoke early after very little sleep. They wanted to be in front of Evan Williams' residence at 6:00 a.m. to begin their surveillance. Miller hoped he would make a move or do something to incriminate himself after the intense interrogation earlier in the morning.

When they arrived on the street where Williams lived, the detectives discussed how they wanted to keep an eye on him. Their initial decision was to inform Williams that he was under surveillance, aiming to pressure him into incriminating himself. However, they decided against it. They speculated that if Williams were aware, he would be more cautious and not lead them to evidence, so they chose to park several houses away.

While they waited for Williams to make a move, they struggled to revive themselves after their limited sleep by swallowing coffee and chomping on bagels. It had been two hours before they saw a light turn on in the home. The activity in the house enlivened the detectives and washed away any sleepiness they felt.

While the detectives watched, they saw lights flash on and off in various rooms as Williams moved through the house. After thirty minutes, Evan Williams backed out of his garage to drive away.

Sergeant Miller pulled away from the curb to begin following. The detectives were disappointed when Williams drove directly to his office without stopping. Miller and Fowler remained outside Williams' office building for three hours before they were relieved by an F.B.I. agent.

Miller pointed out Williams' Audi to the newly arrived agent. He instructed him to call if Williams did anything suspicious. He also told the agent to be discreet because they did not want Williams to discover he was under surveillance.

* * *

Although Evan was exhausted, he made it through the day. Because his office computer was taken as a result of the search, he did not get much work done. Rachel had obtained a replacement for him, but it did not contain any of his software or documents. When he was not attending meetings, he remained in his office with his eyes closed and with instructions for Rachel to hold all his calls. Evan believed he nodded off once or twice.

He left the office at 6:00 p.m., intending to stop on his way home to pick up dinner. Evan was not in the mood and lacked the energy to prepare a meal.

As he pulled out of the parking space in the office building's parking lot, he captured a glimpse of the unmarked cruiser pulling out of a parking slot located on the opposite side of the lot.

"I see you!" Evan muttered.

Evan assumed it was Sergeant Miller or Agent Santiago. While he drove, he kept his eyes glued to the rearview mirror as he watched the car follow him. He made a couple of random turns, confirming his suspicion when he observed the vehicle behind doing the same.

Evan stopped at a local deli to pick up a large ham and turkey sandwich for dinner. When he had parked in the deli's lot, he spotted the unmarked cruiser as it pulled to the curb across the street. He tried to recognize who was in the car, but the clouds and sky reflected off the glass, preventing him from seeing clearly.

He left the deli and continued to go home. Evan chose random turns to create the most circuitous route possible because the police followed. He wanted to annoy them. He arrived home and lowered the door after he pulled into his garage.

***

Sergeant Miller was sitting at a temporary desk that Agent Santiago assigned him when the desk phone rang.

"Miller." He answered.

"Hey, Sergeant Miller. Agent Sinclair. We trailed Williams when he left his office. He didn't take us anywhere. He drove to a deli and then home. I think he knows we're following him. He took the longest route possible."

"That bastard. He thinks he's too smart for us," Miller replied angrily.

"We are outside his house. What do you want us to do?"

"Just stay on him. My partner and I will relieve you around ten. If he leaves, call me on my cell."

"Roger that. See you later," Sinclair said.

***

Evan ate the sandwich he picked up from the deli and drank a few beers while contemplating the searches and interrogation. He thought he should feel worried and scared, but he felt invigorated and determined instead. He looked forward to the *Angel Wings'* mission to Boston on March 10th, but he had not yet chosen a target to kill. He needed to log into *Boredwives* to find another charlatan so he could set up a meeting to continue the quest. The feds had confiscated his makeup kit, but fortunately, the burner phone and laptop sat in a locker at the airport.

He walked to the front window and slightly pulled back the curtain. The unmarked car's presence on the street posed a problem, as he needed to get to the airport to retrieve the burner phone and laptop. He thought bringing them back to the house now would be safe because he assumed they would not do another search. He also had a balance left on the Visa gift card stored at the airport, which he would use during the kill in Boston.

Evan decided to take the risk of going to the airport. He wanted to see if the unmarked car would follow him there. He grabbed his coat and flight bag. He quickly glanced through the curtains hanging over the front windows before heading to the garage.

When he pulled away from the house, he saw the unmarked car's headlights light up. As he drove, he could see the vehicle following behind in his rearview mirror. It tried to remain obscured in traffic. Evan laughed. They honestly believed he had no clue they were behind him. He again took a circuitous route to the airport, wasting their time and gas.

As Evan pulled into the F.B.O.'s parking lot, he noticed the glass windows. He wanted to see if the interior of the pilot's lounge was visible from the parking lot, but he discovered the blinds were closed. He turned off the Audi's engine and walked through the automated doors.

He entered the pilot's lounge, which was empty due to the time of night. He sat on a sofa that faced the parking lot to observe, through a slit in the blinds, the unmarked car parked along the access road. Evan waited for several minutes to see if anyone exited the vehicle.

When he saw the agents or detectives remained in the car, he rose from the sofa and walked into the break room to the locker he had rented. He retrieved the burner phone and laptop, and placed them into his flight bag. He left the Glock and jewelry box behind. He would remove the gun on the morning of his flight to Boston.

He did not want to depart the F.B.O. immediately. He thought if he did, the men who followed him would assume his only reason for driving to the airport was to retrieve something. He knew the F.B.I. would want to obtain a second warrant for a search that included the airport. He could not take an airplane out to fly either. He had had two beers earlier and always adhered to the pilot's 'eight-hour bottle to throttle' rule. There are just some laws he would not break. He walked to the lobby, poured a cup of coffee, grabbed a chocolate chip cookie, and sat on a sofa facing the runway. He would sit watching airplanes all night if he had to.

* * *

When Evan Williams did not leave the F.B.O., Agent Sinclair wanted to walk inside to see what Williams was doing. He first contacted Agent Santiago to get approval to enter the building because he did not want to make a mistake that would get him reprimanded. Santiago approved the request but told him to remain undetected.

Agent Sinclair moved stealthily through the F.B.O. to find Williams sitting on a sofa in the lobby with his back to the door. He was alone and drinking coffee. When he saw that Williams was not doing anything incriminating, Sinclair left the building and walked back to his car. Evan left the F.B.O. to return home after a few hours of observing aircraft arriving and departing the airport, and saw the same unmarked sedan following.

CHAPTER 58

March 7th

Evan was relaxed as he reclined in his chair, watching an old flick he found on Netflix. It was a movie about Robert Hansen, also known as the 'Butcher Baker', a serial killer who lived in Anchorage, Alaska, and owned a bakery. When Evan read the description of the movie's plot, it interested him because Robert Hansen had used an airplane to facilitate killings, much like himself. However, Hansen's approach was much different. Hansen would fly young girls in his plane to remote Alaskan areas, release them, then hunt them down like animals after he had brought his victims to his home to rape them. One of the girls was able to escape. She described him and provided his home's location to an Alaska State Trooper. It was what led to Hansen's capture. A mistake Evan would never make. Evan disapproved of Hansen's murders as he raped and hunted young, innocent girls, nothing like the corrupt women he was killing. While he watched the movie, the burner phone pinged with a message.

Evan had created a new profile on *Boredwives* after returning from the airport the previous week with the burner phone and laptop. Unable to use a disguise because the Feds still had the make-up kit, Evan had to meet his next victim as himself, but it did not worry him. He assumed the F.B.I. did not monitor the website closely and would not be able to locate his photo. Evan took a selfie for his profile without wearing any makeup. He used the name Ken, however. He still did not want the authorities to find him too easily.

The replies to his profile came quickly from many different women. Boston, a highly populated city, had a lot of lonely and bored housewives. He again chose one woman who reminded him of Jenna, with the same hair color and physical build. Her messages, though, contained a lot of sexual innuendo. She even offered to send nude pictures. The woman disgusted Evan. He knew she deserved to die.

The woman's name was Deborah Malloy. She described herself as a forty-one-year-old mother of three who had been married for fifteen years. She preferred to be called Debbie. Although Debbie said her husband treated her well, she said he was always out of town on business, and she liked to have fun while he was gone. As with all the others, she did not look for a new relationship. She just loved to have sex with strange men, saying it excited her.

When Evan had convinced himself that he had her thoroughly charmed, he provided her with the burner phone number before deleting the *Boredwives* profile.

Evan researched area parks in Boston, where the *Angel Wings* mission terminated. He found Baby Back Fens Park and believed it would be the perfect place to perform his ritual. When he mentioned the park to Debbie, she said she knew it well and thought it would be a great place to meet. They made plans to rendezvous at the park on March 10 at 9:00 p.m.

Evan paused the movie he had been watching to pick up the burner phone after it pinged with the new message. It was from Debbie Malloy, confirming their hook-up for Saturday. Evan replied simply with a 'yes'. He did not want to get into a text conversation with her because he wanted to finish watching his movie. Fortunately for Evan, her reply was a short 'okay' followed by a kissing emoji. Evan still passionately hated those emojis, recalling how Jenna and Tanner used them while texting each other. He returned to the movie as he thought about Debbie Malloy dying in just three days.

* * *

Sergeant Miller, Detective Fowler, and Agent Santiago were seated in a conference room while they ate cold, leftover pizza from an earlier dinner and drank warm sodas. It was 10:30 p.m. They discussed Evan Williams and how they could connect him to each of the murders. He remained under constant watch, but the surveillance did not lead them anywhere.

Williams often took an airplane out to fly but always stayed in the Albany airport's traffic pattern, performing take-offs and landings. He did not take any long airplane trips and never left the area. They remained frustrated with their lack of progress in solving the murders and the inability to gather the evidence needed to arrest Williams.

"We have nothing," Sergeant Miller sighed.

"No, we don't," Fowler agreed.

"We can't give up. There has to be something," Agent Santiago added.

"I looked at the dates of the killings, and they are roughly one month apart. If Williams is going to kill again, it will be soon. The last murder was on February 3rd," Miller said.

"We will just keep the tail on him. Watch his every move. He is bound to make a mistake somewhere. Serial killers always do. They even caught the 'Son of Sam' because of a simple parking citation," Santiago replied.

"My superiors are getting impatient. They are looking for me and Detective Fowler to return to Syracuse if we don't make any progress soon," Miller said.

"I said we're not giving up, and I mean it. I have alerts in place all over the Northeast for any murders that fit the M.O.," Santiago said.

"I'd prefer to stop him before someone else gets killed," Fowler said.

"We all do! Let's re-interview his ex-wife, Jenna. Try to get more insight into Evan's mind. Maybe after being away from him, she will see him in a different light and provide some more information to help nail the asshole," Santiago said.

"She relocated to Philadelphia. Do you want to call her, or should we visit her in person?" Miller asked.

"I think we need to talk to her face-to-face. How about taking a trip with me, Sergeant? I can get a flight booked tonight so we can leave first thing in the morning," Santiago said.

"I'm game!"

"I will stay on Williams here. Keep a tail on him," Fowler said.

* * *

Jenna Williams was at her desk working when her administrative assistant, David, knocked on her office door. She was deep in thought, and the knock startled her.

"Jenna, sorry to bother you," David said.

"No problem, David. What's up?" Jenna asked.

"There is an F.B.I. agent and a New York State Police Sergeant downstairs in the lobby. They asked to speak to you."

"An F.B.I. agent?" Jenna asked, surprised.

"Yes."

"I wonder what they want to see me about?" Jenna asked.

"I don't know. What do you want me to tell them?"

"I'll be down in a few minutes," Jenna answered.

"Ok, I'll let them know."

When David left Jenna's office and closed the door, she sat back in her chair. She assumed the police were there to speak to her about Jason's murder last summer, which saddened her. It brought back memories of their time together. However, Jenna wondered why an F.B.I. agent would be involved and why they would travel to Philadelphia instead of calling. She knew the State Police were handling the murder because they had called several months earlier, asking about Evan. Jenna closed her laptop, donned her suit jacket, and walked to a bank of elevators.

As Jenna rode on the elevator from the fifth floor to the lobby, she recalled her conversation with the New York State Police Sergeant when he asked about Evan. She shook her head as she couldn't imagine Evan as a suspect, let alone a killer.

When Agent Santiago and Sergeant Miller saw Jenna approach the lobby, they rose from the sofa.

"Mrs. Williams?" Santiago asked.

"Yes, I am Jenna Williams," Jenna replied.

"Nice to meet you. I am Special Agent Hector Santiago with the F.B.I., and this is Sergeant Stephen Miller with the New York State Police," Santiago said as he held out his hand in greeting.

"Hi. I remember you, Sergeant Miller. Weren't you the one who called me some time back? I'm a little surprised you are here. Why do you want to talk to me?" Jenna asked nervously.

"Is there someplace we can talk in private?" Santiago asked.

"We have a visitor's room. We can go in there if it's not in use."

Jenna, Santiago, and Miller walked across the lobby to a conference room surrounded by glass windows. The room was small and contained a round table with four chairs. It was unoccupied, and they entered. Jenna took a seat in the chair closest to the door. The detectives sat in chairs across from her. Agent Santiago pulled a small notepad and a pen from his breast pocket.

"Mrs. Williams. We are investigating several homicides that involved married women. We can tie them to the killing of Jason Tanner, someone we believe you were dating at the time of his murder," Agent Santiago began.

"Okay," Jenna said, still visibly nervous.

"We also believe your ex-husband was involved," Sergeant Miller added.

"He's not officially my ex-husband yet. New York requires a one-year separation before it will issue a divorce. We filed the paperwork, but we won't sign the divorce papers for another month," Jenna said.

"That's fine, Mrs. Williams," Agent Santiago said.

"Why do you think Evan killed all these people? I have always considered him a very compassionate man. Never hurt a fly. He barely yelled at me when he found out about my cheating on him. He never raised a hand towards me, and I never saw him get into a fight with anyone about anything," Jenna said.

"He has been placed in every city where the homicides took place. We don't have any concrete evidence, but we find it a coincidence we cannot ignore," Sergeant Miller said.

"What do you mean? Every city? I know Sergeant Miller called me about another murder in Schenectady, but that's all I know about," Jenna asked, astonished.

"That is why I am here, Mrs. Williams. We have a woman killed in Penn Yan, New York, and another in Nashua, New Hampshire."

"Why would Evan kill these women, and how could he, in these other places? If he really wanted to kill a woman, it would have been me as his first," Jenna asked.

"We believe he is using his flying skills to move around the Northeast. The same gun that was used to kill Jason Tanner was also used to kill these women," Agent Santiago said.

"We have searched his house, car, and office, but cannot find a gun. We believe he has one, but we don't know where he could hide it. That is why we wanted to talk to you. Is there any place you know of that Evan has access to that can conceal a gun?" Sergeant Miller plainly asked.

"I don't think he owns a gun. I've never even seen him fire one. That's why I don't think he could have killed Jason or these other women." Jenna softly replied.

"Are you positive he has no gun, Mrs. Williams? He could have purchased one without your knowledge," Agent Santiago said.

"Well, no, I don't think he ever bought one. But now that I think about it, he brought one back from Long Island after he cleaned the family home when his mother died. It had belonged to his father. When he showed it to me, I begged him to get rid of it and so he did," Jenna said.

Jenna surprised herself when she mentioned the gun to the police. She had forgotten about the night Evan brought it home in his suitcase until that very moment.

After she let it slip, Jenna regretted it. She didn't want to cause problems for Evan. They were on the verge of divorce, yet she still cared for him and ended up almost putting him in trouble.

Agent Santiago and Sergeant Miller raised their eyebrows at the mention of a gun. Until now, they have not been able to put a weapon in Evan Williams's hand. They could not find gun registrations or purchase transactions for Williams during their investigation. They both felt rejuvenated after obtaining the information about an unknown gun from Jenna Williams.

"Mrs. Williams, did you see your husband discard the gun? Did he tell you if he sold it or how he got rid of it?" Santiago asked.

"No, he just said he got rid of it, and I never saw it again. I believed him when he told me," Jenna answered.

"Do you know what kind of gun it was? Was it an automatic or a revolver?" Miller asked.

"I don't know anything about guns. I'm terrified of them. I really couldn't say what kind it was," Jenna replied.

Detective Miller removed his gun from his shoulder holster and placed it on the table. It was a forty-four-caliber revolver. When Agent Santiago saw Miller put his gun on the table, he followed and pulled his nine-millimeter automatic from his side holster. He set it on the table alongside the revolver. Jenna's eyes widened, and she gasped.

"I know you're afraid of guns, but if you look at these two here, could you point out what your husband's gun looked like?" Santiago asked and continued, "This one here is called a revolver, and this one is an automatic pistol."

Jenna carefully studied both handguns lying on the table. She tried to picture in her mind the gun Evan brought home from his mother's house, but she was so startled to see him holding it in his hand that she turned away quickly and pleaded with him to remove it from the home..

"It might have looked like that one," Jenna said cautiously as she pointed to Agent Santiago's nine-millimeter automatic, "but I can't really be sure. I wasn't happy to see Evan with it."

"Do you know of any places other than at home where he would keep it?" Miller asked.

"No, I can't think of anywhere in particular. We never had storage sheds," Jenna replied.

"Thank you, Mrs. Williams. I think we have everything we need. Here is my card. If you remember anything else, please call."

Agent Santiago smiled when he handed Jenna his card. He had discovered something else to bring him closer to the arrest of Williams.

The three of them left the office. Agent Santiago and Sergeant Miller exited the building while Jenna walked to the elevators. Jenna was distraught because she couldn't comprehend the idea of Evan as a killer. She returned to her office, closed the door, and sat at her desk. She covered her face with her hands, sobbing.

Agent Santiago and Sergeant Miller returned to their rental car for the drive back to the airport. While en route, they discussed the discovery of Evan Williams having access to a weapon, possibly the same type used in the homicides. Although Jenna could not tell them especially what type of gun Evan had shown her, they believed they had made significant progress with their investigation.

Santiago and Miller discussed possible locations where Williams could conceal a firearm. They had searched everywhere they thought Williams could hide it. He was under constant surveillance and never led the detectives anywhere besides his home, office, and airport.

"The gun has to be somewhere," Miller said to Santiago.

"The only place we haven't searched is the airport, but I don't think there is anywhere he could keep it there," Santiago said.

"No, I've been in the F.B.O. There is nowhere I could see. Again, he couldn't leave it on the airplane since everyone in the club could access it. We'll find it.

I know we will. It's just a matter of time before he screws up and leads us right to it!"

CHAPTER 59

Evan had contacted the young boy's family the previous evening to inform them that he would be picking them up at the Plattsburgh Airport at 5:30 p.m. for their flight to Boston for the *Angel Wings* mission. Evan chose that time because it was a three-hour flight and would place him in Boston at approximately 8:30, giving him thirty minutes to order fuel, obtain an F.B.O. courtesy car, and drive to the park to kill Debbie Malloy. He needed to depart Albany no later than 4:00 p.m. to be in Plattsburgh by 5:30.

For dinner, Evan had grilled himself a thick, juicy steak and a baked potato with a side of broccoli. He ate earlier than usual since it would be a lengthy day of flying and killing. He wanted to have a full stomach before he left home. Steak had become his meal of choice on the days he killed. However, if everything went according to plan, he would try to grab a bite to eat in Boston before returning to the airplane for the return flight to Albany. He heard from many people about all the Irish pubs in Boston

Commons that made delicious shepherd's pies, something he would enjoy.

After he cleaned up the dishes, he grabbed his coat, keys, and flight bag. Before he headed to the garage, he peeled back the living room curtains to search for the unmarked car parked in its usual spot up the road. He chuckled as he said to himself, "You should just park in front of the house. I know you're there!"

Evan backed out of the garage to begin the drive to the airport. As he expected, the unmarked car pulled away from the curb to follow. He again took the longest route possible to the airport. He enjoyed playing with them.

When he arrived at the F.B.O., he walked to the pilot's lounge. He was distressed to see a young couple seated on a sofa. He wanted to get to his locker to remove his Glock without being noticed and had hoped the lounge would be empty.

When he entered the room, the young couple looked over, smiled, and said hello. Evan smiled back. He sat on a couch near the break room door and stared at his phone to appear as if he was reading an email. After a few minutes, he glanced back to find the couple no longer looking his way. They had returned to their deeply involved conversation, which allowed him to walk into the break room discreetly.

Evan quietly opened the break room door and moved to the row of lockers. He looked around, opened the locker door, and pulled out his weapon when he knew he was alone. He slid it into his flight bag. He retrieved his laptop from the flight bag and placed it inside the locker. With the computer returned and the gun secured, he exited the break room to see the same couple still conversing. They did not seem to be aware of anything happening around them. Evan walked out of the F.B.O. to his plane.

It did not take Evan long to complete the pre-flight check and receive the instructions for him to taxi to runway one. It was another fortunate runway assignment because it would have him headed north toward his route. He performed the airplane's run-up and was off the ground by 3:55 p.m. and on his way to Plattsburgh. The skies were clear, with the winds calm.

Another fantastic day for a noble mission, thought Evan, taking in the views through the plane's windscreen.

* * *

Sergeant Miller and Detective Fowler followed Evan Williams as he made his way to the airport. They knew he was aware of the surveillance because he took them on the most extended route to the airport. They watched as Williams entered the F.B.O. through the front door.

The detectives remained in their car for several minutes before they followed Williams inside. When they entered, they looked around and spotted him outside on the tarmac. Miller and Fowler sat on a sofa and watched as he walked around the airplane, checked the plane's surfaces, and examined the fuel tanks.

When he heard Williams fire up the airplane's engine, Sergeant Miller stepped from the sofa and approached the F.B.O.'s counter. He wanted to inquire about his destination. The young girl told Miller that Williams said he was heading to Plattsburgh, New York, for an *Angel Wings* mission. Miller thanked her for the information and returned to Fowler, who remained seated on the sofa.

"He's headed to Plattsburgh. Let's let someone up there know to keep an eye on him," Miller said.

"I'll call Santiago. Have him contact the F.B.I. field office up there," Fowler replied.

"Sounds good. All we can do now is wait. Let's go grab some chow," Miller said.

"Yeah, I'm starving, and Williams won't be back for a few hours."

Sergeant Miller contacted Agent Santiago, telling him about Williams' flight and destination. Agent Santiago informed Miller that he would have an agent on site in Plattsburgh. When Sergeant Miller and Detective Fowler saw Williams' plane take off, they left the F.B.O. for dinner at a local diner.

***

Evan arrived at Plattsburgh Airport earlier than he had expected due to a fortunate strong tailwind at altitude that pushed him through the air. The airport was a former military airfield with a twelve-thousand-foot runway situated on the western edge of Lake Champlain, just east of the highest Adirondack Mountain peaks.

The views out of the cockpit as he approached the airfield were breathtaking. The skies were crystal blue and reflected brightly in the lake's water. Evan could see Whiteface Mountain's famous Olympic ski jump far off to the west. The snow that remained on the mountain tops was pure white and unmolested by dirt and grime.

Evan found his passengers seated inside Eagle Aviation Services, the lone F.B.O. that serviced the airport. The small boy needing the *Angel Wings* mission looked sickly, with pale skin and bones protruding beneath his clothing.

When Evan approached, his mother and father stood to greet him with solemn smiles. Evan believed he felt his heart crack slightly at the sight of the family. After introducing himself, Evan told them he needed to have the fuel tanks topped off before they could leave for Boston.

Evan placed his order for fuel, and as he turned away from the counter, he noticed a professionally dressed woman seated at the far side of the lounge. She was the only other person in the facility. Evan sensed that she was watching him. She quickly lowered her eyes to a magazine on her lap when he looked directly at her. Evan returned to the family to sit down beside them.

While seated, he looked at the woman again, and again, she quickly averted her glance from him, looking back at the magazine. It gave Evan a slight tingle, and the hair on his arms rose slightly. Not because he thought she was attractive, but because she seemed out of place. He had the same feeling he was being watched in Plattsburgh, just as he had been in Albany.

With the airplane fueled and his pre-flight routine completed, Evan walked the family to the Skyhawk. He placed the boy's mother and father in the plane's back seat. He helped the boy into the front seat alongside him. Evan believed it would be more enjoyable for the young boy to be seated in front of the controls, having a full view from the cockpit window. He was small and needed to stretch to see out over the cockpit's dash. However, Evan spotted the first smile radiating from him since meeting him. It made Evan feel terrific to know he helped a family in need.

* * *

Special Agent Dawn Sommer sat inside Eagle Aviation Services, watching Evan Williams as he ordered fuel for his airplane. She thought he looked unassuming and was surprised he was considered a suspect in several murders. She continued to watch as he sat with a family, chatting softly with a young boy who looked seriously ill. Williams appeared to be a compassionate man, not someone who could be a serial killer.

When Evan Williams left the F.B.O. with his passengers, Agent Sommer walked to the service desk to inquire about his flight. She introduced herself as a Federal Agent to an older man who worked behind the counter. The gentleman was friendly and tried to help. However, he said he did not know many details.

The man did tell the Agent the young boy needed to go to Boston for emergency heart surgery. He assumed they would fly to Logan Airport, although Hanscom Field would be an alternate place to land. She asked if he knew how long it would take to reach Boston in the type of airplane Evan flew. Like Evan, the man also flew Skyhawks and told Agent Sommer it would take approximately three hours.

When Agent Sommer saw Williams' airplane taxi to the runway, she exited the F.B.O. and walked to her car. She stood outside watching the airplane take off and fly overhead towards the east. When the aircraft disappeared into the horizon, Agent Sommer climbed into her car, pulled out her cell phone, and dialed Agent Santiago in Albany to give him her report.

"Agent Santiago," the agent said when he answered the call.

"This is Agent Sommer in Plattsburgh."

"Agent Sommer, did you see our suspect?"

"Yes. Evan Williams arrived at the airport around 5:00. He met with a young couple and a small boy who appeared to be very sick. Are you sure he's a suspect in multiple murders? He didn't look like a crazed serial killer to me. His communication with the family, especially the young boy, was genuinely caring and compassionate."

"He's our suspect. Don't let his looks fool you. Is he still in Plattsburgh?" Santiago asked.

"No, he left with the family and is headed for Boston. The boy needs emergency heart surgery. Someone at the airport told me Williams would more than likely land at Logan Airport, but he could not confirm it. He said it wasn't typical for Logan to allow small airplanes into their airspace. An alternate airport would be Hanscom Field, outside of Boston," Sommer said.

"Do you know how long it will take him to get there?" Santiago asked.

"About three hours," Sommer replied.

"Okay. Thank you. That's all we needed. Your assistance is very much appreciated, Agent Sommer. Have a good day," Santiago said and hung up.

Agent Santiago informed Sergeant Miller and Detective Fowler of Williams' travels when he ended his call with the Plattsburgh agent. He said he would contact the Boston field office to have an agent waiting for Williams' arrival at Logan Airport. He would also have an agent located at Hanscom Field in the event he lands there.

* * *

The flight to Logan was uneventful. With the clear blue skies and light winds, turbulence was virtually nonexistent. It appeared to Evan that his passengers enjoyed the flight. After he wished the young boy good luck with his heart surgery, Evan said goodbye to the parents and told them he would look for a request for their return flight. He enjoyed their company and would love to be able to fly them back home.

When the family left, he walked to the men's room to splash water on his face. He looked into the mirror, smiling. He was eager to go to the park, feeling refreshed when he exited the restroom. He approached a counter where he ordered fuel for his airplane and requested a courtesy car to drive into the city. They had one available and handed him the keys.

Evan found the red Ford Escort parked near the building and climbed into the driver's seat. He plugged a portable GPS into the car's cigarette lighter to power it up. When the screen came alive, he entered Baby Back Fens Park.

The park was a convenient twenty-minute ride from the airport. Evan arrived shortly before Debbie Malloy and positioned himself in a gazebo in the center of the park. He chose this location for the rendezvous.

Evan could not see what type of vehicle Debbie Malloy drove to the park because the parking lot was not visible from where he sat. However, when she arrived, Evan assumed it was a luxury vehicle based on her choice of clothing. He was sure she was just another spoiled rich bitch who took her husband for granted and screwed around on him behind his back. It affirmed his desire to end her life and her infidelity.

Debbie approached the Gazebo, and Evan said hello, but no more. He wanted to kill her quickly and be at Boston Commons with enough time to grab some Irish grub. He looked around to make sure they were alone, gave her his speech about cheating on her husband, and squeezed the trigger. He positioned her body as he did with the others, with her arms across her chest, and took her rings. He also found her cell phone and erased all evidence of their connection. Evan was in the car and on his way to Boston Commons within five minutes of confronting Debbie. He had become efficient with his adventures.

* * *

Agent John Meyers had arrived at Signature Flight Services on Logan's airfield too late to observe Evan Williams before he left for the city. When Meyers contacted Agent Santiago to tell him he missed Williams, Santiago was infuriated.

"How could you miss him? I told you to be there before 8:30!" Santiago screamed into his phone.

"There was a massive pile-up on I-90, and I was trapped in traffic. I was able to work my way around it, but by the time I got to the airport, Williams was already gone," Meyers said.

"Son of a bitch! That bastard could be out killing some woman somewhere, and we let him!" Santiago yelled.

"What do you want me to do? Should I wait here?" Meyers asked.

"Yes, stay there. Watch for Williams to get back to the airport. If there is any sign that he killed someone, take him into custody. I don't care if it's a speck of blood from a nosebleed. Bring him in if anything looks suspicious. I want this guy!" Santiago screamed.

"Yes, sir," Meyers said as the call ended.

* * *

Evan arrived back at Logan Airport after having what he thought was a delectable dinner. He only wished he could have enjoyed a Guinness beer to wash down the Shepherd's pie. But when he flew, there would be no drinking.

Evan entered the F.B.O. and proceeded directly to the bathroom to relieve himself. He had a long trip back to Albany and didn't want to have to urinate during the flight. As he stood at the sink washing his hands, he caught sight of a gentleman in a blue suit entering the room.

Evan thought he appeared to be an F.B.I. agent because of the blue suit and stuffy appearance. While standing at a urinal, he continually turned his head to glance towards Evan. Evan quickly rinsed the soap from his hands, grabbed a paper towel from the top of the sink's counter, and promptly dried his hands. He tossed the used towel in the trash can as he left the restroom.

Evan quickly moved to the service counter, dropped the courtesy car keys on top, and asked to pay for the fuel.

After he paid, he left the F.B.O. and quickly walked to his airplane.

Evan trembled as he performed the aircraft's pre-flight check. He tried to keep an eye on the F.B.O.'s windows. He could see the man in the blue suit watching as he moved around the airplane. Evan knew the guy was a Fed, but he couldn't figure out how Santiago knew that he would be there. Evan guessed they had asked Albany Aviation about his flight or used the FlightAware software to track the plane using its tail number.

Evan finished the pre-flight check in record time. He was sure he had missed a step or two, but his primary concern was the Feds. Evan climbed onto the airplane, started the engine, contacted ground control with his flight plan, and received his taxi instructions.

Evan had clearance for take-off and rolled onto the runway. He placed the airplane on the white center line and pushed the throttle forward. When the aircraft released its grip of the ground, Evan was relieved to be in the air, away from the prying eyes of the F.B.I.

* * *

Agent Meyers pulled his cell phone from the breast pocket of his suit. He dialed Agent Santiago as he watched Evan Williams taxi to the runway. There was nothing outwardly apparent to justify placing him under arrest. Agent Santiago was disappointed but less angry than earlier. He thanked Agent Meyers for his assistance and ended the call.

* * *

The airspace was reasonably devoid of other aircrafts during Evan's return flight to Albany. The airplane's radio remained relatively quiet due to the reduced number of commercial flights arriving and departing at that time of night. Evan should have felt calm and peaceful as he flew through the silent skies, but all he could think about was the F.B.I. agents who watched him in Plattsburgh and Boston.

The Feds would most definitely make the connection with his presence in the same city and at the same time as the murder of Debbie Malloy. There wouldn't be any evidence placing him at the crime scene, but he knew Agent Santiago and Sergeant Miller would bang on his door as soon as they heard about the murder.

Evan tried to think of anything he might have left behind at the scene. He thought about his cell phone, but he had left it on the airplane. Agent Santiago would undoubtedly ask why he did not bring his cell phone when he drove into the city. Evan would say he forgot to take it from his flight bag and always left the bag on the airplane. He expected another intense interrogation heading his way.

It was 1:30 a.m. when Evan returned to Albany and found the F.B.O. deserted. He walked to the break room located in the pilot's lounge, which was also empty, opened his locker, and placed the Glock inside along with the rings he ripped from Debbie Malloy's finger. He had broken apart the burner phone and dropped it from the airplane into a large lake while en route from Boston.

When he walked to his car, Evan saw the Feds parked up the street. He expected to see them, but it still made him angry. He just wanted to be left alone so he could rid the world of women who disrespected their husbands.

Evan got into his Audi, fired up the engine, and pulled out of the parking lot. He took a direct route home because he was exhausted from the long day. He watched his followers behind him in the rearview mirror. He was sure they were happy he did not take them for a long ride.

*   *   *

Sergeant Miller sat in his car, waiting for Evan Williams to return from Boston. After a short nap, he arrived at the airport a little after midnight. Miller knew it would be a long night and wanted to get as much sleep as possible. The time he spent following Williams cut into his evenings, but he was not about to give in.

When Miller saw Evan leave the F.B.O. at 1:40 a.m., he perked up and became attentive. He watched as Evan looked to see him parked along the road. Although Miller knew Evan was aware he was under surveillance, it did not stop the effort to catch him when he made a mistake. When Sergeant Miller saw the Audi headlights light up and the car move, he started his own and followed.

Sergeant Miller watched as Evan pulled into his garage and closed the door. Miller could see lights turn on and off inside the house as Williams worked his way from room to room, eventually ending in the bedroom. His bedroom light was only lit for five minutes before the room darkened.

He had hoped Evan would lead him to the weapon Mrs. Williams had mentioned when he interviewed her in Philadelphia, but it was not tonight. He must be hiding it somewhere, and Miller was determined to find it. Sergeant Miller assumed Evan Williams was in for the night, sighed, and drove away. He would send Detective Fowler back to Williams' home before 6:00 a.m. to begin another day of shadowing.

CHAPTER 60

March 12th

Lieutenant Marc Adams, the lead homicide detective for the Boston Police, was seated at his desk as he studied the murder of Deborah Malloy when his desk phone rang. He hoped it was the call from the lab he had waited for, with a ballistics report to help him with the investigation. Lieutenant Adams picked up the receiver.

"Lieutenant Adams."

"Good morning, Lieutenant Adams. I am Special Agent Hector Santiago with the F.B.I. out of Albany, New York."

"The F.B.I.? How can I help you boys?" Adams asked.

"We are investigating several homicides from around the Northeast. We believe you had a homicide over the weekend that may match our suspect's M.O.," Santiago answered.

"Yes, we had a homicide of a woman in a park. It doesn't appear to have been a robbery. I was waiting for the Ballistics Department to call me back."

"This is an odd question, but was the victim posed in any way? Even though it did not look like a robbery, did she have anything taken?"

"Interesting that you ask. I thought the victim looked posed. She was lying flat on her back with her arms folded across her chest like she was lying inside of a casket, and it appeared she had her wedding ring removed," Adams replied.

"That sounds like it could be our guy. Could you send over your murder book and any information you have? I am also interested in the ballistics report. If it were a forty-caliber, then it is most likely our guy. I am working with the New York State Police to solve this. We have a suspect, but we haven't been able to get any solid evidence to make an arrest," Santiago said.

"We don't have much to go on yet. We looked around and could not find any witnesses. It looks like he was in and out of the park in minutes. We found no foreign DNA during the autopsy. We have no leads at all. Who is your suspect, and why do you believe he is traveling around the country?"

"He's a pilot, and we think he is killing while traveling to cities for *Angel Wings,* a charitable organization that provides flights for people with medical needs. It is a bit of a mystery. He is flying people to help them and, simultaneously, killing others.

It doesn't make sense to us, and we don't know his motive. We do know our suspect was in Boston on Saturday. Was that the night of the murder?"

"Yes, it was. The coroner put the time of death between eight and midnight. He cannot be sure because it was a colder night, which slowed down the decomposition and caused a rapid drop in body temperature. A jogger found the body early Sunday morning," Adams said.

"Okay. Please send any information you have as soon as you can. We'll try to determine if the murders are connected." Santiago said.

Agent Santiago supplied Lieutenant Adams with his email address so he could send the requested information. It appeared to Santiago that Evan Williams did indeed kill again while he was in Boston. Unfortunately, the agent who was supposed to keep an eye on Evan missed him when he arrived at Logan.

Santiago was frustrated that they were most likely within minutes of capturing him before he killed again. If the agent had been able to follow him, he could have stopped Evan before he had time to pull the trigger. After his phone call to Boston, Santiago informed Sergeant Miller of the recent homicide.

After Miller heard about the homicide in Boston that occurred on Saturday evening, he angrily slammed his fists on his desk. He did not want Evan to have a chance to kill another woman, not while he had him under surveillance, but there was nothing he could do. He picked up the phone and called Detective Fowler, who was sitting outside Williams' office building in the State Police cruiser.

"Hey, Sarge, what's up?" Fowler asked when he answered his cell phone.

"The fucker did it again. Williams killed another woman while he was in Boston on Saturday. Santiago just got off the phone with the lead detective out there. Same M.O.," Miller said, frustrated.

"Fuck!" Fowler yelled.

"I know. Come back to headquarters and pick up Hector and me. We want to follow Williams as he heads home. We will confront him at his home," Miller said.

"Can we get a warrant for an arrest? I mean, we know it's him. It is getting pretty obvious," Fowler said.

"I will talk to Hector while you are on your way back. See if he is willing to try to convince the District Attorney," Miller said, ending the call.

Detective Fowler returned to F.B.I. headquarters in downtown Albany at the same time that Agent Santiago returned from the D.A.'s office. When he saw Agent Santiago climb from his car with a scowl, Fowler assumed the warrant he requested was not issued. He waited at a bank of elevators for Santiago to catch up to him.

When the two men got on the elevator and the doors slid closed, Santiago told Fowler the D.A. was still unwilling to issue an arrest warrant. The D.A. agreed the coincidences were remarkable, but he said any good defense lawyer would argue that they were just coincidences.

"We have no other evidence that positively identifies Williams as the killer. The D.A. wants more. A murder weapon, a witness, DNA, something other than just in the same city and at the same time as the homicides. The D.A. did approve bringing Williams in for additional questioning. Let's do that immediately," Santiago said to Fowler.

When Agent Santiago informed Sergeant Miller of the D.A.'s decision not to issue an arrest warrant, he was furious, convinced of Williams' guilt. He was also angry because they could not obtain sufficient evidence against him to make an arrest, and they could not locate the weapon he used. This was getting frustrating, more than challenging, for Miller.

The three men chose to split up. Miller and Fowler returned to Williams' office building. Agent Santiago waited outside the Williams' home. They wanted to put additional pressure on Williams with a show of force.

* * *

Evan left work early, still exhausted from the long day on Saturday, the day he had satisfied himself with his unconventional hobbies. As he walked to his Audi, he spotted the State Police cruiser parked several spaces away. He could barely see through the windshield due to the glare radiating off of it, yet he believed he saw two men seated inside who watched him.

"These guys will not leave me alone, and I wish they would," Evan mumbled to himself. *So bothersome.*

As much as Evan wanted to screw with the police as they followed him, he did not have the energy to take a long and indirect route, so he drove directly home. Pulling onto his street, he noticed another unmarked car parked directly in front of his house.

It concerned him, and his hands began to sweat, causing them to slip across the Audi's wood veneer steering wheel. He knew they could not pin the murders on him because he was the smartest of all of them, but it still alarmed him. He did not want to live in a prison. Evan slowed his car, but he knew he couldn't stop because the detectives trailed behind. He decided to continue down the street to his home.

After he lowered the garage door and entered the house, he walked to the front window to see what the men in the two cars would do. Sergeant Miller and Detective Fowler got out of the car that followed him from the office and approached the driver's side door of the car parked in front of the house. They appeared to communicate with someone in the vehicle.

As the two detectives stepped away from the parked vehicle, Evan saw Agent Santiago climb from it. He felt slightly uneasy, but he didn't think they were there to arrest him. They would have brought additional uniformed police along. He assumed they were there to harass him after they heard about the murder in Boston. Evan knew they had nothing on him and vowed they would get nothing from him.

Evan poured himself a couple of fingers of the 18-year-old scotch his mother had purchased for him. He downed it in one gulp and poured a second. He sipped the second glass slowly while waiting for Santiago to ring his doorbell, which he would undoubtedly do momentarily. Evan did not bother to sit down. Instead, he stood at the front door with his hand on the doorknob.

The bell pealed a few minutes later, and Evan opened the door immediately. Agent Santiago and the two New York State Police detectives grinned broadly as the door swung open. It made Evan feel uncomfortable because they reminded him of the proverbial Cheshire Cat ready to pounce.

"What do you guys want now?" Evan asked with frustration.

"We would like you to come downtown with us for more questioning," Santiago answered.

"About what? I answered all of your questions the last time I was there."

"We just want to tie up some loose ends. We were hoping you would be willing to come with us," Sergeant Miller said.

"I'm tired. I just got home from work and want to have dinner," Evan said.

"We'll order some pizza and get some cola for you. We wouldn't want you to go hungry, Mr. Williams," Santiago said.

"I'm not in the mood for pizza, Agent Santiago. I was looking forward to grilling myself a nice thick tuna steak and washing it down with a beer or two. I doubt you can do that for me at your headquarters," Evan replied sarcastically.

"Mr. Williams, we are asking nicely. We don't want to have to force you, but we will, if need be," Sergeant Miller said with authority.

"Am I under arrest? If not, I don't think you can force me to go with you. I have not hired a lawyer yet because I did nothing wrong, but if you keep harassing me, I will," Evan barked.

"Aww, Evan, I thought we were all friends here. There's no need to get testy with us," Santiago teased.

"I am tired of the harassment. You people follow me everywhere I go. If you don't stop, I will hire a lawyer and sue you guys, the city, the state, and the Feds. I'll sue your dogs, too, if you have any," Evan snarled.

"We know you were in Boston last Saturday, and there happened to be another murder there. Another married woman. Quite the coincidence, don't you think,

Evan? Just so you know, I do not believe in coincidences," Miller scowled as he spoke.

"Well, that is quite the coincidence. I guess I'm always in the wrong place at the wrong time. I was in Boston, but only because I was helping a young boy and his family. I certainly didn't go to kill someone."

"Okay, Mr. Williams, you don't have to come with us. I was hoping you would be willing. Have a good night," Santiago said.

"Good night!" Evan said curtly as he slammed the door closed.

Evan walked to the front window to observe the three men talking at the bottom of the driveway. He could see Sergeant Miller's hands move wildly as he spoke. He appeared angry. Agent Santiago, on the other hand, remained calm and collected. Evan watched for three or four minutes before they separated, got into their cars, and drove away.

Evan had finished a second glass of Scotch while the detectives questioned him. He decided to pour a third, sat on the couch, and thought. He wondered if it was time to hire a good defense lawyer. He knew he was guilty of the crimes, and he would need the best money could buy.

"A good lawyer might just get me acquitted. It happened with O.J., why not me?" he said aloud to no one.

***

Agent Santiago, Sergeant Miller, and Detective Fowler walked away from Williams' front door to the bottom of the driveway. When they were far enough away from the house where Evan could not overhear their conversation, they talked.

"That son of a bitch did it. I know it!" Sergeant Miller yelled.

"I know he did, Sergeant, but we can't force him to come with us. We have nothing on him," Santiago replied.

"He looks shook to me. Hopefully, the pressure will force him to make a mistake so we can slap cuffs on him," Detective Fowler said.

"I wish the D.A. would just issue the damned arrest warrant so we can get him in the interrogation room. I want another crack at him. I know I can get him to fess up," Miller said.

"The D.A. wants us to get more evidence on him. Being in the same city isn't enough. There were no witnesses to any of the homicides, nor was there DNA we could use. The only option is to find the murder weapon. I could try to get another search warrant, but the last search yielded nothing. He must be hiding it somewhere. It was not here, at his office, or in his car," Santiago said.

"Well, I am going to keep following him. He'll lead us to it eventually," Miller said.

The three men agreed to meet back at F.B.I. headquarters. Sergeant Miller cursed Evan the entire time he drove, while Detective Fowler sat silently beside him.

CHAPTER 61

Evan awoke later than usual because he didn't set his alarm clock when he went to bed. After the authorities had visited his home the previous night to question him, he was annoyed and decided to take the day off from work. Before climbing into bed, he used his cell phone to reserve an airplane because his laptop was at the airport. He was delighted when he found the Skyhawk and the Cherokee available. He chose the Cherokee since he would be flying alone. He enjoyed piloting the Piper much more than he did the Cessna.

He showered and dressed casually in jeans and a sweatshirt. He went to the kitchen to make breakfast, settling on scrambled eggs, bacon, and a cup of coffee. When he finished eating, he placed the dirty dishes in the sink. He was not in the mood to clean up. He was still irritated by the pressure from the F.B.I. and the constant tail he observed in his car's rearview mirror. He wanted to kill again because it gave him such a rush, but he could not take a chance so soon after he killed Deborah Malloy. He believed that a solo flight in an airplane, soaring through the serene skies, would lift his spirits.

Evan headed to the garage and climbed into the Audi. His flight bag still sat on the backseat where he had left it after his *Angel Wings* mission on Saturday. As he backed down the driveway, he waved toward whoever was seated inside the unmarked car parked up the street. He could not see who was in the vehicle because the bright sun reflected off the windshield. When he pulled away, they followed. Evan decided not to take them on a long ride and drove directly to the airport. He wanted to be airborne as soon as possible.

When he arrived at Albany Aviation, he greeted Linda, the girl who worked behind the service desk. He had gotten to know most of the employees. He usually stopped to chat with her, but instead, walked directly outside to the airplane.

Evan completed all the pre-flight checks and climbed in. He contacted ground control and informed them he wanted to travel north over Lake George and asked for VFR flight following. They approved the request, assigned a transponder code, and instructed him to taxi to runway one.

He received his take-off clearance and soared into the sky. He could feel a smile form as his frustration began to fade away. He was relaxed behind the controls, enjoying the view from the windows. Evan traversed north towards Lake George and the Adirondacks with no particular destination in mind.

***

Sergeant Miller watched Evan Williams as he walked around his airplane and visually inspected the fuel and oil. When Evan climbed onto the plane, Sergeant Miller approached the counter and asked Linda if she knew where he was flying off to. She said she did not, but thought it was just a short, pleasure flight.

Miller sat on a sofa in the F.B.O.'s lobby until Evan taxied from the tarmac and towards the runway. He was slightly concerned Evan would fly somewhere to kill again. However, it had only been three days since the last homicide, so he thought it was unlikely. Miller walked to the refreshment counter for a cup of coffee and to a vending machine, selecting a breakfast sandwich. He wanted to wait at the F.B.O. until Evan returned from his flight.

As Sergeant Miller sipped his coffee and nibbled on the dry and cold sandwich, he wandered through the F.B.O., admiring the various paintings hanging on the walls. He looked through the *TIME2FLY* office window, but the room was empty. Miller then headed to the pilot's lounge. He gazed around the room as he entered. When he saw a door in the back of the room with a sign that read 'break room', he decided to walk over to take a peek. He wondered what kind of break room was required by pilots at an airport. He pulled the door open, stopping dead in his tracks when he saw the bank of lockers on the back wall.

He immediately left the room and jogged to the service desk. He waited for Linda to finish a phone call before he asked her about the lockers.

"I saw lockers in the pilot's break room. What are they used for?" Miller asked.

"Those are for the pilots. They can rent them to store equipment. Many pilots who have flown in for just a day or two don't want to carry their flight bags around, so they rent a locker," Linda said.

"How are they rented? Do you supply a key? Is there a registration?"

"No registration. It's all self-service. You pay with a credit card and take the key yourself."

"So, you don't know who is renting? How long can someone have a locker?"

"Well, I guess as long as they want to. Most pilots rent for a few hours or a day at most, but there is no time limit as long as the person feeds the meter."

"Is a locker rented if it's missing the key, or are there lockers with already missing keys that are no longer used?"

"Keys are available for all the lockers, so if a key is missing, it means someone has rented it."

"Thank you, Linda," Miller said when he read her nametag.

Sergeant Miller returned to the wall of lockers. He examined each of the doors and observed that all keys were present except for one locker in the bottom row. He felt a wave of enthusiasm. He had never considered the possibility that Evan could have concealed his gun in a locker at the airport. Miller yanked his cell phone from his coat pocket, selected Agent Santiago from his contact list, and pressed 'CALL'.

"Agent Santiago."

"Santiago, it's Miller. I think I found where Williams is keeping his weapon," Miller said excitedly.

"Seriously? Where? Did you find it?" Santiago was also excited.

"I didn't find it, but there are lockers here at the airport. What if Williams is renting one of them and is keeping his gun in it? It's so easy. Williams could pick up the gun when he left for one of his flights and drop it off on his way back. We never watched him when he was inside the F.B.O. We always stayed outside."

"That is very plausible. I agree."

"Do you know if I can have the airport open the locker because, technically, they own it, or do we need a search warrant? Do you know?" Miller asked.

"I don't know. Let me contact the D.A. and see what he says. Please do not do anything until I call you back. I don't want to lose our only possible evidence because of a constitutional violation or technicality."

"Agreed," Miller replied.

Sergeant Miller stared at the locker for several minutes, wishing he had X-ray vision like Superman so he could see its contents through the metal. He desperately wanted to open it to find the weapon he had hunted. Miller eventually sat on a recliner in the lounge, waiting anxiously for Agent Santiago's call. He was determined to keep the break room door in his sight.

After what seemed to be an eternity, but, only fifteen minutes, Miller's phone sounded. He looked at the caller ID and saw it was from Santiago.

"I just got off the phone with the D.A.'s office. We need a search warrant. If Williams paid for the locker, expecting to protect his property, he is legally protected," Santiago spoke.

"Are they going to issue us one?" Miller asked.

"Yes, we can have a warrant within the next hour. I am going to the D.A.'s office to pick it up, and I'll meet you at the airport. Do not let that locker out of your sight," Santiago firmly said.

"Don't you worry, it has become my best friend," Miller replied.

Forty-five minutes after Miller hung up his phone with Santiago, the agent was at the F.B.O. with a warrant in hand. He and Miller approached Linda, showed her the warrant, and then asked if she had keys to the lockers. She said she was unsure because no one had ever asked, and wanted to call her manager at home before doing anything that could get her into trouble.

When she hung up the phone after speaking with her boss, she told Santiago that the master keys were hanging on a hook within a locked cabinet inside the hangar. She said she would retrieve them.

Linda returned with the keys and handed them to Sergeant Miller. She asked him to return them directly to her before they left the building. She said they were the only set and she would be held accountable if they were lost. Agent Santiago assured Linda that he would personally return them to her.

When Santiago and Miller were at the lockers, they both took deep breaths. They knew it was a long shot to find the murder weapon inside. Santiago bent down on one knee, inserted the key, and turned it until he heard a click. He looked back up at Miller with an apprehensive stare. He returned his focus to the locker's door, slowly pulling it open.

Agent Santiago and Sergeant Miller's eyes widened when they saw what was inside. There was an automatic weapon, a laptop, a cell phone, a jewelry box, and a credit card. Santiago pulled on a pair of latex gloves and then retrieved the items one at a time.

He first removed the laptop and set it on the floor outside the locker.

"No laptop, huh, Evan, you son of a bitch," Miller growled.

The following item Santiago pulled from the locker was a credit card, noting it was a prepaid $100 Visa card. He then pulled out the cell phone. It looked like the type you can purchase with prepaid minutes, also known as a disposable burner phone. Santiago reached for the jewelry box next and opened it. When he saw wedding rings and a Rolex watch inside, he yelled, "We got the son of a bitch!"

After Miller put on his pair of latex gloves, Santiago handed the box to him.

Santiago then pulled out the automatic pistol. He observed it was a forty-caliber Glock, looked over at Miller, and smiled. He knew he had the murder weapon, and he knew he had Williams.

"This is it. We caught the bastard! The rings, the watch, the gun. It's everything we need," Miller exclaimed.

"I believe we did," Santiago replied, as excited as Miller felt.

"Call the D.A. and get us an arrest warrant before Williams lands his plane. I want to slap the bracelets on him today!"

"Yup, already on it," Santiago replied as he dialed.

"I will call Fowler and have him pick up the warrant. There is no way I am leaving this airport without Williams in the back seat of my cruiser," Miller said.

***

Evan enjoyed his freedom as he sailed through the skies north over Lake George and Lake Champlain. He took in breathtaking views of the Adirondack and Green Mountains.

He didn't have a particular place he wanted to go. He just flew. He sought to get away. When he passed over Lake Champlain's northernmost tip, he turned the airplane west towards White Face Mountain. While he piloted the airplane, he kept his pilot's map open on his kneeboard. As he flew over a small airport, he would locate it on the map to identify it.

When he approached the Lake Placid Airport, he decided to land. He had always wanted to visit the small town, but never had the opportunity or the time. Today he did and aimed the airplane towards the airport.

Lake Placid was an uncontrolled field without a tower. It was best practice for a pilot to announce their position as they entered the traffic pattern when there was no air traffic control to separate aircraft. This procedure helped avoid mid-air collisions with other planes in and around an airfield. He dialed the airport's radio frequency, announcing his arrival over the airwaves to alert other pilots of his intentions.

The approach and landing into Lake Placid was Evan's most challenging yet. Surrounded by mountains on all sides, it gave the illusion that the airport sat at the bottom of a bowl. The famous Olympic ski jump constructed for the 1980 Winter Olympics also appeared to him to be perilously close to the runway. Evan felt nervous flying near it.

The mountains also created strong and conflicting wind currents, causing the airplane to bounce the entire descent to the runway. When Evan taxied from the runway to a parking area, he shut down the plane and looked around. The airport sat deserted.

There was no F.B.O. on the field and no other pilots around. March is not a typical time to visit Lake Placid because the ski season has nearly ended. The temperatures were also too cool for sightseers. Evan climbed from the airplane to stretch his legs. He pulled out his cell phone and opened the UBER app to request a ride into town.

***

Detective Fowler arrived at Albany Aviation with an arrest warrant for Evan Williams. He also brought along several uniformed New York State Troopers with him, which was standard procedure during the arrest of a dangerous subject. Agent Santiago and Sergeant Miller were seated in the lobby when Detective Fowler entered. He waved the warrant high above his head.

"I have it," Fowler exclaimed.

"Great," Miller replied exuberantly.

"I also have these fine gentlemen with me," Fowler said as he swung his thumb over his shoulder, pointing to several uniformed officers who followed.

"Perfect. All we have to do now is wait for Williams to land his airplane. Linda, the girl over there behind the desk, gave me this handheld radio. We can listen to Albany's air traffic controllers, and when we hear Williams' airplane's tail number called, we can go out to the tarmac to greet him. I cannot wait to hear these cuffs ratchet around Williams' wrists and watch his smug smile wiped from his face!" Miller exclaimed as he dangled his handcuffs for everyone to see.

Santiago, Miller, and Fowler, along with several State Police Troopers, took seats on the sofas in the F.B.O.'s lobby, anxiously waiting for Evan to return. Miller had the handheld radio firmly grasped in his hands, listening intently for Evan's Cherokee's tail number.

CHAPTER 62

Evan enjoyed his tour through the quaint village of Lake Placid. He discovered several shops selling antiques, souvenirs, and clothing unique to the North Country. There were small, family-owned restaurants scattered around the village.

Evan walked past an open ice cream parlor full of patrons, which surprised him because of how chilly it was outside. He assumed they were locals. He saw remnants of the 1980 Winter Olympics proudly displayed in windows facing the main thoroughfare.

He reviewed menus posted in front of various restaurants as he passed them, eventually choosing a small tavern that overlooked Mirror Lake. He always believed that pubs made the best sandwiches. As he pushed through the door, Evan observed two men seated at one end of a long, curved bar made of highly polished wood. Other than these two men, the place was empty. Evan imagined the locals were not ready to imbibe so early in the afternoon. These men stared when Evan walked through the door, giving him an uneasy and unwelcoming feeling. He assumed they had seen enough tourists during ski season and were unhappy to see another stranger in town.

Evan attempted to ignore the looks, sitting on top of a barstool at the opposite end of the bar. As soon as he sat down, one of the two men seated when he entered rose from his barstool and disappeared into a backroom. He reappeared a few seconds later, behind the bar, and approached Evan.

"Can I help you, stranger?" He asked.

"Are you serving lunch?" Evan inquired.

"Yes, sir, though it is limited. What's your pleasure?"

"I would love a roast beef sandwich if you have that," Evan said.

"Yes, and we have the best roast beef in town. Nice and rare. Anything to drink?" He asked.

"I would love to have a beer, but unfortunately, I flew my own airplane up here from Albany, so I really cannot drink. I guess if you have coffee, I will take that."

"From Albany, you say. Are you here to ski?"

"No, I just always wanted to see the village and never had a chance. I was flying around aimlessly and decided to land here."

"Nice. Here is your coffee, and I'll get started on your sandwich," he said and walked to the kitchen through a door behind the bar.

* * *

"Where the hell is he?" Miller asked anyone who could hear.

"I don't know. We still have not heard his tail number called," Santiago replied.

"Do you think he is out killing again?" Miller asked.

"I hope not. Williams has always taken a month to cool off between kills. I suppose we could have spooked him into killing again, but I don't think we did," Santiago replied.

"No one leaves the airport until we have him arrested," Miller said to all the troopers seated around him.

* * *

Evan was correct about pubs preparing the best comfort food. The roast beef sandwich served had to be three inches tall, and the meat was deliciously rare. Just the way he liked it. The two men in the bar ended up being quite friendly and chatted with Evan while he ate. It was a wonderful day in Lake Placid, and Evan was pleased he chose to land there. When he finished eating, he bid farewell to the two men and took an Uber back to the airport. He taxied the Cherokee to a self-service fuel farm on the airfield to refuel the airplane before leaving for Albany.

Evan contacted Albany Approach while over the Glens Falls Airport to relay his intentions to land at Albany. He received clearance to continue entering their airspace and was instructed to descend to two thousand feet.

Although Evan enjoyed the day, he was tired and happy to be home. The sun was setting quickly, with building lights beginning to illuminate across the city of Albany. Evan located the airport's beacon as it flashed its one green and one white in the distance.

***

Sergeant Miller jumped out of his seat and ran to the window as soon as he heard Williams' voice come across the handheld radio. Agent Santiago followed behind him.

"He is over Glens Falls, I think, heading back to land," Miller said.

"Yup, I heard. It will probably take him another fifteen or twenty minutes before he makes it back to the airport."

"I hope he likes the surprise we have waiting for him," Miller said with sarcasm.

"I don't believe he will," Santiago laughed.

* * *

As Evan neared the airport, the Albany approach controller asked him to enter a left downwind for runway one and to switch to the tower frequency. A left-downwind instruction meant the airport would be on his left. He would fly over his home. He always appreciated receiving that traffic pattern instruction because it meant he would see his house and neighborhood from the sky. He looked down for it.

Evan was at twelve hundred feet on the landing pattern's downwind leg when his heart started to beat hard with what he saw. Several State Police cars were parked haphazardly in Albany Aviation's lot. Their red and blue lights flashed above them. He did not want to believe they were there for him, but he could think of no other reason for their presence. Evan's mind had become preoccupied with what he saw below.

"November one one four Mike Sierra, I said navigate for final approach now!" crackled over the radio.

"Navigate for final approach, four Mike Sierra," Evan replied.

The tower controller had given the instruction several times before Evan heard it, and she sounded angry. He could not concentrate on flying because he was troubled by all the police cars he spotted. As Evan turned for the final approach, he realized his airspeed was much too fast and did not have the flaps deployed for landing.

Evan quickly hit the switch and lowered the flaps as he pulled back on the throttle to reduce his speed. His approach was out of control and sloppy. The stall warning horn shrieked. He pushed in the throttle while pointing the nose down to avoid a wing stall. When the stall warning horn silenced, he pulled on the yoke to level the airplane. He adjusted the throttle to reduce his airspeed. When he saw the VASI lights displaying red and white, he exhaled the deep breath he had been holding. The VASI indicated Evan had returned to the proper glide slope to the runway.

***

"There he is," Miller shouted.

"Let's go, boys," Santiago said to the troopers as they stood.

Sergeant Miller, Agent Santiago, Detective Fowler, and the State Troopers all exited the F.B.O. in a rush, sprinting to the center of the tarmac to wait for Evan Williams. They watched as he descended to the runway to land. However, just as the airplane's tires were about to touch the asphalt, they heard its engine roar and watched as the aircraft climbed back into the sky.

"What the fuck is he doing?" Miller asked.

"Damn it. He saw us and is running. We should have stayed in the building. We fucked up! He's taking off," Santiago screamed.

* * *

As Evan regained control of the airplane with the wheels nearly touching the ground, he looked over to see Sergeant Miller and Agent Santiago as they stood outside the F.B.O. with several State Troopers alongside them. Evan knew for sure they were there to arrest him. He gave it a quick thought before pushing the throttle hard to the firewall and hitting the switch to retract the flaps. He would not land and give Miller the satisfaction of arresting him.

"November one one four Mike Sierra, are you going around?" Evan's radio shrieked.

A go-around occurs when a pilot has not configured the airplane correctly to land, or the pilot is uncomfortable touching down. When this happens, the pilot will go around for another landing attempt. It was not what Evan had done. He ignored the air traffic controller and gained altitude as he turned the airplane south. He did not know where he would go, only that he knew he could not stay.

"November one one four Mike Sierra. Is there a problem? Are you landing? I did not give you instructions to turn. Please respond!" The controller yelled.

Evan continued ignoring the radio. He looked down and saw that the transponder still held the code given to him when he first contacted Albany Approach over Glens Falls. Radar screens displayed the transponder code for controllers to identify each airplane within the airspace. The terrorists who flew planes into the World Trade Center and the Pentagon on 9/11 had turned off the transponders so air traffic controllers could not track the airplane movements. Remembering what those terrorists did, Evan reached over and turned his off.

"November one one four Mike Sierra, we have lost radar contact. Are you having a problem? Do you need to declare an emergency? Please respond," The controller sounded alarmed.

Evan continued ignoring the calls and even considered turning off the radio, but felt it was more important to listen for other aircrafts flying in the vicinity. He descended to five hundred feet, low enough to remain off most radar screens, and followed the Hudson River southbound. He was not sure where he would end the flight. He just knew he had to keep flying.

*** *** ***

Sergeant Miller rushed back into the F.B.O. and to the service desk. Linda was no longer there. Her shift had ended, and an older gentleman replaced her. Miller approached him and asked if it was possible to contact the control tower. He wanted to find out if they could track Evan's airplane. The man wrote down a phone number on a small piece of paper and handed it to Miller.

Sergeant Miller plucked his cell phone from his jacket pocket and punched the number for the tower. It rang several times before someone answered.

"Control Tower."

"This is Sergeant Miller with the New York State Police. That airplane that was supposed to land but took off, do you know where it went?" Miller asked frantically.

"He stopped communicating with us and turned south. He also shut off his transponder. We tracked him as far as South Albany, but he fell off the radar. We believe he is flying at a low altitude to avoid radar detection."

"Is there any way to find him? Are there other radar screens that can pick him up?" Miller asked.

"Not unless he gains altitude. Also, with his transponder turned off, he will appear as another anonymous blip on the screen. I can ask the regional air traffic control sectors to watch for him. If anyone locates him, do you want to be contacted?"

"Yes, and immediately," Miller barked.

After he gave the controller his cell phone number, Miller ended the call with the tower and approached Agent Santiago, who was also on his phone. He had contacted the aviation division within the F.B.I. to acquire an aircraft that could find and follow Evan, but there were none available in the area. When he failed to obtain one, he sighed heavily and frowned at Miller.

"I tried to get us an aircraft, but none are available," Santiago said.

"I just got off the phone with the control tower. It appears Williams is heading south, but he is flying low and dropped from the radar," Miller replied.

"Where do you think he is going?" Santiago asked.

"I don't think he is going anywhere in particular. I think we spooked him," Miller replied.

"So, all we know is he is heading south. There are a lot of small airports out there. He will be hard to find, and with an airplane, he could be hundreds of miles away in no time at all," Santiago said.

"We have a State Police helicopter based here. Let me call to see if we can get it in the air quickly."

Miller dialed the aviation division within the New York State Police and spoke on the phone for several minutes. He inquired about a helicopter and how long before it could be airborne. Agent Santiago could read Miller's face and knew a helicopter was unavailable. When Miller ended the call, he told Santiago the State Police had two choppers. However, one was out of service, and the other was in use in western New York.

CHAPTER 63

March 13th

As he entered the lower part of the Hudson River, Evan soared past Manhattan's skyline, brightly lit off to his left and the Statue of Liberty glinting on his right. He observed sightseeing helicopters as they flew tourists around the landmark and over the island of Manhattan. It forced him to remain highly vigilant to avoid a mid-air collision.

Although he did not communicate with air traffic control, he had the New York area frequency tuned in on the radio and listened to the chatter of airplanes and helicopters as they flew the Hudson River corridor. He knew that he was spotted when he heard numerous reports of an errant aircraft in the vicinity over the airwaves.

When the Hudson and East rivers disappeared below him, he was delighted to be beyond New York City and out of the New York area airspace. As Evan flew over New Jersey, he made the decision to continue to Philadelphia to confront Jenna.

He had ample time to reflect on his life and the events of the past few months. He placed all the blame on Jenna. If she had not decided to join *Boredwives* to meet Jason Tanner, he would not be in the position he was in. She betrayed him and ruined his picture-perfect life. Jenna had released the killer that was lying dormant within him. He wanted to confront her.

He knew it would be his last opportunity to see Jenna. He muttered to himself, "It all began with Jenna. It will all end with Jenna." Evan had been flying south for a few hours and was exhausted. It was dark outside, and the fuel tanks were dangerously low.

Evan looked at the flight sectional. He searched for an uncontrolled airfield near Philadelphia where he could land the airplane. The airport would need to have a fuel farm available so he could refuel the plane after he confronted Jenna and flew away

"Where would I fly after my confrontation?" He wondered aloud. He was not yet certain, but he knew it would not be Albany.

The airport he chose to land at was named Wings Field, located outside the city limits of Philadelphia. He quickly calculated the heading he had to follow to bring him to the airfield.

***

Agent Santiago and Sergeant Miller continued to receive reports as Evan's aircraft was spotted. Reports came in from Poughkeepsie, New York City, and Newark, NJ. It appeared he was headed south, but they still did not know his final destination.

Sergeant Miller contacted several aviation experts to inquire about the fuel range for a Piper Cherokee. Based on the current winds and direction of flight, he learned that Evan would not make it much further than southern Pennsylvania. Unfortunately, they were aware that Evan could have landed at any number of uncontrolled airports for fuel, undetected, while he escaped.

Agent Santiago called the bank that issued Evan's credit cards to have alerts issued with instructions to contact him immediately if Evan attempted to use them. He also obtained a search warrant for cell phone activity and tracking. However, it looked like Evan either turned his phone off or had discarded it. The detectives were frustrated, having been so close to arresting their long-suspected criminal. He slipped through their fingers due to their poor decision to be on Albany's tarmac in full view as he approached for landing.

***

After much difficulty, Evan eventually picked up the green and white light flashing from the Wings Field's beacon and navigated towards the field. When he was close enough, he dialed in the airport's frequency and tapped the mic button seven times to illuminate the runway lighting. He learned that was how uncontrolled airport lighting functioned. These lights would automatically turn off after fifteen minutes to conserve energy.

The windsock was limp with calm winds, allowing Evan to land on the single runway from either direction. He chose runway one-eight because it allowed him to navigate straight in for a final approach. He heard no other aircraft on the frequency and landed without issue. He decided to taxi directly to the fuel pumps to fill the tanks before he parked the plane. Evan wanted to be ready to leave quickly if law enforcement ended up on his tail.

With the fuel tanks topped off, he taxied back towards the runway and left the plane as close to the runway as possible, but not on it. He did not want to cause an issue for other airplanes that might want to land. With the plane full of fuel and near the runway, his escape from the area would be quick. He grabbed his cell phone and nearly powered it on, but stopped himself. If Miller or Santiago had a trace on the phone, they could track him to this location. He looked around, spotted lights streaming through cracks in an old hangar door, and walked to it.

When Evan arrived at the dilapidated hangar, he tapped on the metal walls. Evan heard someone stir inside. After a few moments, the left hangar door slid open. An older gentleman appeared. He introduced himself as Danny, and Evan introduced himself as John. Evan did not want to use his real name.

Evan gave Danny the excuse that his cell phone battery had died and asked if he could make a call for a taxi for him. Danny said he was more than happy to oblige and walked to a phone sitting on a large tool chest. When he hung up the receiver, he told Evan a taxi would arrive within ten minutes.

Danny and Evan chatted briefly about airplanes and flying while he waited for the cab to arrive. He asked where Evan was from and where he was going. Evan told a story about flying in from Pittsburgh to visit a friend. None of which was true, of course. The truth was that Evan flew in from Albany, and Jenna was certainly not a friend.

The taxi arrived quickly, within ten minutes of Danny calling. Evan climbed into the back seat and gave the driver Jenna's home address. Fortunately for Evan, Jenna had called to give him her new address after she had moved. The driver said it was nearby, which pleased Evan, who was unsure of his exact location. He knew Wings Field was outside Philadelphia, but not the actual location. The driver did not exaggerate how close the airport was to Jenna, arriving at her rented townhome after a twelve-minute ride. Evan paid the driver with cash and climbed out of the taxi.

* * *

Agent Santiago, Sergeant Miller, and Detective Fowler sat around a conference table at Albany Aviation, feeling dejected. Evan's airplane was last spotted just south of Newark, New Jersey, after it flew through New York City before it fell from the radar screens for good.

They found a large map of the northeast and sprawled it across the table's top, looking at cities around Newark. The map showed airports everywhere, making it impossible to determine where Evan might land.

"He could be at any one of these. He could have turned west after he flew over Newark or continued south. There must be hundreds of airports where he could have landed and refueled. How the hell do we find him?" Santiago lamented.

"I don't know. We can't visit each one, and if we asked the local police to inspect every airport, they would laugh us off the planet. It would take them days," Miller said.

CHAPTER 64

March 13th

Evan stood outside Jenna's townhome, staring at the front door. He tried to understand why he was there. He did not know if it was to apologize to her, howl at her, or kill her. However, he would have to improvise if he were there to kill her. He did not have his gun. Evan knew Miller most likely found it in the locker when he saw the police presence as he attempted to land in Albany.

Evan finally decided to knock on Jenna's door. He assumed Jenna was in bed because the home was dark. After a few moments, the porch light lit. Jenna appeared in a nightgown. He must have awoken her, because her hair was a tangled mess, and her eyes were red and barely open. When she saw him, a smile briefly formed, but quickly turned to a grimace.

"Evan! What are you doing here?"

"Hi, Jenna. I was hoping we could talk."

"It's late, and I was already asleep. How did you get here?" Jenna asked.

"I flew."

"This late? Why?"

"Can I come in so we can talk?"

"Sure."

Evan glanced around Jenna's townhome. He was surprised to see it fully furnished. It looked like she had lived there for years. Jenna was able to move on with her life quickly and easily, infuriating Evan. His life had been a struggle since she left him. When he walked past the fireplace to sit on a sofa, he spotted an old picture of them that was snapped in Lake George when they had visited one summer. Evan was surprised to see it displayed. Jenna settled into a recliner.

"I remember that trip," Evan said as he pointed at the photo.

"I do, too. We had some great times," Jenna said.

Evan continued to look around the room before he settled his eyes on her left hand, noticing she did not have her rings.

"I see you're not wearing your rings. Did you sell them?"

"No, I don't wear them. We're not married any longer. And no, I didn't sell them. I have them in my jewelry box in the bedroom. I don't think I could ever get rid of them."

"Too bad you had to screw it all up and fuck some asshole," Evan said with sarcasm dripping from his words.

"I'm sorry, Evan. I'm sorry for the pain I caused you."

"Yeah, well, sorry, just doesn't cut it. No one dares to leave me."

"I fell out of love with you, Evan. It was nothing you did. We just changed."

"You changed. I didn't," Evan yelled.

"Please don't raise your voice, Evan. Why are you really here?" Jenna asked.

"I'm sorry. I'm tired and a little thirsty. Could I get a glass of water?" Evan asked.

Jenna rose from the chair and walked into the kitchen with Evan following. When he entered, he spotted a knife block near the stove. It was then that he knew the purpose of his visit. He quietly moved to it and leaned against the counter in front of the knives.

It was that moment when Evan realized that just because he loved Jenna so much, he couldn't kill her first. And killing all those women just made him stronger, not-so-emotional, and more prepared to face Jenna like that.

When Jenna placed a glass in the refrigerator's dispenser to fill it with water, Evan reached behind, quietly pulling the largest knife he could detect from the block. He clutched it behind his back. Jenna turned back towards him to hand him the glass.

"You've probably been hearing bad things about me," Evan said as he took the water from her.

"I have Evan. The police keep saying you are a serial killer and killed Jason and all those other women. I don't believe it, of course. You could never kill anyone."

"Well, Jenna, I hate to burst your perfect vision of me, but it's true. And you did that to me."

"No, Evan. Don't say that. It's not even funny," Jenna said nervously.

"It's true. You turned me into a killer. I was so angry that you had the nerve to leave me. And you used that damned app. I still can't believe you would join that garbage. You destroyed our marriage. All women on that wicked site are doing the same thing to their husbands, and they need to pay," Evan yelled.

After telling Jenna the truth about himself, she began crying uncontrollably. Evan felt sorrow for her because she had once loved him. He also felt anger for her decision to throw him away. It was time; just the right moment. He stepped closer, plunging a butcher knife deep into her chest, piercing her heart.

Evan watched Jenna fall to the floor as blood spurted from her chest with the rhythm of her heartbeat. He believed he saw pity on her face. Pity for what he had become, he assumed. He continued to stare until she gurgled on her blood and took one last deep gasp.

Evan walked to the bedroom and found Jenna's jewelry box. He peered in and saw her rings. He removed them, sliding the rings into his pants pocket. He located Jenna's cell phone on her bedside table in the bedroom and used it to google local taxi companies. He found the one that had taken him there from the airport. He pressed the phone icon on the website and requested a taxi for a return to the airport. The dispatcher said someone would pick him up within five minutes.

Evan studied Jenna's body for a few more moments, turned on his heels, and walked out the door with a smile.

***

Agent Santiago stood in front of the coffee machine, pouring another cup of poorly brewed coffee. He started to walk away when his cell phone sounded. He pulled it from his shirt pocket to check the name displayed on the screen. It was from the Bank of Albany. He knew it was about Evan Williams' VISA card.

"Agent Santiago."

"This is the Bank of Albany. We have recent activity for the VISA account you requested."

"Where?" Santiago asked excitedly.

"A small airport outside Philadelphia. It was used to purchase seventy-five gallons of aviation fuel. The transaction occurred at 9:50 this evening," The voice on the other end of the phone replied.

"Do you have an address or name of the airport?" Santiago asked.

"Wings Field, 1501 Narcissa Rd, Blue Bell. It is a small town just outside Philly," the voice replied.

"Thank you," Santiago abruptly ended the call.

Santiago rushed to the conference room where Sergeant Miller and Detective Fowler were still seated as they continued to scan the map. He pushed hard on the door to open it, slamming it against a doorstop screwed into the floor. Both detectives jumped at the sudden sound.

"He is down outside of Philly. He purchased airplane fuel a little over an hour ago at a small field in Blue Bell. I think he went there to confront or even kill his ex-wife. Or to seek refuge, in the most unexpected way. I don't know. Get her on the phone. I will call the local authorities and get them to the airport and Jenna Williams' home ASAP," Santiago barked.

Sergeant Miller picked up his cell phone from where it sat on the conference table and scrolled through his contacts list. He had saved Jenna Williams' number to be prepared to contact her if necessary. He was pleased he did. When he found her name, he pressed it to place the call. The phone rang several times before it went to voicemail.

When Miller could not contact Jenna, Agent Santiago contacted the Whitpain Township Police Department in Blue Bell, PA. He filled in an officer who answered the phone about the search for Evan Williams with the potential danger to his ex-wife. Miller ordered the officer to have all available personnel dispatched to the airport and Mrs. Williams' home.

Santiago, Miller, and Fowler anxiously sat, swilling coffee while they waited for news from Pennsylvania.

CHAPTER 65

It was just after midnight when Evan left Jenna's townhome. He rode in the back of the cab in silence. The taxi driver attempted to engage him in conversation, but Evan said he was not interested in talking. The look on Jenna's face when he killed her will be forever seared into his mind. Not two years ago, he was a happily married man with a beautiful wife and a satisfying career. He thought he had his psychopathic tendencies held in check and believed it was Jenna who had released them.

Evan slowly walked to the Cherokee, but was not sure where he would go. He felt he wanted to die. He did not want to end up in prison for the rest of his life. He continually repeated the joke about being *'too pretty for prison'*, but the truth was, he was frightened by the thought of others taking control of his daily life. He also did not want to give Sergeant Miller or Agent Santiago the pleasure of arresting him. As he approached the airplane, he heard sirens in the distance. He ignored them until he saw red and blue lights flashing off trees lining the airport's access road. He knew they had found him.

Evan quickly jumped onto the airplane and twisted the key to start the engine. He did not take the time to perform a pre-flight or run-up. As he began to taxi onto the runway, he spotted a police car pulling alongside the airport's fence. Two uniformed policemen climbed out with their guns drawn. When he pushed hard on the throttle, Evan barely had the plane on the runway.

Evan pulled back on the yoke as he struggled to lift the airplane off the runway. The aircraft fought back, and he bounced the nosewheel several times. Evan was too anxious and needed to let the airspeed build until the airplane had enough air moving around the wings to lift it into the sky.

The plane finally released its grip on the asphalt, and Evan climbed skyward. He looked over his shoulder at the police officers as they stood at the edge of the runway, watching him escape their clutches.

Evan turned the airplane on a northerly heading. He knew what he had to do. He wanted to avoid being arrested and spending the rest of his life in a loud, putrid, filthy prison with nasty murderers, rapists, and thieves. He knew he was a killer and found it ironic that he did not want to live with others like him. He did not consider himself a vicious or brutal killer, the kind who would be his roommate for life.

I never killed an innocent woman. Evan reassured himself.

Evan decided he no longer needed to hide from the law and climbed to three thousand feet as he continued north. He reached over, turned on the transponder, and entered 1200, the universal transmit code for non-communicating VFR aircraft. He was not concerned about appearing on radar screens. He encouraged it.

* * *

"God damn it. They missed him. He took off from the airport just as the officers arrived," Miller screamed.

"Did they see what direction he headed?" Santiago asked.

"He took off towards the north, but they lost sight of him once he was over the horizon. He could have easily turned to go anywhere. He has gone with the wind," Miller said.

"We should contact the FAA again and have the controllers watch for him," Santiago said.

Santiago contacted the FAA to request notifications for any errant aircraft spotted flying around the Northeast. He knew it was a long shot, but he had no other options. Everyone wanted to bring Evan in desperately, but with his airplane, they knew he could be anywhere quickly.

* * *

Evan was exhausted, and his back ached. He had been on an airplane for hours in a cramped cockpit, sitting on poorly padded seats. It was not a comfortable place to spend long periods without an extended break. He believed the only reason he did not fall asleep was because of the adrenaline rushing through his veins.

The confrontation with Jenna went just as he had planned, but he did not get what he thought he needed. He wanted to punish her for ruining his life. Evan believed he would get closure from her death. He had often heard the phrase *'closure'* used while watching all the reality crime shows. Evan learned there was no such thing as closure. The rage still churned within him. It was a really bad addiction with no point of rehabilitation.

Evan continued to fly northward over the Hudson River. When he neared Albany International Airport, he worked around its airspace to avoid the need to contact the approach traffic controller. On radar, he would look like any VFR aircraft with 1200 displayed on the radar scopes. He navigated towards the Adirondack Mountains and Lake Placid when he was past Albany's airspace.

He had a considerable amount of time to think, and with the hum of the airplane and the twisted sense of calm, he had decided what he needed to do. When he had flown into Lake Placid the day before, he had become enchanted with the beauty of the mountains, enormous pine trees, and serene lakes of the

Adirondacks. Evan imagined it would be a wonderful place to stop living.

* * *

Agent Santiago was frequently on the phone with airport control towers scattered across the Northeast as he unsuccessfully searched for Evan Williams' airplane. He spoke with every air traffic control sector, which reported that several VFR aircraft had moved through their control areas without a flight following request. They all told Santiago it was very common for private pilots to fly without assistance, especially on clear nights.

Sergeant Miller felt demoralized as he drank bitter coffee dispensed from a vending machine. He could not grasp the fact that he had Evan in his clutches just a few hours earlier, only to have him slip away so easily. He listened as Santiago made his calls, feeling angry that they could do nothing. It had become a waiting game. A game Sergeant Miller did not like to play.

* * *

Evan was in an overwhelming state of calmness. It was the first time he had felt that way since the night he tried to kill his father. He was only bothered by the knowledge that Sergeant Miller and Agent Santiago had found out he was their killer. He knew he was smarter than law enforcement. The only mistakes he made were leaving a pattern: posed bodies, missing rings, and using the same weapon. Although it was adventurous, it made him a suspect too quickly, even after leaving no evidence on the crime scene.

He also knew they would continue to search for him until he was caught or dead. The time he spent on the airplane throughout the night made him realize he could never go to prison. The only way to end it all was to end his own life. Once he made the revelation, he felt a calmness wash over him.

Evan saw the side of White Face Mountain directly ahead and the village of Lake Placid below. He thought about his mother and how she would have loved to visit the quaint little town before she had died. He also thought about Jenna. They had always dreamt of a spontaneous car ride on the Northway to spend time hiking the very mountains he flew over. They had dreamt about having wine while they sat in front of a fire at the edge of Mirror Lake. Dreams that never came true.

When Evan neared the mountain's side, he prayed to God to forgive him for what he was about to do. He never really believed in the Heaven and Hell concept, but he wanted to pray for his soul in the slight chance they did exist and hoped it was enough to save it.

Evan pointed the airplane at the side of the mountain, pushed the throttle full forward, and closed his eyes. Evan had heard about a person's life passing through their mind just before they died, but he discovered that was untrue. All he saw reflected on his closed eyelids was the remnants of a crashed airplane, with its pieces scattered on the side of a mountain as smoke billowed from the trees.

He was perilously close to the mountain's cliffs when he opened his eyes and lost his courage. He yanked the yoke against his chest and twisted his hands to the right as far as possible. The plane climbed vertically while in a right-hand arc. He felt the landing gear scrape against treetops. The stall warning horn blared, but he needed to climb a few more feet to clear a tree line that was quickly filling the windscreen. When he flew above and past the last towering tree, he gently pushed the yoke forward and straightened it to level the plane. The stall warning horn silenced, and Evan regained control of the airplane.

Evan had breathed heavily and perspired through his clothes. It was the closest to death he had come. Experts say it is not easy to take one's life, and they are correct. He could not remember when he pulled on the yoke or turned the airplane. It just happened without a thought. The natural survival instinct took over his body, with his muscles subconsciously turning him away from the mountain and certain death.

Once Evan controlled his breathing, he tried to think about what he should do. He considered going to Canada to hide, but knew that probably wasn't an option. He considered landing the airplane in a remote area, but he lacked the skills to survive in the wilderness. He had never even been on a camping trip. He knew he would not know how to start a fire or hunt for food. Evan decided to land in Lake Placid to rest, purchase aviation fuel, and consider his next steps.

As the fuel poured from the pump and into the wings, he had time to consider his options. He decided to turn himself in to the authorities. Although the thought of spending the rest of his life in prison haunted him, he knew he could not look over his shoulder until the day he died. He discovered suicide was not an option. With the tanks filled, he climbed back onto the plane and started the engine. He would no longer run or hide. He departed Lake Placid Airport, steering the airplane to the south for a return to Albany.

CHAPTER 66

March 14th

Evan looked down at Lake George as he crossed over it and admired the beautiful lakeside homes. It would be the last time he would see the lake with the knowledge of what he had prepared to do. When he arrived at the southernmost tip of the lake, he dialed in the approach frequency for Albany International Airport.

"Albany Approach, November one one four Mike Sierra, over Glens Falls at two thousand, landing Albany," Evan said into the microphone.

"*November one one four Mike Sierra, squawk three one two four,*" The controller replied.

"Squawk three one two four, four Mike Sierra," Evan replied.

"*Radar contact. Fly heading two one zero, navigate straight in, runway one niner,*" The controller instructed.

“Straight in one niner,” Evan answered.

Evan turned to the provided heading and continued inbound for Albany while searching through his flight bag for Sergeant Miller’s card. Evan wanted to call him to let him know he would surrender peacefully, but he did not find it.

“Albany approach, four Mike Sierra with a request,” Evan called.

“Four Mike Sierra, go ahead.”

“I would like someone to contact Sergeant Miller with the New York State Police and let him know I’m on my way in to surrender.”

“Did you say you want us to call the New York State Police?” the controller asked, stunned.

“Affirmative, Sergeant Miller, let him know I am on my way to surrender peacefully.”

“Affirmative, four Mike Sierra.”

***

Sergeant Miller dozed on the sofa in Albany Aviation’s lobby. Agent Santiago was on his way to a nearby donut shop to pick up breakfast and coffee that he deemed drinkable. They had remained all night in the F.B.O., eager to hear anything about Evan, hoping he would attempt to fly back to Albany unnoticed. Miller sprang alert when he thought he heard Evan on the handheld radio. He jumped from the sofa and rushed to the glass windows to search the skies for his airplane. He raised the handheld's volume, placing it to his ear. He did not want to miss a word.

When he heard Evan ask the controller to contact him, he was exhilarated and shocked. Evan Williams wanted to return to the airport to turn himself in. He immediately called Agent Santiago to inform him of Evan's return and intention to surrender. After Miller's call, Agent Santiago abruptly turned his vehicle around and returned to the airport. Coffee and donuts were no longer a priority or desire.

Santiago raced through the F.B.O. doors minutes after he received the call from Miller, bolting to where he peered out the window.

"I can't believe he wants to turn himself in," Santiago exclaimed.

"It's what he said. I heard him on the radio. I also received a call from the control tower."

"Detective Fowler should be here. He has invested as much time and effort as we have," Miller added.

"I have already called him. He's on his way here with a couple of Troopers."

"Excellent. Now we wait. Any idea how long before Williams lands?" Santiago asked.

"The tower said it would be approximately twenty minutes. They are giving him priority handling," Miller answered.

* * *

Albany provided Evan with a direct approach to runway one-nine. He navigated straight in since arriving air traffic was light at that time of the morning. The only other aircraft Evan heard were departing airliners and a UPS airplane on final approach, delivering and picking up packages for the Albany area. He lined himself up with the runway's centerline and followed the VASI's guidance down to the runway.

Evan touched down smoothly and smiled. It was his best landing ever, and he felt proud. His joy quickly turned to melancholy as he realized it would be the last landing he would ever make on an airplane he piloted himself. He also knew it was the last time he would operate anything, whether it was a car, boat, plane, or a simple bicycle. Evan was exhausted. He was also delighted that he had spent his last free hours flying.

It took Evan several minutes to taxi to the F.B.O. because it was at the opposite end of the runway from where he touched down. Although the control tower instructed him to exit at the first available taxiway, he chose to roll the airplane slowly down the entire length of the runway because he was not in a rush for Miller to arrest him. As he turned off the runway and onto Albany Aviation's tarmac, he could see Agent Santiago, Sergeant Miller, and Detective Fowler walk from the

F.B.O. with their guns drawn. Evan felt uneasy and hoped they understood he would not give them a struggle.

Evan stopped the airplane in the center of the tarmac and shut down the engine while he eyed Sergeant Miller. He made Evan nervous because Miller had mistreated him during the interrogations. Evan knew that if he did anything that appeared slightly aggressive, Miller would shoot without hesitation.

"Evan. Show us your hands, please," Santiago yelled.

Evan raised his hands slowly so they could see they were empty.

"Great, Evan. Now, exit the aircraft slowly. When you are completely out, please drop to your knees and place your hands on your head, interlacing your fingers," Santiago instructed.

Evan understood Agent Santiago was in charge. Sergeant Miller and Detective Fowler stood silently, guns raised.

Evan climbed from the airplane and onto the wing, then jumped to the asphalt. He bent to his knees and laced his hands together over his head as instructed. He wanted to follow Santiago's instruction precisely. Evan did not want to get shot.

The three men approached slowly, and when they stood over him, Sergeant Miller placed handcuffs on his wrists. The ratcheting sound they made caused Evan to wince. It would be a sound he knew he would frequently hear for the rest of his life.

Sergeant Miller yanked Evan to his feet with unnecessary force, grinning broadly. He was smug with the enjoyment he had of having arrested Evan. Evan just smirked back. They led him through the F.B.O. and to a State Police cruiser, placing him in the back. Sergeant Miller climbed into the driver's seat and drove Evan away.

EPILOGUE

August 4th

Evan Williams chose to plead guilty to all charges. He knew he was guilty and the evidence against him indisputable. He believed sitting in a courtroom to fight the charges against him would only prolong the inevitable outcome. He knew there wasn't a lawyer alive who would have won him an acquittal. Evan's plea deal also took the death penalty off the table, and he agreed to life in prison without the possibility of parole. He accepted the fact that he would never be free again.

Evan was right about prison. It was noisy, smelly, filthy, and rough. It took him a long time before he could get a decent night's sleep because of the banging of bars, the snoring of sleeping men, and cries from others. The smells were awful, too. The odors of sweaty men who did not worry about relieving themselves of gas filled the walls.

Evan was beaten up a few days after he arrived, primarily to make sure he knew who was in charge. After a couple of weeks, Evan was left alone and mainly kept to himself.

Evan made a couple of friends with other inmates who felt that their incarceration was unjust. He just listened as they droned on about how terrible and unfair the justice system was and how they would be released someday.

Evan occasionally played poker, using cigarettes as poker chips. He didn't smoke, but cigarettes were a currency he used to purchase items from other inmates. Those items included books, potato chips, candy bars, and extra food at mealtime.

Evan liked to sit in the communal area across from a small-screen television. He had to settle for whatever the toughest inmate wanted to watch, but he did not mind.

When he was in the prison yard with other inmates, he would find himself looking skyward when he heard an airplane flying overhead. Evan often dreamt about the time he was in the skies. He used to enjoy the freedom the private rides provided. Now, his freedom was gone, and he would never have an opportunity to fly airplanes again. That was the most difficult consequence for him to accept from everything that had occurred and he sometimes pondered if he really should've let his plane crash.

* * *

Evan's case quickly became a statewide news story, drawing attention not only because of the murder but because of the shocking contrast between a volunteer pilot and the crime he committed. Although the public expressed disgust at *Boredwives'* business model, most people agreed that what the app offered had nothing to do with Evan's responsibility for his crimes. Many expressed disbelief that he had taken it upon himself to act as a self-appointed moral judge—selecting victims, tracking them, and ultimately killing them in a twisted attempt to punish behavior he found unforgivable. Evan became the subject of study just as he had once expected of his psychopathic tendencies.

Sergeant Miller and Detective Fowler went back to Syracuse two days after Evan's arrest. They returned to Albany to be present when Evan entered his guilty plea and received his life sentence. The court's bailiff escorted Evan from the courtroom in handcuffs for the last time, and Sergeant Miller, Detective Fowler, and Agent Santiago all smiled and waved to him with satisfied expressions. Sergeant Miller ended up receiving a promotion to Captain due to his work on Evan's case. Agent Santiago and Captain Miller became close friends and often traveled to each other's homes for parties and celebrations.

Sheriff Brown, the Yates County sheriff who first contacted the New York State Police for assistance with Anne Roberts' homicide, received a commendation from Penn Yan's mayor for having the insight to seek support from the State authorities. He retired soon after the conviction of Evan Williams.

* * *

Angel Wings submitted a press release statement admonishing Evan Williams and the actions he took while flying for their organization. They firmly stated that the pilots who volunteer to help others should be recognized and commended for their time and effort. "*Angel Wings* continues to provide free travel to help patients nationwide with their medical needs."

* * *

Boredwives did not respond to any requests for comment. They continued offering married men and women the opportunity to meet indiscreetly.

THE END

I want to acknowledge the following people:

My good friend and former co-worker in the world of
IT, Jill Byron, for the hours she spent reading, re-
reading, correcting, and supplying me with suggestions
to make this book something I am proud of.

My wife and best friend, Michele Matzen, who allowed
me to take time from our active retirement life to fulfill
a dream of publishing my own book and spending her
days reading the manuscript as I wrote.

ABOUT THE AUTHOR

Don Vallee is a retired IT professional and instrument rated private pilot. He resides in Austin, Texas with his wife, Michele.

When not writing, he and Michele dabble in part-time acting and modeling, appearing in small roles and as background characters in film and on television. They have also appeared in T.V. commercials, social ads, and print advertisements. They are known in Central Texas as Cast-a-Couple, a brand they created for themselves. Cast-a-Couple can be found on Instagram and Facebook.